D0428018

"Hello," Reed repeated. Nothing. "Hello, is anyone there?"

Agents and detectives were making notes, whispering, consulting their computer screens. Digits of the computer clock timing the call blurred by as exhaustion and grief overcame Reed.

"Annie?" Reed said.

More silence passed. Reed squeezed his temple with his free hand. "This isn't funny!" he shouted into the phone.

A male voice responded. "No, it's not funny, Mr. Reed."

"Who is this? Where's Ann?"

"She had to pay."

The negotiator stared hard at Reed, gesturing for him to keep the conversation alive, keep the guy at the phone while the PD scrambled cars.

"Pay?" Reed said. "Pay for what?"

"You'll have to figure it out, Mr. Ace Reporter."

"Where is she? Let me talk to her. Jesus, please! I'm begging you! Please don't hurt her. Just let me talk to her. Please."

"That's not possible."

"What do you want? Please let me talk to my wife."

"You won't be speaking to her tonight."

"Where is she? Please let me talk to her. What have you done?"

"You won't be speaking to her ever again."

The line went dead in Reed's hand.

Other books by Rick Mofina

IF ANGELS FALL

COLD FEAR

BLOOD OF OTHERS

"Rick Mofina brings a gritty realism to the printed page . . . flawed but sympathetic characters draw readers into the action." —*Publishers Weekly*

"Mofina . . . brings back crime-reporter hero Tom Reed from his earlier thrillers. Mofina has something Mary Higgins Clark can't touch: a thorough grounding in police and forensic procedures that lends his pages weight and depth. It all adds up to another riveting read from one of the leading thriller writers of the day." —*Penthouse* Magazine

NO WAY BACK

Rick Mofina

PINNACLE BOOKS
Kensington Publishing Corp.
http://www.kensingtonbooks.com

PINNACLE BOOKS are published by

Kensington Publishing Corp.
850 Third Avenue
New York, NY 10022

All Kensington Titles, Imprints, and Distributed Lines are available at special quantity discounts for bulk purchases for sales promotions, premiums, fund-raising, and educational or institutional use. Special book excerpts or customized printings can also be created to fit specific needs. For details, write or phone the office of the Kensington special sales manager: Kensington Publishing Corp., 850 Third Avenue, New York, NY 10022, attn: Special Sales Department, Phone: 1-800-221-2647.

Pinnacle and the P logo Reg. U.S. Pat. & TM Off.

First Pinnacle Books Printing: June 2003

10 9 8 7 6 5 4 3 2 1

Printed in the United States of America

For Ron and Mary

And when you look into an abyss,
the abyss also looks into you.

Beyond Good and Evil
—Friedrich Nietzsche

1

The register at the San Francisco Deluxe Jewelry Store whirred as sales clerk Vanessa Jordan slid the credit card receipt to the woman admiring the custom order she had bought.

"Your husband is going to adore it," Vanessa said.

"I hope so." Her eyes glistened. "I wanted something special for our anniversary."

Vanessa thought her customer was beautiful. She was wearing a tailored mauve suit, had lovely brown hair, pearl studs, a matching two-row necklace.

"Trust me, he's going to love this. I'd be happy to gift wrap it for you."

Studying the exquisite craftsmanship, the woman considered the offer when the store's front door chime sounded, diverting Vanessa's attention to the security monitor under the counter. The video screen showed two people waiting at the entrance. A big woman in a long beige coat standing behind a man in a wheelchair. Access through the front door required staff to activate a remote lock. The store's guard had just left for his usual fifteen-minute break to get a bagel at the corner bakery. Vanessa followed the security procedure, scanned the other monitors, and inventoried the store: She had her customer at the cash register. Across the floor, a man in his sixties was alone, looking at watches. There was a couple in their late twenties near the engagement diamonds, cooing at rings. Through the window to the street she saw nothing unusual. Everything was fine.

Vanessa glanced over her shoulder down the hall at the manager, a kind soft-spoken man who wore frameless glasses. He was working in the back office, which had the same closed-circuit monitors and a speaker for the front chime. Upon hearing it, he left his desk to help, nodding an okay for Vanessa to open the door. She pressed the button under the counter. The woman and the man in the wheelchair entered.

At that moment, the customer at the counter had reached a decision. "Yes, I would like it gift wrapped. Will it take long?"

Vanessa didn't answer.

"Excuse me, miss? I'd like it gift wrapped."

Vanessa was staring at the front door. The manager had arrived behind her, adjusting his jacket, stopping dead in his tracks.

Once inside the store, the old man leaped from the wheelchair. The woman pushing him folded it, wedging it so the automatic door could not lock behind them. She was over six feet tall, wearing a kerchief over her thick blond hair. She had large dark glasses. Her face was smeared with layers of freakish white makeup that no longer disguised the Adam's apple of a man as his long coat snapped open and he produced an automatic assault rifle.

"This is a holdup! Everyone on the floor!"

Someone screamed. The gun came alive, exploding with rapid fire, destroying every security camera including those hidden in the store's custom-made grandfather clock and the overhead light fixtures. The smell of cordite and the clinking of debris and spent shells filled the air. The wheelchair man stepped forward, silver talons of hair reached from his fedora, huge dark glasses hid much of his face, which resembled fiery red plaster. He opened his coat to a Kevlar vest with a hand grenade clipped to each side of his chest.

"Don't touch any alarms," he said to the manager, who ceased inching toward the counter.

The shooter replaced his empty magazine, let go a staccato burst above the manager's head. Rounds ripped into the wall, smashing an array of expensive Swiss and Austrian clocks. Then he directed gunfire at every display case, glass rained everywhere. The engaged woman screamed, her boyfriend shielded her with his body under a table. The old watch shopper lay facedown on the carpet, his hands trembling above his white hair. The red-faced man came around the counter, pressed the muzzle of a handgun to Vanessa's head while shoving a canvas bag in her face.

"Fill this with everything from the displays now," he said, then turned his gun on the manager, thrusting a bag at him. "I know your vault's open. I know what you have. And I want all your videotapes. Let's go!" They disappeared into the back.

In front, Vanessa hurried from display to display, her fingers bleeding as she swept rings, necklaces, earrings, bracelets, watches, into the bag.

In seconds the manager returned, hands above his head. The wheelchair man was behind him, pressing his gun to the manager's neck, clutching the canvas bag laden from the vault and security tapes. One of the grenades was missing from his vest.

"Please don't hurt anyone," the manager said. "You have what you want. Just go." The gun's grip thudded into his lower neck, dropping him to the floor. Vanessa cried out as everyone's attention was jerked to the front.

Outside, a loudspeaker sounded the word *"Police."*

The red-faced man hurried from the manager to the side

of the entrance window, cursing at what he saw down the street.

"What is it!" said the shooter, darting to the window, eyeballing the problem. "Damn it!" He tightened his grip on his automatic rifle, scanned the customers and staff, assessing their situation. "What the hell are we going to do? How do we get out of this!"

The red-faced man went to Vanessa, seizing the bag from her. "You're done. Get on the floor." .

He then squatted to appraise the female customer near the counter. In her thirties, well-dressed, nice figure, brown hair. Flawless skin that smelled real good as he leaned into her face to push his gun against her head.

"Did you drive here, lady?"

She nodded.

"Alone?"

She nodded.

"Is your car near?"

She hesitated, blinking at the black lenses that hid his eyes. The muzzle drilled hard into her skull.

"Please don't hurt me."

"Do you want to live?"

"Yes."

"Is your car near?"

"Yes."

The woman felt herself being hoisted to her feet, felt the gun jabbing into her back, rushing her to the door where the man opened the wheelchair, then forced her into it as she pleaded in vain. At gunpoint, he ordered her to produce her keys from her purse, then her driver's license, registration, and insurance information identifying her car, the make, model, year, color, plate number. He snatched her wallet, surprised as he fanned her cash. He flipped through personal items, credit cards, bank cards, pausing at the color snapshot of a boy. He looked ten or twelve, brown hair like hers.

"This your kid?"

Tears came. She squeezed her eyes shut, nodding.

"Where's your car parked?"

"Please."

"Where?" He thrust his gun against her neck.

"To the left at the end of the block. This side of the street."

He drew his face within inches of hers. She stared into his dark glasses, seeing nothing in the blackness but the reflection of her fear.

"Make a sound and I'll go to your home and kill your kid. Understand?"

He threw a blanket across her lap, the bags under the seat, then handcuffed her wrists to the armrests.

As she felt the metal clamping hard against her skin, her mind reeled. Did she kiss her son this morning? Her husband? Tell them how much she loved them? She saw their faces. Heard their voices. Tears rolled down her cheeks. She couldn't move her hands to brush them. *This isn't happening. It's not real, I'm dreaming. Wake me. God, please wake me now.*

The shooter's head shook, his blond curls jiggling. "This is all messed up, man. Don't be a fool. We're not taking her."

The handgun flew into his face, scraping his makeup-caked chin. "You're with me. Or you're dead. Right here. Right now. That clear?"

"Okay, okay, it's cool. It's your party."

The red-faced man whirled, plucking the remaining grenade from his vest, holding it up. "Just like the one I left at the back." He affixed a magnet and trip-wire mechanism to it at the front door's inside handle. "The trip retractor sets automatically when I close this door. Open it from either side, it detonates, killing anyone within twenty-five feet."

They left.

The heist took minutes. The victims remained inside the jewelry store. Glass tinkled in the aftermath. Vanessa wept softly. The old watch shopper's hands were still trembling above his white hair. The manager's mind blurred with worry for his customers. *Grenades on the doors. Lord, help us. They took that lady. She was just buying her husband a special anniversary gift; now she is a hostage. Oh, God, please help her.* Struggling to make sense of it all, the manager heard the engaged woman murmuring to her fiancé under the ruins of a display case, her words growing audible.

"Our Father, who art in heaven—"

They all flinched at the sudden pop of gunfire coming from the street.

2

Now what do we have here?

Waiting for the light to change, Officer Rod August saw a large, butt-ugly woman and a man with long hair and a goatee hefting a big old-timer from a paneled van into a wheelchair. The woman got behind the chair and pushed the old man down the sidewalk. The goateed man remained in the van, which was parked illegally in a red zone. No hydraulic lift, no commercial, delivery, or handicap designation on the plate or window.

What's wrong with this picture?

The light changed. August eased his black-and-white SFPD patrol car forward. He pretended from behind his sunglasses that he didn't catch the prison tattoos on the van driver's arm, extending from the window with a stream of cigarette smoke. He let on as if he'd missed the tailpipe jitter of the idling engine. He memorized the California plate number.

It never hurt to be vigilant. There'd been a spate of burglaries in August's zone of this business strip in the Richmond District north of Golden Gate Park. Out of sight to round the block, August radioed his dispatcher to run the tag. Routine. The job was 99 percent tedium, 1 percent adrenaline.

August yawned. The tag was probably nothing. Could be that Mr. Tattoo there was a good boy doing a good deed for Granny and Gramps. But what the hell? He had an hour before his meeting with his lieutenant to discuss his desire to detail into robbery. To move up the ranks. August had five years on the street and had developed the instincts of a detective.

Now Billy, his son, was talking about becoming a cop, like the old man. August flipped down the visor to the small color school photograph of a blond-haired six-year-old, bright blue eyes radiating hope over a mile-wide grin missing a lower front tooth. *You and me, pal. Partners.* August got Billy this weekend. They were going to Big Sur, or to see a ball game, or just hang. Whatever Billy wanted. It was going to be great being with him.

Static crackled over August's radio.

"Your number comes back ten-thirty from Bakersfield PD. Stand by."

A roller. I knew it. Stolen. Gotcha.

"Complainant Victor Trang reported plates stolen from his 2000 Neon a week ago."

August came around the corner, then crept up on the parked van. Its motor was still idling. Time to go to work. He put the transmission in park, called in his location, a description of the van: a white Ford mid-1990s, and the hero in the driver's seat whose cigarette hand was tapping the side mirror. The tapping stopped when August activated his emergency lights, hit his siren to yelp twice. He unbuckled his seat belt, then his holster, gripped his Beretta, then used his loudspeaker.

"This is the San Francisco police. Shut off your engine and step out of the vehicle now with your open hands visible above your head."

Nothing happened.

August repeated his order. Nothing happened. The side mirror adjusted. August caught a pair of cold eyes watching him. August's game face betrayed nothing. *All right, asshole. I'm not asking three times.* August opened his door to shield himself as he stepped out, taking stock of the street around him. It was empty until he saw someone approaching.

Instinct told him to call for backup. *Naw, hold off. I can handle this.*

August's radio crackled with the first report, from a barbershop, of shots being heard in the San Francisco Deluxe Jewelry Store. At that moment August recognized the wheelchair people returning to the van, which began swaying because the driver had suddenly changed his position inside.

In that terrible instant of knowing, August's thought process accelerated to absorb, comprehend, analyze what had befallen him, for there were now *three* people nearing the van.

August's pulse raced upon seeing a terrified woman handcuffed in the chair under a blanket, which was folded back by a breeze, revealing the canvas bags. He saw how the large woman pushing the chair had locked on to him from behind her dark glasses as the old man in the hat shot out his arm to fire a handgun repeatedly into the van at Mr. Tattoo. August's brain commanded his body to leap back into his patrol car, call for help. The big woman was now training an automatic assault rifle on him. August heard the handcuffed woman scream, saw the muzzle fire, his windshield blossoming with round after round, felt burning sledgehammers pound his arm, his vest, wrist, shoulder, throat. *Christ.* The glass popping, gunfire, screams. Warm liquid flowed all over him. *What was that?* His body numbed. His dispatcher was calling, her voice quivering. August was gripping his open microphone as he lay in the front seat of his patrol car gazing up at his son's face smiling down on him.

3

The police scanners sizzled at the *San Francisco Star*.

The young reporter assigned to them was doing her best, deciphering codes, making calls, jotting notes as the chatter spilled over the glass walls of the small office tucked in a corner of the newsroom. Experienced listeners kept the volume low but when a story broke things got hot.

No one knew that better than Tom Reed.

From far across the metro section he picked up on the emotion in the dispatchers' voices. It was a skill he'd never lost even though it had been ages since he did a shift at the police radios, the most dreaded job in the newsroom. The noise irritated the burnouts who wanted them silenced, a blasphemy to diehards like Reed. Scanners were sacred. They alerted you to the first cries for help, pulling you into a story that would stop the heart of your city. Or break it.

Reed sensed something was up. But he forced himself to shrug it off. None of it mattered to him anymore. Today was the day he was going to quit.

He took stock of the newsroom, the editors, deskers, reporters. At their computers, keyboards clicking, phones ringing, people taking notes, conversations flaring, large TVs locked on to twenty-four-hour news stations on overhead shelves. The smell of news and coffee in the air. Reed loosened his tie, draped his jacket over his chair, settled in.

You're going to miss this.

Milestones stared at him from the half walls around his desk, a faded clipping, with the head FORMER GREAT FALLS NEWSPAPER BOY NOMINATED FOR PULITZER PRIZE. It resurrected boyhood memories of Montana, the Rockies, Big Sky Country. Crisp editions of the *Trib,* bulging in that bag, gray with newsprint, slung over his shoulder as he trudged the streets of his neighborhood, dreaming of becoming a big-city crime reporter.

Next to the clipping, a snapshot.

Reed saw a cockier, younger version of himself grinning in front of the Golden Gate Bridge with the gang from the San Francisco bureau of The Associated Press. It was his first job after college and where he broke the story on crime networks on the West Coast that got him short-listed for the prize. He didn't win but it boosted his ego and prompted the *San Francisco Star* to hire him as a senior crime reporter. A dream realized.

The yellowing tear sheets of his bigger stories layered the walls around his desk. So many. Cases that had led him into the darkest regions. *The way Virgil guided Dante's descent into hell.* Headlines above Reed's byline screamed of earthquakes, fires, executions of unrepentant killers, drug wars, blood-drinking cults, shooting rampages, babies whose corpses were found in the trash. *Or worse.* It was a world of pain and Reed was one of its chroniclers, on the scene each time a new horror surfaced, ensuring that an accounting of it bled in the black ink of the *San Francisco Star.*

Over the years, he felt each story fracture the armor he wore as protection from the tragedies he covered. It became an internal battle to keep his distance, especially from the ones whose acts were so hideous the details never made it into print. Instead, they wormed their way into his dreams.

When he tried to drown them with Jack Daniel's Tennessee Sipping Whiskey, his life began disintegrating.

In the newsroom late one night, after finishing a story about a crack-addicted bodybuilder who threw his ten-month-old daughter against a cement wall, Reed had found himself confiding to the *Star*'s religion editor.

"You know what I cover?" Reed said. "I cover evil."

"Maybe you should change beats."

"I can't. I thought about it. I just can't."

"Then be careful. Remember Nietzsche's caution."

"Yeah, what's that?"

"Just don't get too close to your subject, Tom."

That was several years ago, when the stories grew darker and his drinking grew heavier, exacting a toll on his wife, Ann, and their son, Zach.

He picked up the small framed photograph of the three of them, ran a hand over his face. Ann left him during that time. Took Zach and moved to her mother's in Berkeley for a few months. He never blamed her. It needed to be done, so he could see what he'd become. And it worked. They reconciled, pulled through, rebuilt their lives piece by piece. Ann's children's clothing stores were prospering. Reed promised to leave daily news reporting within a year, to stay home and write books. But with his drinking in check, his marriage strengthened. So did his reporting and writing. He had some dry spells, he also whacked a few major stories out of the park. When he'd taken a few months off to write a book, Ann never spoke of the promise he'd made until the weekend before his leave of absence ended. They went for a Sunday drive along the coast. They walked along a rise overlooking the Pacific, Ann took his hand, entwined her fingers with his, then chose her words carefully.

"Tom, you haven't said it, but I feel you're thinking about not quitting."

Gulls cried above them as Zach ran ahead.

"Things are good for us now. We're stronger. Happier," she said. "The stores are doing well. But I'm afraid."

"What are you afraid of?"

"That if you don't get out now, you'll never leave. And if you don't leave, you'll get too close again."

"Ann—"

"Tom, you immerse yourself into the most horrible stories, until they become a terrible obsession. What you achieve for the newspaper comes at a price, and Zach and I pay it."

He said nothing.

"And if that happens again, if it turns bad like the other times, Tom, I just can't go through it. We won't survive it."

The roar of the surf and salty sea breezes tumbled over them.

He couldn't find the words to tell her the truth, that he feared he couldn't quit. Couldn't quit something that deep down he believed he was born to do. Something that had *chosen him*. That despite the bad times, he was convinced there was a greater meaning in it all and he couldn't stop until he found it.

"It's your call, Tom."

He searched the horizon for the right answer.

"This week, Ann. When I get back this week, I'll tell them I'm finished."

Reed set the picture down next to his computer screen.

Across the newsroom somebody was shouting about a jewelry store. The police radios blared. Reed ignored them. An editorial assistant hurried by. "Hey, Tom, good to see you, man."

In the few days since his return, Reed had accepted a stream of "welcome backs" and updates on newsroom gossip, all the while not breathing a word to anyone that he was poised to quit. Three large boxes of unopened mail awaited attention on his desk. He still hadn't gotten through it all, or his hundreds of e-mails. He hadn't even had the chance to talk to the *Star*'s new metro editor, Bob Shepherd. On Reed's first day back, they'd met for a moment. Shepherd wanted a private meeting, then got tied up.

Reed fished out an outdated newsroom memo on Shepherd's appointment. He had joined the *Star* six months after leaving the *Washington Post*. He'd also been a features editor at the *Wall Street Journal* and a metro news editor at the *New York Daily News*. He was a respected first-class legend with twenty-four years in the business. He knew how to break a story and how it should be written. A reporter's dream. Too bad they wouldn't get a chance to work together, Reed thought, wondering if he should begin drafting his letter of resignation when his line rang.

"Tom, it's Bob. Sorry for the delay. Been having a lot of meetings. Got a little time now, if you're clear."

"Sure."

Approaching Shepherd's office, Reed felt his stomach twist with the final story he was about to break. The end of his newspaper career. As he glanced at the controlled chaos of the newsroom, Reed's years at the *Star* blurred by. Shepherd's door was open, he was waving him in while talking into his phone.

"We've got people on it? Have a seat, Tom. Photogs? Good. Keep me posted." Shepherd hung up, extended his hand to Reed.

"Tom, I'm afraid I've only got a few minutes. My apologies. A lot of meetings but I didn't want to put ours off, again. Welcome back, belatedly. How'd the book go? Crime fiction, was it?"

"Yes. It was good, and, well, it's fantastic you're here, Bob, but I think, right off, there's something I have to tell you."

"Sure." The phone rang. "Hang on." Shepherd took the call. Reed noticed the framed awards, certificates, pictures of Shepherd holding the Pulitzer Prizes he'd helped his former papers win. He ended his call.

"Sorry, Tom. I'm going to have to take off to see the publisher. Look, there are some long-range and immediate ideas I need to kick around with you, now, if I may."

"Well, I—"

"Some of my recent meetings dealt with this paper's slipping circulation, loss of readership to the Internet, television, lifestyle, habits, everything. Newspapers breathing their death gasps and what we can do about it."

"Right."

"The numbers don't lie, but I still believe that for the money, newspapers are the best narrative vehicle for reflecting the daily meaning of contemporary life. I know you believe it, because I saw it in your stuff, and the work of some *Star* staffers when I was at the *Post*. I believe there's untapped potential to produce outstanding work on a regular basis here."

"Really?"

"It's part of the reason I sought this job. My wife and I have family here, but a few months after I left the *Post*, I realized I wasn't ready to walk away from this business. I think people like you are its hope for the future."

"You think so?"

"Tom, it's in your stories, your digging, your writing. You get under the skin of the most difficult stories to cover, tragedies. You find the details that haunt readers, that make a small anguish seem epic. You find its soul. I don't know what the *Star*'s priorities were over the years, but I think they missed out by not taking advantage of the natural storytelling talent in this newsroom. I don't intend to make that mistake. I need you to help me save this paper from becoming irrelevant, to make it matter to the city it serves."

Reed couldn't believe what he was hearing.

"Tom, I'd like you to consider trying your hand at something today. We've got a jewelry store heist unfolding."

"I heard some commotion on the scanners."

"Shots fired. People wounded. Details are still coming. Maybe a standoff. We've got people on it already. Depending on how this goes down, we'll get the hits and siders for tomorrow. I'd like you to go down there now with the aim, we'll keep it loose if things change, but go with the intention of producing an anatomy of a heist. Say, from the perspective of the suspects, the cops, the victims. Consider a Joycean stream-of-consciousness approach."

A James Joyce stream-of-consciousness approach. Reed liked that.

"What do you say?"

A literary approach to a heist story by the *Star*. Shepherd's predecessors, the clueless idiot Benson, and Brader the manipulative snake, would have laughed at such a concept, if they could even grasp it. It sounded wild. But Reed couldn't take it. He'd come to resign.

"What is it, Tom? Do you object?"

"No, it's not that."

"The point is to take readers into the heart of a heist, to let them experience what is happening on the streets of their city." Shepherd glanced at his watch. "Sorry, I have to run."

Reed glimpsed the wall behind Shepherd, trying to count his Pulitzer Prizes.

"You were going to say something, Tom?"

"Welcome to the *Star,* Bob."

Reed hustled back to his desk, still employed as he grabbed his notebook, cell phone, and jacket. Heading for the elevator, glimpsing one of the TV screens with the BREAKING NEWS graphic under a jittery aerial shot of the scene of a van, an SFPD black-and-white, driver's door open, windshield laced with bullet holes . . . "We're taking you live now to KTO's news chopper and Sky Parker over the scene in the Richmond District—Aaron, sources have just confirmed to KTO a San Francisco police officer has been shot; that is confirmed . . .''

The elevator doors opened, Reed stepped in.

4

Blood oozed from the suspect holed up in the van near the jewelry store, matting his hair, lacing his face, and drenching his torso. Every few moments he waved a handgun randomly into the evacuated street, ignoring the bullhorned order to surrender.

Officer August lay across the front seat of his idling patrol car, its lights flashing. No way for paramedics to get to him. No need to. Half of his head was gone. Much of it covered the rear widow, filling the rifle scope of the tactical team sniper on the roof of the bakery down the street. He adjusted it to read August's bloodstained nameplate on his chest, then blinked twice. *Stay focused.* He inched his scope over to the van's windshield, catching sun glare. The vehicle rocked. Parts of the suspect jerked in and out of his crosshairs. A hand. A shoulder. A knee.

"Suspect hyper. No clear kill ʾshot," the sniper said through the throat band of his LASH headset to his team leader at the command post. It was set up at the end of the block. On the third floor of a Web-based graphics office with bay windows overlooking the hot zone.

Since the 406 call went out, every available officer from Richmond Station and others across the city had hurried to the scene. They had sealed an outer perimeter, diverting traffic a few blocks back, while evacuating people from homes, stores, and offices. Bay Area radio stations broadcast bulletins. TV news helicopters whooped by overhead. Rubberneckers with binoculars and camcorders gathered at the yellow police tape, straining to see something. Anything.

Far from public view, the tactical team had set up the inner perimeter. The scouts were the first to go in, ascertaining safety points for team members that followed, the sharpshooters, the gas team, the utility man, and the breacher. They communicated with hand signals. Each TAC member took a covered line on the gunman. Each battled to keep his mind on the job because a few yards away they faced the aftermath of their dead colleague. Early in the ordeal they heard the eerie unanswered calls over his radio as his dispatcher tried to raise him, her voice echoing in the deserted street painted red by the patrol car's pulsating emergency lights. She kept trying until she was advised to stop. In the quiet, the TAC members heard nothing but their own breathing while waiting for the tactical plan to emerge from the command post.

Lieutenant George Horn was working on it. He stood over a large table of detailed street maps, floor plans, and notes, while consulting the TAC team leader, the district people, the negotiator, the entry team leader, and the supervisor for EOD, the explosive ordinance disposal team—the bomb squad. High-ranking bodies from the Hall of Justice were said to be on the way. Horn was unfazed. He owned the scene. He knew his job. Keep it simple. Keep it flexible. Peel it down.

What you know: five victims trapped in the jewelry store because the suspects trip-wired the doors with grenades. EOD is working on the back door. Got an armed bleeding suspect waving a handgun. You can't get at him. Got a dead cop lying out there like he was trash and officers struggling not to lose it.

Okay, what you don't know: The shooter could have explosives, a hostage, or an unseen accomplice in the van.

Horn made a call to a tactical team technician on the street, crouched between a parked Cherokee and a Beetle, holding a powerful parabolic dish aimed at the truck's cab. It amplified sound from a distance by some seventy-five times.

"Anything new?"

"From what we're picking up, he's alone but agitated."

"What's he saying?"

"A lot of swearing. He doesn't sound too good."

These were Horn's options: Continue trying to talk to the shooter, which seemed futile. Gas him, and risk further casualties. Make an assault on the van and risk further casualties. Green-light a marksman, and risk casualties. Wait him out. *But you don't know what else is in that van. Could be an injured hostage or accomplice. There's a casualty risk at every turn.*

That's when the district lieutenant lost his patience. "Horn, are you going to take the mother down or buy him dinner?"

"Darnell—"

"You listen here." Darnell's eyes shone. "That's Rod August out there. One of my best. Thirty-two years old. Five years on the job. He wanted to be a detective. I'd be talking to him right now in my office, if—"

"We know," Horn said. "Take it easy. We all know."

"Sure we do. Make an assault and the shooter goes down. It's over in two minutes. If he lives, it's two decades and three million bucks of taxpayer room and board before it's over. And we all know, it's never over."

"Darnell, come on," Horn said.

"Rod's boy was being dropped off at the station today to meet him after his shift. Billy is six years old. He ain't never ever gonna forget today."

No one at the command post knew what to say, until the man leaning against the far wall broke the silence.

"No one's going to forget today, Darnell," Homicide Inspector Walt Sydowski said. "But the best we can do now is let people do their jobs. Now, buddy, just step back before you say something you shouldn't."

"You saying you want that piece of garbage to live?" Darnell said.

"I *need* him to live." Sydowski tapped his notebook on his palm. "We got two armed homicide suspects, fugitive with a female hostage. The bleeder was the wheelman. If he lives, we may learn where his friends are destined."

Darnell was considering Sydowski's point when one of the command post phones rang. Horn put it on speaker.

"It's Logan," the bomb squad tech said from the store's rear entry. "We're ready back here. Let's get them secured."

"Stand by." Horn pushed a button on the console for the direct line to the jewelry store's office and the manager.

"David," Horn said, "everybody hanging in there?"

"Yes."

"Good. We're ready to get you out. You're on speaker. The EOD people are taking it from here, okay?"

"Okay."

"David, it's Logan again. One more time, we need you to describe the grenades."

The jewelry store manager's voice betrayed his anxiety as he detailed what he saw. "Round, about the size of a baseball. Light blue with white markings and a lever that is light blue with some black and brown at the end."

"Yeah. M69s, the training version of the M67 frag," Logan said.

"What's that mean?" the manager asked.

"We think they're nonlethal."

"You *think*?"

"We're not taking any chances, David," Logan said. "Your floor plan shows you have a walk-in vault. Reinforced with a one-ton steel door. Can you squeeze everybody in, keeping the door cracked for air by wedging it with something thin and metal?''

"Yes."

"That door must remain open. Understand?''

"Yes."

"Listen carefully.''

Logan explained that a police siren would sound with three short bursts. The end of the third one would give the manager exactly two full minutes to get everyone into the vault. The bomb squad would then blow the store's rear door. Under no circumstances was anyone to leave the vault until police came for them. If the grenade detonated they'd be safe. The blast would be loud and they'd feel a vibration. Then police would send in the slow-moving remote-control robot to check for the rear grenade before moving on to the front door. It would remove the devices in a bombproof trailer, take them to a safe area, and neutralize them.

"All set, David?''

"Let's do it.''

Inside the store, Vanessa helped David move everyone into the vault. It was the size of an elevator car. The silence after the last siren yelp was unbearable, quickening everyone's breathing.

"Oh, God, please.'' The young engaged woman slid to the floor, clenching her fiancé's hand, knuckles whitening. *I can't live without him. Please, God, if we have to die, let us die together.*

The manager checked his Timex and began counting down the seconds, bracing his customers. The old watch shopper grabbed a shelf bracket to steady himself for the impact.

"Five . . . four . . . three . . . two . . ."

The vault shuddered with a *thud!* Then a tiny *ratta-tap-tap* like a metal ball bouncing on a hard floor nearing the vault's door. The manager's eyes widened, fear sliced through him as through the crack he saw the grenade come to rest against the steel door. The safety clip sprang open.

"Oh. No!"

The manager pulled the vault door shut.

At the command post, Horn reviewed the tactical plan with the TAC team leader for an assault on the van.

"The instant we've got the vault people safe, we'll try one more time to talk him out," Horn said. "If he doesn't give it up, then throw some chemicals in the van. If that doesn't work, we'll green-light the marksmen. If that fails, flash-bangs, ground-level assault, and extraction."

The TAC commanders relayed the tactical plan over the radio.

After the smoke cleared from the jewelry store blast, the six-wheel-drive remote-control robot, the size of a lawn mower, hummed as it lumbered like a tortoise over the remains of the rear door. At the end of the robot's coax cable, the police officer at the control station manipulated its joysticks and switches to study the store's interior through the remote surveillance camera. He felt relieved at the sight of the detonated grenade outside the vault door. *An M69 practice unit. Just hunky-dory. Just a bang and puff of smoke. No shrapnel. No danger.* The officer used the camera's zoom to examine the vault door. The instant he focused, alarm crept over him. The door had sealed. *What the hell?* Alerting his supervisor, he rushed from his control station into the store.

A 911 emergency dispatcher patched through a locksmith with the vault's security firm. Police had contacted him earlier, requesting he stand by a phone in case he was needed. Calmly he guided the tactical officers through steps to open the vault door. Their first attempt failed but not the second. The officers swung the door open as far as it would go.

"Thank you! Thank you!" The engaged woman cupped her hands to her tearstained face.

"Oh, thank God," Vanessa said.

"Everybody okay?" a TAC officer said, directing them out to the back alley. "Paramedics are down the block. It's all over, folks. All over."

News helicopters thundered in the distance, while TV and still photographers situated in alleys and rooftops half a block away recorded the rescue. Police hurried the robbery victims from the scene as EOD used the robot to recover the second grenade from the front door. Like the first, it was a nonlethal training model.

"What about the woman the robbers took?" David, the manager, asked a TAC officer. "Is she okay? We heard gunshots in the street."

"I don't know, sir."

In the street the bleeding gunman in the van ignored the negotiator's final plea for surrender.

"Okay," Horn said, "do it."

The order was relayed to the TAC gas teams, prompting the *thunk-thunk* of tear gas canisters from each side of the street into the van's cab. The truck rocked, clouds billowed from the driver and passenger windows. Coughing. The driver's door cracked. A handgun emerged, a boot found the ground. More coughing. The door opened. A bullhorn crackled.

"Throw down your weapon!"

The man emerged, coughing, staggering into the street, disoriented, soaked in blood, still gripping his pistol. Snipers lined him in their crosshairs. When he doubled over to vomit, the TAC team moved in, shoving him to the street on his stomach, kicking his gun clear, boots crushing the back of his neck, legs, pinning him to the pavement, searching him, handcuffing him. He moaned, squirming in a growing pool of vomit and blood. The rest of the team cleared the van.

"Nothing," one of them said.

A siren blasted and two ambulances crawled to the carnage.

Sydowski arrived just as paramedics began working on the shooter.

"He alive?" Sydowski flashed his star. "Sydowski. Homicide."

They heaved him onto a gurney.

"Barely. Looks like he's lost a lot of blood."

They slid the gurney into the ambulance.

"I'm going with you."

"What?"

"I'm going with you." Sydowski pulled himself into the rear, searching for something to sit on near the shooter's head.

"Walt!" His partner, Inspector Linda Turgeon, arrived. "Leo called me in. Horn briefed me. What's our game plan?"

The paramedics were closing the rear doors.

"I'm going to the hospital with this guy. I'll call. You contain the scene."

"All right." She gave a small wave.

As the ambulance doors were slammed, Sydowski saw TAC team members and uniformed officers from the district huddled near the patrol car of their slain friend.

Turgeon was relieved no one had contaminated her homicide scene. She pulled on latex gloves for an initial inspection of the officer's corpse, his open eyes staring at his visor. She followed his death gaze to the snapshot of a boy, his grin splattered with his father's blood.

5

Reed watched it go down, crouched against the rooftop railing beside Henry Cain, a *Star* photographer.

They had slipped by the outer police line to a California Sierra Bank, half a block away, climbed the service ladder to the roof and a good view. Cain's face was clenched behind his digital Nikon camera as he gently rolled its long lens, shooting the jewelry store rescue and the TAC team jumping on the gunman, all unfolding within yards of the dead police officer.

"Do you believe this, Tom?"

Reed didn't answer. He was jotting down details in his notepad, pages lifting in the breeze as he sketched a little map of the event. A stickman for the dead cop, next to: *How old? Years on the job? Family? WHAT HAPPENED?* It was winding down fast, ambulances and police cars were moving in everywhere. Reed closed his book, heading for the ladder.

"Henry, I gotta get to the victims."

"Hang on, I'm coming with you."

Grasping the metal handles of the ladder, they began

descending to the street when they spotted a tangle of emergency vehicles at the end of the block.

"Hold it." Cain stopped, raising his camera to shoot.

In the distance between two ambulances, Reed saw a young woman. Distraught, cupping her hands to her face. A paramedic and a female police officer were comforting her.

The rapid fire clicking of Cain's Nikon, the choppers, flashing lights, the biting ammonia traces of tear gas, made it crystalline for Reed.

This is my job.

He had wrestled with self-doubt since he had taken time off. The last few months had been agonizing. Sitting alone all day in an empty house at his keyboard, staring at a computer screen, listening to the clock tick down on the rest of his life. No sirens, no crime scenes, no yellow tape, no anguished victims forcing him to navigate his way through tragedy so he could report it. No trips to the Hall to battle detectives like Walt Sydowski, no prison interviews with murderers, or face-to-face meetings with drug dealers, thieves, pimps, hookers, gangsters, and hard-core losers. No sources calling him at all hours with tips that he turned into front-page stories under his byline. It had all evaporated.

One morning at breakfast, Reed's son, Zach, looked up from the *Star*.

"Doesn't it bug you, Dad?"

"Does what bug me?"

"Your name's never in the paper anymore."

At that moment, something flat-lined. Was it really over for him?

Sure, somewhere in the reaches of his memory lay good reason for him to leave daily crime reporting. Ann was right, his job *had* exacted a toll. But that was behind them. He had worked hard to get it all under control.

Now, as Cain's camera whirred, as the helicopters pounded in time with his pulse, Reed knew the truth. He couldn't quit. Not today. Not in the middle of a story like this. A botched jewelry store heist, a dead cop, bombs, and a blank check to write the hell out of it. *Joycean . . .*

"Okay, Reed, let's go," Cain said.

Moving down the alley, Reed was determined to find one of the victims, someone to give him a sense of what went on inside. His cell phone rang. It was Molly Wilson, a *Star* reporter, at the opposite end of the scene.

"Hey, Tom, I'm near the command post. I've got witnesses to the cop shooting, where are you?"

"In the alley. Going for the store victims. Gotta go."

"Hold on, ask about a hostage, Tom."

"A hostage?"

"My witnesses say a woman was taken hostage by the suspects who shot the cop when they fled. Police are going to put out descriptions and a vehicle when they have more."

It took half a second for Reed to absorb what Wilson was telling him.

"Okay. Thanks."

A hostage? Fugitives? *Man. It just keeps getting better.* Reed slid his phone into his pocket as they neared the area where police and paramedics were comforting the victims. Concentrating on what he had to do, he searched the group for any news competitors who had beaten him there. No sign of anyone else yet. He cast an eye around for any uniforms who might keep him away. Clear so far. Reed flinched at the sharp horn blast behind them. A police equipment van wanted to crawl by. Cain stepped into a doorway, indicating he was staying put to take photos. Reed moved for the police van, then walked alongside it, using it to bring him to the edge of the circle around the victims.

Can't get any closer than this.

Expecting to be ordered away at any moment, Reed drew on his years of working crime scenes. *Just blend in. Keep out of the way. You're not even here.* It was happening so fast. Reed didn't produce his pad, but noted everything: the manager recounting events to a detective, then the old man getting his vitals checked by a paramedic. The young couple, sitting in the rear of an ambulance comforting each other. Then, in between the crackling of the emergency radios, Reed heard a gasp.

Next to him, leaning alone on the fender of a patrol car, was a young woman. Her nameplate said VANESSA JORDAN. It looked to him that the female officer inside the car was on her radio trying to contact someone for Vanessa, who stood there, quietly sobbing, fists clenched, arms folded, holding herself together, tears streaming as she raised her face skyward, inhaling air as if she had surfaced from something cold and horrible. *This could work.*

"How you holding up?" Reed said.

"I need . . ." Vanessa's voice trailed. She was trembling.

"Sorry, Vanessa," Reed said, checking to make sure no one was approaching. "Can I help you with anything? Tom Reed from the *San Francisco Star.*"

"I need to call Stephen, my boyfriend. I need him."

"Use my phone, Vanessa."

She accepted his phone, her fingers trembled over the keypad, and she passed it back. "Could you please dial for me?" She dictated the number carefully. Reed dialed, waited until it began ringing, then gave it back. Vanessa pressed it to her ear.

"Stephen? Stephen, it's me. Oh, baby, come and get me. Please come now," she said, bending her head to hear as Reed led her to a quieter spot between two ambulances, almost out of sight.

"I'm okay but that woman . . . What? Yes, that was us on the TV news. They got us out okay but, baby, it was horrible . . ."

Reed glanced around, loving every second of his luck but fearing he would be discovered.

"They put a gun to my head. I thought I was going to die and never see you again—" A hand went to her mouth, stifling a sob. "I let them in, they looked like an old couple, this woman pushing an old man in a wheelchair, only it's a man, dressed like a woman, and they had a machine gun and started shooting and they made me get the jewels. They had hand grenades.''

Hand grenades. Reed's skin began to tingle.

''Oh God, they took my customer. She came in to buy a gift and they put the gun on her head and took her. What? I don't know. I'm with the police people. Stephen, please, I need you to come and hold me, please. Please.''

Vanessa passed the phone to Reed, who noticed TV cameras at the end of the alley. Damn. Others were arriving. He'd heard a detective shout something about keeping the press back. Vanessa Jordan buried her face in her hands.

''Vanessa, can you tell me some more about what happened? Would it be okay? I'll take some notes.''

''Reed?'' Her blinking eyes peered over her fingertips at him as she nodded. ''Tom Reed?''

''That's right.'' He pulled out his notebook and pen. ''Just quickly, they're going to move everything in a second, I just need to know a little more about what happened.''

''That older gentleman was looking at watches, that couple was looking at engagement diamonds. David, the manager, was in the back.''

''They took a woman?''

Vanessa nodded, clutching a tissue to her trembling mouth as she worked on recounting details for Reed.

''The woman had come in to pick up an order when the robbers came in, shouting that it was a holdup. They ordered everyone on the floor and started shooting the displays. One of the robbers had these hand grenades clipped on his chest, he was wearing like a bulletproof vest. I was sure we were going to die. . . .''

Reed's mind raced. It had to be a sign, this story coming to him on this day, the very day he was supposed to quit. Christ, he realized he could never quit. This was more than his job, this was what he was. And God help him he loved it. He didn't look up from his notes, writing frantically as he encouraged Vanessa to keep talking.

''. . . one of them looks out the window, gets all freaked,

something's wrong, something's wrong, so they go to my customer.''

"The woman?"

"Yes and oh God, they put a gun to her head, asked about her car, her family, I think they looked at pictures of her son in her wallet and, like, threatened her. She begged them to just take her car but they handcuffed her to the wheelchair, took her. And then—oh God—"

"Then what happened, Vanessa?"

"Then we heard the shooting in the street. Dear God, that poor woman, what happened? Is she hurt? Did they find her?"

"What can you tell me about the woman, Vanessa? Her name?"

The story was gripping, coming together nicely, Reed mapped in his mind, envisioning how in a heartbeat everyday people found themselves facing death. Police began shouting at the news crews to get back.

"She was very pretty, very nice suit, pearls, early thirties, brown hair." Vanessa brushed her hand to indicate the cut and Reed noticed the crumpled paper in her hand was not a tissue.

"What's that? Do you know her name?"

Vanessa swallowed. Looked at the slip of paper. "I forgot. This is hers, her credit card receipt. I picked it up. I was holding it for police—"

"May I see it?"

"I'd better show it to police first—"

"Just to get her name, please?"

Reed glanced around. More cops were shouting at reporters to back off.

"I don't know if I should."

"Police will want it out. To help find her, if she's a hostage. Just let me look, I won't tell anyone."

Vanessa gazed down at the receipt in her hand and began uncrumpling it, respectfully smoothing it, holding it in her opened palm. He moved his face closer to see the full name.

Ann Reed.

His mouth began to say something but an avalanche of information overwhelmed him. Brown hair, early thirties, pearls. He studied the signature he had known all of his married life, that familiar capital *A,* the clear double *n,* the elegant *R.* His skin prickled and the tiny hairs on the back of his neck stood up as the realization hit him full force.

''That's my wife.''

6

Sydowski leaned closer to the stretcher as the ambulance pulled from the scene, siren wailing. He had one chance here and it was slipping away.

They turned a corner. The suspect's head swayed. An oxygen tube ran under his nostrils. They had wrapped his gunshot wounds with pressure bandages, started him with two large-bore IVs.

But it wasn't good, the paramedic monitoring his vital signs shouted into Sydowski's ear over the siren and working engine. "He's lost a lot of blood, he's got massive internal bleeding and organ damage. He's not going to make it. He's going to code." The paramedic got on the radio to alert the hospital.

Sydowski assessed the dying man. No ID in his pockets. White, about five feet eleven, medium build, small teardrop tattoos under his left eye. Both arms were sleeved in tattoos, suggesting he did time. Probably recent and hard time, Sydowski figured, given the pallor of his skin. His eyes fluttered open, his mouth began moving. The paramedic nodded to Sydowski, he was clear to try obtaining a dying declaration.

This was critical.

He fingered a minicassette tape recorder from his pocket, set the volume to maximum, then pressed record.

"This is Inspector Walter Sydowski, of the San Francisco Police Homicide Detail, star number—" He summarized the time, date, location, circumstances, and identification of the paramedic who served as witness.

"Tell me your name?" Sydowski asked the wounded man. The response was liquid gurgling. It wouldn't be easy. Dying declarations never were. "Can you tell me anything?" Sydowski said.

"Wha—"

"Say that again."

"Why did he shoot me?"

"Who shot you? Tell me who shot you."

"Kra-kra—"

"Did the police officer shoot you?"

"Nnnn."

"Did the police officer shoot you?"

"No."

"Who shot you?" Sydowski leaned closer.

"Kra—"

"Tell me their name."

"Kraze."

"Kraze? Kraze shot you?"

"No."

"Did you shoot yourself?"

"No."

"Who shot you?"

"The kraze—"

"Go ahead, tell me."

Sydowski put the recorder an inch from the man's mouth.

"Ka— crazy psycho fahker kler."

"That's who shot you?"

"I'm the wheel. Why shoot me, you fahk— What—"

"Tell me the shooter's name." Sydowski was losing him.
"Where did they go? Where were you supposed to drive?"

"Grage."

"Tell me again."

"Grage. Drive to the grage."

"What is that?"

"See."

"Where?"

"Seek."

"Is it in San Francisco?"

"Secret. Can't—"

"Where? Give me an address?"

"Hewz wha—"

"What's the name of the man who shot you?"

"Ka-crazy fahker. Stoopid mother— Why?"

"Where did they go? Tell me."

"I dunno why the fahkerrrz— I kep' tellin' — Heez pyscho mother—"

The ambulance hit another corner. Sydowski steadied himself.

"Where do you live?"

"Don— God— I'm gonna die."

"Where do you live?"

"Don let me die!" He raised a hand; then it dropped.

"Tell me your name and where they were supposed to go."

"Don let me—" His head lolled to one side.

The ambulance creaked to a stop at the hospital. The rear doors swung open. Staff worked swiftly, rolling him into an emergency room. Sydowski went to the nearest counter to make notes. He had a dead cop, a robbery homicide with a hostage, two fugitive suspects, and a third critically wounded. He was tired and ran a hand over his face.

"Would you like a coffee, Inspector Sydowski?" A nurse set a ceramic mug with a health campaign logo on it next to his notebook. "It's fresh."

Sydowski smiled, showing his gold crowns. At six feet

three, a trim 180-pound build, a tanned face with wavy salt-and-pepper hair, he was a good-looking man. "Thanks."

The nurse left him to his work. Sydowski hated hospitals. His wife, Basha, had died in one several years ago. It nearly finished him. But he hung on to his girls, his old man, the job, his birds. Then there was Louise.

He'd met her nearly two years ago at the Seattle bird show. A beautiful sixty-something grandmother and part-time actor who looked like her forty-year-old daughter. What Louise saw in an old flatfoot like him was a mystery. He slid on his bifocals, popped a Tums in his mouth, and flipped through his notes.

Louise wanted to sell her place in San Jose, get married, and move in with him in Parkside. After months of talking about it, Sydowski had finally agreed. In two days, they were supposed to fly to Las Vegas to get married. But he was getting cold feet. Living together would be fine, but he didn't know about the marriage part. He wasn't sure how to tell Louise.

Earlier today, Sydowski was getting ready to drive down to the Sea Breeze Villas seniors complex in Pacifica to ask his old man for advice when he got the call from the homicide detail. A police officer had been murdered in a jewelry store heist and he was the primary. All vacation time canceled.

Sydowski called Louise. Las Vegas would have to wait. She detected the measure of relief in his voice and understood. She was an intelligent woman. It was one of the things he loved about her. She had him dead to rights on everything. Sydowski sipped his coffee and returned to his notes.

They had to ID the dying suspect, chase down his network. Sydowski's gut roiled telling him his case was going to get worse. He crunched on another Tums. It never stopped. In over two decades in homicide, he had surpassed four hundred homicides, held the highest clearance rate in the state, and had seen just about every kind of murder there was to see. But they just kept coming. His cell phone rang. It was his boss, Lieutenant Leo Gonzales.

"What do you know, Walt?"

"I'm at the hospital with the suspect from the van."

"How's it look for him?"

"Not good."

"What do you figure happened?"

"I figure the crew is robbing the place, when August happens to roll up on the getaway van."

"That's the early indication from dispatch."

"So they grab a hostage for a vehicle and unload on August and their wheelman to try to erase their tracks."

"Fits. You got anything we can jump on for the hostage?"

"Not yet."

"This is shaping up to be a major ball buster. Make you wish you retired and went fishing in the mountains. Feebees are going to big-foot it. The national networks are calling."

"Wonderful."

"I need you back to the scene, work your homicide, throw robbery and the feebs anything on the hostage. We need a lead on her to blast out data on her vehicle."

When Sydowski finished the call, a doctor in surgical greens, face mask undone, straps draping down his chest approached him.

"You're Inspector Sydowski, with the shooting victim?"

Sydowski nodded.

"Dr. Verdell. The patient's internal injuries were massive from five gunshot wounds. I'm afraid he didn't make it."

Sydowski nodded.

Now he had a double homicide. He turned to the counter, making a note in his book. And if they didn't find the hostage soon, odds were good he'd have a triple.

7

Reed refused to believe it was Ann.

For the longest time he stood alone telling himself that it was a mistake. Numb to the chaos, he began slipping into shock as though waiting for someone to wake him. Ann. He had to find her.

Reed left the alley, went around to the street, ducked under the yellow tape, and headed straight for the crime scene.

"Hey!" Alarm on the face of a huge uniformed officer. "Hey, you can't go down there!" Keys jingled behind Reed. Police barked into radios. "We've got press breaching the cordon!"

Trotting now, Reed was blind to the storefronts blurring by. A deathlike stillness arose from an evacuated ghost zone, void of traffic, of people, of life. Nearing the patrol car with the dead cop inside, he saw detectives probing it like somber reapers, the air punctuated with radio bursts, heavy with the smells of the bakery, the gunfire, tear gas, natural foods store, candles, flowers.

And fear.

A vise tightened against his chest as he came to the over-turned wheelchair next to the empty parking space, clutching the jewelry store receipt he had snatched from Vanessa Jordan. He stood there running his fingers over Ann's signature. *The last thing she touched. It can't be true.* He searched in every direction, praying for her to emerge from a doorway, an alcove. *Please.*

Ann.

Homicide inspectors and crime scene techs working over the murdered officer locked on to him. ''Hey, that's Reed from the *Star*. How'd he get in here? He's trampling all over our scene. Get him out of here.''

A big detective marched toward him. ''Hey! Reed! You trying to be an asshole!'' Sydowski eyeballed him. ''Get the hell out of here, or I'm going to charge you.''

''It's Ann. Walt. They took my wife from the store. She's the hostage.''

Reed told Sydowski what the clerk had said, then handed him the receipt. Sydowski passed it to his partner, Linda Turgeon. Then two huffing uniformed officers clasped Reed's shoulders, yanked at him. ''Sorry, he got by us. Let's go, pal.''

Sydowski raised a hand. ''Hold off.''

Robbery detectives arrived. ''You're the guy who was just talking to our witnesses, then ran off with evidence.''

''Listen up.'' Sydowski stopped them. ''You better hear this.'' Sydowski passed the receipt to them, noting the time on it, going over the story again with Reed. The huddle of cold serious faces grew as Reed repeated his story.

''We're just getting that from the victims,'' a robbery detective said. ''Do you have the particulars on your wife's car?''

''Yes.''

Reed slid the papers from his wallet for the detective who turned away to call a dispatcher to put out information on the vehicle used by the 187 suspects. ''The 851 is a 2003 Jetta. Four-door silver. California tag—''

Sydowski asked Reed if Ann had a cell phone.

"Yes."

Turgeon took the number and called the service provider. Sydowski called the 911 dispatcher, then said to Reed: "Try calling Ann, get her to call 911 now, so we can maybe get a fix on her whereabouts. Can you do that?"

Reed nodded, fumbled for his phone.

"Push up your volume, set your phone on the trunk of this car here. I'll listen with you and tape it after you make the call."

Reed nodded, barely noticing another detective he didn't recognize standing behind Sydowski. Listening carefully. FBI credentials were clipped to his suit jacket. Reed steadied himself, then dialed Ann's number carefully. He set the phone down, then leaned into it with Sydowski, who placed his small recorder next to it. The sound was loud and clear. One ring, two, three . . . "Hi, this is Ann. Please leave me a message." Reed glanced at Sydowski, who shook his head slightly. Reed left no message and ended the call.

"It doesn't mean anything right now, Tom," Sydowski said.

Down the block, to the pissed-off newspeople held back behind the police line, it looked like Tom Reed of the *San Francisco Star* was given some kind of exclusive access to the scene.

"That's not the case," an officer returning to the tape said.

"Oh, really?" Vince Vincent, a TV reporter with *News 99,* stuck out his chiseled chin. "Then tell us what the hell is going on."

"Give us some time here."

"You got about thirty seconds." Vincent shot his finger at the officer. "My desk is on the line to the chief right now, so you better tell us what's up with this bullshit."

"Take your finger from my face, sir, and take my word. You don't want to trade places with him at this point."

"That so? Why don't you let me be the judge of that while you start telling us what's going on down there?"

"You'll know everything in a short time."

Not soon enough. Molly Wilson pulled out her cell phone and punched Reed's number, breaking from the pack at the tape when it began ringing, watching Reed with the police in the distance.

"Hold it," Sydowksi cautioned Reed after the first ring, then said to the other detectives, "Keep it down. Okay, Tom, same as before."

They both leaned near to the phone ringing on the trunk, the tape-recording light glowing red as Reed pushed the phone's talk button and said, "Tom Reed."

"Tom?" A woman's voice, but distant, unclear.

"Ann? Ann, where are you?"

"No, Tom, it's Molly. What're you doing in there? You're drawing a lot of heat."

"I can't talk right now."

"Wait. Tom, you got some kind of scoop. I don't understand."

"Molly, I have to go."

"Damn it, Reed."

"Get off the line, Wilson. Don't call me again." He hung up.

Glancing up from his notebook, one of the robbery detectives said, "The suspects have Ann Reed's home address."

The circle of investigators grasped the significance.

"Better get people over there and clear it," the lieutenant commanding the scene said. "Tom, you expect anyone to be at your home at this time of day?"

"No."

The commander recited the address into his cell phone. "I want this off the air." He ordered cars to set up for TAC to clear the house.

Reed began listing Ann's children's clothing stores in

the Bay Area. Calls were made. Detectives and cars were dispatched.

"Tom," the detective next to Sydowski said, "Steve McDaniel, San Francisco FBI. We're going to help set up on your home phone in case Ann calls or the suspects make demands or contact. We're going to need you at home."

"Hold up. Something else." The robbery detective flipped through his notes. "Witnesses said when the suspects went through your wife's wallet they saw a photo of your son. Where is he now?"

"Zachary. Oh God! He's in school right now."

"It'll be all right," McDaniel said.

"They'll know where he is, what he looks like. I have to get him. I have to be the one to tell him."

"Take it easy," McDaniel said. "Come with me, we'll go there now. We'll call SFPD district people to sit on the school. What school is it? We'll call the principal to quietly remove Zachary from class, and hold him so you can pick him up. Let's go."

"I don't want anyone to know yet," Reed said, telling McDaniel the name of his son's school so calls could be made.

"No one's going to know, Tom," McDaniel said as they hurried from the scene.

A few feet above them, the TV camera lens peeking between the crack in the billboard covering the balcony withdrew unseen. It had recorded everything.

For unlike the reporters held back by police, this TV crew had been ensnared by events as they unfolded around them. They'd captured everything, including every word Tom Reed and the police had exchanged.

"You get the address of the school?" the young pretty reporter said to the cameraman.

"Baby, we've got it all."

The young woman grinned, her full red lips unable to contain her white teeth and glee over the gold they had mined today.

8

Ann Reed's heart hammered against her ribs in the aftermath of the shooting.

Please, God. Help me.

The red-faced man had forced her to the backseat floor of her car. He had handcuffed her wrists and held her head down with his leg, pressing her face against Zach's baseball glove, ripping the cover of his sports card magazine under it.

"One wrong move, one sound, and we'll kill you."

The metal of the gun muzzle knocked against her skull.

The white-faced man drove while his partner passed him items from one of their duffel bags. Ann tried to think. *Be smart. Be calm. Remember details.* Maybe she could plead with them? But they'd shot a police officer before her eyes. She was a witness.

Somebody, please help me.

Before her head was forced down, she had seen the driver yank off his wig, wipe away his makeup with a wet cloth, then slip on a ball cap. All within seconds. She saw his outline but could not identify details. From the movements of the man holding her, Ann sensed he was now also removing his disguise.

It wasn't long before the car gathered speed as it clicked, then hummed along an expressway to disappear into the streams of traffic that webbed across the metropolitan Bay Area. How would police find them?

No one spoke.

They monitored radio news reports. Ann heard a police scanner identify checkpoint locations as they drove and drove. Which way? South down the peninsula? North? East across the bay? Which way?

Ann closed her eyes, trembling at the odds mounting against her, remembering that she'd just filled her car with gas. The jewelry store called on her cell phone to say her order was ready. She'd been headed to the bank. The deposit bag was in the front, locked in the glove compartment. It had cash from her stores. She gasped in silence, choking on a sob. She tasted the salt of her tears rolling down her cheeks into Zach's glove. She inhaled its leathery smell, which mingled with Zach's scent from his shampoo and traces of Tom's cologne from game nights. She heard their voices, saw them rushing off to the diamond. Ann brushed her cheek tenderly against Zach's ball glove. Oh God. It felt as if they were with her now.

Why is this happening? It can't be real. Would she ever see Tom, Zach, and her mother again? All Ann could feel was the metal of the handcuffs and the car's motion taking her further and further from her life.

It was as if she were falling from earth.

God, please. Help me.

At that moment Ann tightened her fists, realizing she was still clutching the piece of jewelry she had bought for her husband.

9

Reed followed FBI Agent Steve McDaniel to his car.

"I'll need directions to the school," McDaniel said.

"South of the park. Turn left at the light."

McDaniel was in his mid-thirties, dark tanned, average height and build. Wore a navy suit. Reed noticed a few stray bullets on the carpet that likely got away from him when he loaded for the standoff.

"I forgot your name," Reed said.

"Steve McDaniel. I'm new here from LA Division."

"You're new to this city and you're the case agent on my wife?"

"Sir, I've had three years with VCMO in Los Angeles, most of them on kidnapping cases. Before that I was with SEAFAT in Seattle. We brought in a lot of violent fugitives."

"Make a left after the next light."

McDaniel's cell phone rang, he took the call, then said to Reed, "It's the principal at Zachary's school. She's got him in her office. How far away are we?"

"Fifteen minutes."

"Fifteen minutes," McDaniel said into the phone, then hung up.

Reed watched the street flow by. Watched the world continue turning even though his had stopped. Ann had been stolen and here he was giving street directions to the FBI agent on the case. Why didn't he grab Sydowski? The old homicide bull was the best. Why didn't he quit the *Star* yesterday, or sooner, like Ann wanted? He could've been with her today. What were the last words he'd said to her this morning? What were they? He couldn't remember. Something was shaking. Coming apart inside. Why did they take his wife?

"Tom, did you hear me?"

"No."

"More people will meet us at your house. We'll get your son, then set up a trap on your home phone."

"What for?"

"Ann might call home. You know that with a trap we'll get a lock on the number."

"You think she'll call?"

"In many cases, it's the first place people try to call if they get to a phone."

"What about the *other* cases?"

"Tom, the suspects might try to contact you."

"You really think so?"

"I do."

"I think I know what her chances are."

"They may have needed her car, needed her as a shield to buy time and distance."

"They already killed a cop in cold blood and you think they'll spare my wife?"

"Tom, a number of scenarios are possible. We don't know what we're dealing with just yet."

"We *do* know what we're dealing with. Cold-blooded murderers."

The fear inside Reed began rising again, flaring with images. They could rape her. Kill her. Toss her body into a dumpster. He stared at his cell phone in his helpless hand. Silent. The green power light blinking like a heartbeat. Reed covered his eyes with one hand. Ann could be dead already.

"There it is." McDaniel pulled alongside the two SFPD black-and-whites at the front of the school.

He badged them, passed the school security officer, who was chatting with two SFPD uniforms. McDaniel and Reed strode through the entrance, down the polished floors of the locker-lined hall. It echoed with the din of classes in progress. Passing an opened door, Reed exchanged quick glances with a male teacher, tapping chalk in his palm.

"Who can tell us what Thomas Jefferson meant when he said . . ."

Reed couldn't recall the last time he had come to Zachary's school. Ann usually took care of all the parent-teacher stuff.

He blinked at the murals on the hall walls under student renderings of the Stars and Stripes, the California state flag, the city flag. The theme was "Our Nation Is Great Because of . . ." Color photos of smiling eleven- and twelve-year-olds beamed from their handwritten papers on topics of Love, Truth, Friendship, Freedom, and Courage. Reed stopped. Zach's face smiled from his paper on Courage. How would he tell him?

They came to the small lobby of the main office where a tall silver-haired woman in a coral pantsuit, holding her folded glasses in one hand, Zach's file in the other, greeted them with concern on her face.

"Hello, I'm Lenore Lord, Zachary's principal. Can you tell me what this is all about?"

"We'll tell you more when we know more," McDaniel said.

"Should I be concerned with the other students?" Her brow creased.

"This is a police matter that only involves one student."

"Is it Zachary's mother, Ann, Mr. Reed? Is she hurt?"

"I don't know much."

"Does this have anything to do with the emergency north of the park? Some teachers in the lounge said there'd been a shooting."

"We really can't divulge any details," McDaniel said.

"I see." The principal's attention went to McDaniel's badge. "And you're with the FBI. Perhaps I should talk to the San Francisco police."

"Ms. Lord, I'd like to see my son now."

"This way."

They followed her into the labyrinth of administration offices. Before stopping at the final door.

"Give me five minutes alone with him," Reed said before he entered.

Zach was on a sofa, hands clasped between his knees, surprise blooming on his face when he saw Reed. The parent who never came to school.

"Dad?"

Setting eyes on his son, Reed saw how much he looked like Ann. Then it came upon him full force like a dagger piercing his heart.

"Hey there, Zach."

"Why are *you* here?" Zach stood.

"It's okay, you can sit down."

"Am I in trouble?"

"No, you're not in trouble." He put his hand on Zach's knee. "I'm going to take you home."

"Home? What for? Where's Mom?"

"Zach, I'm going to need your help on something, something very important."

"I don't understand, Dad."

"Son, it's your mother."

"Mom?" He blinked. "Mom? What? Is she all right?"

"We don't know."

"You don't know? Dad?" His chin crumpled. "Where is she? What happened, Dad? Where's Mom!"

After Reed told him everything, Zach stared at the wall with the flag, the president's picture, the governor's picture.

"Son, it's very, very serious. It's a bad situation. The FBI are going to take us home in case Mom calls, or there's new information. They're getting Grandma in Berkeley and bringing her to our place right away to wait with us. Do you understand?"

"She was buying you a present."

"What's that?"

"Mom. I heard her talking on the phone the other day. She had a surprise present to pick up today at the jewelry store. It was for you."

"I know that now."

Reed put his arm around Zach's shoulder. "We have to be prepared, son. We have to hope for the best that she's going to be all right, that maybe they just needed her car. But we also have to be prepared for anything, okay? You understand?"

Zach was at that awkward age, that period of passage from boyhood into adolescence just before the intense years to manhood. Yet it soothed Reed to feel his son's arms clamp around him. He needed a hug too.

"I'm scared, Dad." Tears rolled down Zach's cheeks.

"Let's go, son."

They were joined by McDaniel when they left the school and hurried down the steps to the car. For a second Zach was overcome by the gravity of the situation brought on by the sight of the San Francisco police and second FBI car with its dash-mounted cherry flashing. He flung his arms around his father. At that moment Reed looked across the street, into the lens of the sole TV news camera shooting from the side of an SUV that didn't have any station logo on it.

After McDaniel drove off with Reed and Zach, the woman turned to the cameraman.

"Did you see how the kid's arms went tight around his dad? The emotion in the kid's little face with his father next to the FBI agent? Did you get all that?"

"Got it."

"It's just so freaking good." Contorting her face before her compact mirror, she engaged in a few touch-ups. Eyes, cheeks. "That's just terrific. It just keeps getting better." She smiled at herself and the prospect of her career skyrocketing.

10

At the edge of the Tenderloin District, just short of the promise of gentrification, but beyond the sidewalks dotted with syringes and islands of vomit, is San Francisco's newest TV news bureau.

Take the creaking stairs of the old Paradise, the aging hotel that morphed into an office building now called Golden Boulevard Plaza. Go to the third floor. Head for the rear and the dark green wooden door fractured by years of police raids. Check out the sign. WORLDWIDE NEWS NOW.

That was the local flag of the new international tabloid TV show headquartered in London. Trafficking in celeb dish, scandal, gruesome crime, and tragedy, *Worldwide* aired successfully to some ninety million viewers in thirty-six countries including the U.S., where it was struggling to carve itself a share in the planet's most lucrative market. To no one's surprise, exclusive dramatic video footage, obtained by any of its bureaus, routinely activated cell and bedside home phones up the corporate masthead in time zones around the globe.

That was the case in the minutes after the San Francisco

bureau shipped off its raw footage of the jewelry store murder abduction to New York, which sent the pictures to London's night desk, who alerted the execs.

"This is New York, stand by, San Francisco," *Worldwide*'s speakerphone said.

"We're standing by."

Tia Layne, chief of the two-person bureau, put her feet on her desk, lit another congratulatory Camel, waved out her match. She squinted through her smoke stream at Cooter, the cameraman working at the computer. Tia pushed the mute button on the office phone keypad, dropped her voice as a precaution.

"This is our ticket. Hear back from the others yet?"

Keeping his eyes on his computer screen, Cooter scratched his two-day growth, then adjusted his foot-long ponytail. "Two San Francisco stations, affiliates to the networks."

"How much?"

"Five thousand each. Wait. A broker in LA will go ten."

"Tell them all the all-news people are up to twenty. Stress that they think the story has legs and we've got access. I'm going back on speaker."

Cooter cut a trace of a grin as he typed. After all this time, he thought he knew Tia. They'd met on the set of a "no-budget" sleaze film in Thailand three years ago. She'd got there by way of losing her job after one month as foreign correspondent. Her Sydney-based news agency fired her because she couldn't prove several people she'd named in her stories existed. Tia then worked as a drug courier, then as an actor in multi-X-rated movies where Cooter was the cameraman. After some one hundred films Cooter thought he knew every inch of Tia. But today she was revealing something he'd never seen. She was a business shark who'd done her homework. Guess being an American caught up in a police investigation that nearly lands you in a Thai prison, or worse, kinda changes your tactics.

"Still standing by in San Francisco," Tia said. "What's going on?"

"London's the holdup. They want William in on this."

Tia raised her eyebrows and began jotting numbers on a pad, recalling how not so long ago her life had gone to hell in Bangkok. Her dream of starting her own production company died when all the money she'd saved from her "acting" career was seized by the Royal Thai Police during a huge money-laundering probe. Her manager was washing her earnings with those of his drug lord friends.

Never again, she vowed.

She and Cooter got back to the U.S. a week before the entire Thai crew would have been charged and jailed. They arrived in Los Angeles penniless and out of work. In the early days, Cooter fell into a hazy California shell-shocked type of existence crashing and getting high with his old TV news friends who worked at LA's biggest news stations.

Through Cooter's friends, they learned *Worldwide News Now* was searching for freelance stringers in San Francisco. They'd helped Cooter make Tia a few on-camera audition tapes that created the impression she had a little "on-camera" experience. Well, it wasn't really a lie. Some of the LA gang vouched for them.

At twenty-seven Tia looked good, possessed a naturally sultry voice that she used as a tool of seduction. She would give those hairdo college girls a lesson in how to perform in front of a camera.

Tia and Cooter got the job. Sort of.

They weren't staff; instead they got a twelve-month free-lance contract. No salaries. They'd be paid for assigned stories but could negotiate a price for anything they generated themselves, provided *Worldwide* had first right of refusal. Tia had worked out the deal. Bangkok crime lords had taught her well. Nobody would ever screw her again. At least not without her consent and contribution. Tia crushed her Camel with the heap of others in the take-out wrapper on her desk.

"Hello, America." The speakerphone came to life again. "This is London. Love your pictures. Stand by."

Tia shook her head, glanced at her watch, reread their contract again. They had been with *Worldwide* three months. Given the show had more than seventy bureaus around the world all competing to get their work on a daily thirty-minute program, it was a victory just knowing that the execs were considering your work.

"Seth in New York, are you there? It's Nigel in London."

"Go ahead."

"William Banks will be joining us. He's at a convention in Monaco. We just picked up five more countries, so he's very positive. He's on a yacht."

"Nigel, Banks here. Let's get going. Everyone ready?"

"Ready in San Francisco."

"The pictures are good," Banks said, "Can you brief me?"

Layne tapped a nail to Banks's photo in an annual report. He headed *Worldwide*'s entire news operation. The top news guy.

"It's your stuff, Tia, go," Seth in New York said.

"We had a line that several Hollywood names were charting their movie choices under the advice of a low-profile San Francisco fortune-teller."

"I like that," Banks said.

"We were in her neighborhood getting establishing shots, b-roll, when a jewelry store was robbed, a San Francisco police officer murdered, and the wife of a celeb reporter taken hostage. We got it all."

"Yes, I saw your pictures. Outstanding," Banks said. "How old is this?"

"Couple of hours."

"Too late for tonight's show in America. How exclusive is it?"

Cooter had been monitoring the Bay Area casts. Nothing.

"Absolute exclusivity," Layne said.

"Yes, well, what about security cameras or amateur footage?"

"Police are holding a news conference soon. We'll learn from them what they have."

"Right, we could start teasing *Worldwide* for tomorrow's show. Nigel? Seth? Set it up for Europe and buy extra time in America."

"Certainly, William."

"Fine then," Banks said. "Very nice work, sorry, your name in San Francisco?"

"Tia Layne and we're not done here, Billy."

From New York to London, to the yacht on the Mediterranean at Monaco, the silence fell thick on the line.

"Excuse me, Miss Layne?"

"I've got our contract in front of me. All I'm required to do is give you first right of refusal on our work. Which I did. Now you tell me how much you're going to pay for it, because I can get thirty thousand from the U.S. networks. This is supreme stuff and this story could go long."

It took about half a second for Banks to realize he was dealing with someone nearly worthy of his time.

"Who did you say this celeb reporter was, whose wife has been taken hostage?"

"Tom Reed, a *San Francisco Star* newspaper reporter, Pulitzer nominee, a big crime reporter."

"Never heard of him. Have you, Nigel?"

"Not at all, sorry. Seth, is he relevant to Americans?"

"Well, he was on Larry King, he'd broken a few big crime stories."

"San Francisco?" Banks said. "We'll go fifteen."

"Thirty, because I know that's what the U.S. brokers can get us."

"And how would you know that? Have you been shopping?"

"I'm aware of the market."

"Ms. Layne, is it? I get the feeling you're extorting us and to be blunt, I don't much like it."

"To be blunt, your annual report states the corporation earned one hundred million dollars in profits last year and your challenge is to secure footing in the U.S. market. Now my deal requires me to offer you first right of refusal on our work and release it to you if we've agreed on a sum. If we don't agree, I'm free to shop it. Now, I've showed you our work and I've told you our sum. Thirty thousand.''

''Twenty.''

''No. Thirty. You consider this: thirty thousand and you tease it all over the U.S. tomorrow. We bury it two-thirds into the show, pull in more numbers, spike your ad rates a bit. After we air this stuff—and you damned well know it's good—every major American news network is going to want to use it. You license it to them stipulating full duration credit to *Worldwide News Now* and you've just got more free advertising in your critical market than you could possibly dream of. You consider this, you got advertising twerps in New York you pay more than thirty thousand a year and they couldn't come close to touching what I'm giving you: the recorded murder of an American police officer, the kidnapping of a celeb wife. It'll be controversial, there'll be national newspaper editorials. The day after you use this, *Worldwide News Now* will be the most talked about show in America. So you want to dick me around for thirty thousand and then watch what you could've had, flashing in your face on CNN or FOX? I think shareholders would love knowing about that after they read it in the *Wall Street Journal*. You've got thirty seconds.''

There was nothing but silence all the way around. Cooter was shaking his head, wondering if this was the same woman he had recorded in more sexual acts than he could remember.

''Agreed. Thirty thousand, Ms. Layne.''

''On one condition.''

''No conditions.''

''Fine. You do get CNN over there?''

There was a tense audible sigh.

''What's your condition, Ms. Layne?''

''Thirty thousand for each additional exclusive portion of footage we deliver to you on this story.''

"Fifteen."

"Thirty."

"Thirty. But it must be exclusive."

"Agreed. Then you'll make today's payment for sixty. We've got Tom Reed exclusively picking up his son at school minutes after Ann Reed was taken hostage."

"Fine. And, Ms. Layne?"

"Yes, Mr. Banks?"

"This deal is null and void if we determine your footage is not exclusive at airing, or if a single frame has been previously shopped. I've got your contract in front of me too."

"Then we have a deal."

"Indeed we do."

After the calls ended, Tia Layne and Cooter watched their exclusive footage again, the murder of a San Francisco police officer, the kidnapping, Tom Reed picking up Zachary.

"Hold it, Cooter, run that again. See? Look at the kid's face." Tia bit her thumbnail. "People are just going to eat this up."

Tia lit another cigarette, watching and thinking of any way to keep this story going. To her, Tom Reed's anguish and his wife's life were mere articles of commerce. Product. And she was determined to produce more.

11

Ann Reed smiled at the reporters packed into the Police Commission Hearing Room in the Hall of Justice for the first press conference.

News cameras pulled in tight on her photo, which had been reproduced from her driver's licence, enlarged, and posted on the corkboard. Nothing in her pretty face betrayed the fact that death was so near. On the board next to her were the pictures of SFPD Officer Rod August and Leroy Driscoll, the dead suspect from the van. The cameras tightened on them too.

As they settled into chairs, reporters gossiped, sharing their disbelief and theories over what had happened to Reed, scanning the pack to see who the *Star* had assigned to cover the story of one of its own. The reporters who knew Reed wanted to convey their sympathy. Those who didn't wanted an inside angle.

Lieutenant Leo Gonzales of the homicide detail began by summarizing the case. He pointed to the color photos on the board of a car identical to Ann Reed's. He detailed her physical description, including the clothing and jewelry she was wearing at the time of her abduction.

The last time she was seen alive.

Then Gonzales cleared his throat, leaned into the mountain of microphones, and dropped a stunner.

"We're hoping Officer August's final radio call will help us solve his murder and find Ann Reed. We're going to play the last seconds of those dispatches for you. We believe the voices in the background are those of Ann Reed and the suspects. We hope someone will recognize them and we're appealing to the public for help."

The revelation rippled through the room. Gonzales explained how in the moments after August had called in his location and a vehicle check, SFPD dipatchers received a 911 call from a barbershop of a 211, an armed robbery in progress. The caller reported gunshots in the neighboring jewelry store. When the dispatcher tried to alert August, who was in the area, she maintained an open line to his unit radio. It recorded the gunfire that killed him. It also recorded the seconds that followed and what detectives believed were the voices of the suspects passing by with the hostage.

Gonzales nodded to an officer who set a tape player before the microphones. The tape rolled, its volume boosted. First came defeaning popping, then crashing, glass breaking, then chaos, and then August. "Four, oh, six—request—" then his death gasps, then his dispatcher's frantic futile calls to raise him over radio cross talk. "All units report of a 211 and 406—in the—" Arising from the static hiss between recording beeps came new voices from the street. Distant but clear, beginning with a woman, her cries growing louder as they neared the police car.

"Oh God, please let me go!"

"Shut up! I told you to shut up! Where's your car!"

"Please. Don't, just please!"

"Are you sure you got him?"

"Christ, it's all going to hell!"

"Keep moving, come on!"

The voices faded, drowned out by police alerts, people shouting in the street, then sirens. The tape clicked off. Silence filled the room. Gonzales was now ready for questions from the press.

"Do you have any leads on the whereabouts of Ann Reed?"

"Nothing so far."

"Any contact or demands from her abductors?"

"Nothing."

"What are the odds she'll be found unharmed?"

"We won't speculate. This is a priority. We've got several agencies working together on the case."

"A task force?"

"Yes."

"Do you have anything on who the two male suspects are?"

"Nothing concrete so far, it's only been a few hours."

"The dead man in the van, Leroy Driscoll, how did you identify him?" asked a young man from an Internet magazine, who looked to be in his teens.

"Fingerprints."

"His picture has a CDC number. Is it a prison photo?"

"Correct. He did time in Folsom."

"His offense?"

"He stole cars."

"Can you confirm who shot Driscoll? Was it August?"

"Officer August never discharged his weapon."

"This is for Lieutenant Darnell," a columnist from the *Chronicle* said. "Sir, what can you tell us about Officer August? How many years of duty?"

Lieutenant Moses Darnell swallowed hard and gathered his thoughts, before his words came out in a deep baritone as if he were giving a eulogy.

"Rod August was sworn in five years ago. He was an outstanding officer who was on his way to becoming an outstanding detective. He was a devoted father to his six-year-old son, who was supposed to meet him at the station today when he finished his shift. He was thirty-two years old." Darnell swallowed, looked away. A few awkward seconds passed before a reporter from the Associated Press asked if investigators knew how much had been stolen in the heist.

"We're still doing inventory with management. It will take some time."

"Given the average jewelry store take is upwards of a hundred and fifty thousand dollars, where would you put this one?"

"Substantial."

"Seven figures?"

"Substantial."

"Does the fact grenades were used suggest terrorist involvement?"

"We don't think this is a terrorist act, but we can't rule it out yet."

"What's the robbery history of the store?"

"This is a first-time hit."

"How would you rate its security?"

"First-rate. But this was a planned, brazen, violent attack. As we told you, the suspects were disguised. They destroyed all security cameras and took the tapes with them."

That bit of information on video hit home with Tia Layne. "Officer, are you saying you have no images from any security cameras or amatuer video of the suspects?"

"We're still checking cameras in the area, but nothing's surfaced so far. We're asking anyone with any information to contact us."

Layne immediately collected her bag and headed for the door. She nearly tripped over the feet of some woman who appeared to be out of it. As if grief-stricken by the story. *Taking this a little personal there, aren't you, hon?* Layne thought as she brushed by her. Then, passing Cooter at the back of the room amid the fence of tripods and TV cameras, she shot him a barracuda's grin. He winked back.

Both knew the police tape with the dead officer, his killers, and the hostage would enhance their exclusive footage with dramatic sound.

In the hallway, Layne found a private corner and slid into it. Indifferent to public smoking regs, she lit a cigarette, then pressed her cell phone's speed dial for *Worldwide* in New York. They'd love this. A "worldwide exclusive," that's what they called their hottest stuff. Layne dragged hard on her Camel. *It's going to be so out-of-this-world compelling. Damn.* She exhaled. *Be there, Seth. Got to get started promoting this. More important, you got to cut me that freaking check.* Layne tapped a glossed fingernail to her teeth. The way that woman was screaming, pleading in the audio. Beautiful.

Absolutely beautiful.

12

Molly Wilson drove from the Hall of Justice to Reed's home near Golden Gate Park, brushing at the tears drying on her cheeks.

Reed was her best friend at the *Star*. Her confidant. They sat next to each other, worked with each other, knew the details of each other's lives. She stopped at a light, hands tightening on the wheel. *Get ahold of yourself.*

But nothing made sense. In a matter of hours everything had gone nuts. It started when she stomped back into the newsroom searching for Reed so she could rip into him for acting so weird at the scene. Then Acker, the deputy assignment editor, rushed up and told her. Tom's wife was the hostage.

Molly was dumbstruck, standing there staring at Tom's empty desk, his computer, the framed photo of him with Ann and Zach, as the news exploded around her and frenzied editors put more people on the story. At the news conference she could barely take a note. She sat there in shock catching her breath when they played that tape of the gunfire, the officer, the killers, then Ann pleading.

A horn blast startled Wilson. The light had turned green just as her cell phone rang. It was Acker, even more frantic since watching the press conference, which TV had carried live.

"Molly, did you get to Reed yet?"

"No."

"You've got to get to him. How far away from his house are you? TV's going live from the house. Everybody's there."

"Acker, listen to me."

"We called his house, his cell, her stores, relatives. Nothing."

"Stop phoning him at home. Homicide told me he can't talk now, the FBI has a trap on his phone in case Ann calls, or they make demands."

"He'll talk to you."

"Acker, his wife's been kidnapped."

"And that's news, Wilson. This is the biggest story in the state right now. It's ours and you better not drop the ball."

Another horn blast. Wilson pulled over.

"Acker, what does Shepherd say? Let me talk to Bob."

"He's in meetings. They want you to get to Tom, Molly."

"Acker, are you listening to me? He won't talk to anybody."

"You're his friend. Get in his house as his friend, Molly, and get us the edge on this story."

"Acker, I just told you—"

"Did you see the press conference?"

"What?"

"Hear that tape? It was unbelievable. Did you hear the tape?"

"Yes, I heard the damned tape. *I was there.* You sent me there."

"Then you get to him and get us an interview before deadline."

"Acker—"

He hung up.

Wilson's bracelets chimed as she thrust her phone into her bag, cursed, her eyes burning as she left six feet to rubber and squealed back into traffic. Emotion rolled over her, forcing her to admit her problem.

Wilson came to the *Star* from a Texas daily, where she'd worked on the police beat after finishing her master's degree in English literature. In San Francisco, she was assigned to the crime desk with Reed. After years of intense stories together, Reed had become more than a mentor. And there were so many times she wanted to tell him.

Especially during Reed's dark days when he was drinking and Ann had taken Zach and left him. Wilson reached out to Reed, made her desires clear, but he worked things out with Ann. Wilson was happy for him. She was. But as time and superficial relationships wheeled by, she thought of Tom.

It's wrong. You've got to stop this, she told herself as she came upon the knot of police cars, news trucks, and neighbors in front of Reed's house. Part of her could barely stand being here, yet part of her didn't want to be anywhere else. A couple of uniformed officers held the press back on the sidewalk in front of the house.

"Latest word is, Mr. Reed's not making a statement," a cop told reporters.

Wilson scanned the area, relieved to spot Sydowski from homicide approaching from down the street. She went to him.

"Hi, Walt."

"Wilson."

"Have you been in?"

"In and out a few times."

"It's so horrible. Any word on Ann?"

Sydowski eyed Wilson. He was looking for a notebook or tape recorder. Didn't see one. "No word on her."

"How's Tom doing?"

"It's rough, Molly. Sorry, I gotta get inside."

"Please, Walt. Can you tell him I'm here, that I want to see him?"

"I don't think this is the best time."

"Please."

"I'll see what I can do."

Wilson watched him enter the home through the same door Ann Reed had opened for her so many times in the early days, when she and Tom hosted parties. Or when she'd drop by to visit. So long ago.

Wilson walked behind a TV news van, hugging herself to wrestle down the truth that was gnawing at her.

13

Zach Reed stood unnoticed at the kitchen doorway listening to his mother's pleas hissing on the tape police were replaying for his father.

"Dad?"

The detectives and FBI agents at the table turned. The tape was switched off and Reed's red-rimmed eyes met his son's.

"Yes, son?"

"Maybe they'll let Mom go when they get far enough away, you think?"

Reed was at a loss. The investigators exchanged glances to see who among them had the right answer.

"It's a pretty good theory," Sydowski said.

Zach nodded.

"Zach," Sydowski said, "the most important thing now is to keep working on positive theories like that one. Think you can do that?"

"Yes."

Ann's mother, Doris, came to the doorway. She put her

arm around her grandson. Lines of worry creased deep into her face.

"Zachary, some pizza's just been delivered. I'll bet you're hungry."

"Not really."

"I think it's your favorite with extra cheese and there's cherry soda."

Reed found the words to say, "Go with Grandma, Zach, have something to eat."

"Okay, Dad."

Outside the Reed home, satellite trucks and a small crowd lined the street. Inside, technicians put in extra phone and fax lines. Uniformed officers and detectives came and went. People worked on laptops, talked on cell phones, drank coffee, consulted files, shared notes, and monitored TV and radio news reports. As they worked, not one cop in the house dared breathe a word of the horrible reality behind cases like these: that the odds of Ann Reed contacting them were astronomical. The odds they would find her were even greater.

Reed's home phone rang. All activity ceased.

"It's coming from within the city," said an FBI agent reading from a computer screen. "It's a business. Stand by."

The FBI had put a trap and trace on the Reeds' home phone to immediately give them the number and a fix on details of any incoming call. Tape recorders connected to the line were rolling. Sound-level needles bounced. An FBI hostage negotiator wearing a headset was ready to listen in. He had a clipboard and pen, prepared to jot instructions. Reed looked at the negotiator, who nodded. Reed grabbed it on the third ring.

"Hello."

"Is this Tom Reed, of the *San Francisco Star*?"

"Yes."

The FBI agent working at the computer screen indicated it was a press call. McDaniel and Sydowksi nodded.

"Tom, it's J.D. Mark with Bay Action News Radio."

"I'm sorry. We can't really say anything right now."

"But if you could tell the cop killers who took your wife one thing, Tom, what would it be?"

"Please."

"Tom, just a few words."

"Release her. I'd say just release her. Please. And, if anyone has any information, just call the police. Please."

Reed hung up, then plunged his face into his hands. It was the thirty-ninth press call since the news conference. When Reed regained his composure, McDaniel passed him a thin file folder on the dead suspect, Leroy Driscoll.

Reed studied the information, glancing at Driscoll's NCIC number, his CDC data. Served time for stealing cars. Driscoll's profile, then his mug scowled at him. Chin tilted, stone-cold expression, three small tattoos running like tear tracks under his left eye.

"Tom," McDaniel said, "is Driscoll in any way familiar to you?"

Reed shook his head.

"And the voices on the dispatcher's recording, they ring any bells?" Sydowski said. "Want us to play the tape again?"

"No. I keep telling you. Why do you keep pushing this on me? You guys have said this is random. Why do you keep asking me this stuff? Do you really think there is some connection to me? Is there something you're not telling me?"

"No," Sydowski said. "It's procedural. You know that, Tom. We're checking all possible links."

"Sounds like you got jack. Sounds like you're desperate."

"Take it easy. We're doing everything we can."

"What about his prison and parole records? Find out who his friends are? Fingerprint the store, the van? Find out where he lived? Did you fingerprint his gun, trace it, the shell casings? Anything like that? Or you just going to ask me stupid questions?"

"Keep it down, Tom. We've got people doing all of those things and more. We're going to need a little time."

"Ann doesn't have any time! It could be too late! *You know it. I know it!* Hell, they murdered a cop and their getaway man and took my wife. Now you tell me, how much time does she have?"

Reed felt hands on his shoulders pushing him back down into his chair.

"Keep it down, Tom," McDaniel said. "You got to think of your son."

"Tom, we've got no evidence to indicate anything right now," Sydowski said as his cell phone sounded. He took the call, listening, then saying: "No, I haven't told him yet. Just hang on." Then to Reed. "Molly Wilson and Henry Cain from the *Star* are out front. They want to see you."

"Let them in," Reed said.

"Aren't they press?" McDaniel was shaking his head. "No, Tom, we've already given a press briefing today."

"I'll talk to them."

"Tom, we need to all be on the same page on releasing information."

"They're friends. They were there. I'll talk to them."

When Reed saw Wilson and Cain, something swelled inside so he nearly lost the little control he had as Wilson hugged him tight and Cain shook his hand, squeezing it firmly. Hours ago the three of them were covering the thing. Now, it was as if he were receiving them at Ann's wake.

"Tom, all the photogs send their best, man," Cain said.

Wilson and Cain sat on the sofa, Reed sat in the adjacent chair, circled by detectives.

"You've got ten minutes, Ms. Wilson," McDaniel said.

She kept her head down, opening her notebook, flipping past used pages, stopping at a fresh one. She uncapped her pen, her hand quivered slightly, waiting to write.

"Tom, how—" She stopped. Started again. "How did you learn it was Ann?"

Reed struggled as he recounted everything, answering

Wilson's questions while the FBI counted down the time. Ann's mother joined Reed, standing next to him, taking his hand.

"We're praying," she told Wilson, as Zachary slipped between his dad and his grandmother, telling Wilson that he wanted the bad guys to "please just let my mom go."

Cain's Nikon flashed repeatedly on them, capturing Reed's anguish, Zach's young heartbroken face, Ann's mother dabbing her eyes.

Ten minutes passed and McDaniel said, "Time's up."

"One last thing, Tom." Wilson stood. "You said you learned it was Ann from the receipt. What did she buy at the jewelry store?"

"I don't know. A surprise gift for our anniversary."

"We're going to hold that information back for now," McDaniel said.

At the door, Wilson searched Reed's eyes, embracing him again, whispering to him. "I'm so sorry, Tom. They wanted us to do this."

"It's okay," he said. Reed understood. Maybe better than anyone else.

Hours passed without any contact from Ann or her abductors. Reed went to the window looking out at the street, feeling nothing.

Bob Shepherd, Reed's editor from the *Star,* called.

"Everyone at the paper sends their prayers, Tom. The publisher's setting up a reward fund for information, or for anything you might need. If there's anything I can do, call, no matter what. Call."

"Thanks, Bob" was all Reed could manage.

Night came and police told Reed they were following scores of tips from the news conference. Sightings and police stops involving cars and women fitting the descriptions. But nothing concrete. Detectives continued working quietly as Reed gazed at the satellite trucks, unable to count the stories where he had pursued anguished relatives and friends of crime victims.

Reed had lost track of the time. Zach had refused to go to his bedroom, falling asleep on the sofa, his head in his grandmother's lap. Eventually, she drifted off too. Reed ached from exhaustion, lack of eating, then grappling with the sudden strange hum of his nerves being strained as the phone jangled, jolting everyone from the quiet.

The agents were instantly alert.

It was 2:35 A.M.

"Call is coming from San Francisco," the FBI agent at the computer said.

It rang a second time.

"A residence in the Mission area."

SFPD dispatch was alerted. The negotiator nodded to Reed, who swallowed, then answered.

"Hello."

No response. But the line was open. The sound-level needles on the recorders did not move.

"Hello," Reed repeated.

Nothing.

Zach sat up, rubbing his eyes, watching his father, reading his face as he spoke into the silence at the other end of the line.

"Hello, is anyone there?"

Agents and detectives were making notes, whispering, consulting their computer screens. Digits of the computer clock timing the call blurred by as exhaustion and grief overcame Reed.

"Annie?" Reed said.

More silence passed. Reed squeezed his temple with his free hand. "This isn't funny!" he shouted into the phone.

A male voice responded. "No, it's not funny, Mr. Reed."

"Who is this? Where's Ann?"

"She had to pay."

The negotiator stared hard at Reed, gesturing for him to

keep the conversation alive, keep the guy on the phone while the PD scrambled cars.

"Pay?" Reed said. "Pay for what?"

"You'll have to figure it out, Mr. Ace Reporter."

"Where is she? Let me talk to her. Jesus, please! I'm begging you!"

Silence.

"Please don't hurt her. Just let me talk to her. Please."

"That's not possible."

"What do you want? Please let me talk to my wife."

"You won't be speaking to her tonight."

"Where is she? Please let me talk to her. What have you done?"

"You won't be speaking to her ever again."

The line went dead in Reed's hand.

14

The FBI locked on to the exact location of the call within seconds.

"A residence in the Mission off of South Van Ness." The agent at the computer read the address from his screen to the SFPD dispatcher. "Advise them no sirens."

They had three black-and-whites and two ghost cars in the zone. It took four minutes for them to hit the location.

One of the unmarked cars drove by the address, a neglected bungalow, its paint peeling, the yard a jungle of wild grass, entwining weeds, shrubs, trash, patches of an overgrown hedge. It had a small ramshackle garage with swing-out doors shut tight and secured by a heavy padlocked chain.

The SFPD tactical team was rolling. ETA was thirty minutes.

More police vehicles converged on the area establishing an outer perimeter to choke off all traffic in and out. The late hour was an advantage. Residents in houses in the line of fire were awakened and evacuated.

As the TAC team moved into position, the commander

was informed that the house had no complaint history and the rez, Ray Archer, aged sixty-four, did not come up in anyone's system.

"We've got a white male, lying on a bed in a bedroom in the southwest corner. Watching TV. No weapons. No other occupants," one of the TAC scouts reported.

After weighing all scenarios, the commanders decided that surprise was critical given that a hostage could be used as a shield in a protracted standoff.

"Everyone set," he said. "Go in hard. Go."

Entry teams came in from the front and the rear, clearing the small two-bedroom house, within seconds coming upon the sole occupant.

A disheveled man, wearing dark pajamas and a white robe, lying in his bed watching TV. The air in the place had the hospital smell of disinfectant.

The man was not alarmed seeing four heavily armed TAC team officers, their weapons trained on him, standing in his bedroom. Unshaven, mostly bald, save for the foot-long strands of gray-white hair writhing wizardlike from the sides of his head, the man seemed pleased to see the officers.

"Book 'em, Dano," he said, raising his hands, palms open.

One officer looked at the man's wallet on the table near the bed.

"You're Ray Archer?"

"I am and I want a lawyer. I know my rights."

The officers surveyed the room. The tables and dressers were cluttered with scrapbooks bulging with news clippings. On one, the San Francisco telephone book was splayed open. One of the white pages was folded back to the listings for Reed. Tom Reed's number was in the book, but no address. His listing was underlined in red. Another officer flipped through the scrapbook. Clippings of Bay Area crime stories, some of them *Star* stories with Reed's byline. The TV was tuned into *Dragnet*.

"You have the right to remain silent," Ray Archer was told.

Several empty medication containers were among the newspapers. The name of the doctor listed on the prescription was read over Archer's bedside telephone to a police dispatcher.

The doctor was awakened, the call patched through. It took a few moments to absorb what was happening with Ray Archer, her outpatient from Golden State Coastal Psychiatric Institute.

"He suffered a head injury from a motorcycle crash years ago," she explained to the TAC team leader standing in Archer's bedroom.

"Ray used to be a scriptwriter in Hollywood. Cop shows. I'm sorry. He does this from time to time when he's off his meds. Calls real people he learns about from the news and assumes a role. He's harmless."

"Who loves ya, baby?" Ray Archer grinned.

The TAC team officers exchanged looks.

Some of them had been friends with Rod August. Two of them would be pallbearers at his funeral.

15

Details of the call were immediately relayed to Reed's home.

"False alarm. It came from a psychiatric patient," Sydowski repeated into his phone, turning to Reed, who acknowledged the report by closing his eyes and shaking his head wearily.

He went to the window, unsure if he could hold up much longer. Ann's mother, Doris, joined him and placed her hand on his shoulder. "I know what you're fearing, Tom. I fear it too."

Reed put his arm around her and they comforted each other.

"Ann's a fighter," she said. "You know that. She's smart. We can't give up. We have to be strong for her now and keep praying."

Nodding, Reed tried to smile. Doris squeezed his hand.

"Zachary's sleeping in his room," she said. "I'm going to lie down with him. I don't want him to wake up alone," she said. "Promise me you'll try to get some rest, Tom."

Reed promised but lingered at the window staring at the

street, convinced at times he saw Ann's silver Jetta approaching. His heart rose. He wanted to run into the street, take her into his arms. But when he blinked he saw satellite trucks and police vehicles.

It was coming up on 4:30 A.M. Sydowski stood beside him.

"You should try to get some rest, Tom," he said. "McDaniel left to change. I'm going to do the same. We've got to get ready for a major case meeting in a few hours at the Hall."

Reed gazed into the night. He had covered so many crimes, he knew the odds in cases like Ann's. He knew he had to prepare for the worst.

"It looks bad for her, doesn't it, Walt?"

Sydowski stared out the window.

"Each case has its own circumstances, Tom."

"Don't bullshit me. Not now."

"We don't know the details on this one. Where it's headed. We've got no evidence to suggest she's been harmed."

"You've got two corpses."

"Tom. You're exhausted."

"Why would they keep her alive? Why?"

"This doesn't help."

"You take her car, you kill her. I mean maybe you rape her first, you know; then you kill her, dump her body."

Sydowski had seen this in victims before, near hysteria and exhaustion.

"Tom. Stop it. You need to think of Zach, of Doris."

"Why? That's what I can't figure." Reed ran a hand through his hair. "None of it makes sense. Why take her? They could've just taken her keys, her car, her wallet."

"Likely they didn't trust her saying she had a car, and also needed her as a shield. Remember, August was all over the van, ruined their getaway plans, they panicked, improvised."

"So what now? They were disguised, you've got no sketches, no security tape. Nothing."

"Tom, we've got their dead partner. We've got some of the stuff they left behind. We got a start. They're not going to get away with this."

"Right, you'll get your vengeance for August, but will I ever see Ann again?" Reed searched Sydowski's face. "Will I?"

It was a question no one could answer.

Sydowski took Reed's shoulders. "Get some rest."

Reed nodded.

But when Sydowski left, Reed anguished over his fear that Ann was already dead. It made him too afraid to face the bedroom alone. *This can't be real. It can't be.* You just don't wake up to another day, go along living your life then—bang—without warning, without a chance to prepare, in a heartbeat, everything changes.

Now, more than ever, Reed sensed Ann's fragrance, pulling him into their bedroom, beckoning him to face the inevitable. He swallowed and entered, feeling himself floating in the darkness.

He took her pink bathrobe from the chair. The one she wore every morning when she stepped from the shower after belting out a Springsteen song. He pressed its terry cloth to his face, saw the glint of the framed family photo she kept on her side of the bed, next to the bracelet she decided against wearing.

He stood over their bed, which she'd made that morning, as she did every morning. He could see the comforter's floral pattern that she had adored. He stood there in the darkness holding her robe, pretending she was in it, scolding him about something.

He swallowed hard, reluctant to roll back the sheets, knowing there were more traces of her there. He settled for lying on top of them, staring at her side of the bed, imagining her there, seeing the curve of her back, hearing the rhythm of her breathing. Hearing her voice from the tape.

"Oh God, please let me go!"

Here it comes. He couldn't stop it. Image upon image swirled in his mind. The dead officer, the bleeding suspect. They took Ann.

"Oh God, please let me go!"

They could rape her. Kill her. Dump her. A thousand fears preyed upon him, feasted on his soul. *Stop. Please.*

"Oh God, please let me go!"

Reed was beyond exhaustion but could not sleep. Because if he slept he would lose her. He ran a hand over his face, now stubbled with whiskers.

"Dad?"

Zach stood in the darkened doorway like an apparition.

"What is it, son?"

"Can I sleep with you?"

"Sure, buddy."

Zach climbed onto Ann's side. Reed draped her robe over him and put his arm around him.

"Dad, are you scared?"

"Yes."

"I was thinking about the tape when we heard Mom."

"What about it?"

"Well, it means she's still okay, right? That's why the police played it, right?"

"They played it for lots of reasons, but that's right."

"Well, I know that she's thinking of us and she's going to be okay."

"How do you know?"

"Because I asked God to take care of her and the little boy whose dad got killed."

Reed took a moment.

"That's good, son. Get some sleep now, okay?"

Reed pulled Zach to him. Zach, warmed by a prayer to heaven, warmed by his mother's robe, warmed by hope, Reed drawing strength from him, lying there in the same clothes he had put on that morning to quit his job, the same clothes in which he'd salivated for the story that had become his tragedy. Was this punishment for breaking his promise to her? Reed said a prayer for Ann, feeling Zach stir. Then he noticed something fall out of his son's relaxed hand. Reed retrieved it, held it up to the light.

A small photograph of Ann smiling at him from the darkness.

Reed covered his face with his hand holding her picture and wept.

Ann. Forgive me.

16

Ann Reed felt the car stop.

The engine was switched off. Doors creaked open, the vehicle sprang with the shifting weight of two people stepping from it and walking off.

Ann's heart jumped. The ringing in her ears resumed as she struggled against the dull pain that enveloped her. *What are they going to do to me?*

Her face and hands were slick with sweat. Her clothes were drenched in the stifling air. She held her breath. Her skin prickled. She could hear murmuring but couldn't distinguish a word. She flinched at the sudden *clank-clank* of heavy metal objects tossed to the ground nearby. Then she heard grunting, thudding, and scraping, repeated over and over.

What are they doing?

Ann was blind in her darkness where she tasted the salt of her sweat and tears that had seeped through the duct tape covering her mouth. They had bound her hands and feet too.

Cry out. Kick. Scream.

But she had. Her legs and wrists burned. Overwhelmed by terror since it happened, she had struggled until they were raw. It was futile. She had to think of something. Anything. But there was nothing. Absolutely nothing she could do. This was not like any of the movies she'd watched at home with Tom. It was real. It was happening.

Please, somebody, help me. It's so hot. All she could hear now was thudding and scraping. *Be strong.*

She went back, trying to remember details of everything. About twenty minutes after the robbery she'd felt the car gain speed like they were on an expressway. Not long after, she'd felt it slow down to exit. They couldn't have driven long enough to leave San Francisco. After getting off the freeway they'd made several turns as if driving in a neighborhood. Then they'd come to a complete stop.

Ann had feared they had purposely taken an indirect way to her home to threaten her family. But before she knew what was happening, a bag, or hood, was slipped over her head. She couldn't see. They'd bound her more securely with tape, hefted her from the car and into the back of a larger car, which was cooler as if it had been in sheltered parking. Then she heard them move the cars, felt them toss bags into the second car. Doors thudded closed. She realized they'd switched cars as they'd pulled away into the noise of heavier traffic and the hum of an on-ramp, an expressway, gathering speed. They drove and drove with Ann drifting in and out of consciousness.

She'd lost all sense of time and direction, clinging to the hope they would let her go or that somehow someone would deliver her.

Now they had finally stopped and all she could hear was thudding and scraping. How many hours had it been? It felt like night. Where were they? The heat. Were they near a factory? A boiler? An oven?

She thought of Tom, Zachary, her mother.

I love them so much. Let me see them again, God, please.

The thudding and scraping stopped. Someone approached.

The rear door popped open. The hood was pulled from her head and Ann saw the stars, more brilliant than she had ever seen them before.

The air was still hot but fresher. She inhaled it, feeling it swirl around her. A flashlight beam pierced the darkness and burned into her face. She squinted at the two silhouettes blotting out the heavens and froze.

Large work-gloved hands hoisted her out by her shoulders and calves, carrying her around the car for several yards before laying her on the ground, rolling her onto her stomach.

She saw nothing in the night. She'd no idea how long or how far they'd traveled. No hint of where she was.

She lay there, cheek pressed to the hot ground, minutes passing in silence. A horrible chilling silence slithered along slowly before it reared to shriek to her: *A decision has been made.* Ann's heart nearly burst, her eyes widened, her pulse throbbed in her ears.

Oh God. No, please. Please.

The flashlight beam hit her eyes, forcing her to lift her head and turn it, to see the pick, the shovel.

The fresh grave.

17

By 6:00 A.M. Sydowski was at his desk at the Hall of Justice going hard on the latest reports, making notes before the case status meeting.

He knew Reed was right. There was little hope. At any time Sydowski expected his double homicide to become his triple, depending on where they found Ann Reed. He'd met her a while back. Nice lady. Too good for Tom, who was as close as you got to being a friend without being called one. Even though Reed was a pain-in-the-ass reporter, Sydowski liked him. Would make a helluva detective, he thought, opening his file on the murdered officer.

Rod Jerome August. Born in San Francisco. Recognized for bravery after jumping into the bay to pull out two Japanese tourists whose van went off a pier. Sydowski turned to another citation when his telephone rang.

"Walt, it's Harm. Figured you'd be in." Harm DeGroot and Sydowski had graduated from the academy together. Harm was a sensitive guy who had once been August's supervisor. "So, how'd it go?"

Word had gotten around that Sydowski had accompanied

the chief, Darnell, the chaplain, a POA rep, and a crisis counselor to deliver the news to August's ex and their son.

"You know how it is, Harm. They never go well," Sydowski said. "She's a real estate agent near Belmont. She knew the instant she saw us pull up. Wouldn't let us in. Stayed on her side of the door, yelling, 'He's not my husband anymore, don't you bastards know he's not my husband anymore?' We tried to calm her, to get her to let us in. Everything went all quiet inside for a few moments; then the door swings open and August's six-year-old boy, Billy, is there kneeling beside his mother. She's weeping in a heap on the floor. Billy looks up at us and says, 'Is my dad the one that got shot?' The chief gets on his knees and tells him his dad died a hero."

DeGroot cleared his throat. "Christ almighty, Walt. We got to find these guys. Got anything on them?"

"Working on it."

"We got to go flat out on this."

"Harm, I got a task force meeting coming up. Got to go."

"Thanks, Walt."

Sydowski removed his bifocals, rubbed his eyes, then reached for Leroy Driscoll's file. Car thief. Armed robbery suspect. Murder victim. August and Driscoll. Honored hero. Convicted felon. Later, Sydowski would be witnessing the autopsies on both men.

Inspector Linda Turgeon set a mug of fresh coffee before him. Reading that faraway look in her partner's face, she attempted conversation to bring him back. "So, Walt, you and Louise getting hitched?"

"Thinking about it. How about you?"

Turgeon sipped her coffee. "Thinking about it."

Sydowski drank some coffee. It was strong the way he liked it. "This case delays things. I called Louise. We're putting Las Vegas on hold."

"She good with that?"

"She's got no choice, Linda. Can't get married alone, can she?"

"Easy there."

Sydowski popped a Tums into his mouth. That was breakfast. He collected his files. "Time to go to the meeting, Linda."

In room 400 of the Hall, enlarged photos of August, Driscoll, Ann Reed, a 2003 silver four-door Jetta, Driscoll's van, and the San Francisco Deluxe Jewelry Store were posted on wheeled corkboards. FBI agents and SFPD detectives from homicide, auto theft, and robbery took places around the table, others lined the wall. Several dozen investigators in all. As information sheets were circulated, Bill Kennedy, Deputy Chief of Investigations, kicked it off.

"The department took a hit on this. It hurts. But until we arrest the suspects we've got a deadly situation here. Let me remind everyone in this room that we have concurrent jurisdiction with the FBI. They'll focus on the abduction of Ann Reed, we'll focus on the homicides and robbery. We'll work together on everything. Leo, bring us up to speed."

Lieutenant Gonzales listed major steps taken so far. The SFPD Special Services Unit went to their street sources, the unit in state parole on fugitive parolees was shaking down all avenues. "We've got nothing on the two suspects. No prints, not even a composite. No security video. Nothing so far. We hope that will change. We're checking traffic and toll cams," Gonzales said.

"We've got August's final transmission, and we've got the tape of Driscoll's last words in the ambulance. He was incoherent and there was a lot of background noise. Voice analysis is trying to clean them up," he said.

"We're talking to Driscoll's parole agent, working through his employers, his associates, inside and out. We got an address but it's outdated. We haven't got any clean latents yet from the van, which was stolen out of Fresno.

Or the plate. Stolen from Bakersfield. Preliminary work at Hunter's Point shows the cartridges found in the van are the same as the casings found in the store and on the street. The thinking is the bullets recovered from the autopsies will match, which will link the van to the heist and shootings.''

None of Ann Reed's credit or bank cards had been used since the heist.

''She had a large amount of cash in her car at the time. She apparently was en route to make an unscheduled bank deposit from one of her stores that raised money through a sales event for charity.''

Gonzales said robbery detectives were going through the jewelry store's employee lists for the last several years. They also inventoried the jewels stolen in the robbery to put out on the FBI's jewel and gem database, which would alert police and jewelers' associations nationwide.

''The take was above average, nearly one million. They're going to want to unload this stuff, or it could have been a commissioned job. Either way we need a fix on a buyer pool. Might give us a lead on their destination.''

The FBI was working with ATF, military police, and records on the grenades used. ATF was trying to trace the dead suspect's weapon.

''Last night we got a lead on the wheelchair. Stolen from a hospital in San Jose. We're checking with security there,'' Gonzales said.

FBI Agent McDaniel left the room to take a call after his cell phone began vibrating on his belt. A few moments later, he returned to the meeting. ''Excuse me,'' McDaniel interrupted. ''We may have something.''

''What do you have?''

''Anyone hear of the TV show *Worldwide News Now*?''

''It's a new show,'' Turgeon said. ''Dishes up trash on the stars. Why?''

''Our liaison office at the U.S. embassy in London says the program has footage on our heist.''

"So what," Sydowski said. "So do all the local stations, I don't get it."

"No, not after the fact, Walt, actual footage of the shooting on the street. The whole thing, start to finish. Our people say the show is set to air it."

Sydowski grabbed one of the room's phones.

"Who you calling, Walt?" Turgeon asked.

"Our media people. I think this outlet had a reporter at the news conference. Seems to me someone asked specifically about security cameras or amateur video of the suspects." Sydowski jabbed at the extension. "Damn. We learn about this *a day* later. I don't believe it."

18

Reed woke clawing his way through the fog of not knowing where he was, then remembering why Ann's side of the bed was empty and cold. It was his first morning without her.

He sat up, fingers gripping the sheets. Still wearing the clothes he wore when he'd rushed to the jewelry store, he went to the living room, which adjoined the kitchen. Investigators were poring over reports faxed from the case meeting, working on their laptops, talking on their phones. Zach sat before the TV with an FBI agent. Doris was making scrambled eggs. The aroma of coffee was in the air.

Reed braced himself, then said, "Anything?"

"Nothing, sir," a young FBI agent said.

Reed went to the window, saw more news crews outside, then went to the kitchen. Doris hugged him. He hugged her back.

"Did you get some sleep?" he asked.

Doris ignored his question with what he thought was a chilly wave of resentment. He dismissed it when she said, "Have some breakfast, Tom."

He wasn't hungry. Headlines from the Bay Area papers screamed at him from the counter. The heist was the lead item in every one. Huge news pictures. In the *Star,* Molly's story ran across six columns. It began:

His assignment was to take you inside yesterday's deadly jewelry store heist but when veteran Star *crime reporter Tom Reed arrived at the scene of a murdered police officer and a dying suspect—*

He couldn't read it.

"Dad." Zach came to him. "Maybe all the news, it will help find Mom."

"Maybe." Reed put his arm around him. "I'm going to take a shower. I'm really not hungry right now, thanks, Doris."

Somebody's cell rang.

"Tom, it's McDaniel for you." A female agent held out her phone.

Reed's stomach tightened. Was this it? Was this the call?

"Tom, do you have a VCR?"

"Yes, why?"

"We've got something to show you before the whole country sees it."

The FBI in London had taped the San Francisco heist report from *Worldwide News Now,* then bumped it to FBI headquarters in Washington. Technicians there fed it to the San Francisco field office, where it was transferred to a VHS tape, which McDaniel inserted into the machine at Reed's home, then told him what to expect. Reed and Doris had decided to let Zach see it with them. He should know and see what everyone else would see.

The show's generic intro rolled with a montage of some of the world's most famous faces, fading to Amanda

Christianson, the hostess. She smiled from *Worldwide*'s glittering set in London.

"Welcome back. Now, our world exclusive report of a shocking tragedy. Somewhere in America the kidnapped wife of one of the nation's top crime journalists is facing a life-and-death struggle with the cold-blooded killers of a police officer. The drama began yesterday when jewel thieves launched a commando-style robbery on a San Francisco boutique that left two people dead and sparked an intense manhunt." Footage of the scene rolled in slow motion next to Christianson's pretty face. Then Reed saw himself talking to detectives. "But the story takes a bizarre turn as the horror was compounded for Pulitzer Prize-nominee Tom Reed, a newspaper reporter dispatched to cover the robbery. Please be warned, the images you're about to see may be disturbing. With more, here's our San Francisco correspondent, Tia Layne."

The show threw to Layne, standing in front of the jewelry store.

"Amanda, Tom Reed is a newspaper reporter for the *San Francisco Star*, whose work put him on the short list for American journalism's greatest award, the Pulitzer Prize. For years he has covered the toughest of all beats, crime on the streets of San Francisco. But yesterday when he rushed from his newsroom to cover this terrible case, he found himself facing the story of his life. One that is still unfolding. . . ." Layne detailed events.

Reed was stunned as the pictures rolled. Ann handcuffed in the chair, the suspects, like players in some freakish macabre production, one popping his handgun at the van, the other rattling his M16 at the officer, the police radio crackling with their voices, their faces disguised in brilliant red and white, Ann's pleas ripping into him.

The item showed Reed getting Zach at school, the police press conference, news crews keeping a vigil at Reed's home, the report ending with a fading ghostly image of Ann's face.

Zach was transfixed. His jaw muscles pulsed. Reed pulled him tighter, his heart breaking for his son. Reed was helpless to protect him. Zach still held the tiny photograph of his mother. Refusing to let go. Refusing to give up.

"This segment airs tonight at 7:30 P.M. Pacific time," McDaniel said when it ended. "Three hours sooner in the East."

They played it several more times for Reed in the hope he might notice something the detectives missed. They slowed parts. Froze frames.

"What about their shoes, Tom, anything familiar?" McDaniel asked.

"No."

"Their walk? Body build? Clothes?"

Reed concentrated but recognized nothing.

"Their voices?"

Over and over, as he had the previous night, Reed listened to the tinny scratchy blasts of conversation. "No. Nothing."

"Body movements? The wheelchair?"

"Nothing."

"Is that definitely her car?"

"Yes."

"Is Ann trying to communicate anything?"

"No."

After they finished, McDaniel stepped away to make calls. Reed sat alone in an alcove, on a love seat at a bay window overlooking the flower garden Ann tended. This was her favorite spot to read, or just sip tea. She'd wanted to put in more roses. *No. Don't think of her in the past tense.* That footage. He wanted to reach into it and pull her to him. But it was futile. *How do you fight a nightmare? How do you battle a hurricane? She's gone.* He saw her face, heard her voice entangled with the voices of those who took her. Did he recognize them? He searched his memory but found nothing. He ran his hand over his face. His eyes burned and the flowers Ann had nurtured began to blur.

19

In the San Francisco bureau of *Worldwide News Now* Tia Layne was typing on her keyboard with the phone pressed between her ear and shoulder.

"I told you. My account should show a large deposit. I called the bank in New York, they've assured me the money's there, but I don't see it, hon."

Someone knocked on the door.

"Cooter, get the door," Layne called out but heard no movement. "I have to go," she said into the phone. "I'll call you right back and when I do my damn money better be there."

Layne slammed down the phone, cursing the bank and Cooter's absence. She opened the door to Sydowski and McDaniel. They held out their identification. "Can we come in, Miss Layne?" McDaniel said.

She considered closing the door. Instead she swung it open.

The two men positioned two cheap stools in front of Layne's desk. She lit a fresh Camel and rocked in her chair. "What's up?"

Sydowski looked her over. "Why didn't you alert police to the fact you had pictures of the murder of a police officer and abduction of a citizen?"

"Why? Because I don't work for you, that's why. Freedom of the press."

"You cost us twenty-four hours. Critical time that may have saved a life."

Layne dragged hard, thinking Sydowski wasn't bad looking for an old fart. She was wondering about his stamina when McDaniel said, "Miss Layne. We'd like you to volunteer us your raw, unedited footage."

"Would you?" She flicked ash on the floor. "What's in it for me?"

Sydowski leaned to her. "We don't go looking up your name on Interpol, your alleged links to organized crime in Thailand. Your acting career."

"My, my." Layne smiled. Sydowski was dangerous. She liked that. "The tape's not my property. Being competent investigators, you'd know that." She opened a drawer, tossed two business cards on the desk. "You have to call the show in New York."

Sydowski ignored the cards. "How about I call the DA right now and get a warrant?"

Layne crushed her cigarette in an empty container for take-out food. "There's a coffee shop around the corner," she said. "You go there and give me thirty minutes to make some calls."

"Fifteen." Sydowski popped a Tums in his mouth. "Then I'll make some calls."

After they'd left, Layne grinned as she reached for her phone. This was good, she thought, waiting for the connection to *Worldwide*'s New York office. The cops must have zero leads. She lit another cigarette.

"Mr. Morten's office."

"It's Tia Layne in San Francisco, put me through to him."

"He's on another line, Ms. Layne."

"Tell him it's me."

"But he's on another call, Ms. Layne."

"Now, please." The line switched to elevator music. Three seconds of something from a Broadway musical.

"Seth Morten."

"It's Tia in California."

"Tia, I just got off the line with London. They loved your item. Networks are already calling. It's fantastic."

"Yeah, listen. A couple of Joe Fridays just paid me a visit. They want our raw footage, all the uncut stuff, or they'll get a warrant. I think I should volunteer it."

"Why?"

"We can capitalize on this. In my next piece we can say police need our pictures to help solve the crime. It reinforces us as owning the story."

"Let me call legal."

"There's nothing in it we haven't used."

"I don't know. It's the show's property. What if it gets leaked?"

"Seth, the police will want to take their time going through it. There's nothing there. The best pictures are in the piece. If we refuse, they'll get it with the warrant in a few hours anyway, believe me."

"All right. My other line's going. Tia, I'll talk to legal. You stall the cops, suggest they view it in your office with the promise of all unedited tape after the show airs in the Pacific zone. That should cover us."

"Fine. There's one more thing."

"What?"

"Tell the editors to insert a super of our toll-free tip line for viewers with any information to call us at the end of my item."

"Why? We're not a crime and cop show."

"Do it, Seth. This story's going to be huge."

20

Jill grabbed a water bottle and a beer from the fridge, then stepped from her boyfriend Warren's tent trailer. *Tell him tonight,* she thought, squinting into the sun sinking over the caravan of four-by-fours that had settled in for the night at the southern edge of Death Valley, California.

"Thanks. You sure everything's fine?" Warren touched the can to his moist forehead.

"It was a long haul today. I'm just going to stretch my legs."

"Where're you going?"

"I'll walk for a bit down the prospector's trail to the old cabin." Jill held up the map. "It's not far at all."

"It's not. I thought the plan was for all of us to go there in the morning after breakfast?"

"Thought I'd have some alone time."

"You need to be alone?"

"I'm restless. I'll get a sneak preview of the cabin."

He regarded her for a long moment. Whatever was bothering her, Warren realized that he would never pry it out of her, so he resumed preparing chili, his contribution to the group's potluck campfire dinner. ''Be careful, Jill. I think the girls ran over to see the Murrays. If you see them, remind them, we'll be eating in an hour.''

''Will do. But they're vegetarians, dear. Remember?''

He didn't return her smile. She pecked his cheek, adjusted her sunglasses, and set out alone, knowing that their relationship had ended long before this adventure to the desert with his daughters.

Jill took a pensive pace along the sandy trail, a miner's road from the 1890s, snaking through a series of rocky hills at the fringes of the barren Silurian Valley near the Mojave. *What am I doing here?* She was a thirty-four-year-old corporate lawyer for a conglomerate in Philadelphia. Never married. Devoted to her work. A fitness freak who held a black belt. A curious soul who loved reading mysteries. Warren was the attorney for a large private humanitarian foundation in Pasadena, ten years her senior and recently divorced, he had told her over dinner in Chicago at the conference where they'd met several months earlier. They commenced a cross-country romance. At times it was intoxicating, with an intensity that had burned itself out. Or had it?

This trip was Warren's idea, a chance for Jill to get to know his girls. Emma was sixteen and Taylor was twelve. Both in braces. Beautiful like their mother, who was an engineer for the city of Los Angeles, specializing in strengthening community buildings against earthquakes, therefore, a saint, Emma had informed Jill at the outset of the trip a few long days ago.

''My parents will likely reconcile and remarry,'' Emma had said to her while Warren gassed up their rented Grand Cherokee outside of Bakersfield. ''Oh, and I think corporate greed is vile. In fact, I saw your firm targeted on an anti-globalization site.''

Taylor giggled, betraying to Jill that the attack on the other woman had commenced. From that point on Emma never removed the headphones of her CD, while Taylor immersed herself in books.

Jill accepted the hostility as natural, but it emphasized that she and Warren were separated by more than a continent. It wasn't the girls. It was just over. Jill missed her independence. Missed no complications in her life. She had a tight circle of friends, a penthouse condo. Her job directing corporate donations was fulfilling. Three times a year, she volunteered at Philadelphia shelters. *So there, Emma.* She stuck out her tongue.

Jill crested a hill, stopped to rest on a rock. The temperature hadn't dipped much, still in the high nineties. A hot breeze was kicking up. She patted her damp brow, then sipped from her bottle.

"What's that?"

A glint of metal caught her eye. Not far off. Looked like a rusted-out old car. Jill started to it, glancing at the map as she walked. It appeared to be at the mouth of an abandoned mine entrance. Her curiosity grew as she neared it. The thing was half in the darkness of the mine and half in light. Must've been left here from the prospector days.

A car. Definitely a car. She ran her fingers along its body. It smelled bad. *Hold it. That's not rust.* She examined the black residue on her fingertips. Sooty. *This car's not old. It's practically new.* Jill stepped back. *Someone's torched it.* Likely stolen from LA. Maybe an insurance fraud thing. The plate was gone. She could see the serial number on the dash and slapped her pockets for a pen or something, making her water splash.

Her heart skipped.

Guttural growling threatened her from the darkness.

She froze.

Something was scratching in the dirt behind the car.

A coyote?

What now? Run away like a girl? Wouldn't Warren's daughters love that? Jill searched the area for a large rock. She found a couple and bowled one with all her strength under the car. It resulted in yelping; then a little scrawny coyote pup lurched away.

"Get outta here!"

Jill's second toss of a smaller rock hit its target and the coyote disappeared. She rolled several more rocks under the car and waited as the desert wind gusted, stinging her arms and legs with sand.

Confident all was clear, she dropped to her knees behind the car, removed her sunglasses to see what the animal had been pawing at. There was something. She wiped grit from her eyes. Something in the dirt near the rear tire. The wind began buffeting, flapping against her T-shirt as she fished out her key chain, hoping she'd replaced the battery of her penlight. It worked. Good. The light was strong.

Sand began swirling. Jill aimed her small light, until it caught something small, silvery, and reflective, half buried.

What is that?

Jill blinked, reaching in, feeling the object. Hard. Metal. She tugged lightly. It was embedded in the ground. Strange. The dirt was soft. Loose. She dug at it some, until she had a firmer grip on the metal thing with her fingers, and tugged. It moved a bit. She dug more dirt away. Pulled. It moved a bit more. It was attached to something. A stick or log? *What the heck is it?*

Jill repositioned herself. Still on one knee, she wedged her other foot against the car's tire, gripped the metal object, pulling with all of her strength, her scalp tingling, the earth ripping open, revealing that she'd seized a chain, linked to a handcuff, clamped around an arm, attached to a shoulder, now rising from its shallow grave until Jill stopped pulling and began screaming.

21

Just before sunrise Sydowski and Turgeon rang the bell at Reed's door. An FBI agent let them in. They went directly to Reed's bedroom.

Sydowski switched on a bedside lamp, which bathed the room in soft light. Reed woke, squinting. His hair was messed. He was wearing a T-shirt, sweatpants. He stood before them. They didn't have to speak. It was written in their eyes.

Sydowski let a moment pass, thought of a star falling from the sky.

"Tom, a woman's body—"

Reed's knees buckled. Sydowksi and Turgeon caught him, sat him on the bed. He thrust his face into his hands, took a deep ragged breath, groaning as he let it out, not feeling Turgeon's hand take his shoulder, nor Sydowski take the other. Sydowski squeezed hard until Reed felt it and met his eyes.

"Listen to me. Nothing's been confirmed. Are you hearing me? Nothing's been confirmed. A woman's body was found.

Tom, you've got to hear me now. Identification hasn't been confirmed.''

''No. No!''

Sydowski sat beside Reed, gripping his knee hard.

''Tom, you've got to be strong here, for Zach. For Doris.''

Tears fell as Reed gasped, nodding, swallowing, gulping air, the room spinning, Turgeon and Sydowski comforting him until he managed to speak.

''Where? How?''

''San Bernardino County. Hikers in the desert, north of Baker.''

''Did she—'' Reed looked at the ceiling. ''Did she suffer?''

''We don't know any details. County people are still working on it. We're flying down.''

''I'm going down there.''

''You should stay here, wait for word.''

''I've got to see for myself.''

''Tom,'' Sydowski said, ''we advise you to stay here.''

''No one on earth will stop me.''

Sydowski saw Ann's robe, her slippers, her framed picture near the bed, and knew Reed must go.

''Walt, I have to know.''

''Tom—''

''What flight are you taking?''

''There's a direct jet to Las Vegas that leaves in ninety minutes.''

''I'm going to be on that flight with you. Let me tell Doris and Zach first.''

Moments later, Zach's cries and Ann's mother's muffled moans reached to the living room where Sydowski and Turgeon waited for Reed to dress, pack, and do what he had to do.

When the bell chimed at the front door, Sydowski opened it to two plain-dressed women wearing concerned faces. One middle-aged, one barely in her twenties. They were crisis workers from victim services he had called after San

Bernardino alerted him to the discovery of the corpse in the desert.

The 737 thudded down at McCarran International.

Agents from the FBI's Las Vegas field office led them through the terminal amid clanging slot machines to a waiting full-sized four-by-four. Doors slammed, tires squealed, and the federal vehicle roared south on I-15.

"We got coffee, fruit, bagels, donuts, if anybody wants anything," the agent in the front passenger seat offered.

Everybody took something except Reed, who watched the mammoth casino resorts and metro sprawl melt into the desert. It took well over an hour to reach Baker. Its big thermometer dominated the restaurants, motels, and gas stations that marked a rest stop between Los Angeles and Las Vegas.

Approaching the sheriff's substation on Baker Boulevard, Reed saw the news trucks from Barstow. A small cluster of press people were waiting. They were greeted by Baker deputies and members of the San Bernardino County Specialized Investigations Division, who'd been at the scene much of the night. Agents from the FBI's Los Angeles division were waiting inside.

A young man in dark glasses thrust a microphone toward him. "Tom, what's your reaction to the discovery of the body?"

"Could you give us a statement, Mr. Reed?" a woman holding out a cassette recorder said.

Overhead, a small prop plane crossed the sky.

"No statements." Sydowski waved off the questions. "Excuse us, please."

Inside, conversations ceased when the San Francisco group joined the others crowded around a small table. Sydowski's case binder slapped down. A man in a navy polo shirt rose and introduced himself to the new arrivals as the lead investigator.

"Detective Marv Gutteres, Sheriff's homicide detail."

"Marv." Sydowski introduced himself, then said, "This is Tom Reed."

Glances were traded around the table.

"Tom's got a few questions, which I thought we could take care of right away," Sydowski said. Gutteres extended his hand.

"Mr. Reed, I'm terribly sorry."

"Is my wife dead?" Gutteres had quick, intelligent eyes, an honest face. Reed didn't know if he was a God-fearing, compassionate family man who took his kids to church on Sundays but he wanted to believe it. Christ, he needed to believe it. He couldn't accept some pension-tabulating clock watcher. "Did you find my wife?"

"Please, Mr. Reed, have a seat."

"Just tell me, Detective."

Throats were cleared. Local officials were annoyed that Sydowski had brought a victim's relative this deep into their case. The air conditioner rattled and hummed.

"This is a bit unusual because of the stage of our investigation," Gutteres said more to Sydowski, "but I'll tell you what I can, Tom. A female hiker from Philadelphia found a car. It was not your wife's Jetta. According to the VIN, it's a Buick, stolen from a Sacramento mall lot."

"What about the owners?"

"No one's missing. Our arson people say the car was set ablaze. In a shallow grave near it, a body was found. It appears to be a white female."

"Was the body burned too? Was she alive at the—" He stopped.

"We're not certain of any details. The coroner's investigators haven't removed it from the scene for an autopsy. We haven't confirmed the victim's identification or cause of death. It may take a while. The find was made just before sunset. We've still got our scene people working out there, combing the area for anything to help us find the suspects.

We've canvassed where we could, gas stations, restaurants, motels all along the corridor.''

Reed nodded, noticing that Gutteres had a file thicker than the others.

"You're not telling me everything. What else do you know?''

Gutteres blinked coldly at Sydowski, then opened his folder and slid a plastic evidence bag to Reed. He covered his mouth with his hand.

It was Ann's wallet.

"Tom,'' Gutteres said, "we haven't confirmed identification but you should prepare yourself.''

Reed nodded. "Can I talk to the person who found her?''

"The witness was distraught and went to Los Angeles to catch a plane home. I apologize that we don't have more for you.''

"I want to go to the scene. See it for myself.''

"I understand, Tom, but we've got to start briefing the other agencies as quickly as possible. We've got armed, dangerous fugitives suspected in three homicides now.''

Suspected in three homicides now. There it was.

Reed removed his glasses and rubbed his eyes.

"Tom, maybe you should rest up. That San Francisco footage broadcast by that tabloid show has drawn a flood of calls and national press attention. This place is getting busy. We've reserved some motel rooms, maybe if you waited there—''

"I need to see it for myself.''

"Marv,'' Sydowski said, "it might be best if we all saw it now. Familiarize ourselves, so we can start on the same page.''

A second of knowing passed between the detectives. Get the relative in and out; then get back to work. Gutteres understood.

"It's about an hour's drive from here.''

* * *

Reed sat in the rear of a four-by-four behind Sydowski as the convoy of police vehicles worked their way along the dirt roads north of Baker.

To break the silence, the deputy at the wheel explained the region.

"Baker substation is a satellite of Barstow, responsible for Nipton, Primm Valley, Sandy Valley, parts of Mojave and Death Valley National Parks. Serves about two thousand residents. Only get four or five homicides a year, if that. We work mostly with the California Highway Patrol on the freeway. Our jurisdiction covers about five thousand square miles of remote, uninhabited desert terrain where the temp has been recorded at 130 degrees Fahrenheit. See, there to the east you got the Avawatz Mountains, to the west, the Silurian Hills. It's quite beautiful, really."

No, it's not, Reed thought.

Threading their way up and down a rolling serpentine trail, they stopped next to a couple dozen parked vehicles, including two police four-by-fours parked sideways to block the press trucks. Photographers had climbed to the rooftops of their vehicles for a better shot, turning their cameras on the new arrivals.

Heat rose from the desert as if it were a blast furnace, moistening Reed's skin in seconds after he got out and began walking with the deputy and Sydowski. They came to a hill with a clear view of the large white canopy and several scene people in coveralls and white gloves working under it. Silence filled the air after the last car door was shut.

"I think we'll stay back here for now." Gutteres arrived beside them. "We want to preserve the scene. We've taken tire casts of impressions left by a second vehicle. We've found a few other items of physical evidence we want to analyze."

A small plane rattled across the sky.

"That's us. Aerial shots of the scene," Gutteres said.

"The guys tell me the LA and Vegas newspeople have been flying over too."

Reed stood there staring at the charred remains of the Buick. The tiny hairs on the back of his neck bristled. *None of this is real. It just can't be. Wake up.* Some ten minutes later, a radio crackled. Someone called Gutteres, who walked back to the cars, talked in muted tones to other officers, then returned. "I think we should go now."

"No," Reed said.

"Tom, you don't want to see any more."

"I'm staying."

"Tom, they're going to move—"

It was too late.

Oh, dear Jesus.

Reed stared at the scene, his vision obscured by legs and arms, his eyes widening as white-gloved hands reached into the shallow grave and hefted a dirty corpse into a black body bag. Blood thundered in Reed's ears. He couldn't hear Sydowski calling his name.

Reed was falling into infinite darkness.

22

By the time Tia Layne got to the desert scene everything was over. Reed was long gone, the corpse had been removed, the burned-out car loaded on a flatbed. Nothing out there but bored cops, a damned hole in the ground, and sand. Layne dragged on her cigarette.

Now this. She shook her head. More satellite trucks and news vans from Los Angeles, Las Vegas, San Bernardino, San Diego, and San Francisco.

"This sucks, Cooter."

"It's not your story anymore, babe."

"Our pictures brought everybody running to this hellhole, I'll be damned if I'm giving it up." Layne crushed her cigarette in an empty coffee cup. "Pull into the restaurant. I want to eat, go to the motel for a shower, then figure out how we can get in front again."

Inside, a booth became available after two guys squeezed out. The one wearing a *Los Angeles Times* T-shirt let his eyes linger on Layne.

The waitress arrived. "It's like a press convention. I bet

you're reporters too," she said, wiping the table, taking their orders.

Salad for Layne. A cheeseburger for Cooter, who spotted friends from a Los Angeles station and went to visit while Layne checked her phone for messages. She had four, all from *Worldwide* in New York. "Tia, you must be out of range. It's Seth. Every network's paid to use your footage. I have a new offer to discuss. Call me on my direct line." She called Seth's number but got his voice mail. Damn. She left a message. Cooter returned.

"We've been beat by the real news pros, babe."

"What're you talking about?"

"My buddies were at the scene and got long shots of Reed seeing them pull the body out of the ground. Strong stuff. He's gone back to San Francisco, to wait for autopsy results."

"Damn it. Are you sure? Damn it. So we missed every damn thing."

"Face it, Tia. We don't know the news game. We got lucky once. Right spot, right time. The real newspeople are all over this thing big time. We're choking in their vapor trail, kid. Let's go back to chasing celeb trash."

The food arrived. Layne lost her appetite. She pushed her salad aside. Through the window she saw a female TV reporter, gripping a mike, talking into a camera, filing a piece from the streets of Baker. *Look at her.* All teeth and gloss. Miss Fresh-Out-of-College, Daddy paid for. Never had to do the things Layne did just to survive.

"You know, Cooter, we're just as good as they are. Maybe better because we work harder. No way am I letting this go. No damn way," she said, lighting up a cigarette, then jabbing the numbers on her phone, trying New York again. Cursing at the busy signal.

"Excuse me, miss," the waitress said, "smoking's not permitted."

"Wonderful." Layne stood. "I'm going next door to the motel."

Cooter grunted, more interested in his food and watching the pretty young reporter in the sun, wishing he were still making movies.

At the motel, the maid's cart was parked several units from Layne's. She began inserting the key but her door opened; then Layne's jaw dropped. So did the maid's, who had her hands in Layne's suitcase.

"What the hell are you doing?"

The hands withdrew.

"I'm sorry, this is not what you think."

"You were going through my things. I'm calling the manager."

"No. Please. It's not what you think. Let me show you." The maid's hands plunged into Layne's clothes, sifting, until she produced a tiny bottle of the motel's shampoo. "See? I forgot to leave one here when I made up this room. I came back, it slipped from my hand and fell into your bag."

She was in her mid-twenties, a little overweight, had ill-fitting clothes, stringy hair, bad skin, and a bruised cheek. A sad case. Still, Layne didn't believe her. She picked up the phone.

"I'm calling the manager."

"No, please. If I lose this job, he'll hit me again."

"Who?"

"My boyfriend."

"Cry me a river, hon."

"I'm begging you. Please. Please listen."

Layne held the phone on her hip, letting the maid plead.

"I've got a kid, a little girl, and I'm leaving him. I got two jobs. I'm saving up. I got to get away but if I lose this job, I'll lose my other one too."

"What's your other job, pickpocket?"

"Cleaning the sheriff's office at night."

Layne replaced the phone in its cradle.

"You clean the San Bernardino County Sheriff's office here?"

"Yes."

Layne hit on an idea. "You know all about the body in the desert?"

The maid nodded.

"What's your name?"

"Lucy."

"Lucy, I won't call the manager."

"Oh, thank you."

"If you agree to the deal I'm going to offer you."

"What sort of deal?"

It was simple, really. Nothing illegal or even wrong, Lucy kept telling herself that night as she began cleaning the sheriff's office. Layne just wanted a few minutes to go through the trash and recycle bins. Stuff that's already garbage, Layne had reasoned. But if she found anything useful, then she'd forget about the misunderstanding in her room *and* she'd give Lucy six hundred dollars in cash for her help. It would go toward that dealer's course in Las Vegas and a chance for Lucy and her daughter at a new life. No more searching luggage for loose cash.

Lucy began her routine. First she checked to see if they had any customers in the cells. Thankfully, they were empty tonight. Next, she watered the plants. Then she began cleaning up the coffee station, which was messier than usual given all the extra detectives in on the big case. She began humming "Suspicious Minds," her favorite Elvis song, while scrubbing the sink, but stopped when she heard a knock at the door. It was Layne.

"We're alone," Lucy said. "You'll hear the police radio and the highway patrol going. It's an hour before the deputies' shift change."

Layne took stock of the small office. Lucy had lined up several recycle baskets on a meeting table. Layne began a flurry of paper rustling, finding highway traffic reports, court schedules, notices on changes to state legislation, county regs. Absolutely nothing relating to Ann Reed's case.

In what looked like the boss's office, Layne found vacation schedules, memos on equipment, memos on new pension matters for county employees. Nothing to give her a jump on the story.

She went to the trays for the fax machines and computer printers.

Nothing. Her heart sank when she saw a shredder. That's what they did with the important stuff. Layne bit her lip. She could switch on some computers. Forget that, too risky.

"Find anything?" As much as she wanted Layne to leave, Lucy was secretly counting on the money.

"Nope."

Both of them held their breath when one of the fax machines beeped to life just as the headlights of a car shot into the office.

"It's a deputy." Lucy opened the back door and Layne stepped outside.

Brad Roup, the rookie Baker deputy, breezed through the front.

"Hi, Brad."

"Hey, Lucy. Looks like they left you quite a mess."

"No problem. Everyone's been busy."

"Thought I had extra flashlight batteries in my car. Wrong. Hey, what's with the fax machine?" Roup went to it, his utility belt making leathery squeaks, keys jingling.

"I don't know. It just started beeping. I didn't want to touch it."

"Out of paper. No biggie." Roup refilled the machine, pressed a reset button, then began rummaging through desks. "Batteries. Batteries."

"All quiet out there, Brad?"

"Yup. Here we go." Roup found batteries and began

loading them into his flashlight when the fax machine came to life extracting pages. Roup, still loading his flashlight, bent over the tray to read the information.

"Something wrong, Brad?"

"Naw. It's the latest specialized investigations stuff on the big case south of DV park. Just spit out an extra copy for us. I'll leave it with the boss."

Roup grabbed it, put it on the supervisor's desk, then took a call on his radio. California Highway Patrol wanted to meet him for coffee.

"Remember to lock up now, Lucy. See ya."

After his lights disappeared, Lucy let Layne return. She photocopied the fresh report from the fax machine, sat down, and began flipping pages, not believing what she was reading. "We've got an exclusive here."

"I'm not sure you should—" Lucy stopped at the sight of the cash Layne pulled from her purse.

"Hold out your hand." Layne piled twenties in Lucy's palm, stopping when she'd counted to six hundred dollars.

Layne went out the back door and hurried to the motel to wake Cooter and show him the report. Once he'd read it, they checked out and set off for an all-night drive to San Francisco.

"Tia, I had it all wrong," Cooter said as they drove. "Without a doubt, you *own* this story, babe. Did you ever talk to Seth, see what he wanted?"

"He said that the numbers were so good on our first exclusive, William Banks feared we'd go elsewhere with our next one. So the show will double our fee for each additional exclusive on the story."

"Double! Hot damn, Tia. Then this is it!" Cooter slapped the stolen report on her lap.

"Yes, when we get Tom Reed's reaction on camera, we'll have it."

Layne gazed into the desert night, feeling the words, the details and facts of the report hot on her lap. She couldn't bear to read it again. God, the unspeakable horror Tom Reed's wife faced out there in her final moments. Then Layne thought of another sixty thousand dollars and hated herself for smiling.

23

At home Reed lay on his bed running his fingers over Ann's robe.

Dread hammered inside his chest so hard that he knew he was losing his grip. Something had fractured, was going to shatter, something that could never be repaired. His fingers began tightening on the pink terry cloth.

Be strong.

Reed picked up the phone and called Ann's mother, working to move the words from his mouth, not letting go of Ann's robe.

"I'm back, Doris."

"Was it Ann?"

"There was a body. It's at the coroner's office. They'll let us know when they've confirmed identification."

He couldn't believe he'd said the words.

Ann's mother gasped.

"Doris, I need to be alone at the house just now, I'm sorry."

"I know, Tom."

"Are the counselors with you and Zachary?"

"Yes."

"Please don't tell him anything yet. I'll do it. I'll join you there as soon as I can. There are some things I have to do now, then some things we need to do together."

"Oh, Tom."

"I know."

Reed hung up, released Ann's robe, stroked it, then looked at the ceiling and swallowed until he found the strength to stand. Exhausted, he moved through the empty house like a man sinking in a black ocean. Most of the detectives had been reassigned, or had afforded Reed some privacy by waiting in their cars, or in the rear yard where earlier Sydowski and McDaniel had dropped him off, out of sight of the cameras in front.

"Tom, you must be prepared for the worst, brace yourself for it," Sydowski had said.

Reed knew from all of his years of crime reporting that's how police, who always knew more than they revealed, alerted the relatives of victims, to psychologically move them toward the horror before they drew back the curtain. *"Nothing's been confirmed, but you should prepare for the worst."*

Reed knew.

Leaving the bedroom, he went to Ann's small office in the house and sat at her desk. He saw her pen, her business stationery, saw her handwritten calendar notes, *meet distributor,* then *Zach's scout meeting* and *charity dinner.* He traced his fingertips over the words she'd written.

The San Bernardino County Coroner, their SID people, had Ann's medical records, and the list of her personal items, her mauve suit, her pearl earrings, necklace, watch, her silk blouse, her shoes. They were checking it all against the scene and the TV footage. The FBI again confirmed no calls had been received from her or the suspects. Her cell phone, her bank and credit cards, had not been used. There was nothing to hope for other than to pray she did not suffer, had not been in pain. That they hadn't—*Stop it.*

He glanced at the pamphlet Marv Gutteres, the San Bernardino detective, had handed him before he left Baker. Crumpled and creased because he had jammed it in his pocket. Reed smoothed it. It was from the coroner's office and explained procedure. Reed glimpsed, *We extend our deepest sympathy to you at this time.*

Keep moving, he told himself. He reached for the Yellow Pages on Ann's desk, plopped the book in front of him, and flipped through the *F*s. *Flooring, Furniture,* back, *Funeral. Funeral.*

It came upon him, crawling through his insides, scraping out his soul.

Ann is gone.

In the street the newspeople waiting in front of Reed's house were bored. The officers in the marked patrol unit were discussing the 49ers and the Giants with some of the TV guys. No one noticed the dirty four-by-four that rolled to a halt a few doors down.

Tia Layne stepped out, crushed a cigarette under her shoe waiting for Cooter to grab the camera from the rear, check its battery, slam in a fresh tape, do a quick balance.

Layne opened her mouth to three quick pumps of breath freshener. She grabbed her hand microphone and her file.

"Ready, Cooter?"

"Let's go."

Hearing the doorbell, Reed lifted his head from the Yellow Pages, rubbed his eyes. He didn't move, hoping whoever it was would go away. The bell rang a second time.

Reed opened the door to a woman, and a man who was squinting behind a camera lens aimed at Reed. He recognized the woman and the look in her eager face. Something cold and terrible passed between them.

She was that reporter from *Worldwide News.*

"Mr. Reed," Layne began.

Reed shook his head, closing the door. "I've got nothing to say right now. Please leave."

"Tom, just a statement on the confirmation from San Bernardino."

"What?" The door stopped. "Nothing's been confirmed."

"Yes, it has."

"No. No one's told us yet. We have nothing official yet."

"I have it."

"You have it? But—"

"It's been confirmed. I'm sorry but it is your wife."

Reed's eyes drilled into hers.

"Here." Papers rustled as she handed them to Reed.

"What's this?"

"A police report. I'm sorry. You have my sympathies."

Standing there, his face unshaven, hair messed, eyes reddened, shirt untucked, he began reading the words under the San Bernardino County letterhead, a summary by the homicide detail on the discovery by Jill Fuller, Philadelphia, Pennsylvania, of *unidentified female human remains.* His pulse began galloping at the list of items that matched Ann's—mauve suit, silk blouse, pearl earrings, necklace, shoes; then the pain burning inside him began raging as the next phrases screamed at him.

Indications of violent sexual assault . . . victim's head and hands removed. Not located at scene . . .

Jesus God Almighty. Reed's heart stopped.

"Do you have a statement, Tom?"

His legs were weakening, he stepped back as if he'd been punched, gripping the door.

"Tom."

Spotting Reed at the door, the other newscrews were approaching, cameras were hoisted onto shoulders. Reed retreated into his house, slamming the door shut, his back thudding against it as he slid to the floor, everything going black.

Through the door, the small press pack heard an anguished groan. The youngest-looking reporter among them, a twenty-something with traces of acne, turned to Layne.

"What was that? We miss something?"

Layne gave him a half smile, then walked back to her four-by-four with Cooter. When they were alone inside, she exhaled, then lit a cigarette.

"Looks like we've nailed another exclusive, Cooter."

He said nothing. He just stared at Reed's house.

Layne let go a stream of smoke, then reached for her cell phone to alert New York.

24

Reed rubbed his face and the memories swirled.

That night on the campus after taking Ann to see *Casablanca*. Her brown eyes in the moonlight after he kissed her. For the first time. Then on their wedding day. Then in the delivery room, kissing her as she held Zach.

Then the other morning.

Seeing Ann in her suit, looking good, smelling so nice. He was reading the paper, eating an orange. She grabbed his chin to turn his head to hers before she set out for the day. She rubbed his whiskers. "Good luck telling them at the paper and don't forget to shave, pal." An extra moment in the good-bye; then she added, "I love you." She kissed him. For the last time. *I love you. For the last time.*

No. Not for the last time. Please. She was fine. This was a dream. A wild dream. It just *seemed* real. Like the report in his hands. Felt so real, man, it was scaring the hell out of him. He had to shut this nightmare down. Reed got to his feet. Only one friend could help him now. That was J.D. He rubbed his lips. Find him because this was a bad one.

These papers in his hand were so real and their words were eating into his heart. *J.D., it hurts bad, you gotta help me.*

Reed went to a top shelf in the bedroom closet. So high, Ann needed the chair to reach it. He rummaged through it, knocked things over, magazines, old papers, Ann's old cassette tapes, hats, old purses. Ann smiled at him from the old snapshots spilling from the photo albums. Opening her first store. *Stop it.* Painting the nursery. *Stop it.* Hands searching, reaching into an old purse. Nothing there. Ann with her arms around Reed and Zach. Laughing. *Come on.* Fingers feeling inside a canvas bag until he gripped his neck. *J.D. Old friend.* A hidden bottle of Jack Daniel's Tennessee Sipping Whiskey.

The report fluttered from his hand as he caressed the label, the glass, while sounds and images exploded in his brain. Ann in the wheelchair. Gunshots. Muzzle flashes. Voices on the police tape. Ann's plea searing him.

Please. Don't, just please!

Seeing them lift the dirt-covered corpse in the desert.

God, help me. Pull me out of this. The images, the sounds from the tape. Ann's pleading, piercing him, making his ears ring. The phone. The phone was ringing. Thank God. It'd wake him up. It'd end now. The ringing continued. Reed was underwater, swimming to the ringing phone. *Wake up. You're supposed to wake up now, damn it.*

"Dad?"

His son's voice staggered him.

"Dad, are you there?"

Reed couldn't wake up. *Why? Jesus, wake up!*

"Dad, please answer me."

Reed's words crashed together in his throat coming out in a liquidy bubble. "I'm here, Zach."

"Dad, when are you coming to Grandma's to get me?"

Reed's fingers tightened on the phone and the bottle.

"I'm on my way now. I'll be there."

"Hurry, please, Dad. I need you here."

Reed hung up.

His breath came in hot, raw gasps as he hurled the bottle, the glass shattering, its contents blossoming, bleeding down the bedroom wall, dripping like tears from Ann's nightstand to the floor and the San Bernardino County Sheriff's report, unable to douse the words burning on the pages.

Indications of violent sexual assault . . . victim's head and hands removed. Not located at scene.

Sunlight strobed through the steel girders of the Bay Bridge as Reed drove east on the lower deck, a few hundred feet above the blue-green waters of San Francisco Bay.

The skylines that necklaced the Bay Area would never again be the same for him. During his years as a crime reporter Reed had seen every manifestation of evil. In each case he'd edged as near as he could, feeling its power brush against him, enjoying the privileged access of an avid observer while in the secret, darkest regions of his heart, he had thrilled at its touch. Now the karmic wheel had turned full circle on him, coiling around him with a hold so overwhelming that every moment Reed had lived until this point evaporated in the presence of its awful majesty.

Just don't get too close.

Be strong for Zach, Reed urged himself in Berkeley, after pulling on to Fulton and parking in front of Ann's mother's house. He found strength in their presence.

"There's some place we need to go." That was all he said to Zach and Doris after a tearful embrace.

Few words were spoken as they crossed the Bay Bridge, taking 101 South through San Francisco. Reed found a classical music station and they listened to Mozart as they continued south on Highway 1 at Daly City.

Columns of sunlight shot through the clouds above the ocean as they rolled along the coastline of the peninsula beyond Sharp Park, passed Pacifica, the curling highway hugging the coast. Then somewhere after that, Reed stopped at a quiet stretch of beach and shut the car's engine off.

Gulls cried, gliding in the sea winds as the surf rolled and hissed over the sand and rocks.

"She loved it here," Reed said, putting his arm around Doris, who searched the horizon.

"Her father and I would drive here when she was a little girl to fly her kite. She used to joke that it was Ann's beach."

"Dad." Zach was standing away from them near the car.

"Doris, give me a moment alone with him. Come on, son."

Doris hugged her grandson, seeing her daughter's face in his; then Reed took Zach's hand. They began walking along the beach. They walked for some time, leaving two sets of footprints fading in the surf. Reed's search for the words to begin ended when Zach came to the point.

"Mom's not dead."

Reed stopped, put his hands on Zach's shoulders, and met his eyes.

"Zach—"

"No, Dad. I don't believe it."

"Zach, we have to accept it. She's gone. Mom's gone."

"Stop saying that. Everyone's wrong."

"No, no, son, they're not wrong."

"You're a liar."

"Zach—"

"I don't believe it. Did you see her?"

"Yes. In the desert."

"No. She's not dead."

"I know it's the hardest thing in the world to face."

"Dad, she can't be dead. She's my mom. She can't be."

Reed felt Zach slip to the sand and slipped there with him, both of them on the beach holding each other as the Pacific rolled over the sand and the gulls cried. Reed rocked his son in his arms, not knowing how they would survive this, only that they had no choice, that maybe they should move here to somehow honor her dream of living by the ocean and oh Jesus, he thought he felt her, could hear her calling him *Tom* over the ocean. *Tom.*

"Tom!" Doris was trotting. Her face was serious but not sad. "Tom!" His cell phone from the car was in her hand. She was breathless. "Tom, Inspector Sydowski."

Confused. Putting the phone to his ear.

"Tom, it's Sydowski. I'm so sorry."

"Why didn't you call, or Gutteres?"

"We just got word from San Bernardino."

"It's too late now, so go to hell."

"No, Tom, that reporter Layne, she came to us for comment after what she did to you. I went to your house. We missed you."

"Doesn't change a goddamned thing, Walt."

"Tom, all she had was a crime scene summary."

"So?"

"It's not Ann."

"What?"

"The victim was not your wife. I swear to you. I've got the San Bernardino coroner's completed autopsy report in my hand. I just spoke with the coroner, Gutteres, McDaniel. The results are conclusive."

"I don't understand."

"The woman murdered in the desert isn't Ann Reed."

25

After talking with Reed, Sydowski started on a Tums.

Maybe they should charge that tabloid TV reporter. Christ, what she did to Reed was unforgivable. But Sydowski couldn't let the mess distract him. *Push it aside. Let San Bernardino handle it.* A press statement was coming to summarize the facts. It would contradict any fabrications that woman dared to put out.

Turgeon was at her desk talking on her phone. "Ten minutes to the conference call, Walt."

He acknowledged her over his bifocals. He munched on his Tums and went over the fresh pages spread across his desk. Updates from the FBI, ATF, Sacramento, and the county.

Who was the victim in the desert?

They had confirmed that the clothing and items found with her belonged to Ann Reed, but the remains were not those of Ann. Blood typing confirmed it. Ann was A-positive. The victim was O-negative. The victim was a white female in her mid-twenties. Based on what they had of her, the coroner estimated she was five feet eight inches, 115 pounds. Ann Reed was five feet four inches, about 105 pounds. The victim had the lungs of a longtime smoker. Ann detested smoking.

So who was the Jane Doe? Sydowski swallowed his Tums as Gonzales came out of his office. "Let's go."

They took the conference call in an empty meeting room down the hall from the homicide detail.

"Okay." Gonzales led it. "We've got SFPD, San Bernardino, Sacramento Justice, FBI, Los Angeles, ATF. Everybody acknowledge."

They did.

"It's critical we ID our Jane Doe," Gonzales said. "We're counting on it to give us a lead on our suspects."

"It's going to take time," Gutteres in San Bernardino said. "Given her condition, no dental records, no fingerprints. Coroner said she has some surgical scarring, that she's undergone an appendectomy."

"We saw that, Marv," McDaniel said. "We've put out an alert to medical networks, associations, and societies to urgently consult records that fit her description. And every major U.S. police agency, including Interpol and the RCMP, is going to their missing-person files. Vice and drug units are putting out the word far and wide in case she was a known hooker, user, or both."

Gutteres offered an update on the work done in the desert. "The tire impressions not carried off by the wind at the scene indicate a larger vehicle, possibly an SUV, was used by the suspects to leave. We're working with highway patrol, everybody near us. Walt, what's up at your end?"

"We're still awaiting our lab people at Hunters Point to clean up the tapes of the wheelman's last words and police radio," Sydowski said. "They're imaging all the shell casings into the database working with ATF."

"How you doing on your dead guy, his associates and kin, Walt?"

"Nothing to get excited about so far. He kept a low profile. We're going through everything."

"Still working our way through the jewelry store's client and employee lists," Gonzales added. "Let's throw this open, brainstorm here for a bit before we get back to work."

"The thing is, why?" Turgeon said. "Why go out of your way to make it look like Ann Reed's murder?"

"To prevent identification," Gutteres said.

"Why leave another victim?" Sydowski said.

"Could it be something ritualistic, a serial or cult thing?" Gutteres said.

"Not with a robbery," Sydowski said. "What do you think, Dean?"

Dean Roth was the FBI's profiler for the region.

"I think you're most likely right, Walt. The homicides at the San Francisco heist scene are logical, robbery related, if you will. Even the abduction of Ann Reed, the need for a means of escape, fits. But it's the behavior we see later that takes it to another level."

"How, aside from the brutality?" Gutteres said.

"That the fugitives would risk driving across the state with a victim in a high-profile case is brazen to us but might be regarded as normal for the team, an exhibition of its power. Now, look at their subsequent behavior. The disguising of the Jane Doe victim, that's key."

"How so?" Turgeon said.

"It suggests that they could be linked to her, a friend, an associate, a witness to the crime, so yes, to prevent identification is right."

"We got that?"

"But it goes beyond a witness," Roth said. "I believe she was somehow instrumental, or a player in the crime. Hence the need to annihilate her and ensure you have a difficult time identifying her. That's one level."

"But what about Ann Reed?" Sydowski said. "Why take her in the first place? Why not kill her?"

Roth thought about it. "That's where we run into something different. With this case you may have come upon something more than a robbery."

"What?"

"I think something was decided—triggered might be the better word—triggered in the heat of the moment at the heist when August rolled up on the getaway van."

"What do you mean?"

"Yes, the Jane Doe knew, or was connected to the heist, so she was removed. And, on one level they used mutilation and Ann Reed's belongings to disguise identification. But there's an indication that their plan changed, on the spot. That whatever the fate of the first victim was, Ann Reed *made a better victim,* if you will. And in some way, they wanted acknowledgment."

"I don't know," Gutteres said.

"There's a team dynamic," Roth said. "It goes beyond robbery-for-profit logic. I suspect we've got two disturbed personalities that exploded at the robbery and melded into a deadly new entity. It's possible that one personality will dominate the entity, or the two will battle for control."

"Cripes." Gonzales shook his head.

"The suspects' behavior at the robbery could relate to their pasts, their upbringings, experiences. Could be a combination of things that have been festering. Then the sudden circumstances providing an opportunity to exact vengeance on individuals, or society, for any past grievances," Roth said.

"Can any of this be directly related to Ann Reed?" Sydowski said.

"She appears to be a random victim," Roth said, "but rule nothing out. If anything, it appears that abducting her has boosted their drive, like putting gasoline on fire."

"Will they kill Ann Reed?"

"Not immediately."

"What do they want to do? Torment her pursuers?" Gonzales said.

"Something like that. They know all bets are off. It's a death penalty case. That's a given. They've already bet the house. They've got nothing to lose. To be blunt, I think they want to play, inflict pain.''

"So this isn't over?" Sydowski said.

"On the contrary. It's just beginning.''

26

Dexter climbed into his old Dodge pickup, headed south out of Winslow on Route 87 to a secluded spot he knew along Clear Creek.

He loved driving in the high desert with the window down, breezes snapping his T-shirt, radio loud on his favorite Flagstaff country station. He adjusted his straw Stetson as he turned the truck off the road, easing her into the shade of an old oak that sheltered the picnic table. His old man first brought him to this fishing spot on his sixth birthday. Helped him carve his name in the tree before walking out on him and his mom a couple years later.

Dexter killed the big V-8. The engine ticked in the tranquillity as he reached into the bed for his rod, tackle, bag with two cold cans of beer and two of Juanita's big soft tacos, made just the way he loved 'em, extra cheese, stringy lettuce, tomato diced thick, wrapped tight in waxed paper.

Dexter was pretty sure he loved Juanita, he thought, his line whizzing out as he cast, then sat down and started into one of her tacos. Heck, he loved her. No doubt about it, they'd known each other since high school.

Couple days ago after the storm, the whites were hitting pretty good. Dexter cast again, chewing on the fact Juanita had a point. He was a twenty-five-year-old grown man. Time to think about moving out of his mom's double-wide at the edge of town. He felt a tug. Call him crazy but he liked using a rig, or sometimes a spinner did the trick. Nope, nothing. He cast again, then opened a beer. Thing was, he had never thought about moving out until Juanita started all this talk of quitting the diner, moving to Los Angeles to try acting, telling him he should quit living with his mom in the trailer, quit his mechanic's job at A.J.'s and go with her to seek adventure.

Was that another tug?

Why did Juanita have to push so hard, make him feel like he was going to lose her? The line locked. His rod bowed into the letter C. Snagged something. He began reeling it in. The veins in his tanned arms rose, the object pushing a considerable wake. Dexter moved to the bank, glimpsed something brown as he brought it closer, lifting it out, water cascading from it. A boot. A big old work boot.

People will throw anything in the water. He cast again. Maybe he could try Los Angeles. He considered it for another half hour, not reaching any decisions by the time he'd finished his beers, tacos, and fishing for the day. He stood and stretched, put his rod and tackle box in the back of the truck, returned to the picnic table, crumpled his cans, and walked to the trash bin at the roadside.

The first thing Dexter noticed was the buzzing of the flies.

A dark cloud of them dotted with a few bees and wasps orbiting something atop the garbage filling the steel mesh basket. It was a big purse, a nice-looking designer bag, resting atop the greased, stained fast-food bags, drink cups, and beer cans. Looked new, out of place. Its flower pattern bulged a little with whatever was inside. He tried to peer in the top but it was zippered shut. The handles looped invitingly from the garbage.

Dexter looked around. He was alone. What the hell? He

waved away the buzzing cloud with his hat, then hefted the bag. Felt like it had seven or eight pounds of something inside, he figured, after taking a few steps, setting it down, reaching for the zipper, sliding it open.

27

Several hundred miles away, just off a lonesome freeway exit that vanished somewhere into the night, two men sat in the Old Glory Truck Stop, studying laminated menus and their circumstances.

The first man was Del, a six-foot-three-inch, 230-pound ex-con with a muscular build. He'd decided to have steak as he scratched his whiskers. It had been a few days since he'd shaved and he pondered another goatee, like the one he'd had when he was in Folsom where he had met the man sitting across from him.

John. The guy who was running this show. Or thought he was.

At six feet two, 220 pounds, John was Del's physical match. But something lethal and dark beyond measure was coiled inside. Cold eyes burned from his taut baby-smooth face, clenched like the fist of a man who had to smash his way into a world that wanted him dead. Long before they'd met, John was condemned to die on Florida's death row. He'd been found guilty of murdering a corner store clerk near Miami. But John studied the system, used it to fight back until the court tossed his conviction. He walked off death row free to resume a life of crime, which led him to Folsom and his destiny with Del. In the realm of born losers, John was a prince.

But not to Del. Not anymore.

He regarded him the way a mongoose regards a cobra.

Del no longer trusted John. Since the San Francisco job went wrong, John kept pushing things in a dangerous direction. But Del knew they couldn't part, knew that he couldn't let his guard down, not until this ride to hell was over. For now, he'd take his pleasures where he could find them, he thought, enjoying the curves on the approaching waitress.

"I almost didn't see you fellas," she said. "Sitting all alone in the dark. This section's closed."

"Well, darlin'," Del said, "hope you don't move us, 'cause we like it here."

"It's fine, dear." She pretended not to notice Del's malformed ear. "What can I getcha?"

"Steak sandwich and milk sounds good."

"Fine. And you?"

John's face was buried in newspapers.

"Buddy, the lady asked what you want."

"I'll have the same," John said to his newspaper.

"That's easy. Say, where you boys from?"

"California," Del said.

"New York," John corrected.

"California *and* New York. What's the story?"

"We're headed to California," Del said. "Been on the road a spell."

"What's in California for you?"

"Miss." John cut her short. "That big TV on the shelf work?"

"It works."

"Could you switch it on to news and switch off your questions?"

Her face reddened. She collected the menus.

"Wait, miss. Hey, buddy," Del said. "I'm sorry, miss, he's just a little stressed and tired."

Most of the warmth drained from her. She'd seen her share of jerks. She gave Del a hint of a smile, then left him thinking how if he was alone, he'd date her tonight. Just like the hundreds of other women he'd dated over the years. Like the one they had left in Death Valley, the one that was in the paper John couldn't stop reading.

Ever since San Francisco, John checked every newspaper, every radio station, every TV newscast for the latest on the heist. Sometimes he'd chuckle to himself. It pissed Del off that he'd never speak to him.

"You know." Del dropped his voice. "That was stupid with the waitress. She's going to remember you."

John ignored him and moved on to another newspaper.

"Did you take care of business and call the client?" Del said.

"Called him when you took a piss."

"He still interested, even with all this heat?"

"Don't worry about it."

"You told him we got it?"

John raised his head, the glow of the TV news broadcast lighting the smooth surface of his face. "Shut up."

Del clamped his teeth to hold back his anger. *Walk away now,* he urged himself. *It's all gone bad, just walk away. Look at what's happened.* When they started, four were in on it. Now it was down to just the two of them and John was pushing it. Always changing things. It didn't smell right. Was he setting him up? Would John do that? No way. They were tight, man. They went all the way back to C Yard where they covered each other's back. Kept each other alive. But why couldn't John look him in the eye anymore?

"John." Del kept his voice low even though no one was close enough to overhear. "I just don't get it. You're leaving a goddamned chum line for them."

"Don't worry about it."

"That's all you say. That don't cut it."

John watched TV.

"As long as we're traveling heavy I'm going to enjoy myself. It's been a while," Del said.

John's attention never left the television. "Not until I say so."

"I got needs."

John's eyes met his. "Not until I say."

They ate without speaking. Del ordered two slices of banana cream pie for dessert. When the waitress cleared their plates he licked his fingers and told her he still craved something sweeter.

"Look who I got for company."

John was peering into his black coffee as if it held answers for him.

"You fellas have a safe trip," she said. "Cook's wrapping up your takeout. You can pick it up at the cash." She snapped the check from her pad.

After she left, Del started on John again. "You going to tell me what's really going on?"

John sipped his coffee and looked beyond the window at the darkness.

"I want to know, John. You're taking risks, acting like it's some kind of game now," Del said. "My life is on the goddamned line here. You're pushing it to the edge and I want to know why."

"I got my reasons."

"You got your reasons!"

Del's jaw began pulsating as he stared at John, then began gnawing on a thumbnail. "What're your reasons?"

"I'll tell you when the time's right."

"That might be too late." Del got up. "I'll meet you at the truck."

John watched him walk across the big parking lot and figured sooner or later he'd have to tell him the truth about why things had changed; make him understand why it had to go down his way. On one point, Del was right, they were putting it all on the line, but it was no game. Not for John.

He glanced at the headlines before gathering the newspapers and the check, chuckling to himself at the irony. For the first time in his life, he was in control.

The truck was at a remote dimly lit section of the lot, bordering a wooded rest area with outdoor washrooms. Probing his teeth with a toothpick, Del glanced back at the restaurant and thought of the waitress, the curves of her body, the way strands of hair had slipped from her ponytail, the dark grove of trees where nobody would hear her scream. But there was no time.

Del spat and kept walking. He faced a bigger problem with the heist as he tried to assure himself that despite complications, they were going to pull it off. They'd been smart, careful to adjust to things on the run. They'd left no paper trail by using cash. It was dumb luck that lady at the jewelry store had so much. It meant no friction on the road.

The SUV was obtained through Driscoll's connection at a parking lot near LAX. The truck's owner was out of the country on a three-week vacation. They still had sixteen days before it would even be reported stolen. It was John's idea to get a couple of small magnetic signs for the front doors that read SUPERVISOR. NATIONAL LANDSCAPE SERVICES. Meant you could store just about anything in the back without attracting suspicion.

Del checked to be certain no one was nearby in the remote area of the lot, then slid the key in the tail door and opened it. The rear had been adjusted to accommodate several items.

Del took inventory under the huge tarp, pleased that nothing looked out of place among the few large bags of sod, wood chips, seed, large rolls of silver duct tape, canvas bags, shovels, a pickax, chains, ropes, a circular power saw. A close inspection of the sawblade's teeth would reveal flecks of dried blood, mixed with minute traces of bone and viscera.

The largest item, a full-sized sleeping bag, was zipped

closed. It writhed slightly and issued a muffled whimper, prompting Del to bite down hard on his toothpick.

"Don't worry, darlin'. I'm going to get to you. Just like the other one. Only with you, I'm going to take my time."

28

Reed stepped into the elevator at the Hall of Justice and leaned against the wall unprepared for whatever awaited him as he ascended to room 450.

Homicide.

How many times had he taken this ride in pursuit of a murder story? How many times had Ann begged him to quit? He shut his eyes to think clearly. He'd refused Sydowski's and Turgeon's offer to pick him up when they called him to come down. He was still angry over the incident with Tia Layne before Sydowski explained that it wasn't Ann.

Was she still alive?

Turgeon was the first to meet him. She was wearing a dark business suit and holding an empty mug. "I'm getting fresh coffee, would you like one, Tom?"

"No."

Turgeon offered him the chair next to the metal desks where she worked alongside Sydowski. The same creaky chair where he'd sat so many times and pumped them on someone else's tragedy.

Sydowski was on the phone, leaving Reed to take stock of the homicide detail, a place of battle. He reflected on the city's motto, *Oro en paz, fierro en guerra.* Gold in peace, iron in war. The filing cabinets, the shelves laden with binders, the walls papered with memos, notices, lookouts, clippings, some with his byline. It was as if he were seeing it all for the first time. A dark jacket matching Sydowski's pants was draped on Sydowski's chair. His desk was cluttered, there was a fanned poker hand of phone messages. He hung up.

"Sorry, Tom. Let's go in an interview room where it's private."

"Whatever you have to tell me, you can tell me here."

Reed drew looks from the people working nearby.

"We'll go where it's private," Sydowski said.

The barren room where inspectors questioned murder suspects and witnesses was a white cinder-block rectangle. Not much larger than a prison cell. It had chairs and a small table with a wood veneer finish. The only uplifting thing were the roses on Turgeon's coffee mug.

"Tom." Sydowski unbuttoned his collar. "What that reporter did was unconscionable. We want you to know—"

"I just can't believe," Reed said, "that nobody gave me so much as a hint on the condition of the victim. Not you. Not Gutteres. Not the FBI. And you all knew, didn't you? That's the thing. You all knew yet no one told me. You went with the assumption it was Ann. Prepare for the worst, you said. Left me to plan a funeral and tell my son his mother's dead. Then this woman comes to my door and throws details in my face. Details I should have been given."

"Nobody's happy about what happened," Turgeon said.

"How in hell did she get that sheriff's report?"

"Stolen," Turgeon said. "San Bernardino says she worked something out with a cleaning lady. There may be charges."

"Stolen?" Reed shook his head.

"Nobody had control over this," Sydowski said. "Everyone's sorry for what happened. Look, if you've got questions on anything, we'll try to answer them."

Reed took a breath. Fatigue replaced his anger. "Do you have any leads on where Ann is?"

"Nothing solid yet," Sydowski said.

"Do you think she could be alive?"

"Honest to God, we just don't know."

"You have anything on the suspects who took her?"

"Nothing more than their voices," Sydowski said.

"Did you get an ID on the desert victim?"

"Not yet. It's going to take time, given the circumstances."

"What about the task force? Is anybody any closer to anything?"

"The FBI's entered details of the items from the heist into JAG."

"The jewelry and gem database?"

"Yes. A lot of the stolen stuff has the jeweler's mark."

"That might save the jewels."

"Tom," Turgeon said, "everyone's going flat out."

"My wife's been abducted in a triple homicide and you think I should cheer up because you *didn't* take a nap."

She let Reed vent. A moment passed before his next question. "Anything more on Driscoll, the dead driver?"

Sydowski opened a file folder.

"Latest from CDC is after he did his time in Folsom, he was on supervised parole for three years. That ended a few years ago. They've gone through LEADS, the registry, community services, his addictions treatment counselors, talked to his former PA. No violations. No drugs. No crime. On paper, he was clean. FBI's going through his visitor-contact history, last addresses list, phone records."

"And?"

"Nothing official, but something lit up."

"What?"

"They got a line from informants through the LAPD and LA County that just before the robbery here, he was shopping for something from an auto-theft ring hitting the less reputable lots near LAX," Sydowski said.

"It's a small piece of the puzzle," Turgeon said.

"What about the suspects? Don't you have a shred of a trace?"

"There's no paper trail," Sydowski said. "No clear latents in the van, the heist, or the wheelchair. Nothing so far from the shell casings. We're still going over a lot of areas but we've got nothing solid right now."

Reed stared in his empty hands.

"Tell me why. Why did they take her? Why take her when they just needed a car? Why make it look like her in the desert?"

"There are a million possibilities," Turgeon said.

"It's like they're playing with you, with me. A game to inflict the most pain. When I saw them remove that corpse, I—" Reed's shoulders began to shake and he covered his face.

Turgeon touched his arm until he regained his composure.

"So why did you need me today?"

Sydowski traded a quick glance with Turgeon before pulling a cassette tape from his breast pocket.

"What's that?"

"The voices of the suspects picked up on Rod August's radio."

"I've already listened to it."

"We know. But it's been cleaned up even more. Much of the background noise is gone, or reduced. We'd like you to take it home, listen to this enhanced version."

"Do you know how hard it is for me to hear Ann's voice?"

"We know," Sydowski said. "But we'd like you to take your time and listen to it, please."

"Why? We've been over this."

"The voices are much better, maybe you'll recognize one of them from all the crime reporting you've done over the years."

"Now you think there's a connection to me? What's changed?"

"No." Sydowski's eyes met Reed's. "Tom, at this point we're not certain of anything, which means we've got to check everything. All we need is a break."

"A break? And you think I'm the one that's going to give it to you? After all that's happened? This"—Reed nodded to the tape—"this is the best you can do?"

"Dozens of people are working round the clock on this case," Sydowski said. "You know how these things go. All we need is one break to lead us to the suspects. It's not important how we get it, or where it comes from. I know it's difficult, but would you please just listen to the tape again?"

For the first time, Reed noticed a postcard-sized agenda sticking from the side pocket of Turgeon's jacket. It was for August's funeral service.

It dawned on Reed that Sydowski and Turgeon had lost a member of their police family. At least he had a glimmer of hope of seeing Ann again.

Reed reached for the tape.

"All right. I'll listen to it."

29

A dark somber river of uniformed officers flowed into St. Mary's Cathedral for Officer Rod August's funeral. Their polished badges were crossed with black mourning bands, their polished shoes shuffled on the expansive stone entrance steps as police pipers droned a series of dirges into the clear blue sky overlooking San Francisco.

"Must be a thousand of them. It's never going to end." Tia Layne gnawed on her second wad of gum to fight her unbearable cigarette craving. "This sucks," she whispered to Cooter.

His right eye was tight to his camera's eyepiece as he recorded the massive procession entering the church, known for its striking parabolic arches that swept toward the heavens.

Layne and Cooter had been careful to take a position near the cathedral but at some distance from the other Bay Area news crews covering the funeral service.

The San Francisco police, the San Bernardino County Sheriff's office, and the FBI had all lodged formal complaints against her to *Worldwide*. No charges had been filed yet for taking the San Bernardino police report.

"Any word?" Cooter said.

"Nope."

Layne was told by *Worldwide* New York that the matter might be mitigated because she and the show had volunteered their uncut footage to the police. But there was no guarantee. She checked her watch. The district attorney's office and *Worldwide*'s lawyers in New York should've wrapped up their long-distance discussions on the stolen report by now.

"Seth will call." Layne indicated the cluster of news crews and chatty cops nearby. "Look at them. Looking over here, laughing at us. Screw 'em."

"It was your idea to come."

Layne was searching for Tom Reed, hoping he would have attended.

"I'm not going to back off now," she said. "We're just as good as they are and we have just as much right to cover this story as they do."

"Maybe, but there're less risky ways to earn bread."

"I'm not going back to making movies, Cooter. I'm through with that part of my life. Got it?"

Cooter repositioned the camera. His shoulder ached and he cursed himself for not bringing his tripod to record the pageantry, the hearse, the scores of black limos, the honor guard. He was counting the one hundred gleaming police motorcycles marshaled for the procession to Colma when Layne felt her cell phone vibrate.

"Tia." She kept her voice low.

"It's Seth."

"Well?"

"It's not good and they're not done yet."

"That's it?"

"They're very serious about charging you."

"You're kidding. After we played ball with them on our footage? Look, I explained what happened. I was invited into that police station and saw that report in plain view and asked for a copy."

"Tia. Come on."

"Didn't the lawyers tell them about freedom of the press?"

Layne recognized California's attorney general entering the church.

"Tia, the show was flooded with calls and e-mails after the news wires reported what you did. London isn't paying you the sixty thousand."

"Why?"

"Inaccurate reporting."

"We clarified that in the next report. Get me my money, Seth."

"The damage was done. You pissed off a few people, Tia. The lawyers are working hard to prevent charges. For now, you and the show will send formal letters of apology to everyone aggrieved. *Worldwide* will quietly send sizable donations to several nonprofit groups that aid crime victims. And they'll settle out of court, five thousand, I think, with that maid who claims you extorted her to obtain the report."

"That's a lie. She was stealing from me."

Layne saw San Francisco's mayor enter flanked by a couple of police commission members.

"Doesn't matter now. That's how it's going down, Tia."

"This sucks. Now what?"

"They're going to talk some more later next week. The DA's people have a major case in court. You're not off the hook yet."

"So what do I do here?"

"Some of the editors in New York wanted you off the story. London overruled them after Nigel pointed out that *Worldwide News Now* is not CNN, or *60 Minutes,* or the BBC. That this is more about ratings, public appetite, and product than credibility."

"Well, duh. I knew that from the get-go, Seth."

"I sent them our numbers since you started reporting on this case."

"And?"

"They're soaring. London was intoxicated by them. You've got them a share of the U.S. market. The story and your controversy are drawing a crowd. I sent them today's op-ed piece in the *Post*, citing our cop-murder footage and your doorstep ambush of Reed. The usual harping on ratings-driven tabloid sleaze. It was golden. It led to more attention."

"I told them this would happen. So what now?"

"Stay with it, but try to stay out of jail."

"What about my money?"

"You'll get what you've earned legally."

"And the terms for future work?"

"It's negotiable but I told London that because of your ratings your fee is likely to start at one hundred for each exclusive and *legally obtained* report they want. I mean this will be hot around the world for them."

"What did they say to that, Seth?"

"I really shouldn't tell you."

"Come on, Seth."

"They didn't even blink."

"Beautiful, because this story is far from over."

She hung up. One hundred frigging thousand dollars. Layne grinned from behind her dark glasses just as a group of officers and San Francisco's police chief escorted the murdered officer's ex-wife and little boy into the church.

30

The Dodge pickup swerving into town on 87 caught Winslow City Police Officer Ken Flannagan's attention.

The driver was flashing his high beams, honking his horn, had his arm out the window waving his hat at his patrol car. *Looks like Dexter Pratt from A.J.'s*, Flannagan thought, pulling alongside the truck.

"What's the trouble, Dex?"

"Out by Clear Creek. I'll show you."

"What is it?"

"Come on."

Truck tires squealed. Flannagan followed him. He hadn't smelled alcohol. Young Dexter was never any trouble but he looked like he'd seen a ghost. What could it be? Flannagan wondered, pulling off at the spot near the oak tree. Dexter stayed in his truck and pointed to the bag.

"It's inside. I haven't touched anything. You look at it."

Flannagan stepped from his cruiser.

"You going to tell me? 'Cause if this is a prank—"

"No prank, I swear."

Flannagan walked to the bag. He'd been on the job two

years. In that time he'd seen suicides, fire victims, traffic
fatalities, and such. He knew the gagging stench of natural
deaths, an odor that hit him as he reached for his baton and
pen to spread the bag's sides apart.

He saw fingers. Slender like a female's. Then hair as eyes
wide in terror met his. Flannagan's stomach tightened, he
stepped back and dry-heaved.

Navajo County responded first and took control. It was
their jurisdiction. The FBI dispatched people from Flagstaff
to assist as word rocketed through police circles that the
find was linked to the homicide-abduction case in California.

The FBI's Evidence Response Team rolled out of Phoenix
Division with a full contingent of forensic experts. Others
were coming up from Tucson. They worked quickly examining the evidence, photographing, mapping, analyzing, and
organizing spiral and grid searches. They interviewed Dexter
Pratt, took a statement, impressions of his shoes, his tires,
fingerprints to compare them with everything they were
collecting from the area.

The FBI people brought an entomologist, an expert on
insects. With certain species of flies, the adult female will
leave her eggs on the nostrils, mouth, and eyes of a corpse.
The eggs evolve into wormlike larvae that feast on the
decomposing flesh before they hatch in a cycle that takes
about twenty-four hours, which, after factoring in other conditions, can provide a means of determining the time of
death. In the Clear Creek find of a woman's head and severed
hands, it was estimated that the time of death exceeded forty-
eight hours. Moreover, it did not occur at the scene.

As for identification, well, that's where the case broke
wide open.

The good condition of the hands made it relatively simple
for the FBI to obtain fingerprints. They were immediately
submitted to the national database, known as AFIS, the
Automated Fingerprint Identification System, and to a

number of regional, state, and local programs. In California the prints were accessed by California's Department of Justice, the SFPD, and the San Bernardino County Sheriff's office. They were checked through the DMV, Cal-ID, and a number of other systems.

It took less than three minutes before California got a hit. The DMV system confirmed the fingerprints matched those on the driver's license of:

Carrie Dawn Addison. DOB 02/05/76
Height: 5 feet 7 inches. Weight: 116
Eye Color: Brown. Hair Color: Brown
Address: 707 Short, San Francisco CA

31

As mourners filed out of St. Mary's Cathedral, Sydowski's cell phone vibrated.

Within the hour he and Turgeon stood at the front door of the large dark green Victorian in the Upper Market where Carrie Dawn Addison's apartment was located. Sydowski pressed the buzzer a second time.

"Let's try next door." Turgeon indicated the man polishing a metallic lime green '57 Vette. "Excuse me, sir. Do you know the people at this building?"

The man looked to be in his late fifties, salt-and-pepper brush cut of a retired marine. The Stars and Stripes hung from his garage.

"Who's asking?"

"San Francisco police." Sydowski held out his ID.

"There a problem?"

"We're checking on the welfare of someone listed at the address."

"Gosh. Is Ellie all right? I just saw her a little while ago."

"Who would that be?"

"Ellie Brunner, she owns the place. Rents out the rooms upstairs. Mostly young women. College girls, nurses."

"Any of them named Carrie?"

"Yes. There a problem?"

"What can you tell us about her?"

"Carrie? Not much. In her twenties. Moved in two years ago, I'd say. Keeps to herself. Quiet. Every now and then I see her working on her laptop on her balcony, catching some sun. I think she's a student. What's the problem?"

A burgundy Chev sedan stopped at the house. A slender white-haired woman with round frameless glasses stepped from it. She was wearing a print dress and carrying a plastic bag, celery stalks sticking from it. On seeing the strangers, a question formed on her face.

"Mrs. Brunner?" Sydowski said.

"Yes, can I help you?"

Turgeon held out her ID.

"Can we have a quick moment in private?"

"Police?" Her attention bounced between the inspectors.

"Can we talk privately, please?" Sydowski said.

They went inside. Minutes later Brunner led Sydowski and Turgeon up the exterior wrought-iron staircase at the rear to Carrie Addison's second-floor apartment. As Brunner worked the key into the lock, the detectives tugged on green latex gloves. It was a small, neat one-bedroom.

"She live alone?" Sydowski said.

"Yes."

"Have many visitors?"

"None. She's quiet, moved in over two years ago. You said it was urgent police business to check on her welfare but—"

"It is, Mrs. Brunner." Turgeon took stock of the furnishings, the mail on the table.

"Do you know where she's employed?" Sydowski said.

"Not exactly. I think she's got several part-time jobs."

"Can you tell us about any of them?"

"Addictions counselor. She told me she helped people with substance-abuse problems."

"You know where?" Turgeon said.

"In the Mission, I think. Officers, I really feel uncomfortable and you're worrying me. Was there an accident?"

"Something like that," Sydowski said. "Again, when's the last time you saw or spoke with Currie?"

"A few weeks ago."

"What do you remember? Her demeanor? Any details?"

"She was leaving town for a few days to visit a friend. She seemed happy. Before that she told me that she might be leaving the country for some sort of job in South America. That she'd let me know soon."

"When was that again?" Sydowski gazed at the mail.

"About two weeks ago."

"Have you spoken to her on the phone since you last saw her?"

"No."

"You remember what she was wearing that day?"

"Goodness. Faded jeans, maybe. A yellow top. Short-sleeved. I'm not sure. She was carrying two travel bags."

"Walt?" Turgeon nodded to some travel books on the Caribbean and Central and South America lying on an end table near the sofa.

"Ma'am, is her phone wired through your line, or is it separate?" Sydowski said, examining the telephone answering machine.

"Separate."

"Do you know if she received many packages, or deliveries?"

"None that I know of."

"She have trouble paying the rent?"

"No, never."

"She have any male visitors?"

"None that I saw. Please, you're worrying me."

"I think we better get a warrant."

Brunner sat down at the small kitchen table. "Please tell me what's happening."

Turgeon pulled out a chair and sat across from her. As a seasoned homicide detective she knew how to keep a professional distance without being cold. Ellie Brunner seemed to be a good-hearted woman, but this was not the time to tell her that the head and hands of her tenant had been found inside a designer bag in a roadside trash bin near Winslow, Arizona.

"Mrs. Brunner. Ellie, we have reason to believe Carrie may have been harmed. We're trying to sort things out. We don't know everything yet. Once we do, we'll tell you."

Sydowski's cell phone trilled.

It was Terry Witherspoon, one of the SFPD robbery inspectors chasing the victim's ID. He was calling from San Francisco Deluxe Jewelry.

"Walt, we're down at the store with the manager going through the employee list again."

"And."

"Carrie Dawn Addison is on it."

"Bingo."

32

At home alone in his study, Reed slapped the police tape into his machine, pushed the button. The reels rotated counterclockwise.

Sydowski had said the enhanced tape would be released to the press later. The lab had set it up to play the segment continuously. The tape hissed; then Ann's pleas exploded from his bookshelf speakers, the clarity of her breathing, her gasps put her in the room with him.

"Oh God, please let me go!"

"Shut up! I told you to shut up! Where's your car?"

"Please. Don't. Please!"

"Are you sure you got him?"

"Christ, it's all going to hell!"

"Keep moving! Come on!"

That was it. Three seconds passed; then it played again. Then again. Reed had to stop it a few times, forcing himself to ignore Ann's voice to concentrate on the male voices. It seemed futile.

After nearly an hour, Reed ran his hand through his hair. As the tape rewound, he switched on his small television, muting it to the local coverage of the police officer's funeral. There was the SFPD honor guard. August's coffin, the police chief, the mayor, the attorney general, an ocean of blue. The tape resumed.

"Oh God, please let me go!"

"Shut up! I told you to shut up! Where's your car?"

Strange. Out of nowhere, for an intense half second, he thought maybe, he'd recognized a cadence, a certain tone, an inflection?

"I told you to shut up!"

Reed had heard that voice somewhere. Hadn't he?

"I told you to shut . . ."

Hadn't he?

"I told you to . . ."

Come on, hadn't he?

"I told you. I told you. I told you."

Did he know that voice? The possibility slithered deep into the dark regions of his memory, then vanished. Damn. His mind was playing tricks on him. It was desperation. How many times had he listened to the segment?

Reed stood, watching the police funeral, feeling the seams of his world coming apart. He was anguished, exhausted, grappling with the fact he was utterly helpless. The tape continued.

Why had Sydowski insisted he listen? Was there a connection? Why did the suspects go out of their way to make it appear Ann was the one they had buried, tormenting him, making it a game? Why? The camera pulled in on the woman in black, the murdered officer's ex-wife, holding the hand of her little boy. Thoughts of Ann and Zach pierced Reed.

"Oh God, please let me go!"

The phone rang, jolting him.

"Tom, it's Molly."

"Molly?"

"Tom, I'm sorry," she said. "Did you hear about Arizona?"

"No. What about Arizona?"

"You're going to hear something on this, I wanted to tell you first."

"Christ, Molly, what?"

"A source of mine just called me and said the Navajo County Sheriff's office and FBI ERT were called out to a find."

"What—where?"

"Near Winslow. It's happening now!"

"What? What did they find?"

"Her bag. Ann's bag."

Reed collapsed in his chair.

"Tom. I hate this. I'm so sorry. I'm calling you as a friend. When we heard what that reporter from *Worldwide* did, I just wanted you to know."

Reed steadied himself. "Molly, did your source tell you anything more?"

"They found something in the bag. I don't know what but it's connected to the site in Death Valley."

Reed's room began spinning: the police funeral. Ann's voice.

"Oh God, please let me go!"

33

Ann Reed lay in darkness in the back of the idling SUV.
She'd learned the names of the men who'd kidnapped her.

John and Del.

How many hours—*days?*—had it been? Ann didn't know. She existed between the worlds of sleep and fear. She became expert at feeling, sensing and identifying travel movements, sounds, and rhythms. She glimpsed the vehicle and its plate during a late-night bathroom stop.

They'd driven almost nonstop, constantly monitoring radio news reports. In the rare instances the men talked, they spoke in low tones. She had to strain to hear them.

But that's how she got their names.

John and Del.

They'd pulled off of the highway and had been parked for several minutes. One had left the truck for about five minutes, then returned.

She strived to hear, catching words.

"Cabin . . . left at the pool . . . passed the trees . . . private . . . number ten . . ."

The transmission engaged, the truck crept forward, making gentle turns before creaking to a halt. The engine was turned off. The suspension sprang as they stepped out and walked off. She listened. Several moments passed before they returned. A key slid into the truck's rear lock and the door opened.

She held her breath.

Please, God. Help me.

Someone began tugging at the sleeping bag, jerking its zipper open. She felt warm night air; then a cloth hood—*a pillowcase?*—was pulled over her head.

The duct tape around her ankles was cut and torn away but the bonds around her wrists and tape covering her mouth remained. She was manipulated into a sitting position, her legs moved over the tail and bumper, until she found her footing and was pulled to her feet. She heard the faraway drone of a highway and the chirp of crickets. Shaking with fear, she fought to assemble details, as if she could fashion them into a means of escape.

Someone gripped her upper arm and forced her forward.

They moved over a pebbled surface, then soft grass, then ascended *one, two, three* squeaky wooden steps until she sensed a threshold and they entered a room with soft flooring. Carpet freshener, furniture polish, and the scent of pine were mixed by an air conditioner. Its fan rattling and humming.

The room's door was shut, locked, bolted, and chained. Curtain hooks whizzed in the track. A light switch clicked. There was quiet movement, a bag was dropped nearby on a linoleum floor. Then someone drew near. Close. Body odor and cigarette breath invaded her nostrils.

Without warning her head twisted and the hood was yanked off. She blinked, adjusting to the dim light that made everything in the room appear tinged with blood.

A tall, muscle-bound man stood within a few feet of her. He was unshaven. He had short black hair, a disfigured ear, and sideburns tufting to his jaw in thick forests that thinned into a sea of growth reaching the beginnings of a moustache drooping over the rotting teeth of his sneer. His eyes traveled up and down her body.

Ann felt the vibrations of her heart.

The room was large. It looked clean. Two queen-sized beds. Large TV. A coffee table. A desk. A telephone. *A lifeline?* A sofa and sofa chair from where another big man studied her. He was in blue jeans, white T-shirt. Muscular, tattooed arms. Shaved head. Clean-skinned smooth face. His dark eyes locked on to hers, following them to the telephone.

"Forget that," he said. "You'll do what you're told. Understand?"

Ann blinked once. She had it now from their voices. This one, the shaved-headed smooth-skinned one, was John. He seemed to be in charge. The other one with the misshapen ear and bad teeth was Del.

"We're going to take the tape off of your mouth but don't think about trying anything or making a sound. One: no one will hear you. And two." John glanced at the man standing before her. "You'll be punished."

The duct tape binding her wrists began clicking from her trembling.

"Understand?"

Ann shut her eyes.

It's a dream. A bad dream.

"Do you understand, *Ann*?"

She opened her eyes to meet his, then nodded once.

"Good. All right then."

Del fumbled with the duct tape over her mouth, his big clumsy fingers stripping it, the adhesive side resisting, stretching her skin as though he were peeling it from her skull. It stung but she swallowed her pain, working her sore jaw up and down as he sliced the tape from her wrists.

"Go take a shower," Del said.

Shower? Then what? The beds. The threats. Don't make a sound. You'll be punished. Then what?

Ann didn't move until the air conditioner rattled to a dead-silent stop, making her flinch.

"You do what we say," John said. "Get in there. Shower. Put on fresh clothes from the bag."

Ann blinked back her tears, turned to the bathroom. Maybe there was a phone there? A window, door, a vent? *Please, something.* Del shoved her toward the bathroom.

Inside, Ann locked the door, then fell against it to study the room. Beige walls and tile. No windows. No doors. No vents. Just a bathroom.

No way out.

Think. She had to do something. Anything.

She started the shower, then turned to the vanity mirror over the sink, seeing herself for the first time since it happened. Shock and anguish had carved dark lines deep into her skin under blotches of dirt, nicks, and scrapes. Her hair was matted, gritted with sand and grime. She covered her mouth with her shaking hands. Her eyes glistened, remembering Zach and Tom—their faces—would she ever see them again? Their voices—would she ever hear them again? Aching to be with them. Hold them. The hot water hissing, her face fading in the steam clouding the mirror, until she was gone.

Don't give up.

In the shower Ann sobbed, releasing her fear and panic. Del with the rotting teeth, deformed ear, and sideburns had whispered to her, "Don't worry, darlin'. I'm going to get to you. Just like the other one." Ann tingled with fear. She scrubbed furiously under the needles of hot water. *"Do what we say"*—as if she could cleanse herself free—*"you'll be punished"*—scouring as she gasped for her life—*"just like the other one"*—feeling the first molten drops of rage burn in her gut against the indignity, against the violation her captors had inflicted.

Don't give up. Fight back. For your life. For Zach. For Tom. But there were two of them and they were big men. Strong men. Powerful men.

Then think. You're smart. Think. This is your life.

Drying herself, Ann wrapped a towel around her, then

examined the soiled, foul-smelling clothes she had worn. She retrieved Tom's small gift from the jewelry store. She'd hidden it in her shoe, then her bra. It was her talisman. She squeezed it.

That first night in the desert they'd yanked off her white silk blouse and tailored mauve suit, replacing them with dirty, torn jeans, a ripped and stained short-sleeved yellow blouse. The stains had dried brown. They had exchanged her clothes for something—*someone*—in the desert. *The other one*. Ann swallowed, then went to the bag. A dark green canvas bag. The tag inside said *Carrie D. Addison*. A San Francisco address.

Who was she? What happened to her?

The shovel. The pick. Digging. Ann knew. Carrie was *the other one*. Wasn't she? *Oh God. Oh, Carrie, dear God, whoever you are, I'm so sorry. So, so sorry*. Ann fought back her tears, her skin tingling as she struggled to push it all from her mind. She had no time. She swallowed. Took a deep breath.

Think.

She found fresh underwear, socks, clean jeans, a polo shirt, there was a woman's toiletry bag. It had tampons, deodorant, toothpaste, a toothbrush, but she chose to use her fingers to clean her teeth. She found a hairbrush. After a few quick strokes, she rifled through the bag for anything to help. A cell phone. A gun. A knife. Something.

There it was.

She spotted it, seized it. Her mind accelerating, darting like a fleeing swallow. *Hurry*. This was hope. Her only chance. *Come on*. This was something. *Come on—God, please help me*.

Ann jumped at the hammering on the bathroom door.

"Get your ass out here!"

34

Reed left another message on Sydowski's cell phone.

"Walt, it's Reed. Call me."

He couldn't reach anybody since Molly called him about Arizona. Not Sydowski. Couldn't reach Turgeon, Gonzales, or McDaniel. He tried Molly again at the paper. No luck.

The investigators keeping vigil in his living room knew nothing more than he did, or were keeping tight-lipped. Nothing came up on the newscasts. Reed had accessed the *Star*'s system from his home computer. Nothing about any breaks in the case on the wires. He hated being left in the dark. It felt like he was betraying Ann. Failing her. *Do something.*

Reed searched the directories on his desk until he found a Phoenix number and dialed it.

"Associated Press."

"I'm calling from the *San Francisco Star*. You hearing of anything breaking in your area that might be related to our jewelry store heist?"

"Maybe. Just a minute." A hand muffled the phone.

Reed's question was repeated to someone else. "Hang on. I'm going to transfer you."

The line clicked.

"Hi, this is Julie Juarez. I think I know what you're talking about. Hold on a sec." Her keyboard began clicking.

"Thanks."

"No problem. Here we go. Near Winslow. We should be moving something soon. We've got an alert from our stringer there. A report of police sealing an area after a discovery at Clear Creek."

"Discovery of what?"

"Doesn't say." The keyboard tapped. "A police source told our stringer it's related to that Death Valley homicide, the one linked to your heist. Says here Winslow and Navajo County are on it with the FBI's evidence team out of Phoenix. Must be a corpse, or something like that."

A corpse.

Reed hung up. His chest heaved. How much more of this was he supposed to take? From his study, he could see their bedroom. His eyes stung and he shut his door just as the phone rang. As the detectives had instructed from the outset, he let it ring twice before answering.

"Tom, it's Sydowski." On his cell, grunting like he was ascending steps.

"Walt, is it Ann? What they found in Arizona, is it her?"

"No."

Reed closed his eyes, then opened them.

"Are you absolutely sure this time?"

"Absolutely."

"Tell me more."

"A guy fishing near Winslow found the rest of the remains of the victim you saw in the desert. We've ID'd the victim as Carrie Dawn Addison of San Francisco."

"How do you know?"

"Just got it confirmed through her fingerprints. Does her name mean anything to you, Tom?"

"No. Should it?"

"Just checking."

"What about Ann? Was there any trace, anything?"

"No. I'm sorry."

"Any sign of where Ann is?"

"Nothing yet. Tom, I don't have much time. But there's something you need to know, and you'd better be sitting down."

"I am."

"The remains the fisherman found were the head and hands."

"Jesus."

"They were in Ann's bag. He found it in a picnic area trash can at Clear Creek, near Winslow."

No words came to Reed.

"Tom, are you with me?"

Reed managed to utter, "Yes."

"Tom, I'm telling you because it's all coming out in a few hours. The task force is holding a media briefing at the Hall. We think Carrie Dawn Addison's the connection because she once worked at Deluxe, the jewelry store. It's a break. I wanted you to get it first from us. I've got to go."

Reed hung up, took a few deep breaths, absorbing the information, forcing himself to hang on and focus. After a long moment, he called Doris, alerted her to Arizona and the news conference. She wept for the dead woman's family and for Ann.

"I'm coming back to your house to be with you and Zach."

Reed admonished himself for being selfish. How could he forget what Ann was enduring, what had happened to Carrie Addison, Rod August, their families? Thinking of them, he steadied himself for what he had to do: tell his son what had happened before the entire Bay Area was informed.

An F-18 jet fighter hung by a thread from the ceiling of Zach's room. A large model of the aircraft carrier the USS

Kitty Hawk sat majestically on one shelf, the walls were papered with the flag, posters of the 49ers, the Sharks, the Raiders, and U2.

Half hidden by a curtain, there was a tattered poster of Reed. An ancient thing that had gone in *Star* boxes to promote his investigative series on unsolved homicides. Reed was usually blind to it. A younger, cockier version of himself haunted him. Not because it took him back to his dark, drinking days but because he was a better reporter at the time. He took on everybody and won. A far cry from where he stood now, helpless to do anything to find Ann. Reed grasped a measure of comfort that at least his son still deemed him worthy for his wall of champions. Zach was sitting in the window seat looking at pictures from their recent family trip to Hawaii.

"I heard you on the phone, Dad. They didn't find Mom, did they?"

"No. It was about the other woman in the desert."

"What about her?"

Reed was apprehensive but told him the details. Zach's face reddened. He blinked. "What about Mom?"

"There's nothing new," Reed said. "And soon everyone will know the things I've just told you. It'll be on the news and stuff."

Zach nodded.

Reed sat on the edge of his son's bed and fell into his thoughts, swallowed by a thousand fears—the religion editor's caution on getting too close, Ann's warnings, *"You get the story but we pay the price."* Joking about cases with the homicide detectives at the Hall. The karmic wheel turning full circle on him, fate punishing him, locking its fingers around him, tightening.

"Dad?"

Zach stood before him and put his hand on his shoulder.

"Sorry, Zach," Reed said. "I'm trying to make sense of everything. I just don't know what it means."

"I do. It means Mom's not dead."

"I want to believe that."

"It means you have to find her."

"Find her? Me?"

"Yes, because that's what you do. You're as good as anybody at finding people, even bad guys. You found lots of them, Dad. Now you have to find Mom."

Reed searched Zach's eyes. They were radiant with the unshakable belief his mother was still alive. Did he possess some intangible link to her by virtue of having entered this world through her? His eyes were brown, like Ann's, and at this moment, the way they caught the sun spilling through the window, Reed swore he was looking into her eyes, hearing her calling to him.

Find me, Tom.

Zach gripped his shoulder.

"You can find her, Dad."

35

Ann stepped from the bathroom into darkness.

John was in the sofa chair watching the large muted TV, the room's only light source.

"Sit down and keep quiet."

Del was gone.

For an instant Ann considered hurling herself through the window to run screaming for help. But the curtains hid its size. Was it a big window? Was it barred? Could she get by *him* before he stopped her?

She saw that the phone had vanished. So had the phone book, the motel's color brochures, offer cards—all the items that would identify the location. In the TV's flicker she saw newspapers scattered on the veneer coffee table before it. *USA Today* and the *New York Times*. National papers available most anywhere. No sign of a local daily.

She sat in a hard-backed chair at the small table well across the room on the other side of the beds, as far away from him as she could get. Her stomach growled with hunger pangs. John's attention remained on the TV. They sat that way for nearly half an hour until Del returned with two brown bags filled with Chinese takeout, six-packs of canned beer, cigarettes, and snack food. He started pulling everything from the bag, setting it on the coffee table.

"Before you eat, go check the bathroom," John said.

"Why?" Del said.

"See if she tried to leave anything."

"I'm hungry." Del got at the food, shoveling plastic forkfuls into his mouth. The aroma of deep-fried and stir-fried chicken, pork, and beef dishes filled the room. "I'll do it later."

"Do it now."

Del cursed, bit into an eggroll, tromped to the bathroom, banged around, then exited and returned to the food. "Nothing."

John turned to Ann, dropped a soda can and two containers of food in one of the grease-stained bags, then tossed it to her. Rice, mixed vegetables, and ginger ale.

"Anything on the news while I was out?" Del said.

John shook his head. The two of them smacked their lips, guzzled beer, belching. Food and sauces rained on the carpet as they surfed between news and sports channels. When they finished eating, Del lit a cigarette, lay back on the couch, opened another beer, downed half, and looked at Ann.

"Everything all right over there, darlin'?"

She kept her eyes on the TV and didn't respond.

"You're a pretty one, aren't you?"

Ann said nothing.

"Well, you just let me know if there's anything I can do for you."

"Leave her alone." John went to the bathroom.

A moment later he came out holding a small piece of folded paper. He tossed it to Del.

"Read it."

The air tightened.

"What's this? Where'd you find it?"

John's jaw was clenched. "Just read it. Out loud." He glowered at Ann.

"Please call the FBI now," Del read. *"My name is Ann Reed, I was kidnapped by two men from the San Francisco Deluxe Jewelry Store armed robbery. I saw them shoot a police officer. We're going east. Men are named John and Del. Two white males about six feet driving a red late-model SUV with Calif. plate starting*—Jesus Christ—" Del leaped from the sofa. "We got to drop her now. Right now."

"Sit down." John grabbed the note. "I'll handle it."

"John, I'm telling you she's too goddamned dangerous. She's going to bring us down."

John stared at Ann.

"We had a plan, John, and this crap with her was never part of it."

"Shut up."

"We passed that warehouse. It had a row of dumpsters. We could put four hundred miles behind us easy before sunrise."

John's eyes never left Ann's.

"No witnesses. That's what you said, John. It's what you promised."

"I said shut up."

John started toward Ann. She stood, pressing her back to the wall. He held the note before her face. It was written on a page torn from the address book she'd found in the bag. She'd hidden it in the bathroom's dish of complimentary soap and shampoo.

"This," he said, "is going to cost you. Get on the bed."

She didn't move.

"Get on the goddamned bed."

Ann shook her head. He swatted the small table aside. It thudded to the carpet, spilling her food everywhere as he grabbed her. In one lightning motion she was catapulted to the bed, his large hands pinning her to the mattress. "I warned you not to try anything."

Del stood over them, a beer in his hand, grinning.

"Hand me our stuff, Del."

There was a chink of metal as he tossed him the bag they'd used in the armed robbery. John took out two sets of handcuffs and a chain; locked her wrists into the cuffs, which he linked to the bed's metal frame, leaving her enough length to sit up or lie down.

Before Ann could brace herself, the back of John's hand cracked hard across her face, stinging, making her head throb. Stars blurred through her pain and tears. John's face came within inches of hers.

"Now you listen good." He grabbed a fistful of her hair, yanking her head back until his eyes burned into hers. "You try anything like that again or make a sound, you're gone. Got that?"

Ann sniffed. Sobbing, she nodded.

He stroked her hair. "No matter what you do, Ann, I'm in control, understand?"

She understood.

John flushed her note in the toilet, then returned to the TV and more beer with Del. He lit a fresh cigarette, shooting glances at her on the bed.

Ann stared blankly at the TV. Long moments passed in silence. They'd found a channel showing the movie *The Getaway*, the Alec Baldwin, Kim Basinger version. Ann wept through much of it, watching the growing parade of empty beer cans lining the table near Del. He was engrossed by the sex scenes, loving the story line of the wife of the vet who appeared to enjoy having sex in front of him with the criminal who'd abducted both of them.

"Look at that, darlin'," Del said to Ann between slurps of beer. "Bet your husband's fit to be tied about now."

"Shut up," John told him.

After the movie ended, John collapsed in the bed next to Ann's. Del stayed on the sofa, his snoring soon punctuated with belches and farts. Ann's chain jingled when she turned to the wall. In the darkness her reality was crystalline.

I'm going to die. I'm wearing the clothes of a dead woman.

I've been kidnapped by killers who've revealed their faces to me. They face the death penalty. They have nothing to lose. I'll never see Zach and Tom again.

No. Stop it. Fight back. How? Escape? How? If they wanted you dead, you'd be dead by now. Maybe they wanted to hold her for ransom, torture her, play some perverted game. How could she know? They were monsters. She had to get away.

Ann froze.

A large hand reeking of tobacco clamped over her mouth and pressed her head into the bed. She inhaled the stench of beer, cigarettes, and rotting teeth. She opened her eyes to Del's, gleaming at her from the night. His other hand closed like a vise on her inner thigh.

"Shh. We can be quiet, darlin'."

Ann shook, making the chain clink.

"You're going to like it."

No. Don't. No.

Del's free hand reached for the zipper of her jeans. She struggled as he pulled it down, then reached for her lower stomach.

No!

The click of a gun's hammer stopped everything.

"I told you to stay away from her." John's gun was pressed to Del's head.

"Take it easy." Del withdrew his hands and got up. "Take it easy. I was just having some fun."

"Stay away from her."

"Hell, John. You want to go first, or what? Huh? What is your thing with her? You going to tell me, or just let her mess up everything?"

"You'll know everything soon enough."

Del was urinating in the bathroom with the door open.

"That's too late, partner. Too damned late."

He returned to the sofa. John returned to his bed. Soon both of them were snoring.

Ann sobbed into her pillow. Then, so the chains wouldn't

ring, she slowly pulled her zipper up, fastening her jeans. *God, please help me.* She reached into her bra for Tom's gift and a small folded piece of paper. Her second note. Without making a sound she slipped it under the sheet, praying that the motel staff would find it when they changed the linen.

It was her only hope.

Before sleep took her, she clutched Tom's gift until she saw his face and those of Zach and her mother.

36

Tyler Vaughn, electrician for AJRayCo, stepped from his van at the Sundowner Lodge near the Rio Grande in Albuquerque, New Mexico. He leaned on the fender to study his work order for cabin 10. Finish off a small rewire job.

He flipped through the pages on his clipboard to calculate how much cable he'd need, when the cleaning maid's cart squeaked to a halt beside him.

"Have you got work to do in there right now?" she said.

Vaughn looked her over. " 'Fraid so."

"Well, if that don't beat all." Her shirt and jeans complemented her figure as she looked back at the long asphalt path she'd climbed. "I push this heavy thing up here, 'cause I always start with number ten first, and find you. All set to go in and mess it more."

"Whoa, I won't be long. We can work in there together."

"You going to mess things up?"

"No, but I'll have to cut the power; can give it to you when you need it."

"You won't mess it more, make me have to come back?"

"Promise."

"All right."

Inside, Vaughn went to the panel, figuring he could replace some of the ancient knob and tube wiring without a hitch. He'd definitely use Bx cable outside. He checked the outlets and the walls, flipped through his work sheets, then put them on the round table near the bed. It was all configured nicely. Yeah, this was a piece of cake.

The maid began in the bathroom, surprised at how clean the guests had left it. Scrubbing the sink, she enjoyed the way the electrician's utility belt hung from his slim waist. He must have a girl.

Vaughn worked fast inside, then went outside. You definitely wanted that exposed old stuff replaced with Bx. He worked expertly with his strippers between peeks through the window at the maid tugging at the linen. She was easy on the eyes.

"Darn," she said.

The bedsheets had whipped over the table nearby, scattering his paperwork on the carpet. She collected everything—supply page, schematics, job order. And what was this odd one? Seemed out of place. Folded lined notepaper. Looked like a woman's handwriting. Maybe a love note from his girlfriend? She was tempted to read it, when he reentered.

"Sorry. I messed up your papers." She smiled, tidied them together, including the little note, then handed them to him.

Vaughn folded them, shoved them into his jeans. "Nothing in there to worry over." He smiled right back.

Vaughn got the maid's name and number before he finished the cabin job. During his next job at the trendy Desert Dog restaurant to fix the stove, then the inspection at the Kennedy high school, the cooler at the corner store, and the two residential orders, she was on his mind.

By the end of his day, Vaughn had forgotten that some of his installation work counted as hours toward his senior master electrician's ticket. Judy pointed it out to him at the shop when he added all of his papers to the leafy collection she had from AJRayCo's nine other electricians.

Judy the red-haired beauty. That's what the guys called her. She was the shop's sixty-four-year-old drill sergeant and den mother. Held the place together, looked after them, even went along with their elaborate practical jokes, like the time they wired Christmas lights to the switchboard to flash with each incoming call, the time they convinced a local radio station that she was Marilyn Monroe's long-lost baby sister, and that one where they hired an Elvis impersonator to phone her on her birthday. "Baby, why'd you break my heart, baby, why?" She never let on, but she loved the Elvis call.

The gold chains on Judy's bifocals jiggled as she flipped quickly through the work orders, pages snapping as she completed her end-of-day billing tally before the boys waiting by the garage bay door clocked out. It was business as usual, until a solitary slip of notepaper fell from somewhere in the pile.

What's this?

Judy unfolded it. Reading the words, she gasped.

Please call the FBI now. My name is Ann Reed, I was kidnapped by two men from the San Francisco Deluxe Jewelry Store armed robbery. I saw them shoot a police officer. . . .

Dear Lord. Judy had seen the news reports. She reached for the phone as she continued reading. Wait a minute. Her hand stopped. She turned the note over. *This can't be—*

"Hold on there!" Judy marched down the hall to the garage bay to confront the men waiting to leave. "Everybody freeze!"

She came upon them, bitching or bragging about tricky jobs, sports, and weekend plans. Conversations trailed and all eyes went to Judy and the small scrap of paper she held up.

"Whose work is this?"

Judy read the note aloud:

"Please call the FBI now. My name is Ann Reed, I was kidnapped by two men from the San Francisco Deluxe Jewelry Store armed robbery. I saw them shoot a police officer.

We're going east. Men are named John and Del. Two white males about six feet driving a red late-model SUV with Calif. plate starting. . . ." It ended there.

"John and Del? Come on, Sparky, this is your style."

Sparky Dane was a crusty old electrical man who loved to push Judy's buttons. He knew John was her despised no-good two-timing wig-wearin' former boyfriend and that Nat Foosey was the shop's young joker who'd set up the Elvis call. Judy expected they'd produce the rest of the "note" to say *Two white males about six feet driving a red-haired woman crazy!*

Sparky shook his head, as if he hadn't a clue.

Judy turned to young Nat.

"Foose, is this you?"

He shrugged. "No, ma'am."

"Sounds like you better call the FBI, just to be sure, there, Judy." Sparky sounded dead serious.

But Judy was sure she'd detected a twinkle and trace of a grin. She took stock of the others. They seemed to be watching the clock, or checking their watches. As usual they never betrayed the joke, milking it. The test was how long they could keep a straight face, as they fiddled with sun-glasses, jingled keys to their cars and pickup trucks.

The buzzer sounded. Quitting time.

The men departed, leaving Judy alone in the shop shaking her head as she went to the big corkboard. Sooner or later, she'd get to the bottom of their latest trick. She grinned, posting the note with a map pin to the board.

As she walked back to her desk, it began gnawing at her that it was a strange way to make a joke. She shrugged it off. Those boys were always finding strange ways to get her going. Less than an hour later, Judy activated the twenty-four-hour on-call message, cut the lights, locked up, and left.

On the shop's corkboard amid the clutter of labor regs, health forms, union news, and tool offers was Ann Reed's plea for her life.

37

In the *Star* newsroom, Molly Wilson's phone rang, breaking her concentration on the story she was writing after the latest press conference.

"Wilson."

"It's Tom."

She stopped typing. "Oh, Tom. How are you holding up? Everyone here's praying for Ann, for Zach, for you."

"Molly, I need your help."

"Anything."

"I watched live coverage of the conference on Carrie Addison."

"It's horrible. They've got to catch the bastards."

"What do you know about her?"

"Just what they said. She was a former employee of San Francisco Deluxe Jewelry. They think she's the link."

"But how? Inside info?"

"Seems most likely. I wish I knew. We're working on it."

"Molly, I need to know if any of your cop sources have

told you anything more on Addison's ties to the people who took Ann.''

"Got nothing right now, Tom. They're scouring her apartment for prints, paper. Checking her phone records. Your sources are way better than mine.''

"What's Addison's address?''

"It's an apartment in the Upper Market, 707 Short.''

"What about the jewelry store? Staff saying anything about her?''

"Nothing. They're screening calls. Won't come to the door. Maybe they're blaming themselves.''

"What about Addison's relatives?''

"Haven't located any yet.''

"Thanks, Molly.''

"Tom.'' Wilson was puzzled. "Do you know something? I mean, aren't the police keeping you updated?''

A moment passed.

"I'm going to find her, Molly.''

"You're going to find her? Tom, it could be risky if you jump on this.''

"Molly—''

"They've got a task force of a dozen agencies in two states now. I understand what you're going through.''

"No, you don't. Unless you're going through it, you can't possibly know what I'm going through.''

"I'm sorry. You're right. I'm sorry. But maybe you should just sit tight, try to hang on?''

"I've got to try to find Ann. I have to go, Molly. Call me if you get anything.''

Reed collected his thoughts, shaping them into his next step as if he were covering the story.

Carrie Dawn Addison was the link to the suspects. Somehow in some way, Addison had to have known them, or the people who knew them. He had to get inside her life and he had to do it fast.

Reed began flipping through previous editions of the *Chronicle*, the *Star*, the *Merc*, looking for names of jewelry store staff members, scanning the first reports on the case, searching for their names in stories or photo cutlines until one leaped at him.

Vanessa Jordan.

The clerk who still had Ann's receipt in her hand when he'd talked to her. She was the one who'd told him. Vanessa was distraught at the scene. She'd used his cell phone to call her boyfriend. Reed dug through the papers on his desk for his cell phone and notebook.

He began punching the phone's keypad. It beeped, calling up the menu, beeping as he scrolled through the call history. That's right, she'd called her boyfriend. The numbers were swimming on the phone's small screen. He confirmed it with date and time. There it was, 415-555-3312.

Reed wrote it down in his notebook so he wouldn't lose it. Then he called the number. What was her boyfriend's name? The call clicked through. What was his name? Reed tried to remember that day. Tried resurrecting the memory of Vanessa in the alley behind the store, police everywhere.

"I need to call Stephen, my boyfriend. I need him."

It continued ringing.

Stephen.

It was picked up between the third and fourth ring.

"Hello." Male voice. Early twenties.

"Stephen?"

"Yeah. Who's this?"

"I'm a friend of Vanessa's."

"Friend of Vanessa's? Which friend? I don't know your voice, man."

"Look, Steve—"

"Don't call me Steve. I don't know you and this isn't a good time."

"Who is it, Stephen?"

Reed could hear Vanessa's voice in the background. She was there. Next to Stephen. Reed had to talk to her, he couldn't lose her.

"Stephen, tell her it's Tom Reed. I need to talk to her.

My wife, Ann, was the lady she was helping at the store when the robbery happened. Tell her, please. Please. Tell her I have to talk to her, that I'm sorry about everything. But it's critical, please.''

Reed overheard Vanessa, distraught, saying something about the police, the press, that they should hang up. Then Stephen was talking to her about Ann Reed. "Hang on man," Stephen said to Reed. His heart nearly burst as he squeezed the phone. "Are you Tom Reed, that guy from the *Star*?" Stephen said.

"Yes. Ann's my wife."

"The one they took?"

"Yes. I met Vanessa at the store, that's how I got your number. She used my phone to call you that day."

"Hang on."

Reed heard more muffled conversation. It went on for several moments, only he couldn't make out any of the words until Stephen came back.

"Look, man, Vanessa says she's sorry for you but she can't talk to nobody about nothing."

"Stephen, it's my wife's life. Please."

"Man, I'm sorry but she's scared to death. Look what happened to Carrie. Three people dead. The FBI's all over this. The SFPD robbery is looking at her. Man, she's waiting on a call from a lawyer. She is scared to death."

"Meet me. Just meet me for five minutes. You come too, Stephen."

"Hang on."

A long agonizing minute passed; then Stephen returned with a location. "You know it? It's in the Haight."

"Yes." Reed knew it.

"Meet us there in ninety minutes. No cameras, no cops. Just you."

38

Eighty minutes later Reed was in the Haight, pacing in front of a boutique displaying lava lamps. No sign of Vanessa Jordan or her boyfriend.

Reed checked his watch again and the location they'd given him. The stretch between the Upper and Lower Haight, next to Masonic, on the side near an exotic carpet store with a bank of newspaper boxes out front. This was the place.

The air carried the smell of incense, herbs, and the sudden earsplitting bass from a passing car that made him jump, pounding on the fact the clock was ticking.

"You Reed?"

He shot his head around finding himself toe-to-toe with a white guy in his mid-twenties. Fullback proportions. Short sandy hair. Stone faced. "I'm Stephen," he said, angling his head to see under Reed's ball cap and dark glasses.

But no Vanessa.

"Where is she?"

"Not here," Stephen said. "Let's go."

"Where?"

"Not far. You came alone, right? No cameras or stuff?"

Stephen stopped to invade Reed's space. "Because this is so far off the record. There is no record."

"I just want to find my wife."

After two blocks they came to a pickup truck. Vanessa stepped from it and came to them. Her face was raw. Her eyes were red. She was gripping a crumpled tissue in her fist.

"Take it easy." Stephen grabbed her shoulders. "Let's go over here."

They went to an alcove that offered some privacy from the street.

"Vanessa, do you have any idea where they might have taken my wife?"

She shook her head.

"But police think Carrie Addison's the link to the robbery," Reed said.

"I swear," Vanessa said, "I don't know who those creeps are, but I think it's related to Carrie's problems with drugs."

"Drugs?"

"She was my friend from grade school. She had a hard life. Her dad walked out when she was, like, twelve. Then her mother married some guy who had three little kids and moved to Boston. Carrie's been on her own since she was sixteen."

"So how does that connect?"

"A while back Carrie and I met at a bar. Old girlfriends. She told me she was having a hard time with money, needed a job. I'd been at Deluxe Jewelry about a year, so I talked to David, the manager—he's a sweet man. He gave her a job."

"But she lost it?"

"I'm going to tell you the truth, only so it might help you understand, you can't put this in the paper, or tell police."

"Vanessa, please. It's my wife."

"Stephen and I party. We used to like a little coke, some pot. Cripes, this is San Francisco. Carrie partied too. She started to score for us, she knew all the connections. Got us the best stuff, best price. It was fun.'' Vanessa's fist went to her mouth as the tears fell. ''We never knew. I mean we never really knew how bad. I—''

Reed struggled to understand.

''Carrie was a hard-core addict, crack, heroin,'' Stephen said. ''She had a five-hundred-dollar-a-day habit and was running up huge drug debts to lots of different people, some in the Mission and Visitation Valley.''

''David suspected she was stealing watches,'' Vanessa said. ''Once, a gang-banger came into the shop and demanded his money. That's when David fired her.''

Reed was shaking his head.

''I saw her, a few months ago, right after she'd lost her job, and she said she was getting counseling and would be leaving California for a new job she had lined up in Florida, working on cruise ships. I believed her. That's why no one suspected her after the robbery.'' Vanessa sobbed.

''We all thought she had straightened her life out and was in Florida. I was happy for her and she promised.'' Vanessa had trouble voicing her words. ''She promised to send me a postcard and I kept watching the mail for it but it never came. Somebody did those awful things to her, killed her and left her.'' She sobbed into Stephen's chest.

Reed ran a hand over his face, overwhelmed, not knowing how this connected to anything. Or how it would help him find Ann.

''How do you think this ties to the robbery?'' he asked.

''We're not sure,'' Stephen said. ''We thought you'd figure it out.''

''When Carrie was having her drug troubles,'' Vanessa said, ''we'd heard a lot of wild rumors through our circles but it all seemed like so much bullshit. It was just so frightening I just couldn't believe any of it.''

''Like what?''

''Like she owed this big dealer thirty-one thousand dollars and he was dead serious she was going to pay it. He said he'd throw her off the Bay Bridge, or turn her out on the street as a prostitute to work it off.''

"What's the dealer's name? Or his street name?"

Vanessa and Stephen traded glances, signaling to Reed that this was the moment of truth. "We *heard* it was Caesar," Stephen said.

"Caesar. You tell the police?"

Vanessa nodded. "They're trying to find him now."

"They think this guy's connected to the heist?" Reed said.

"They think he knows something."

"How would I find him?"

"We've never met him. Only heard that he's dangerous."

"How can I find him?"

"You can't say where you heard—"

"Please just tell me how I would find him."

Stephen handed him a business card bearing nothing but a phone number.

"That's one of Caesar's sellers," he said. "Usually deals out of the Mission or Sunnydale. That's where the police started looking for him after they talked to us."

Reed thanked them.

"Tom," Vanessa said, "I'm praying for your wife."

Reed turned, then hurried to his car.

39

Sydowski studied Officer Don Valdosa as he worked the safe phones in the task force room at the Hall of Justice.

Valdosa wore dark jeans and a dark track jacket. He had a diablo goatee and a New York Giants knit cap pulled tight to his dark glasses. As he shifted in the swivel chair, his gold neck chains chimed as he tried to get information on Leopoldo Merida.

Leopoldo was an elusive Bay Area dealer, known only to a few people on the street. They called him *el viento*, "the wind," because police could never find him. He never dealt on the street level. He was three or four people up the food chain. To some, he was known as Caesar. And the only hope Sydowski had of talking to him was Valdosa, one of the SFPD's best narcotics cops.

Sydowski knew that often you couldn't score on a case unless you passed the ball. Watching Valdosa do his thing for the past half hour convinced him they were advancing.

Alternating between English and Spanish, using his cell phone and pager, Valdosa pumped his CIs, or confidential informants.

"... No, man, I don't want to arrest nobody," Valdosa said into his phone, waving at Sydowski, indicating that he might be on to solid information. "No ... I've got Caesar's old number, man, you know, *el viento,* he changes his numbers like his underwear, man...." Valdosa laughed with his source at the little joke. "Right, man. That's right. I always remember people who help me. That's right. In what denominations do I remember? Oh, that's good, man."

Turgeon entered the room with a few pages of computer printouts on Leopoldo Merida. She did not interrupt as Valdosa finessed his source.

"Man, nobody's at risk here," Valdosa said into the phone. "Didn't you see it all over the news, man? We saw the shooters. The body descriptions, their voices, man, you know, and we know, it can't be Caesar. Right? Looks like big white boys. I just want to talk to Caesar respectfully, man-to-man, 'cause he's so powerful, you know, he may have heard ... right. He *may* have heard. You say you might know where Caesar's at? For how much? That much? Now, that's workable. I'm sayin it's workable. That's right. You call me back on my cell. In one minute. I'm just looking for direction, man."

Valdosa hung up. Stroked his goatee, then talked softly to Sydowski.

"Caesar knows our shooters. He definitely had dealings with them. Word is he took off right after it happened. To Chicago."

"We could tap Chicago PD to grab him tonight," Sydowski said.

Valdosa shook his head. "He might be back now in our yard."

"Where?"

"He's got girlfriends, cousins. Word is he's back. Somewhere here."

"Was he directly involved?" Sydowski said.

"What I'm hearing confirms what you've got, Walt. Carrie Addison owed his franchise big time. Caesar always collects. He knew her connection to the jewelry store and may have parlayed information from her to our suspects.''

"To settle her debt to his business?"

"Right, and maybe one of his own, to the suspects."

"An information transaction?" Sydowski said.

"Maybe a debt, a favor, a trade, with somebody powerful enough to have him bend a knee for them.''

"Your CI good to call you back, Don?"

"He's deep inside the network and one of the smarter ones."

Sydowski checked his watch. "We should be hearing soon if crime scene got anything from Addison's apartment. Some good prints might put us on to our boys right away. You think Caesar had a direct hand in this?"

"Hard to say."

"Maybe he got a cut?" Sydowski said.

"I think he's strictly an organic criminal."

"We're talking about a million-dollar heist."

It was a good point. Valdosa nodded.

"I'd like to know what was in Chicago for him," Sydowski said.

While waiting for Valdosa's guy to call back, Sydowski put in a few quick calls to San Bernardino, Sacramento, Corrections and the FBI. Nothing had surfaced but everybody was pushing hard in all directions.

Turgeon finished reading. "Caesar's got a bit of violence in his past."

"That's what I've heard," Valdosa said.

"File says that to settle a beef in Fresno he jabbed an ice pick in a customer's eye because he failed to pay his debt."

"He doesn't like complications," Valdosa said; then his cell phone trilled and he took the call. "Right, yeah, right, man." Valdosa took notes, then gave big nods to Sydowski. ". . . Got it, right, man. No, I won't forget."

"Good information?"

"Caesar's in the city. Word is, he'll be making a rare personal appearance with his crew in the Mission tonight, trouble brewing over distribution territory with a Fillmore posse. We'll need a lot of help, Walt. He's out there ready to wage war.''

40

Sirens ripped through the night in the Mission where Reed sat alone in his car near Garfield Square.

He was ready. He'd put together six hundred dollars from the house and the automated teller. He tried the connection's number again but got nothing. He looked up at the black sky. This was all he had to find Ann with. Six hundred bucks. And hope. Folded crisply in his shoe. He tried again. It rang three times, then stopped. Damn.

What was he doing wrong? Before leaving Zach with Doris, he'd called the number several times from his home. Then he tried using his cell. All in vain. No doubt the connection had caller ID and would be wary of strange numbers.

Reed drove along the perimeter of Garfield Square rolling by the housing complexes. He spotted a public telephone at a corner, stopped, and called. If the connection saw that the number was from his turf, then maybe he'd have a shot.

The line was answered.

"Yeah."

"Caesar?"

"No Caesar here. Who's this?"

"Tom."

"Don't know no Tom. Wrong number."

"No, wait. I need something."

"Who gave you this number?"

"A friend of a friend."

"What's your name, man?"

"Tom. And I need something right now. I just need to buy something, okay?"

"What do you want?"

Reed told him.

"For you, that's five hundred."

"I thought it was three. Everybody says three for that."

"I'm hanging up."

"Wait. Five's cool. I got that. But I need to do this now."

"Intersection of South Van Ness and Twenty-fourth in thirty minutes. Walk up to the car with the lime fluorescent ball on the antenna. Show us your hands. In thirty minutes."

Reed saw a couple of different cars roll by, the people inside eyeballing him cold and hard. After thirty minutes, the glowing antenna ball trembled over the hood of the late model Chev sedan that crept up to the intersection. Street wisdom dictated that experienced dealers didn't drive status cars to work. You wanted to blend in. Fools drew attention to themselves.

The only things that gleamed on the tan sedan were the darkened windows reflecting the desperation of the addicts who approached it.

Reed flashed his palms, then watched a distorted version of himself melt into the Chev as the front passenger window dropped. The guy at the window was wearing a hooded Chicago Bulls warmup top and an expression devoid of emotion.

"Closer, man," he said to Reed.

Reed stepped closer.

"You Caesar?"

"I'll be whoever you need me to be, baby."

Stifled chuckling leaked from inside. The car was crowded.

"I need Caesar."

"Who are you?"

"Tom."

"Step closer, Tom."

Reed didn't move. "I'll only deal with Caesar."

"Time is money. Get closer," the window guy said. "Gotta shake your hand, man, that's how it gets done."

Reed glimpsed the tiny five-hundred-dollar clear plastic bag in the man's extended hand.

"Now show me your money."

Reed showed him the bills folded and tucked between the fingers on his left hand. Reed's right hand reached for the dealer's drug hand but in an eyeblink Reed's wrist was seized, a fist drove into his stomach, doubling him as a second large man leaped from the passenger rear. He threw a headlock on Reed, shoved him into the backseat next to another rider. The Chev squealed away.

No one spoke.

The car was silent except for Reed's gasps. He dropped his head on the back dash. City lights flowed by. Someone snatched his cash, hands patted him for weapons, probed him for his wallet, which he'd left at home. His stomach ached. He felt queasy. When he managed to raise his head he met the barrel of a large chrome-plated pistol aimed at his face by the man in the front passenger seat.

They took the freeway heading south on 101.

The man holding the gun stared at Reed. He had a scarred face, a wispy beard, and cold eyes. A gold-capped tooth sparkled as he sneered. Reed felt the highway clicking under them. He grunted, then swallowed. No one spoke. Moments and miles passed along with Old Candlestick, then Brisbane. Reed could see San Francisco International as they continued south toward Burlingame.

The gunman contemplated the night, then said something in Spanish to the driver, prompting him to nod and sneer at Reed in the rearview mirror.

They entered San Mateo and exited the highway, driving to an abandoned area near the bay somewhere around Coyote Point.

Reed felt the gun bore into his skull, the pressure growing unbearable as the car turned onto a gravel road, threading through a stand of eucalyptus trees and stopping at the deserted shoreline. All doors opened, hands seized Reed's arms, his ankles, lifting him out, forcing him to his knees. A gun was held inches from Reed's face. Other cars were parked in the darkened area. Other people materialized. One of them walked up to Reed and squatted so their faces were level.

"Who are you? And don't lie."

"I'm Tom Reed. My wife was kidnapped in the jewelry store heist."

"What do you want from us?"

"Help me find her."

"Who gave you the number? Police?"

"A friend of a friend."

"What did this *friend* tell you?"

Reed saw only a shadow. He could not distinguish a face.

"Are you Caesar?"

"Answer me, please."

"My friend said Caesar is respected and feared, and that maybe he knows Carrie Addison and the men who took my wife."

The man spat out a stream of Spanish, then said, "Did the police send you?"

"No."

"Don't lie."

"No."

"I said don't lie."

"I found you myself."

"You lie. I know who you are, Reed. We see the news,

man. Everybody knows who you are. This smells bad. I'm going to get the truth from you.''

"Just tell me where my wife is. Please.''

"The police are trying to put this all on me. The hit, the dead pig, the dead junkie bitch. She owed me, so they think it's me, right?''

"I don't know what they think. I just want to find my wife. Please.''

"You know more. You know what the police know. You're a big-ass reporter. They tell you things, Reed. Keep you in the loop. Let you know what's going down.''

"They don't tell me a damned thing. That's why I'm here.''

"You lie.''

The man produced a gun, pressed it into Reed's head between his eyes. Bay winds tumbled across the black water, pummeling him as jetliners whined their approach to the airport and the man shouted into the night.

"Now you tell me the truth, Reed!''

"I did. I swear.''

"Tell me what you know!''

"Your people sold to Carrie and she's dead in my wife's clothes. I swear.''

"Liar!''

"Please, we have a son.''

"Who's putting it out there that I did the 187s? Tell me, who?''

"People on the street say you sold to her.''

"That bitch owed me thirty-five and she couldn't pay. I told her I ain't no motherfucking bank. Her ass was mine. I owned her and one way or another she was going to pay. But I didn't kill her. So why would they try to put all this on me? I wasn't even there, man.''

"Please.''

Caesar pulled back the hammer.

"Tell me.''

"I swear.''

Reed saw his trigger finger squeeze. He closed his eyes thinking of Ann, Zach, and eternity. He flinched at the *click-thud*. Nothing happened. Reed swallowed air.

"Tell me the truth, Reed."

Caesar showed him a clip of live rounds before slapping it into his gun. "This one's for keeps." The muzzle drilled into his head. "Tell me the truth."

"I did."

No words were spoken. Reed remained kneeling.

The wind and jets roared. Then a cell phone trilled.

Caesar took the call in Spanish. He hung up, then said something to his crew. Reed was pulled to his feet. Adrenaline coursed through him, tears filled his eyes, he struggled to breathe, and his body quaked after they pushed him into the rear seat of another car. Caesar took the front passenger seat.

The tires hummed on the highway. As they neared San Francisco, Caesar touched the barrel of his gun to his lips and pondered Reed.

"I'll help you and you'll help me, Reed."

"How?"

"What I said. You're a big-time reporter, I saw you once on Larry King. I might need a favor one day. So, I'll help you, you help me. It's the only hope you've got."

It was true.

"I have a little brother, Jorge," Caesar said. "A while back, he went to Folsom after a bullshit setup. He's quiet. My mother's favorite son. A white-boy gang went after Jorge inside but this big dude, a white guy, protected him. Word got to me. I let it be known that I considered myself indebted to him for saving my blood. When he got out, he looked me up."

"What did he want?"

"He and his friend had business opportunities in South America. They needed capital fast and he wanted me to point him to a solid source. So I gave him Carrie."

"She knew the store."

"She knew the product, the staff, what time and day was best, when the guard would be gone. It was like I told her, you owe me, I owe him. He saved my blood, that's the way it goes. It was simple. All debts paid in full."

"She paid with her life and my wife is missing."

"So much in this world we can't control."

"Where are they? Who are they?"

"Let your police friends know I did my civic duty and helped you."

When they returned to the Mission the car slowed. Caesar's eyes scanned the streets with an intensity that never betrayed if he was the hunter or the prey. Reed figured something was up with Caesar's call, the one that had spared him. Caesar was searching the night for something, growing impatient. He spoke quietly in Spanish to his crew.

"We're going to let you out."

"But you never told me their names, where they're headed."

"That's up to you. You found me, you find them, and maybe you'll find your wife." Caesar said something in Spanish and his crew laughed. "Maybe. She might even be alive, eh?"

Tires screeched, sirens yelped, and in a heartbeat the sedan was boxed in by unmarked cars and armed police officers. Weapons drawn. Lights pulsating. A bullhorn crackled.

"This is the San Francisco Police Department. Shut the engine off, drop the keys to the street, and step away from the vehicle with your hands raised."

Caesar grabbed Reed, put his arm around his neck and his gun to his head as he cursed in Spanish, glaring defiantly at the officers locked on to him from behind their shotguns and Berettas.

"You are a dead man," Caesar whispered before releasing Reed.

Police ordered the passengers from the car.

"I had nothing to do with this."

"And your wife?" Caesar chuckled. "You better pray she's dead."

Reed said nothing.

"Because after what they did to Carrie, death would be a comfort."

Before Caesar dropped his gun, opened his door, and allowed himself to be yanked to the pavement and hand cuffed, he spat in Reed's face.

41

Reed ordered coffee at an all-night diner near San Francisco General. Sydowski finished his telephone call, then stared at him for the longest time.

"I don't know what to say to you, Tom."

Caesar was being held at the Hall of Justice. Reed looked into the night. He wasn't shaking as much now.

"You've got to let us do our job. We were on him. He knows the suspects. Valdosa was primed to leverage him. Now he's gone mute and called a lawyer. It's going to be difficult for us to pull anything from him."

Reed swallowed.

"Tom, you've got to try and stay in control. Keep your emotions in check and let us do the investigating."

"Are you any closer to knowing who took Ann and where they went?"

Sydowski considered what he should reveal.

"We're working on a lot of things."

"What about Carrie Addison's apartment?"

"We're still going through everything. Tom, you've got to let people do their job."

"I tried that and a reporter came to my door and told me the headless corpse in the desert was Ann."

"Tom—"

"I tried letting people do their job and was left to make funeral plans for a woman no one has found."

"Tom, stop it. You should get some sleep."

"I tried that and all I see is my wife's face, hear her voice, and feel my gut telling me that there's nothing to prove she's dead."

"Tom, you've got to stay out of this."

"Why? Every word is true. I got more help from a drug dealer than from the police."

"Tom, I've taken you deeper into this case than I've ever taken anyone into any investigation." Sydowki popped a Tums. "I really think you should go home and be with Zach."

"He wants me to find his mother, Walt."

"Tom, it's dangerous for you to get involved like this."

"You think I'm going to sit at home and do nothing knowing she's still out there and that there's every chance she's alive?"

"But you can't go round conducting a one-man investigation that's driven by anguish. It can only end badly, like it almost did tonight."

Reed was exhausted.

"I'll tell you a story, Walt. A few years ago, Ann had read some book about a guy searching for his missing wife. The guy's relentless against all odds. He never gives up. A few days after she'd finished, she tells me about it and says, if that ever happens to us promise me you'll never stop searching for me. So I tease her and say I'll just have to start dating again. Later that night she wakes me. She's had a bad dream from the book and this time she's serious that I promise her that I would never stop searching for her. I mean she's crying. So I make a promise and she falls asleep in my arms."

Reed gazed out at the night.

"But I never kept it. Until now, I never started searching for her and no one, not you, or the people who took her, will stop me. No matter what has happened to Ann, I'll find her and bring her home."

Sydowski nodded, then checked his watch.

"I have to get to the Hall, Tom. One of the uniforms will drive you to your house."

At home that night, Reed looked in on Zach, who was asleep in their bed. Doris had fallen asleep on the sofa. He covered her with a blanket, then went to his study to think about his encounter with Caesar, pushing aside the fact of how close he'd come to the edge.

Noticing the enhanced police tape, he slipped on headphones and set it to play. Ann's voice vibrated against his eardrum.

"Oh God, please let me go!"

Then the suspects' voices.

"I told you to shut up! Where's your car! I told you to shut up!"

It played over and over. Reed was certain he'd heard that voice before.

"I told you to shut . . ."

He was sure of it. Folsom. Jorge went to Folsom.

"I told you to . . ."

He was falling asleep with the tape running, voices swirling in his brain.

I told you. I told you. I told you.

Folsom.

42

Somewhere in America, Ann Reed sat motionless in a motel room.

John sat on one of the queen-size beds watching her.

She was bound to a hard-backed chair with quarter-inch yellow nylon rope. Duct tape masked her mouth and bound her wrists.

Ann kept her eyes on John's right hand, the one holding the large pair of scissors. His thick thumb caressed the blades while he studied her face.

Please don't hurt me.

She was still groggy from the driving.

They must've put something in her soda to make her sleep. She had no idea where they were today. She tried hard to find details that might save her but each motel, each cabin, each horrible second, was the same. They always removed the phones and any information identifying their location. They kept her bound and gagged, careful to kill any hope she had of escaping; leaving her to live in terror, never knowing what they intended to do at any moment. Like now.

Why was he holding the scissors and staring at her? Del was gone. Likely to get food. It was the routine. Ann never felt she was any safer alone with John. He stood and approached her.

She held her breath as he raised the scissors to her head.

"Don't move."

The comb in his left hand bit into her silky hair and offered a bouquet of it to the scissors, which began their work. Her locks fell like large snowflakes on her shoulders, her top, her lap, to the green plastic trash bags John had slit open and arranged like a drop sheet underneath the chair. Ann's beautiful jaw-length hair was sliced away above her ears; then he hacked at her bangs. Her eyes stung at the violation. When he finished he brushed the cuttings from her face with a towel. She felt naked. Smaller. Less than what she was.

"Be still."

He lifted her, chair and all, biceps bulging his tattoos as he carried her easily to the bathroom where he placed her in the large shower stall.

He fashioned a hair salon type of apron out of the plastic bags that allowed her head to poke through but was snug around her neck. He produced a large drugstore bag from which he withdrew bleach, a quick-hair-dye kit, latex gloves, vaseline, shampoo, tub and tile cleanser, and several other items.

Ann glimpsed the packaging as John worked on her hair. Sunset Blond. *Blondes Have More Fun.* The picture on the box showed blond tanned twenty-somethings frolicking in thongs at a volleyball net near the beach. Ammonia vapors invaded her nostrils.

When he finished, John cleaned everything up, stuffing it into a trash bag. Then he cut Ann's bindings, startling her when he sliced off her clothes, leaving her in her bra and panties. He indicated the travel bag of women's clothes. "Shower, shampoo, scrub the stall clean of any dye. Dress in fresh clothes and hurry up."

He left, closing the door behind him.

Ann was numb, degraded as she carried out his orders, sobbing in the shower, feeling for hair that had been replaced by chopped straw, refusing to face the reality, dreading to see the truth as she scrubbed at the walls, the floor, the water spray mingling with her tears.

After dressing in capri pants and a T-shirt she forced herself to confront the mirror. She wiped the steam clouds and was hit full force with what had befallen her. She no longer saw herself. Short blond stalks replaced her brunette waves. Fear lines cut like furrows into her skin. Tears spilled from her bloodshot eyes

Who was this woman? This specter?

Ann Reed was gone. Dead to the world. They had obliterated her identity. Just as they did with the dead woman whose clothes Ann was now wearing. How much longer before they put her in a shallow grave?

God. Please help me. Ann covered her mouth with her hands. *Oh, Tom. Oh, Zachary.*

John called Ann several times before she emerged from the bathroom. He regarded her the way an artist regards a finished painting.

"Here." He reached into his breast pocket. "Put these on."

Sunglasses. Dark, nonreflective in the style of movie stars from the 1940s and '50s. Ann slipped them on and sat stone faced in the chair. Everything had been cleaned up and cleared away. The air conditioner hummed as John sat on the bed staring at her. Satisfied with his work. Twenty minutes later Del returned with bags of food that smelled like deep-fried chicken. He stopped dead in his tracks.

Ann was identical to the woman in the color snapshot John had kept in his cell at Folsom.

The picture of his wife.

43

Retired cable car gripman Jed Caverly waved to his neighbor the morning after he returned from his trip to Europe. He stepped outside to take stock of his tidy bungalow in the southern San Francisco community of Excelsior.

"Welcome back, Jed," Lil called from her porch. "Got your mail here. I'll put the kettle on and we'll catch up."

"Be right over, Lil. Just have to tend to a few things."

Jed didn't feel too jet-lagged. Probably get hit with it later, he thought, while inspecting the dells of ferns, roses, and red rhododendrons that flourished in his yard. It might not be like the stately manicured lawns of Crocker Amazon but it was just fine for him.

An avowed bachelor, Jed loved meeting people from around the globe who marveled at San Francisco as he ferried them up and down its rolling hills. He was rewarded with countless names and addresses of people to visit in nearly every country in the world. He'd always thank them. "I'm savin' my pennies so when I retire, I'll come see your town."

Jed had always been frugal. The first thing he did when he bought his house all those years ago was build a very large garage in his rear yard. He rented it to people to store vehicles. He'd had all types of clients. Collectors, bikers, racers, enthusiasts who restored classics. He rolled the income into accounts that yielded nice returns.

He whistled as he strode along his tiled walkway to his garage. In recent years it was generating $400 monthly, allowing him to travel in style. He'd have to rent it out again. His last tenant had assured him he'd have his vehicle out by the time Jed returned from Europe.

"Let's just see how much of a cleanup job we've got here, Percy," he said to the calico cat threading around his ankles.

Jed shaded his eyes to peer through the barred window, not understanding what he saw inside. What the heck was that?

"What's going on?" Jed grimaced, then scratched his head. He looked again, as if a second glance would have a different result.

Strange. The young fella had *guaranteed* he'd be out. Everything would be gone by the time he got back so he could rent it out. Even paid cash up front, which was the only reason he decided to let the guy have a two-month deal. He'd usually insisted on a six-month minimum.

Jed had gotten a weird read off the guy, with his beard and tattoos. He didn't really like how he'd bring a couple of friends around to sit in the garage and talk long into the night. But they kept to themselves. If there's one thing Jed had learned, you can't judge people by their appearance. He shook his head. He'd have to call the guy to see what his plans were.

Before visiting Lil, Jed got her gift from his house. A painting he bought from a Parisian artist who produced street scenes near the Seine.

"This is for you, Lil, for watching my place and taking care of Percy."

"I love it. Thank you so much, Jed."

Lil draped the canvas over a wicker chair to admire it

while she poured tea, passed him a bundle of mail, then began updating him on community gossip. Jed nodded politely, not really caring who had a hip replacement or a pacemaker installed. He sipped his tea, nodding for what he thought was sufficient time before he indicated the stack of *Chronicles* she'd saved for him in the box in the corner of her porch. Jed was an avid newspaper reader.

"Any big local stories while I was gone, Lil?"

"Some stink over a city contract scandal. And the Forty-niners gave a fortune to some player. It's beyond my understanding what professional athletes earn these days."

"So pretty quiet then?"

"Mmm." She caught herself in midswallow. "Oh, a terrible, dreadful armed robbery at a jewelry store a few days ago."

"Where?"

"In the Richmond District. A big story actually. The police are still looking for the robbers. A police officer was shot dead, an accomplice too. Murdered in the street. A woman customer was taken hostage. Might be linked to another woman murdered in Death Valley."

"Wow. I'll have to read that one."

Lil's phone rang. "Excuse me, Jed. I'm trying to make an appointment with a specialist for my arthritis. It's in the papers there."

She went inside to take the call. Jed set his teacup aside and began scanning the papers. He didn't have to go far into them to catch up on the jewelry store case. Most of the articles were on the front page.

It was an engrossing story, Jed thought, flipping past the headlines and photos backward from the most recent item. Unbelievable. Like some kind of thriller movie. Sensational million-dollar heist, deadly shootout on the streets in broad daylight, corpse in the desert, a San Francisco business-woman abducted, a national dragnet for the unknown suspects.

"Good Lord!"

Jed's blood chilled the way it did when he had almost lost control of a Powell car one foggy winter near Mason and California. All the spit vanished from his mouth. He was staring into the eyes of the young man who'd rented his garage. His color photo was on the front page, identifying him as the robbery suspect killed at the scene.

"Jesus H. Christ!"

Jed stood. Unable to take his eyes from the photo.

"Lil! Damn! Lil, I need your phone. I gotta call the police!"

44

"You said you'd have something to us last night. It's now midmorning. What's the holdup?" Sydowski said into the phone.

At the desk next to him, Turgeon had finished talking to Los Angeles County on a tip that was shaping up to be nothing. Not quite accustomed to her new pancake hip holster, she shifted uncomfortably.

"Right," Sydowski said. "Just be damned sure you alert us the second you've got something." He hung up, removed his glasses, rubbed his tired eyes, then turned to Turgeon.

"Linda, somewhere there has to be a trace, a latent, something to identify these guys. I can't believe it's taking us this long to get a lock." He shuffled his reports, then reached for his coffee. "Anything from LA?"

"Nothing."

"Did you call CDC and Sacramento again? They must have something on little Jorge Merida's prison friends."

"They're working on it."

"The FBI or our robbery guys determine who their buyer is?"

"Not yet. They figure it's gone deep underground because of all the attention on the heist."

"You don't pull off something like this without having a buyer lined up."

"Walt. You've had the lead on over four hundred homicides, you know that sooner or later it'll break. We're on the edge of something."

Sydowski shoved his glasses into his pocket, folded his big arms and stared at nothing. "I know the profiler has his theories, but this thing makes no sense, Linda. Why take her?"

"Insurance?"

"For what? You take a hostage if you're trapped in a standoff. They're your shields, your bargaining chips. These guys got away."

"Ransom? She's a businesswoman. Reed's got some profile."

"But we haven't had a single demand. And why make Addison's murder look like Ann Reed's?"

"Throw us off. Buy time. It was a quick discovery. It could've been weeks or months before the Death Valley find."

"Why not let Ann Reed go from the outset? It's easier to travel without her. It's better to travel without her."

"It's possible they've killed her and we just haven't found her yet."

"True. Three homicides with special circumstances, they're facing the death penalty. They've got nothing to lose."

"Maybe they want her as insurance for something later."

"This thing is out of control," Sydowski said.

Lieutenant Leo Gonzales appeared before him with a slip of paper.

"Walt. Linda. This came through 911. Sounds solid."

Sydowski studied the note.

"Jed Caverly. Address near McLaren Park."

"Lives in Excelsior. Thinks he rented his garage to the dead driver. Says the guy and his friends left something in there that we should see."

45

Tia Layne offered her most assuring smile and a little cleavage to the manager of the San Francisco Deluxe Jewelry.

"Look, David, we just want to get some pictures to show you're getting back to business. It's happy news."

The manager guarded the front entrance, keeping the door open a crack. Curtains inside the shop's street windows were drawn. He didn't return Layne's smile and was indifferent to her V-neck T-shirt. He eyed Cooter's hand on his camera.

"I'm sorry, no," the manager said. "It's been too tragic."

Layne's gaze through her sunglasses went beyond him to the staff inside arranging jewelry in the new display cases. The people who knew details on the link to the dead clerk. If she could just get to them. Get them talking.

"Everyone's trying to move on with their lives," the manager said. "We're praying Ann Reed is reunited safely with her family."

"But that's the kind of stuff we need, David."

"How about outside?" Cooter offered.

"Outside?"

"Yeah," Layne said. "You and your staff can tell us how you're trying to cope and, *more important*, are praying for everyone else."

"I don't know." He glanced to the spot where Officer August died.

"We could do it with you as a group," Layne said. "Let the world know that you refuse to let criminals keep you down."

"I don't know, it's very hard. Carrie was an employee. We tried to work it out with her. We had no idea about the degree of her addiction."

"Hold it," Layne said. "David, see, you're already talking about it. It's a natural thing to want to talk about it. Let's just do it with the camera on, okay? And you just look at me like we're just talking."

"Wait, I think—"

The cell phone clipped to Cooter's battery belt rang. He grabbed it, saying, "I'm tied up now, can I call you—*what's that?*" He set his camera down and jotted notes. "Just now!" Cooter said. "Got it, thanks." He hung up, then pulled Layne's upper arm and his camera.

"Cooter!"

"We have to go now. Something's come up."

"What's going on?" Layne said as he rushed her to their SUV.

Cooter squealed from the curb after tossing Layne a folded city map and an address he'd scrawled on his notepaper. "It's in Excelsior, near McLaren Park. Find us the fastest way there."

"What is it?"

"Security guard next to our building listens to police scanners. I slipped him a few bucks to keep me posted on the case."

"Okay."

"That was him. Says he caught on something related to 'the Deluxe 187s,' the SFPD code for murder. Found in a garage at this address."

"He say what?"

"Doesn't know. But he said it sounded good. They're sealing it. Homicide and crime scene are rolling. It's all happening now!"

"What do you think it is?"

"I dunno. Directions! Directions!"

They arrived within thirty minutes to a tangle of black-and-whites, lights wigwagging in front of a stucco house. Other police cars were in the rear. Yellow crime scene tape bordered the neat double-wide garage. Cooter got his gear.

Kids on bikes did laps in the alley around the police cruisers and the tape while neighbors gathered at the edge of the yards to speculate on what police had found in Jed Caverly's garage with the canary-yellow door.

A couple of newspaper photographers and more TV camera operators had gathered a few houses away. A small car with the call letters and logo of a Bay Area radio news station was creeping to the scene. Within minutes more than a dozen newspeople had collected near the garage. Cooter and Layne stood near them, eavesdropping.

"You guys hear about the takedown in the Mission last night?" a female TV reporter said.

"I heard something about it," a newspaper reporter said.

"One of our producers is married to an SFPD officer. She heard an army went out to grab the dealer who sold to Carrie Addison."

"The jewelry store clerk they found in the desert?"

"Right." The reporter dropped her voice, but Layne could hear her say, "They throw down on the car carrying the dealer and his crew and they find a surprise inside."

"What kind of surprise?"

"Tom Reed."

"Reed?"

"The way we heard it is, he's out on his own searching for his wife after he got a lead on the dealer who supplied the gal found in the desert. The dealer freaked and put a gun to Reed's head."

"That true?"

"That's what he told the detectives."

Layne marched to her truck, cell phone pressed to her ear. She'd punched in Tom Reed's home number. She wanted an interview with the reporter who was risking his life to find his abducted wife. It was ringing.

Come on, pick up. She had to *get* this one.

It was worth one hundred thousand dollars.

46

Jed Caverly held a key in his fist when he greeted Sydowski and Turgeon in front of his house.

"Right this way." He led them to the back. Two uniformed officers joined them, explaining that no one had set foot in the place.

"That's right," Caverly said at the garage door, watching the homicide inspectors tug on surgical gloves, then shoe covers. "I recognized this Leroy Driscoll guy from the newspaper. He told me his name was Sean Keeler. I never touched a thing. Never entered. I keep nothing in there and clean it before each tenant. Whatever's in there is his."

"We'll go in alone," Sydowski said.

Dust particles danced in the shafts of sunlight that lit on a 2003 silver four-door Jetta.

"That's Ann Reed's car, Walt."

Sydowski opened the driver's door. Her key ring dangled from the ignition. Sydowski didn't get in. Instead, he reached in and switched the key to accessories. He checked the gas level. Full. Noted the odometer reading. Turgeon opened the rear passenger door, making notes on the condition. Sydowski popped the trunk for her.

"Car's empty. Looks clean, Walt."

The garage was immaculate with a polished floor. Spotless. Sydowski went to the workbench near the window. On it were several cardboard boxes of various sizes, a stack of folded maps, ropes, duct tape, clips, a cooler, files of notes, notebooks, textbooks on alarm systems, gems, catalogues, keys.

Turgeon and Sydowski were careful. They jotted down inventory and sketched maps in their notebooks before taking some snapshots. At the far end of the garage Sydowski found a folded wheelchair leaning against the wall. A second one? They must've practiced. Near it was a small wooden table and four chairs. On the table were wigs, boxes of stage makeup, several plastic trash bags, clips for an M16, then boxes with holsters, a .357 Taurus revolver, clothes, a number of out-of-state plates, blank registrations and ownership forms, a few Slim Jims, tools, chains, handcuffs, several M69 training grenades. A file folder with neatly typed notes about Deluxe Jewelry.

"They switched here. This is where they parked their getaway vehicle. They drove her car here and switched," Sydowski said.

"Looks right."

Sydowski surveyed the place, allowing himself a measure of satisfaction. This was it. The break they were so desperate for. This was where they'd plotted the robbery. Where they launched it, and, judging from the setup, where they intended to ditch the van and use another vehicle for the long-haul getaway. Sydowski grew anxious for the crime scene guys to get here and get them prints, get them identifications, while he pored through the things they left behind. Now that they had some of the pieces, he could start to put the puzzle together.

"Walt?"

Turgeon had locked her flashlight beam on the floor near the vehicle's rear.

Sydowski got to his knees to examine the spot.

"Looks like blood," he said, then turned his head to the garage window at the sound of loud voices outside.

"Sounds like Tom Reed's out there," Turgeon said.

47

The instant Tom Reed saw Sydowski and Turgeon step from the garage, he knew the meaning of their shoe covers, their gloves, clipboards, sober faces.

"Walt."

Reed was several yards from him on the other side of the yellow tape, the ever-present line that over the years had separated the two men at countless murders. Reed called it *Sydowski's circle of death.* Two uniformed officers stood vigil next to Reed as Sydowski lifted the tape, inviting him to cross the line. But he didn't move because he couldn't move. A cloud passed in front of the sun, the emergency lights painted Sydowski's face red.

"Come on, Tom."

A big rubber-gloved hand took Reed's shoulder gently. All of your life you feared a moment like this, a moment when a grim-faced homicide detective lifts the tape and beckons you to step inside. *The circle of death.*

"Tell me, Walt. Is it Ann?"

Sydowski was conscious of the scores of people watching them.

"Can you just tell me if my wife's in there? Can you have the decency to—" Reed ran his hand over his face.

"Not here," Sydowski said. Turgeon took Reed's other shoulder.

"Tom," Turgeon said into his ear, "there's no victim in the garage."

Reed blinked, trying to comprehend.

"What is it then? Was she there? Did they bring her here?"

"Keep it down," Turgeon said.

"What the hell for? What's in there? I have a right to know. No one tells me anything."

Sydowski saw the TV and newspaper cameras taking pictures of them.

"Take a breath and get ahold of yourself." Sydowski dropped his tone. "Linda, ask Mr. Caverly if we can take Tom inside his home." Then to the uniforms he said, "Everyone's too tight. I want the perimeter of this scene widened by another two houses."

The uniforms nodded. One began waving back the press, triggering protests, while the second one grabbed the roll of scene tape, making it whiz as he enlarged the restricted access area around the garage.

Inside, Reed thought Caverly's house smelled like cheese and Old Spice. They pulled out vinyl-covered chrome chairs from a small table set from the 1950s. A stack of mail was piled in the center ready to teeter on the Niagara Falls souvenir salt and pepper shakers.

Turgeon and Sydowski slapped their clipboards on the white tabletop. Facedown. Offended, Reed shook his head, looked through the window at the garage. Police lights strobing red in his eyes as he watched children running around the satellite news trucks and the intense TV lights. Carnival time.

"So what the hell is in there?"

"Evidence," Sydowski said.

"From Ann?"

"It's her car."

"Her car? Is she—what else did you—"

"Just her car, Tom. They drove here, left it, and switched vehicles."

"But how?"

"It looks like they rented the garage from the homeowner here, and planned things from here."

"Is there anything inside her car? A note—something?"

"We don't know yet."

"I'd like to have a look. I might recognize something."

"Can't let you look, right now."

"Why not?"

"*Because it's a crime scene, Tom.* We have to preserve and protect it so the techs and the lab can do their jobs properly. You know this. We just did a preliminary inventory."

Reed stared outside. "So what's in there?"

"Tom, we can't tell you just yet, because we aren't sure exactly what it is and we're holding back."

Reed looked around, keeping his hands pressed flat on the table to keep them from shaking.

"Why didn't you call me?"

"I can't notify you on each step we take."

"Why not?"

"Tom, you're not an investigator on this case."

"You're right. I'd say my stake in this was somewhat larger. So why am I getting my information from tabloid reporters again?"

"That's who called you?" Turgeon said. "Tia Layne from *Worldwide*?"

"Does it really matter? You forgot me again."

"Tom, it's dangerous for you to get too close, to get involved."

"*I am involved.* This is my wife. My life. *I am involved.*"

"Look what happened last time," Sydowski said. "You could get hurt, or hamper the investigation. Tom, please go home."

"And do what? Wait for calls that never come?"

"Tom—"

"Wait for Ann's call that never comes?"

"Did you listen to those tapes, the enhanced ones?"

"For hours."

"Anything register? Ring a bell?"

"Nothing. But you keep asking me about any connection to me. Why? Do you know something?"

"No."

"Something you're not telling me?"

"No, Tom. We just want to be certain we've looked hard at every possibility."

"I've listened to those tapes over and over and I get nothing. It's so painful because all I hear is—"

Reed stopped. Swallowed.

"All I hear is her voice."

"You need to sleep," Sydowski said. Reed was unshaven. His hair was messed. He had been living in the same clothes for days. He was bleary-eyed. "Go home, Tom."

"I can't. It's the not knowing if she's hurt, locked away. *Dead*. Until I know, I can't stop searching for her."

His fingers trembled as he covered his face, then looked out at the neighborhood, at the laughing children and the crime scene, feeling each splash of strobing red like waves of the abyss rolling closer to him.

48

In Mayberry, Barney reached for his gun, triggering the laugh track.

Zach and his grandmother sat before the TV, still absorbing the last live news bulletin from the garage in Excelsior. When Reed returned home, they switched off the set and released the full weight of their fear to him. Doris stood, placed her hands on Zach's shoulders, braced for whatever Reed was going to tell them.

"It's not her."

"Thank God," Doris said.

"They found the Jetta, her car, in the garage."

"Her car? That's it?"

Reed explained what the detectives had told him. A moment passed before anyone knew what to say.

"We saw you on TV, Dad. You looked mad."

Reed put his hand on Zach's head and attempted a smile for him. "I was just worried about what might've been in there."

"Tom." Doris waited until Reed's eyes met hers. "What

happened last night? You went out late to meet a man who might've known something?''

"Yes, I found him."

"Did he know anything?"

"Not much. The police are talking to him."

"Did he work at the jewelry store?"

"No, Doris, he was just someone I had to see."

"Why? What's his possible connection?"

"He's a''—Reed glanced at Zach, then at Doris—''he's from the street.''

"The street."

"You know the crime stories I do—"

"Of course I do. That's why this is happening."

"What? Doris."

Reed followed her to the kitchen, where they were alone. "Doris, please talk to me."

She hurled a copy of the *Chronicle* at him, then the *Star*.

"Doris. Stop it."

"It's all about headlines and stories and everything *you do*! You love getting close to criminals. Ann tried and tried to get you to quit but you ignored her *and now look what's happened*."

"I know but—are you *blaming me* for this? Doris, please."

She covered her face with her hands and turned her back to him. Reed said nothing, allowing her time to decide if she was finished unloading her anger.

"This—" she began, "this street person you saw, did he help you?"

He put a gun to my head and pulled the trigger. Should he tell her that?

"No. It was just—he didn't know much, Doris, I'm sorry."

Reed's body ached. He went to his study. Two of the FBI agents assigned to the house for any call nodded to him from their equipment table as he walked through the front room. One was working on a laptop, the older one was playing solitaire.

"Hang in there, Tom," the older one said.

Reed entered his study and closed the door. He went to his computer to search the news wires for updates from Arizona or San Bernardino. He got as far as entering his password before raising his hands to his face, examining the cuts and bruises on them from his encounter with Caesar. Images of Ann's abduction swirled with the others: the corpse unearthed in the desert, the garage, the gun against his head. He was shaking. Coming apart. He rubbed his dried lips.

One. Just one drink. No. Get a grip. Just one. No.

He took stock of his office. Something had changed. The poster. The ancient *San Francisco Star* poster promoting his special series on unsolved murders. It had been in Zach's room. Now it stood in a corner of Reed's office next to a stack of binders and boxes of his old news clippings, as if someone were looking for something. *He didn't do that, did he?*

His door opened, Zach entered with a sandwich and a glass of milk.

"Grandma made this for you. She went outside to the garden."

"Did you do that?" Reed accepted the chicken sandwich, nodding to the poster and binders and boxes of his old stories.

"Yes."

"What are you looking for?"

"Dad, don't get mad."

"I'm not mad, buddy. Just curious why you got out my old stories."

"I was listening."

"To what?"

"The tapes. Everything, you know. When the police were here and when you're on the phone and stuff, I was listening to you."

"You were?"

"Dad, I heard them tell you to think of anyone who you might have done a story on, to listen to the tapes, in case you recognized one of the guys."

"Zach." Reed set his plate aside. "Come here."

"Don't get mad."

"I'm not mad. I understand. But how could you possibly know, or recognize anyone? I wrote some of those stories when you were in diapers. There are dozens, hundreds even. I can't remember most of them. Besides, I really think—" Reed stopped himself from saying he was convinced Sydowski had given him the task of going over the tapes and searching his memory for anyone recognizable as a pacifier, a futile diversion to keep him out of the way. But he couldn't say that to Zach. His eyes held hope. Unconditional, unyielding hope. In them, he saw Ann and felt something rising inside.

"You all right, Dad?"

Reed nodded. Zach went to the binders, kneeling on the floor.

"Look, Dad, I'm just flipping through the old articles. The computer doesn't go back this far. I'm searching for old stories on robberies that have guys that look sorta like the guys in Mom's case. Some even have pictures with the article. I've put a yellow sticker on them, and I've written down their names, or stuff if it's there. Come here, Dad. See?"

Reed couldn't see. His eyes were blurry. He patted Zach's head.

"You're doing a good job, son. Keep it up. I have to see Grandma."

Reed went to the small garden at the side of the house where Doris was tending Ann's roses. Bordered by a thick hedge, it was an oasis of privacy where Ann enjoyed nurturing her flowers. They bloomed in clusters of white, pink, yellow, and red.

"Doris, thank you for the sandwich."

She nodded, not looking at him. "Her Caribbeans are such a lovely orange," she said.

Reed inhaled gently. Ann always smelled so good after working here.

"You know, she wanted to join the rose society," Doris said, then froze at her use of the past tense. "*Wants,* I mean she *wants* to join. Dear Lord."

"It's all right." He put his arm around her, then told her how Zach was coping.

"I know. He's so much like Ann," she said. "Refusing to quit no matter what."

Reed gazed up at the clear sky, feeling guilty for not doing more to find her, to bring her home.

"She's a fighter," Doris said. "I remember the time when she was five years old and I almost lost her in an accident."

"She told me. She fell off her bike, banged her head pretty bad."

"She had just learned to ride her new two-wheeler on the sidewalk. I was talking to the postman in front of our house and heard a scream and crash, she'd fallen and hit her head. This was in the days before helmets. I remember running, the letters and magazines flying, how she wasn't moving, just lying there, her eyes wide open, not answering me, not moving, feeling cold. Blood dripped from inside her ear."

"It was a bad concussion, wasn't it?"

"I rode in the ambulance. The postman came with me. Her father rushed from his office and met us at the hospital. It was a traumatic head injury. Fractured her skull and she had fallen into a coma."

Reed nodded.

"Nothing could be done. What you do is pray. I held her and stayed with her the entire time, telling her I would never let go, that I needed her, that's what you do. And you make deals with God."

Tears rolled down her face as she worked on her daughter's roses.

"That's what I did. I said, 'God, you can do anything to me, but just don't take my little girl before you take me. Please.' " Doris paused. "Ann woke up after thirty hours and everything was fine."

"A miracle."

"A deal with God."

Reed blinked.

"Two years later, my husband died of a heart attack. I realized that was the deal, that God could do anything if he spared Ann. God exacted his price from me." Doris touched her lips with the back of her hand, holding her shears, and stared at peach roses. "So, I don't think it would be right if he took her now, because—" Her chin crumpled as she struggled to push the words out. "Because I already paid the price. God and I have a deal, you know."

Reed put his arm around her, consoling her in the garden until he noticed a red patch on her baby fingertip.

"Doris?"

"Oh." She saw the tiny wound. "I must have pricked myself on a thorn."

They went into the house. She got a bandage from the bathroom. Zach was playing checkers with one of the FBI agents. Reed retreated to his office.

He collapsed in his swivel rocker, his overtired mind swimming with a thousand thoughts as he slipped on his headphones to listen to the tapes again. It was something. He had to do something. The garage with Ann's Jetta. That had to bring them closer. It was related to the robbery. Surely it would bring them closer to knowing. Or was it all in vain, as he had witnessed in other cases? Anguished families, praying, clinging, surviving for days, weeks, on threads, whispers, leads, hope, only to learn in the end that the victim was murdered within an hour and nothing they'd done had mattered.

Ann's panicked voice floated into his ear.

"Oh God, please let me go!" Then the first abductor. "Shut up! I told you to shut up!"

Listening, Reed turned the chair to face a younger version of himself staring from the poster by the pile of old news articles Zach had been combing through. The words on the promotional poster speaking to him.

Did they get away with murder . . .

He tried to remember, what was that series about? Several cases, all steeped in mystery, unsolved homicides. He spent weeks on each one, years ago.

Should he make a deal with God? Or would the price be more than they could all bear? Reed remembered their ordeal with Zach, his own horror near Coyote Point. Could he handle this? Fear and anger washed over him, as the detective in Reed grappled with the father and husband. The voices of the men who'd taken Ann pounded in his head until exhaustion took him.

Did they get away with murder . . .

49

Ann Reed stared at the strange blond woman in the rear-view mirror, feeling nothing as the sun slipped to the horizon and the highway rolled.

She'd run out of tears miles ago after they'd decided to let her ride sitting up in the backseat. Who would recognize her now? She couldn't even recognize herself. And what did it matter on these hopeless, desolate back roads? Studying billboards and license plates, she tried in vain to determine exactly where they were. Texas? New Mexico? Oklahoma?

Her right wrist was cuffed to the door's handgrip under the window. Her right ankle was cuffed to the bottom frame of Del's front seat. The child-safety locks prevented her from opening the door. Her chains chimed with Del's empty long-neck beer bottles rolling on the floor. His head was lolling against the headrest, mouth agape as he snored. John drove. Between the newscasts, which he kept so low she couldn't hear, he met her often in the mirror. They never spoke. Silence passed with the miles.

Out of nowhere, a highway patrol car passed them. Ann

didn't see its markings. Had no chance to scream out as it disappeared in the distance along with her hope.

At that moment, she thought of Zach, how he felt when she took him in her arms. The smell of his hair, his soft skin. His kiss on her cheek. The way he liked his peanut butter and grape jelly sandwiches cut into four. It was the same way she'd liked hers cut when she was his age. That's how her mother had made them for her.

Ann remembered her mother's smile. Remembered how they'd held each other so tight after Ann's father died. How it took so long before her mother ever smiled again, the sadness never really leaving her eyes. Ann remembered how her mother had raised her alone, working at the Berkeley campus library. She used to love visiting her, sitting in the quiet next to her at her desk, doing her homework eating peanut butter and grape jelly sandwiches cut perfectly into four. All of her life her mother had been her best friend.

Ann blinked at the farm fields rolling by and felt Tom's small gift. Jammed tight in the toe of her shoe. Their anniversary was coming and she wanted this for him. Even though he drove her crazy, made her so angry, she loved him.

It was his wildness, his burning desire to chase what he wanted. He was fearless. Self-confident. But she never realized that what he pursued would take such a toll, almost cost them everything. Still, she loved him. His fury gave her the courage to chase her own dreams. She always believed her love for him could endure anything. She needed him and always would. The truth was that even though she wanted him to quit reporting, she feared his passion would be switched off and the sadness she saw in her mother's eyes would surface in his.

Tom.

She felt his gift with her toe, thought of the warmth of his back next to hers in their bed. The way her name sounded when he said it. His smile. As the fields flowed by she ached for him, for Zach and her mother. What were they doing now? What did they know? Would anyone find her note?

Think, Ann. You've got to get away. Surely they're going to kill you, then bury you like they did with the other woman.

Think. Escape. There had to be a way. All she needed was one tiny chance. One drop of luck. Was it out there? In the twilight, somewhere in the vast ocean of prairie where no one would hear a scream, or a gunshot?

The SUV slowed and took a paved side road to nowhere. Ann surveyed the area in the remaining light, looked behind at nothing. No cars. No signs. No buildings. John consulted a crisply folded map as fields of tall grass blurred by on either side.

Night was approaching when after a few miles John slowed the SUV to nearly a halt as he inched onto a dirt tractor-path of a road. A shovel and pick rattled in the rear. A dust curtain rose over their departure point, as if they'd left the earth.

The SUV toddled at low speed for at least two or three miles along a gradual downward slope that came to a river. John stopped. It was a beautiful and lonely spot. Rushing water sparkled. John began unloading things from the rear— sleeping bags, groceries he'd bought that morning at a truck stop, a couple bundles of firewood.

Del slept.

John opened Ann's door, uncuffed her, walked her to the front of the SUV where he affixed two sets of cuffs and a length of chain to the vehicle's front tow loop. She could let her arm down while sitting on the soft grass with her back against the front tire. The night air was cooling.

John built a fire, guzzled some beer, and set out cans of baked beans, opening them with an opener, then setting them near the flames to simmer. He pulled out a bag of biscuits, nacho chips, napkins, soda, and a six-pack. After the beans were done, they ate in silence by the firelight to sounds of crackling wood, John's beer, and Ann's chains. Sparks flew to the stars.

When she finished, Ann wept quietly. John watched her,

saying nothing. Doing nothing but drinking beer. After a few minutes a soft sound struggled from her heart.

"Please let me go."

The snap of burning wood was her response. John stood, stepped back from the blaze until he was a mirage at the edge of the night. His silence magnified her fear. She wanted to scream at the pain they'd caused, the outrage, the violation. The horrible things they'd left in their wake. Her shoulders shook as her tears splashed on her hands.

"Why are you doing this?"

"Why?"

Ann sniffed and nodded.

"You haven't figured it out yet? Smart lady like you?"

She shook her head.

"You don't know who we are or what we are?"

"No."

"I'm the all-time loser and you're my prize."

"Please, I don't understand."

He crushed a beer can and opened another.

"Some people make mistakes in life." John swallowed more beer. "And some people are life's mistakes. That's me."

"What do you mean?"

"Look at you. Rich San Francisco businesswoman. Grew up in a nice family, went to college. Got married, had a kid. It's in the papers. Big-shot reporter husband, nice house in San Francisco, everything going your way."

"I don't understand."

"I spent nearly all of my life in prison. That's the name this country gives to the place it keeps its mistakes."

John finished his beer and opened another one. Ann lost count and grew worried. What was that flash of metal? His handgun?

"Everything going your nice little way."

"I'm sorry, I don't understand what it has to do with me."

He stepped to her and drilled the gun hard on the top of her skull.

"It has everything to do with you."

"No. Please." The gun's hammer clicked back. She shut her eyes.

"I could have taken anyone's car in the jewelry store, Ann. But when I saw it was you, saw Tom's picture in your wallet, I knew it was meant to be. I'd never have dreamed we'd meet like this."

A long moment of silence passed.

"It was fate giving me my chance to right a wrong. When I saw it was you, everything changed. And now look at you. You're so beautiful."

He took another drink.

Ann sobbed.

"I don't understand. None of this makes sense."

"I know your husband. Tom's the reason you're here and he's the reason you're never going home."

50

Tia Layne was on the phone in the San Francisco bureau of *Worldwide News Now*. The number she'd called had rung once, twice, before it was picked up on the third ring.

"Hello?" a male voice said.

"Tom? Tom Reed?"

"Who's calling? Is this—"

"It's Tia Layne. Don't hang up."

"I've told you no interviews."

"Tom, you of all people should understand. Surely you've made calls like this at times like these?"

"What you did with that sheriff's report was debased."

"I apologize for that. I thought our information was correct."

"It was dead wrong."

"I took a journalistic risk."

"You committed a crime."

"Look, I apologized. And you're going to get it in writing. Would you just remember that I'm also the person who tipped you to the garage in Excelsior?"

Reed said nothing.

"Tom, I'm trying to help you."

"You're trying to help yourself."

"All I'm asking is that you please consider giving us an exclusive on-camera interview about how you're trying to find Ann."

"No. And to imply I somehow *owe you* is sick."

"I'm sorry you feel that way. I understand what you must be enduring."

"You don't know jack."

"I've been reading about you. And I know this: if the tables were turned, you'd be doing exactly what I'm doing right now and you damn well know it. You know how the press functions."

"And I know how *you* function." Reed hung up.

Layne slammed down the receiver, then lit a cigarette, feeling her shot at one hundred thousand fade in her smoke cloud. Getting Reed on camera to talk about his private hunt for his wife was not going to be easy. Then again, nothing in Layne's life was. She wasn't going to give up. Not yet.

The aroma of onions and cooked beef diverted her thoughts.

"How's it look, Cooter?"

"Not bad."

Between bites of his gigantic grease-dripping cheese-burger, Cooter was working on the stuff they'd already shot for a piece on Reed, reviewing and cutting night shots from Coyote Point.

"Look." Cooter chewed, pointing to the small video monitor where Layne saw herself at the shore saying, "Reed's search nearly ended here when they—" The images accelerated as Cooter fast-forwarded to grainy night shots of drug deals on the street, cutting to Layne reporting from a menacing corner over the bass throb of a passing low rider, "From America's mean streets, Reed—" Cooter froze on an image of Layne with her mouth open and eyes closed while he took another bite of his burger. "I have to move stuff around and work in the cop shooting but it's not bad, Tia. What do you think?"

"It's useless."

"Why?"

"We don't have Reed. We have to have him exclusively to make the sale. It doesn't work without him."

Cooter shrugged and worked on his burger.

"Just imagine if we had stayed on him." Layne shook her head, thinking.

"What do you mean?"

"Had we followed him around we'd have stuff of him at Coyote Point, the police takedown with Reed and the drug gang. I mean, can you imagine the power of *those* pictures?"

Cooter nodded, chewing thoughtfully. "It'd be tough to be that close to him, or even anticipate what he's going to do. Even the police don't know."

"We got to think of a way."

"Why?"

"A top crime reporter, a Pulitzer nominee, searching for his wife, kidnapped from the streets of San Francisco in a heist that left a cop dead, a woman's corpse in the desert, body parts in Arizona, Reed in pursuit and nearly killed by drug dealers." Layne stubbed out her cigarette, shaking her head. "It's a world story and it's worth one hundred thousand to us if we can nail it. That's why."

Cooter popped the last bit of his burger into his mouth and shrugged. Layne got up from her desk and began pacing.

"This story is far from over, it can only get better. Reed's not going to let up until he finds his wife," Layne said. "We can't afford to miss his next step, whatever it is. We have to be there."

Cooter sucked the remainder of his soda from his plastic cup, thinking.

"How are we going to do that, Cooter? He doesn't want

to cooperate. He doesn't want us near him. The police don't want us near him. There has to be a way for us to do this.''

Cooter wiped his face, then burped.

''There is, Tia.''

51

Molly Wilson nearly fell, stepping from the shower in her apartment at the edge of Russian Hill near North Beach. Her home phone *and* her cell phone were ringing. Wrapping herself in a towel, she hurried to her living room.

It could be the paper but she prayed it was one of her police sources.

Wilson had to know what the hell was going on with the investigation and Tom Reed. Earlier that day, she'd seen him at the garage in Excelsior. But Sydowski had refused to tell her much, so she called every cop she knew. She went to her home phone on the table at a bay window and grabbed it.

"Hi, just hold on."

Her bag with her cell phone was on a chair next to the table. She pulled it out, pressed the talk button.

"Hello?"

Nothing. Missed the call. Darn. She felt water drip down her back from her damp hair as she went to the other phone.

"Sorry, hello."

"Molly, it's Todd at the paper, sorry to bother you at home."

"What is it?"

"A caller, some woman, wants to talk to you."

"About what?"

"She didn't say. She just wanted to talk to you."

Wilson was running late to meet a police friend from the lab.

"Put her to my voice mail."

"Tried that, she wants to talk to you."

"Take a message, Todd, I'm running late."

"She won't leave any information. She insists on talking to you. I've got her on another line. Can I transfer her to you?"

"Don't give out my home number."

"I won't, can I transfer her?"

Wilson glanced at her watch.

"Yes."

"Here we go."

San Francisco's lights twinkled. Wilson could see the Golden Gate.

The line clicked.

"Hello," a woman said.

"Hi, this is Molly Wilson."

"You're the reporter at the *San Francisco Star* who sits right beside Tom Reed?" Her voice was rough, husky but sober and coherent. Mid-thirties.

"Yes. But I'm running late."

"I've got a message for you."

"I'm listening."

"It's actually a message for Tom Reed."

"Look, I don't have time for this. Why are you calling me?"

"You sit beside him, right? That's what your office told me, right?"

"I sit beside him."

"Then police aren't running a tap on *your* line."

The caller had Wilson's full attention. "Who are you?"

"No police."

"Excuse me?"

"You got to swear no police, or I won't give you the information and Reed *will never know.*"

"Never know what?" Wilson grabbed her bag. *Where's the tape recorder?*

"You protect sources?"

"We protect sources. What's the information?"

"If police are involved there's no information."

"Damn it. What's the information?" Wilson managed to find a notebook and pen. "We get a lot of crank calls. What're you talking about?" She couldn't find her cassette recorder but began scrolling through the function menu on her telephone answering machine. "Could you wait a minute? I was on my way out and you got me tangled up here."

"I'm calling from a stolen cell phone, the call went first to your sports department, then transferred to news, then you."

Wilson found *record conversation*, activated the key, and a bright red indicator light began flashing.

"What sort of information do you have?"

"The kind that has to be delivered in person to Tom Reed, so he knows where it's coming from. But no police."

"Yes. No police. Just Reed."

"It's got to be very soon. Take down these instructions."

Wilson took notes and read them back, wondering if this was a ransom call, a crank, or the real thing.

"Look, you have to tell me, so I can tell him. Is this about Ann Reed?"

"Yes."

"Is she all right? Where is she? Is she hurt? Are you with her?"

The line went dead.

52

Molly Wilson's bracelets jingled as she tore the page from her notebook and approached one of the officers outside Tom Reed's house.

"So?" The cop read the note, indicating other reporters milling nearby. "They all want to see Reed privately. He ain't talkin'."

"He'll talk to me, Molly Wilson from the *Star*."

"The *Star,* where Reed works?"

"I don't want to tie up his phone. But you guys won't let anyone on his property. So would you please send my note in quietly?"

He considered her request for a moment.

"I need to stretch my legs. Give me your card." The old cop heaved himself out of his Crown Victoria.

Fifteen minutes later, no one noticed Wilson break from the press pack to wait at the rear yard gate where the officer said Tom would meet her. He came out of his house alone. They sat on the small bench under a tree. She didn't waste a second.

"Tom, I got a call. It came to the paper. They put it to my home."

"About Ann?"

"Yes."

"Is she alive? Where is she? Do they want money?"

"Hold on, let me—"

"How long ago did you get the call?"

"About twenty minutes, maybe half an hour."

"*Half an hour!* Molly, why didn't you call me or—"

"It was a woman. She said she'd give up information on the condition you didn't tell the police. That's why she called my line. She wants to meet. I couldn't call you without the FBI hearing. I came straight to you to let you decide. Could be a nut. Could be real. I recorded what I could. There's not much. Listen."

After Wilson played the few seconds of instructions Reed said, "Is your car here?"

"Down the street."

"I'll tell everybody in the house that I have to check something in the newsroom. Park at the next block intersection and wait for me."

The caller wanted to meet across the bay in Oakland. Reed's stomach knotted as they crossed the Bay Bridge and he searched the night for answers.

"So what happened at the garage, Tom?"

"You want to know as a reporter, or as a friend?"

"What? God. As a friend, Tom. God, what's happening here? I came to you with this. I told no one about this. For God's sake. It's me, Molly. I sit beside you at the paper and confide my heart to you."

Reed rubbed his stubble, apologized, then told her what happened to him when he chased his own lead on Carrie Dawn Addison to Caesar. Wilson shook her head in disbelief.

"Then I slug it out with Sydowski, who tells me I'm getting too close, that I should stay out of the way. He promises to keep me posted. Then right after that, I find out about the garage. Not from him, but from Tia Layne.''

''That tabloid woman who stole the report?''

''I'm going out of my mind, Molly. I've got to find her. No matter what, I've got to end this.''

The meeting was at a basement bar in a renovated warehouse near the waterfront a few blocks from Jack London Square. Its steps creaked. Its walls evoked the planks and beams of a ship. They found a booth, ordered mineral water, and waited. To Reed, the tattooed, goateed customers suggested parolees.

''You get anything from the drug dealer?'' Wilson said.

Reed told her everything Caesar told him.

''But he never gave you names?''

''No, but it all happened at Folsom. Sydowski figures they'll get a hit from latents in the garage.''

''But they haven't found anything yet?''

''Still waiting.''

''How are you holding up, Tom, really?''

''Hoping and praying, Molly. All I want to—I don't know.''

Reed checked the time on his cell phone. Thirty minutes past the appointed hour and nothing. Wilson checked her phone to make sure it was working and the battery was strong.

Ninety minutes after the specified meet time, Wilson said, ''This is cruel.'' Then they left.

Walking to Wilson's car, Reed gazed across the bay at San Francisco's lights. He was defeated. His hand shook when he touched the door handle. He was losing it.

''Tom Reed?''

A woman stepped from a darkened doorway. White, mid-thirties. Black jeans, black leather waist-cut jacket. Hands in the pockets. Big hoop earrings, short bleached hair.

''I had to be sure you didn't bring the cops.'' She had the face of a woman who'd had a hard life and her tone carried an air of genuine fear.

"Do you know where my wife is?"

"No, it's not like that."

"Do you want money, are you a messenger?"

"Listen—"

"Please take your hands out of your pockets so I can see them," Reed said.

Wilson took stock of the area. Gulls shrieked above. The horn of a tug moaned in the distance.

"You visited my boyfriend in Folsom a few months back and wrote about him. You said his crimes were due to his drug problems. That helped him at his hearing. He heard about your wife and wants to help you, so he sent me to give you information to your face, then take your reaction back to him."

Reed remembered.

"Donnie Ray Ball. The county homicide cop who robbed banks in the East Bay."

She nodded.

"What's your name?" Reed said.

"Angela."

"What does Donnie know?"

"None of it can get back to him, that's why he has to be vague and, believe me, I don't know nothing, okay?" Angela's voice wavered. She was shaking. He exchanged glances with Wilson. This was the real thing.

"Okay," he said.

"Donnie says if his information works out, you've got to remember that he did this good thing for you. *That you owe him.*"

Reed thought about it.

"If it works out, I'll remember that he helped. *If it works out.*"

"He said there were three of them. They all did time in Folsom, that's how they knew each other. He caught wind of it in C Yard. More new information came to him through the grapevine after the cop got shot and your wife taken. It's big news, you know—"

"Angela, who are the men? I want their names."

She swallowed.

"You know the dead one, Driscoll."

"Everyone does. Come on."

"Donnie couldn't give you the names but said I could only tell you where to look for one of them."

"Jesus, Angela." Reed stepped toward her. "Are you going to help me, goddammit! What are their names and where did they go?"

Angela shook her head, swallowed.

"Donnie said he thinks they never planned to take her, that it just happened she was there, that it wasn't part of their plan."

"Is he involved in this?"

"No."

"Then tell me, where is my wife?"

"I don't know."

"*You don't know?* That's it. What the hell are you trying to pull?"

"Wait, no, you've got to listen."

"What are their names? Where did they go?" Reed was shouting.

"Tom." Wilson grabbed his arm.

"All I know," Angela whispered, "and all Donnie said, and I swear to God this is the truth, I'm so sorry, but all he said was you had to look back at some old news stories."

"Old stories? Which stories? I wrote hundreds and hundreds."

"Stories from way back, about guys thinking they got away with murder."

"What?"

"Donnie said the guy behind the robbery is in your stories."

"He's in my stories?"

"Donnie says you met him."

Reed's intestines contracted. *I met him.*

"Oh Christ," Wilson said, drawing their attention to the

SUV half a block down the street. "I think somebody's watching us."

Reed saw a glint of glass at a passenger window. *Binoculars?* What was going on? He turned back to Angela. She was gone.

53

Make the unseen seen. That was the personal code of Officer Nancy Chang, an SFPD fingerprint expert.

Since the robbery homicide, Chang's life was lived in nineteen-hour days, at the Hall, the lab at Hunter's Point, and the crime scenes. She rose at daybreak to join other forensic techs in the pursuit of clear prints that would identify the suspects. The case wouldn't yield anything. Nothing from the jewelry store, the van, or August's patrol car. They dusted and scoped everywhere and everything—the shell casings, the spent rounds, the grenades—but nothing was usable. Same story for the FBI and the San Bernardino County and the guys in Arizona. Nothing.

Chang reached for her coffee mug, a personalized birthday gift from her friends at the ME's office. She loved the enlarged thumbprint logo, over the words *Leave some for me*.

After striking out at Addison's apartment, it had started to look as if these suspects were going to beat them. They were either very smart or very lucky. But luck is like time. Sooner or later it runs out for everyone, Chang figured as she sipped coffee and resumed wrapping up her work on the new impressions investigators found at Jed Caverly's garage.

As with the Addison apartment, Chang first made a set of elimination prints of everyone who might have been inside that garage, starting with Jed Caverly. One team of techs worked on Ann Reed's Jetta. Nothing. Then they got busy on every item in the garage, including the trash where they found fast-food wrappers, take-out cups, cigarette butts, and empty beer cans. The trash yielded dead Driscoll's prints again.

And something new.

Unidentified latents on the beer cans.

The techs had dusted the cans, photographed the prints with an old reliable CU-5, before collecting them with lifting tape. What they had was a good clear set of impressions from the right hand. After Chang studied the arches, whorls, and loops, they confirmed what she'd suspected. Nothing fit with the elimination set from the garage, or any of the other scenes. She double-, then triple-checked.

Definitely a new player.

Chang locked on to the five fingerprints she had of the new sample. Starting with the right thumb, which in a standard ten-card is number one, she carefully coded its characteristics, then those of the other fingers. Then she scanned the prints and entered all the information into her computer. Now she could submit it to the SFPD's automated fingerprint-identification systems, AFIS, for a rapid search through massive local, state, and nationwide data banks for a match.

And here we go. Chang typed a few commands on her keyboard, sighed, and reached for her mug. Her computer hummed as it processed her data for a list of possible matches to study.

After fifteen seconds, it came back with two hits from the SFPD's local data bank. *That's a start,* she thought. It would take about ten minutes before she got results from the California Identification System, Cal-ID, a computerized file holding the fingerprints of some eight million people, which was operated by California's justice department in Sacramento.

It would take longer before her submission was searched through the regional information sharing systems, like the western states network and the FBI's mother of all data banks, the IAFIS, which stored nearly seven hundred million impressions from law enforcement agencies across the country.

Chang went to the coffee room to start a fresh pot of coffee and heat up the mushroom soup she'd brought from home; then she returned to her computer. The search was done. It offered her a list of seven possibles that closely matched her unidentified submission.

Now we're talking.

Chang set out to make a visual point-by-point comparison between the garage print and the seven on the list. Seven. Lucky number seven. Chang's pulse increased. This was when she was at her best, zeroing in on the critical minutiae points, like the trail of ridges near the tip of the number-two finger. Dissimilarities there. That eliminated the first two candidates right off. *We have some lovely parting gifts.* On the next set, she enlarged the samples even more to visually count the number of ridges on the number-three finger. Distinct differences emerged. *Thanks for playing.* That took care of all of the others.

All but one.

Chang's eyes narrowed as she compared her submission with the computer's remaining suggested match. All the minutiae points matched. The branching of the ridges matched. Her breathing quickened as she began counting up the clear points of comparison where the two samples matched. Some courts required ten to fifteen clear point matches. She had twenty-three and was still counting, knowing that one divergent point instantly eliminated a print. By the time she'd compared the left-slanting patterns from the last finger, Chang had thirty-five clear points of comparison and was thinking ahead about testifying in court.

This is a match. I do so swear. So help me God.

Finally she matched the scales of the prints, then used her computer program to superimpose one over the other, the way one would trace a picture. She swallowed, clenched her fist, and touched it to her desktop.

A perfect match. Yes.

Chang then confirmed the identification number of her new subject, and submitted a query into a number of data banks. One of them, the California Law Enforcement Telecommunication System, CLETS, a network run by the justice department's Hawkins Data Center. Chang's query ran through an array of systems, including the FBI's National Crime Information Center, California's department of motor vehicles, the state justice department. It also accessed the various systems of California's department of corrections, including the Parole Law Enforcement Automated Data System, LEADS, and the Automated Criminal History System. The submission could verify parolee history, offender identification, arrest records, convictions, holds, and commitments for other law enforcement agencies, even create all points bulletins and drop warrants.

All in less than a minute.

In Chang's case, it took thirty-seven seconds before the hardened face of a white man glowered from her monitor. She went to the offender's central file summary and read quickly through his offenses.

Good Lord. He was released as a PC 290. Sex offender.

She reached for her telephone. Her supervisor had cleared her to call the primary detective immediately once she had a hit. It was 1:30 A.M. but the line was answered on the first ring.

"Inspector Sydowski?"

"Yeah."

"Nancy Chang. I got a match on a print from the garage. Got a pen?"

"Go ahead."

"Delmar James Tribe."

54

Delmar James Tribe.

Sydowski studied his CDC photos and read his file.

Born June 12, 1964, in Tampa, Florida. Height: six feet three inches. Weight: 230 pounds. Race: white. Hair: brown. Eyes: brown. Nationality: American. Aliases: Paul Ager, Robert Franklin, Jack Soller, Mitchell Cantu. Occupations: former sergeant, U.S. Marines, truck driver, construction worker, explosives/demolitions expert. Scars and Marks: missing left earlobe. Tattoos: one left forearm, cobra coiled around a sword on upper left arm, the words *No Surrender*. On right forearm, *The Grim Reaper*. On upper right arm, a broken heart in hell.

"Heads up, everybody." SFPD Lieutenant Leo Gonzales arrived and kick-started the task force's early-morning case-status meeting. "Let's make it quick. Go, Walt."

Investigators from the SFPD, FBI, the Bureau of Alcohol, Tobacco, and Firearms, U.S. Marshals Service, California Justice, California Department of Corrections, and several other agencies flipped through their copy of Tribe's file as Sydowski updated them.

"Shortly after we got the hit on Tribe's prints we went back on some of Merida's crew about three A.M."

Gonzales held up his hand.

"For the new faces just coming to this, Merida is a.k.a. Caesar, the drug dealer with the link to Carrie Dawn Addison, our desert homicide who was a clerk at Deluxe Jewelry."

Sydowski said, "Merida's people gave us statements. They said Tribe and the dead driver, Driscoll, knew each other from Folsom, that Tribe was the white boy who saved Jorge's ass inside. Merida's guys said Tribe and Driscoll met Merida four or five times to discuss the jewelry store and Carrie Addison. Tribe was accompanied by an unidentified white male who was in charge of the robbery operation."

Sydowski hadn't shaved. He scratched his silver-white stubble.

"Everybody ran Tribe's aliases. We got a hit on one, Jack Soller. It was for a traffic beef across the bay. The Soller hit gave CDC and Sacramento an East Bay PO box used by Jack Soller. When they dropped the address through their health and human services data banks they found a prescription check for Delmar James Tribe was sent to the same PO box."

As Sydowski continued, Turgeon carefully reread Tribe's criminal history to make sure she hadn't missed anything.

While posted to Kaneohe Bay at Pearl Harbor, Hawaii, Sergeant Tribe followed a female corporal from a bar, dragged her into an alley. She fought him, managing to bite off his left earlobe before he raped her, slit her throat, and set her on fire. She survived. After a court martial, Tribe was sentenced to eight years in Fort Leavenworth, Kansas.

Upon release, Tribe joined an antigovernment militia group. He was suspected but never charged in a spree of armed bank robberies in California, Utah, Florida, Colorado, and Texas. His signature was the use of trip-wired hand grenades. In those offenses, a fifty-five-year-old manager in Los Angeles lost his right hand. In Miami, a twenty-four-year-old teller was blinded. Tribe was also suspected in several violent sexual assaults.

According to the facts of his last offense, Tribe was arrested and charged after he raped, then stabbed a twenty-six-year-old San Diego real estate agent with a letter opener from her purse. The assault took place in the agent's family van. She had parked in the lot of a suburban mall where she'd gone shopping for a stroller for her twin baby girls. Portions of the offense were recorded on the lot's security cameras.

The mother survived. She testified against Tribe. But his public defender made a compelling case for Tribe's history of abuse at the hands of his alcoholic father, which led to drug addictions and Tribe's lifelong mental problems. The jury never heard about Tribe's criminal history.

The mother was permanently disfigured, her marriage ended under the stress. Her wounds required her to endure the rest of her life with the aid of a colostomy bag.

Tribe was given a six-year sentence.

A psychiatric assessment described him as a violent, sadistic sexual predator. It cautioned that while he presented a facade of harmless charm, he was a psychotic sociopath prone to flashes of uncontrolled, homicidal rage. There was an excerpt of what Tribe told a psychiatrist about his behavior: "Each woman I met wanted me. What I never understood was why they lied about it. It pissed me off. They didn't deserve to live for what they did to me."

There was a supplemental note that said Tribe loved collecting reptiles. He was partial to snakes and was known to attend shows or join clubs and talked of establishing a reptile farm in Central or South America.

And Tribe was the normal one.

That's what Merida's crew told them last night. Turgeon finished reading, took a breath, and looked out the window. She watched a pigeon perched on the sill. She went to her notes. They didn't know a single thing about Tribe's mystery partner. Not yet. She closed Tribe's folder.

McDaniel gave the FBI's update.

"So far from our work through the jewelry and gem database, none of the stolen product has emerged. But we've picked up several leads on the potential buyers in New York, Chicago, Houston, Boston, Detroit, Miami, and Atlanta. We're aware dealers will tip us to bring heat on a competitor."

"So where do you go with that?" Sydowski said.

"We're circulating Tribe's information and we've started the process of getting search warrants in all the listed jurisdictions for all the telephone numbers of the potential buyers," McDaniel said.

Gonzales turned to Kay Lowenstein, a supervisor with the California Department of Corrections in Sacramento, for a report.

"Tribe was released on supervised parole three years ago. He was PC 290 and registered. The Board of Prison Terms and his parole agent indicate he met all conditions and counseling requirements. Complied with his drug test schedule and was clean. No violations," Lowenstein said, meaning *he was not our mistake*.

"Except we don't have a valid address for him?" Turgeon said. "Parole and community services is required to keep an accurate location history."

"Would you like me to stop to debate parole agent caseload with you now, Inspector Turgeon? Tribe satisfied the requirements of his parole conditions. He obviously intended to deceive us on his last address."

Sydowski got between them. "Please continue, Kay."

"Folsom is assembling an inmate list to give us a pool of whom Tribe may have associated with, or which gangs he was allied with, while serving his sentence. Bearing in mind that Folsom is a level-four maximum-security institution with a shifting inmate population of some three thousand, this could take time. They're focusing on C Yard, where he did much of his sentence."

"What about his employers, his circles on the outside,

all the people in addiction counseling groups? He may have befriended his partner in rehab," McDaniel said.

"Tribe's parole agent is on it." Lowenstein closed her file.

"Anyone or anything else before we get back to work?" Sydowski said.

McDaniel stated the FBI was expecting Tribe's court-martial transcripts, his Leavenworth records, and his marine records from St. Louis. "We'll go through his unit albums, his entire file for associates. NIS and the U.S. Marshals Service is helping us find his buddies who testified in his defense."

McDaniel pulled his cell phone from his pocket, read an e-mailed alert to the task force. "A federal arrest warrant by the United States District Court, Northern District of California, has just been issued for Delmar James Tribe," McDaniel added. "I've talked to our NHQ, we'll get the ball rolling to put him on the FBI's Most Wanted list today."

"We're set," Gonzales said. "We'll hold a news conference as soon as we can to put out everything we have on Tribe. His picture, his history, we'll get it out across the country. Finally, before we get back to work, I just want to remind everyone of the obvious. Tribe is only one half of our problem. We need to nail down his partner to double our chances of grabbing them, finding Ann Reed."

Files were collected, cell phones were put to use, as the meeting broke.

"Walt, can I see you?" Turgeon pulled Sydowski aside. "We'd better tell Reed about Tribe, don't you think?"

"Yeah, he's going to find out. Might as well be from us."

"How do we tell him this? After what he's been through?"

"We just tell him, Linda, that's all we can do."

55

The thread of hope named Angela had disappeared into the night on the Oakland waterfront. And the vehicle that had been watching them had pulled away when they spotted it.

"Tom, maybe this whole thing was a setup," Wilson said as they drove back to San Francisco.

"She was too specific about Donnie Ray Ball."

"But someone was watching."

"Could've been police. I don't care. I've got to follow this. Let's go to the paper."

"Now?"

Reed shot Wilson a look. She pushed the gas pedal and the city loomed.

The *Star* newsroom was deserted. They smelled microwaved popcorn wafting over the sea of empty desks, silent keyboards, and computer monitors whose screen savers flickered in the tranquillity.

Chad, the twenty-year-old news assistant, was the sole

person on duty. His Nikes were crossed atop an early edition on the metro assignment editor's desk. He was reclined on the swivel chair in front of the big-screen TV, watching a John Wayne movie. A portable police scanner clattered next to him, its sound turned low. More interested in keeping his mouth filled with popcorn, Chad glanced at Reed and Wilson. Reed detected a pungent hint of marijuana.

"Paper's gone to bed. What's up, man?"

"We're not here."

"Hope they find your wife, Reed, so you can kick some serious ass."

Wilson went to the coffee room to make a fresh batch. Reed went directly to his desk, logged on to the *Star*'s computerized article archives, uncertain if they went back far enough to contain that series he did. Scrolling through story after story. It was hard to concentrate.

Think hard. Stories from way back, about guys thinking they got away with murder. The guy is in your stories—you met him.

Trouble was, Reed had written hundreds, maybe thousands of stories on crime, murders, rapes, robberies, fires, quakes, mud slides, victims, criminals, profiles, trends, reports, investigations, features on tragedies, anniversaries, and executions. He searched subject, keywords, checking dates, names, or bizarre aspects that stood out. Data flowed by in a blurry river of information. *It's in here. It's just got to be in here. You met him.*

Reed had met thousands of people. Interviewed them at their homes, offices, schools, jobs, at crime scenes, at hospitals, at funerals, the cemeteries, courthouse steps, and prisons.

So many.

It was true. He'd carry the details of some stories until the day he died. Like the way a mother cradles the picture of her murdered child, the way a belly chain sounds when a convicted murderer sits down for his interview on death row, or the way a gun pressed to your head feels when a drug dealer has his finger on the trigger.

Still, there were stories he couldn't recall until, for one reason or another, the actual article he wrote popped up in his face.

"Here, Tom." Wilson set a mug of black coffee down on Reed's desk. "Any luck?"

"Nothing."

"Angela said it has something to do with stories you did about people who thought they had gotten away with murder."

"I recall a series I did years ago but no details. Zach's got a promotional poster for it in his bedroom."

"Got your picture on it?"

"Yeah."

Wilson got on her hands and knees to prospect in the long-forgotten junk zone between their desks. She sifted through the stacks of yellowing editions of the *Star,* movie posters, a couple of classics from Fillmore West, others for Bruce Springsteen, The Rolling Stones. One for the pope. Wilson got up, unfolding one with tattered edges.

"This it?"

It was an old poster with Reed's head and shoulders over a stylized lead, *Did they get away with murder* . . . It had gone into *Star* boxes years ago to promote his investigative series on unsolved homicides . . . *To find out, read Pulitzer Prize–nominee Tom Reed. Only in the San Francisco Star.*

"That's the one."

"It was here when I moved in," Wilson said.

"It hasn't any details. And I just can't remember a single name. What's wrong with me? I'm drawing a blank on this."

Wilson went to her keyboard.

"Tom, I think I referred to one of the cases from your series in one of my old features on Roberta Mind." Wilson entered the archives and pulled up a single hit under her byline, then displayed the item. The reference was near the bottom. *"Roberta Mind,"* Wilson read aloud, *"killed her husband in a domestic dispute in the late 1980s.* Tom, your files would be in the dungeon.''

"The dungeon? I never go down there."

"Chad!" Wilson called. "We need the keys to the dungeon, they should be in the assistant's supply desk."

The dungeon was at the very bottom of the *Star* building, a vast basement warehouse area on the same floor as the presses, which were now rolling with the *Star*'s final edition, making the building tremble and hum.

Wilson and Reed unlocked the battered steel door, threw on the lights, and walked down the rows of chicken-wired storage stalls, each with its own door and lock. Every journalist at the *Star* had a unit for storage. Each one measured four feet by eight feet and had shelves filled with discarded files and material. Editors who were in divorce proceedings hid personal treasures here, like cash, rare coins, or game balls autographed by Bonds, or Montana.

The vibrating presses made the lights flicker and raised dust.

"This place stinks. It's musty," Wilson said. "Here we go." She tapped on a stuffed unit whose door read 647 TOM REED.

"I've never come down here, I just sent junk down," Reed said, pulling out his keys. "I think it's this one." The key worked.

Wilson entered. Large cardboard file boxes, stacked six high, filled the unit. Each one was dated.

"This one, this one, this one." Her pen squeaked check marks on the boxes to start searching. Reed grunted, hoisting them to the floor, tearing them open. They were jammed tight with files, notebooks, printouts, papers.

"Look for Roberta Mind," Wilson said, climbing to a higher shelf where she tore open a box. "That should lead you to the others."

"They're not even in alphabetical order. I just heaved stuff in here. Most of the dates are wrong."

"Keep looking." Wilson was fast. "Together we can get through this stuff. Come on. Anything with Roberta Mind will lead us to the others."

The lights flickered as the presses droned, making the room shake. Minutes became half an hour. Half an hour became an hour, then another hour as the pile of boxes searched became larger than the remainder.

Reed flipped through file after file, dust and sweat stinging his eyes, his body aching, until he came across a file with *Roberta* scrawled in large letters. It was thick. *Now we're getting somewhere.*

He scanned the draft of a story from a dot matrix printer. Roberta Mind was a hairdresser acquitted of killing her husband because of a history of domestic abuse. But detectives said she'd planned his death, plying him with booze and taunting him, even though he had completed four successful months of counseling. Reed remembered that story.

But according to Donnie Ray Ball's tip, Ann's kidnapper was a man Reed had met. That ruled out Roberta. Reed caught a note in her file saying her case was among four in the series he did.

The next one was about Elonzo Haze, a pimp suspected of murdering one of his hookers who was going to testify against him. That one came back to Reed. It involved voodoo or something occult. People who'd had info on the case kept disappearing before detectives could question them. It was never solved. A real bone-chiller. Reed talked to Elonzo on the phone a few times but they'd never met.

A note on the file folder said *More series material in box 3312.*

"That one, Molly." Reed pointed to the box on the top shelf in the corner. "Get that one. Look for two stories from the series. The folders might have something written on them."

Still on the higher shelf, Wilson heaved the box nearer,

opening to the case of Cyrus Makepeace. "Remember that case, Tom? Wilderness guide whose customers died hiking?"

"Yeah, it's all coming back. Cyrus arranged to make himself a beneficiary on their insurance policies before his clients had wilderness accidents. They never charged him even after a couple of exhumations."

"Here's the last one on the series," Wilson said, just as the lights flickered, the floor shook from the presses, and the board she was standing on cracked. "Look out!"

Wilson caught herself but the box crashed, files spilled on the floor at Reed's feet. He bent down to collect them. He reached for a black-and-white mug shot and he froze.

"Jesus Christ!"

Realization rushed at him with all the fury and the earth-shaking thunder of the presses, driving him to his knees as he studied the face that met his in the flickering light.

The face of a long-forgotten enemy.

John Mark Engler.

56

The forty-watt porch lighting of the Moonlit Dreams Motor Inn attracted clouds of frenzied moths but few guests dared to stop. Every few minutes a car or truck passed down the highway, interrupting the crickets but ignoring the vacancy sign beckoning from the darkness.

But for the paint blistering, not much happened here.

The air conditioner didn't work in number 6 where Ann Reed's wrists were handcuffed to the wooden arms of a chair. Duct tape covered her mouth. She blinked away the salty sting of another sweat droplet.

Delmar Tribe couldn't stop watching her. Even when he tilted his head to swallow more beer, he kept a predatory eye locked on to her. It had been twenty minutes since they'd settled in. John Engler stepped from the bathroom after a shower, his hair damp, face reddened.

"Where the hell you going?" Tribe said.

"To phone our guy and get some food, which is your job but you're too damned drunk."

"Screw you." Tribe stared at Ann, then at the fractured TV screen. The set got two channels: a fire-and-brimstone

Bible-thon and professional wrestling. "How long you gonna be?"

"Half an hour. Maybe less so don't get any ideas, Del."

"Why the hell do you pick these rat-hole dumps, huh?"

"To make you feel at home." Engler began collecting the keys, knives. "These places are cheap, out of the way, take cash, ask no questions. Do I have to spell it out for you? Give me your gun."

"What the hell for?"

"Because I don't want any trouble while I step out."

Tribe glared at him before giving up his gun, then opening another beer.

"Slow down there," Engler said. "How 'bout some chicken from that place we passed down the road?"

"How 'bout we get our money and split? I'm sick of this. I want my cut. Let's keep driving and get it done with the buyer."

"No, he's not ready. Take it easy. I'll be right back."

"Get more beer."

Engler drove off.

Tribe lit a cigarette and resumed watching Ann through his smoke cloud. Her breathing quickened. Alone with him, she was vulnerable. Maybe John did this on purpose. Time ticked by as she fought to figure out Tom's link to these men. If she understood, maybe she could reason a way out.

As crickets chirped in the night, Ann felt his eyes on her. Watching. Waiting. She blinked at her mounting fear. Ten, maybe fifteen minutes had passed, providing some relief. Maybe he would leave her alone.

Without warning he stood and stripped off his shirt.

He was huge. He had the build of an inmate for whom bodybuilding was a religion practiced daily in the exercise yard. His powerful muscles strained the tattoos on his arms and shoulders. Being shirtless magnified his deformed ear, underscoring Ann's worry that he was *abnormal*.

"This place is a sweatbox." He touched his beer to his forehead and chest. "I see you're hot too, *darlin'*."

Watching her watching him, he shook his head slowly.

"Damn. You're a looker." He seemed bigger as he stepped next to her, bending over, drawing his face to hers. "Well, it's no secret anymore. I know what you want."

She began to tremble.

Fight. They're going to kill you. Don't let him do this. Fight him.

He held up the handcuff key and his rotting teeth emerged as he grinned.

In a few quick powerful movements he had Ann handcuffed to the bed, using the length of chain for her legs. She managed to scratch him, drawing blood on his shoulder. She got in a few hard punches but it was like slamming her hand against rock. He laughed.

"Might as well admit the truth to yourself," he said, "you want this. You really want this bad. They all wanted it, darlin'. All of them."

He placed one of his knees on the bed between her legs. Her heart galloped. She thought of Tom. Of Zach, thought of the woman buried in the desert. She prayed. Prayed to die now so he couldn't do this, couldn't take her last bit of dignity. She prayed for the other one to return.

His eyes burned into hers, the tips of something so dark and dead it turned Ann's blood cold. He cupped one hand around her neck. His fingers met at the front, like a vise. His big thumb caressed her chin, her lips.

"Darlin', I seen how you've been looking at me and I know what you want. It's been a long time since I had something as beautiful as you. We both have needs. I'm going to help you with yours."

He drew his face to hers, his sweat dropping on her, his breath stinking of beer and cigarettes. He reeked of body odor. As he began tugging at her T-shirt, Ann shut her eyes, feeling his hand, the hand that loved caressing king snakes, moccasins, and diamondbacks, slide down her stomach, then inch lower.

Oh God. It's really going to happen to me. . . .

Loud thumping on the porch planks out front smashed the quiet.

"Hey, Dad, can I get a soda from the machine!"

Startled, he stopped. It was a kid. Right out front. Staccato thudding on the porch continued.

"They got grape!"

A man's muffled voice, then a car door shutting. The man again saying: "No, Frankie, we got juice. Ours is number two. Four doors that way."

"But, Dad!"

"Keep it down. I said, let's go."

More thumping, fading. A door slamming.

"Christ." Tribe left Ann for the window, to peek through the curtains.

Another car door slammed. Engler had returned. He entered in seconds, his eyes going to Ann chained to the bed, her shirt torn, jeans unbuttoned, then to Tribe, bare-chested, stomach and face scratched, zipper down.

"What did you do? What the Christ did you do?"

The plastic take-out bags in his hands dropped, Engler charged Tribe, slamming him to the wall. Muscles and veins bulged, teeth were bared. The two men growled as they struggled before Engler shoved Tribe to the floor. He went to Ann. He was going to tear the tape from her mouth but remembered the family a few doors away and kept his voice low.

"Did he rape you?"

Ann shook her head.

"But he was fixing to rape you?"

Ann closed her eyes, half sobbing, and nodded.

Tribe pulled on his shirt, boots, grabbed some food and beer.

"What the hell is it with you and her, John?" He pointed a plastic knife at Engler. "Why didn't we drop her after the job? Why did we keep her, huh?"

"Sit down and cool down."

"What kind of sick thing you got going? Look. You color

her hair, but not just any color. It's *her* color. What's wrong with you?''

·''Shut up.''

''I'm telling you, John, she is going to bring us down. We should drop her, just like the other one. You let me have Carrie; then we dropped her. Clean. Even played out your little switch game in Death Valley. The way you wanted, so you could get your kicks. But we stuck to our plan with Carrie. Remember our plan, John?''

''Shut your goddamned mouth.''

''Whatever happened to our plan? The one that said no witnesses. I don't recall the part that said drag a transmitter across the country. The wife of some big-ass reporter. What in hell is up with you, you twisted—''

Engler punched Tribe, knocking him to the floor.

''So that's it.'' Tribe rubbed his jaw. ''She's *your* fantasy, your prize. Something's going on. Something happened to you in the joint, brother, something bad got you all turned around.''

''Why don't you put some food in your yap and shut up?''

''Listen to me, I'm going to take her; then I'm going to dump her. *It will happen*. It always does. My needs are so powerful, I ache. But they will be satisfied. Then we'll complete our business, go our separate ways. Got that?''

The room rattled when Tribe slammed the door behind him.

Engler picked up the remaining food, arranged it on the table, uncuffed Ann.

''I'll take the tape off to let you eat if you don't scream.''

Ann couldn't respond. She was shaking.

''You should eat. Take your mind off things.''

A long moment passed before her trembling subsided. She was exhausted. She was hungry. She was terrified. Somewhere she found the strength and nodded.

They ate in silence watching the Bible show as Ann blinked back her tears, stopping herself from saying thank you to the man who'd kidnapped her. When they finished he cleaned up, then handcuffed her to the chair. They stared at the TV set, both of them imprisoned by their fate, watching a fiery minister from South Carolina scream about atonement.

"Will you"—Ann cleared her throat—"will you tell me how you know my husband and what he's got to do with this? Please?"

Engler was transfixed by the preacher and didn't answer.

"What did your friend mean by saying you colored my hair *her* color?"

He didn't answer.

"... if we say that we have no sin, we deceive ourselves. ..."

"Are you going to kill me?"

He didn't answer.

"How do you know my husband?" Ann's voice cracked. "Please, I'm begging you, answer me."

He didn't answer.

The screaming minister was now directing viewers to James, chapter 4.

"For what is your life? It is even a vapor that appears for a little time and then vanisheth away."

57

"Do you know John Mark Engler?" Wilson retrieved the scattered papers and records.

"I know him."

Reed leaned against the wire mesh of the storage stall staring at the dirt-smeared pages in his hand, not believing what he was reading.

Wilson sat next to him, examining the file.

John Mark Engler was born in 1966, in San Francisco, to an unwed teen who gave him up through a street ministry. Engler lived in several foster homes. At age sixteen he told a teacher his foster father, an alcoholic butcher, was abusing him. No one checked into it. Nothing was done.

One night, after sealing the doors and windows with wood screws, Engler set fire to his family home. Two other foster children, Engler's foster mother, and the butcher died in the blaze. Engler was arrested three months later working in an Oregon logging camp. His large stature enabled him to pass for a nineteen-year-old. Because of his claims of abuse, he was sentenced to twenty-one months in juvenile detention.

Four murder victims by age sixteen. Wilson shook her head.

After his release, Engler drifted and worked as dishwasher, cabdriver, construction worker, bartender, security guard, before becoming a drug addict, a drug dealer, an armed robber, and a murder suspect.

In Florida after stealing a car, Engler picked up Tyler Randall Vine, a twenty-two-year-old drifter hitchhiking outside of Miami. The pair consumed cocaine, then decided to rob the Stop N' Skip all-night convenience store.

The clerk, Harold Smith, a twenty-four-year-old med student who volunteered at a clinic, was visited on his job that night by his girlfriend, Anita Lee, also a med student majoring in research of terminal diseases in infants.

At 3:00 A.M., Vine entered the Stop N' Skip, pointed a semiautomatic pistol at Smith, and demanded cash. Smith shielded Lee and complied. Vine shot Smith in the head; then Engler entered and they took Lee hostage. It took five days before Broward County searchers, acting on a tip from a local "who mighta seen somethin' out there," found her body in the swamp, less than fifty feet from the westbound lane of Everglades Parkway, known locally as Alligator Alley.

Six weeks later, Kansas City PD picked up Vine. He was extradited to Florida, where he confessed to shooting Smith but swore to Jesus it was Engler who murdered Lee. Vine was charged with first-degree murder while the FBI issued a warrant for Engler.

Two months to the day after grappling hooks snagged the belt loops of Lee's shorts in the Everglades, Engler was taken down by a SWAT team in Shaker Heights, Ohio, where he was hiding in the toolshed of a retired funeral director who'd called police about a suspicious noise in his backyard.

Handcuffed in the back row of the Miami-bound jet, Engler told detectives escorting him that Vine had done the killing. What Engler didn't know was that Smith had survived his wound and had identified Vine as his shooter. While Smith failed to identify Engler, he said a second man had entered the store after he was shot. A foot impression in Smith's blood matched Engler's shoes and put him at the crime scene. Broward detectives charged Engler with first-degree. Both men were convicted and sentenced to die by electrocution in Florida State Prison's Death House in Starke.

Vine worked the appeal process, never once wavering from his account that he didn't murder anyone. So did Engler, who researched the law with unprecedented intensity, using every avenue afforded a condemned inmate.

But Vine accepted his fate when guards took him to the ready cell for the final three days of his life. He apologized to the families of Smith and Lee for the tragedy. Yet he maintained, as the hours ticked down, that he was innocent of killing anyone. Even after his head and leg were shaved for effective electrical contact, Vine upheld his innocence. Despite the encouragement of two spiritual advisers to unburden his conscience and prepare for everlasting peace, Vine was resolute, right up until the moment he was strapped into the chair.

In the seconds before two thousand volts of electricity were discharged into his body, Vine shouted: "Engler murdered Anita! I saw him! It wasn't me!" His cries were seared in the hearts of the witnesses, forever haunting some of them as the final words they'd hear on nights when sleep wouldn't come.

Two days after Vine's execution, Engler was moved to the ready cell. In Engler's version, *he* was the innocent victim. Vine confessed to shooting Smith because Smith identified him, but Vine wanted Engler to die with him. Engler maintained that Vine was a stranger he'd picked up and tried to help, that he'd pulled up to the Stop N' Skip at Vine's request to buy a snack. Engler said he ran in to help upon hearing gunfire to see Vine forcing Lee to the car at gunpoint. Vine ordered Engler to drive across the

Everglades, ignoring his plea to let Lee go. Engler was scared for his life and complied with Vine.

Engler made his case in an eleventh-hour petition for writ of habeas corpus to the district court. On the afternoon before his scheduled execution, the high court granted Engler's motion, saying that no weapon had been found, meaning the state had only circumstantial evidence against Engler, nothing strong enough to secure guilt beyond a reasonable doubt.

The court acquitted Engler. He walked from death row a free man.

"Jesus, Tom, that's an incredible story. What happened?" Wilson flipped through the pages.

"Engler's public defenders managed to get the other states to sign off on Engler's lesser crimes for time served in Florida. Engler worked his way back to California, went to college, started a small garage business, got married. Years rolled by. I never knew Engler existed."

"How did you get on to him?"

"One day out of the blue I got a call from a source who'd suggested I call the Broward County Sheriff's office in Florida and ask about this old Vine and Engler case. Specifically for any updates."

"What happened?"

"They'd found the gun used to shoot Harold Smith and his girlfriend, Anita Lee."

"Who found it?"

"Some environmental group doing work in the swamp near where they found Lee's body."

"Did it help? In that condition, after all those years?"

"They set their best lab and ballistics people on it. Vine had said Lee struggled with Engler while getting out of the car. He'd banged his gun hand and bled. Angered, he slapped Lee, then asked Vine for another clip, 'to make sure he had enough bullets for her.' The trace blood on the gun and the clip matched Engler's type and they managed DNA and other physical evidence. It supported Vine's account, that Engler shot Lee.''

''So what did you do?''

''As I remember it now, the call came when I was starting work on the murder mystery series. Word got out on the police grapevine that this Bay Area guy had gotten away with a murder in Florida.''

''All good timing.''

''Yeah, I got all the case files I could, made a lot of calls, learned prosecutors in Florida were looking into laying new charges without getting hampered by the double jeopardy clause. They were working a new angle. The last word I'd had was that the case against Engler wasn't strong enough given the time elapsed and that Vine, the only other witness, was dead and couldn't be cross-examined. But I still had a good murder mystery.''

''Big time. How could you forget this case?''

''I don't know, Molly. Maybe I wanted to. I didn't like Engler. Got a bad read off of him.''

''What happened? How did you meet?''

''He was living in San Francisco. I visited him, interviewed him several times. At first he brushed off the gun as sour grapes by police. He claimed it was planted by vindictive cops. Then he got very hostile, warned me not to run the story. Threatened me.''

''We all get that.''

''Exactly, so it wasn't a big deal. I just thought the guy was a prick.''

''Then what?''

''I interviewed his wife. I remember I felt sorry for her. She seemed nice. I could tell by her reaction that she knew nothing, absolutely nothing, about the man she'd married. It was like the real Engler never existed.''

''Must've been a shock.''

''She turned white as a sheet. *That* I remember. Right before my eyes.''

''He must've gone nuts.''

"He came to the newsroom to confront me. Then he got a lawyer. Threatened to sue if we ran the story. There was nothing he could do. We had the facts. It was all true. A murder mystery. We lined the story, I never heard from him. A few weeks later, I tried to call him. His phone had been disconnected. He just vanished."

"That's it?"

"No. About a year went by. I'd forgotten all about him. Then I got a call from Hal Forester."

"The *Star*'s court reporter? He retired when I came to the paper."

"Right. Hal said I might be interested in the case of a man charged in several armed robberies and drug deals by the name of John Mark Engler."

"You go down?"

"I did. To see if Engler would go for an interview."

"And?"

"In court we exchanged glances; then he went cold on me. He crumpled the notes I passed to his lawyer. He got six years." Reed checked the file. "Six years in Folsom."

"Driscoll went to Folsom, probably met Engler there. We got to get this to Sydowski fast. See if Engler's the guy who took Ann." Wilson stood. "I hope to hell it's not him but if it is, it's a lead, Tom. Let's go."

Reed hadn't moved. He was staring at Engler's picture.

"Tom? What is it? Is there something else about Engler's case?"

"A few weeks after he was processed, Engler called me from Folsom, had his lawyer patch the call to the newsroom."

"To say what? Agree to an interview?"

"Molly, we all get crazy calls all the time, right?" Reed swallowed, his eyes stung. "Threats. Like we said, comes with the territory, right?"

"Tom, what did Engler say to you?"

Reed removed his glasses and rubbed his eyes.

"Who thinks anything will come of these things? I mean

I truly believed Engler was a two-time loser who probably did kill that clerk in Florida and was going to Folsom for six years—"

"Tom."

"I've had bikers, drug dealers, killers, threaten me, say things to me, drive by my house. I mean you cover crime, people rise from the sewer and say things—"

"Tom."

Reed's body quaked as the presses rumbled.

"Engler said that one day, when I least expected it, fate would see to it that I felt his pain for what I did to him."

58

In the suffocating night heat of the Moonlit Dreams Motor Inn, Engler ignored Ann's questions until she gave up.

She stared at the cracked walls, the cheap oil painting of a palm-lined beach cove in the moonlight. Engler opened another beer, engrossed by the minister raving on the television.

"—and there shall be no more death, neither sorrow nor crying, neither shall there be any more pain." The minister waved the Good Book around.

Engler raised his sweating can to the screen saying: "Hallelujah, Reverend. I hear destiny calling."

He took a long swallow, switched off the set, and stood before Ann for the longest time, taking inventory of every inch of her from head to toe and back again. Not in the ravenous way Tribe had feasted on her, but with the look people get when they think about something they had loved and lost.

"You still don't understand, Ann, do you?"

She shook her head.

"You don't understand who I am or what I am?"

"No."

"I told you some people make mistakes in life, remember?"

"Yes."

"And some people *are* life's mistakes."

"I don't know what you mean."

"My mother was a seventeen-year-old prostitute. My father was a twenty-dollar trick. I'm the result she dumped nine months later, like something she'd leave in a toilet. I was never meant to be in this world."

Ann looked away blinking. *He's crazy.*

"I was abused in every foster home I was sent to. By the adults and the older kids. Until the last home. Fate intervened and burned it to the ground when I turned sixteen. Then I was on my own. Unleashed myself on America."

Engler walked around Ann.

"I traveled. Had my scrapes with the law. The state of Florida did everything, *every damned thing* within its mighty power to kill me for something I never did. I was twenty hours from being executed when destiny plucked me from the jaws of death and set me free." Engler drank some beer. "I built a new life for myself."

At that moment, the first tiny drop of knowledge fell on Ann. *He'd walked off death row.* Fear and fatigue clouded her memory, but within its deepest corners, she was certain she recalled Tom having once written about a man who'd beaten his death sentence at the final moment.

"How do you know my husband? Did he write about you?"

He froze, glaring at her for several moments.

"*Your husband* hunted me down to question me about the past."

Ann swallowed.

"*Your husband* said he had information about my long-forgotten brushes with the law in Florida. I answered his questions, then begged him to leave me *and my wife* alone."

She was starting to remember.

"*Your husband* refused to let up. Pounded his chest about freedom of the press. Said he had the *facts* and was going to write the *truth* about me."

Tears rolled down Ann's face. It was all coming back.

"Do you know what your husband did? He waited until I wasn't around and ambushed my wife, showed her selected records, told her about the *facts* of my past and asked what she thought of the man she'd married."

Ann remembered how Tom never talked about the story.

"I tried to explain the truth to my wife but he'd done too much damage. I called a lawyer to beg your husband and his newspaper to stop his story. They ignored me."

It was so long ago, but Ann remembered how Tom was bothered by it. Wanted to forget about it.

"They put the story on the front page with our pictures splashed all over it. A long article mixed with facts and police lies. Other reporters found us."

Ann had a vague memory of the story flaring, then fading. Then a long period of nothing on it until Tom got a call about a court case.

"Your husband's story destroyed the new life I'd built. My auto shop business collapsed. Debts mounted. People turned on me. I turned to drugs, I robbed banks. And I was sent back to prison. Folsom."

Engler stared at the moon and palm trees in the sun-faded picture.

"Do you know what that does to a man? I'd survived a wrongful conviction on death row. But twenty hours from execution, I'd triumphed and walked away. I went to school. I started my own business. Got married. Then your husband decides he'll write a story in a newspaper that costs twenty-five cents before people wrap fish in it, or let their pets crap on it."

He turned and faced Ann.

"Have you begun to understand?"

Ann nodded.

"Every minute of every hour of every day inside, I thought

of your husband. Of what he did. Of what he took from me.'' Engler studied his beer can. ''At first I thought I would look for him when I got out. I plotted it, planned it, fantasized about what I'd do, and savored it. It kept me going for nearly four years. But one day, I figured, naw, John, the asshole ain't worth it, that's what I told the prison psychiatrist.

''The shrink said I had deeply rooted vengeance issues.'' Engler's eyes twitched. ''Imagine that, I told him. But I decided, I'll just let it all go. And when I'd done my time, I'd get a stake to build a new life in a place where people can't ever find me.'' Engler swallowed the remainder of his beer.

''But there's one thing, I told the shrink, if fate ever deemed it necessary for Tom Reed's path to cross with mine, then I'll make certain he atones.'' Engler looked upon Ann. *''And here we are.''*

She blinked away her tears.

''Please, I'm begging you, please just let me go.''

''You still don't understand.'' Engler repositioned the coffee table, sat on it so he could lean closer to her. ''A few days after the story appeared, I came home from another useless meeting with my lawyer. I wanted to talk to my wife about moving away. But I couldn't find her in the house. I went to my garage. I saw her, standing there in the upper loft. I thought it was funny, she never went up there. I called to her. She wouldn't answer. It was too quiet.

''I went up the stairs. My eyes had to adjust to the way the sun came through the gaps of the wooden frame. I saw her standing there with her head down. 'Babe,' I said, 'we can pull out and start over somewhere else.' But she didn't answer. Then I saw the rope. Taut to the beam, creaking as she swayed, the toes of her bare feet brushing the floor. A copy of the newspaper splayed out under her. The one with your husband's article.''

Ann looked at the floor. She didn't know.

''I can still hear it, that rope creaking, knocking—the

sound of my world ending.'' Engler pulled his face within an inch of Ann's.

"She was three months pregnant."

Ann shut her eyes.

"Now do you understand?" Engler's eyes became disturbingly tender as he stroked Ann's dyed hair and smiled.

"He took my wife; now fate has given me his. *You're mine now.*"

Engler's eyes grew wide as he pressed duct tape over Ann's mouth before she could scream.

59

Delmar Tribe devoured his chicken dinner while marching aimlessly from the motel across vast fields lit by the stars.

Rage and adrenaline throbbed through his body from fighting with Engler. Sweat and grease put a sheen on his skin and goatee, creating the aura of something dangerous. Something hunting in the night.

Gnawing the last bones clean of meat, he shot a glance over his shoulder at the motel, now tiny on the horizon as he moved farther away. He had been achingly close to having her until Engler ruined the moment. That sick puppy was probably in there with her right now. Man, who could resist a woman like that? It was a wonder either of them had lasted this long. Tribe spat. *Hell. It don't matter.* One way or another he would have his turn. Then he would kill her, which they should've done the first night.

Tribe squinted at the grove of trees about three hundred yards ahead. A series of outbuildings and tents, a large campfire, a couple dozen cars, vans, pickups. Sounded like singing. Tribe tossed his trash aside, popped open one of his beers, downed half, then released a thunderous belch.

He stopped. Undid his zipper and urinated while assessing the encampment. Might as well check it out. He had time and no fear of being left behind. Engler had dropped the truck's keys when they fought in the motel. They were now in Tribe's pocket. He belched again and moved on.

In the darkness, no one at the Heavenly Inspiration Girls Bible Camp saw Tribe lurking at the edge. He was invisible standing beyond the firelight finishing yet another beer.

Girls who looked to be twelve to late teens were ringed around the blaze singing under the stars. Maybe thirty of them, Tribe figured. He scanned the herd. All female. Not a man in sight. Praise the Lord.

The singing stopped, pages with lyrics flapped; then the singing resumed with an old folk song. Tribe heard "If I had a hammer . . ." before his nostrils flared at the sight of a loner. Looked like a leader. Off by herself near a tent that the light barely reached. Looked like she was sewing something.

He began moving in her direction, careful to stay in the darkness. He crept up to within ten yards of her without making a sound.

She was in her late twenties. Tanned. Brunette. Kinda pretty. Good shape. Sewing a button, or something. Alone near a tent behind a car. Perfect. She would do.

Tribe moved like a cat behind her. Six yards, four, three, two. In a heartbeat his powerful hand cupped her mouth and nose. She kicked at the air but she was light and the singing was loud. He liked how she smelled, sweet like flowers, as he forced her into the empty tent and onto her back. He pressed down with his full weight and strength. Her eyes bulged, nearly popping from their sockets, her chest was heaving.

"Don't make a sound and you'll live," Tribe whispered in her ear. "Okay?"

She nodded.

Tribe moved his hand to undo her jeans but in an instant she shifted and he was the one screaming, for in the darkness he'd failed to see she'd been gripping small scissors which she'd plunged into his face, paralyzing every fiber of his body with electrifying pain.

The woman fled from the tent screeching warnings to the others.

The handles stuck out from Tribe's skull two inches under his left eye, the blades piercing his face, embedding in his upper gum until they ground against the roots of his upper left teeth.

Tribe staggered from the tent toward the fire, growling. Blood gushed from his face as he clawed at the scissors. Touching them magnified his pain. Gripping his head, Tribe found his bearings for the motel. Before anyone knew what had happened or which way he went, Tribe disappeared back into the darkness.

In the chaos of the camp, orders were shouted as the singing turned into a chorus of panicked shrieking. "Stranger! Attacker! Get the girls in the cars now!" Doors slammed, locks locked, horns sounded, engines were started. "Get the sheriff! Betty's got a cell phone. Marge's got a CB!"

60

Tribe lurched into the motel room, his shirt crimson, his face a horrible mask with the small scissors still protruding.

Engler, who'd consumed a few cans of beer, started to laugh. "You idiot, this a joke?"

Ann's screams were muffled by the duct tape.

Tribe struggled to speak, shoving his slurred words painfully through his clenched teeth. "She stabbed me. Christ almighty, you got to help me, John!" Tribe scrambled to collect things while holding his face.

"What the hell are you talking about, Del? What're you doing?"

"The camp behind us." Tribe thrust his hand into his pocket, tossing the keys to Engler. "Goddammit! It hurts. John, I went to the camp, the bitch stabbed me. Oh Jesus! Get something from the truck! God, it hurts!"

Engler rushed outside to the back of the motel. Several hundred yards across the fields he saw headlights going in every direction, heard the echo of honking horns, revving engines, faint shrieking. What had transpired was crystal clear: Tribe had gone hunting for a woman.

"Did anyone see you or follow you back here?" Engler gathered things, thinking quickly while Tribe moaned on the bed.

"I don't know. It was fast. Christ, John, help me now. It hurts!"

"You'll live. We've got to go."

"John, help me."

"Hang on."

Engler loaded the SUV while Tribe groaned.

"Jesus, please, John, do something now, goddammit!" Tribe slurred, spraying blood-laced spittle.

On alert for sirens or flashing lights, Engler got the small bottle of whiskey he'd kept hidden with the jack in the truck. He also got a pair of pliers, a screwdriver, and a small first-aid kit from Carrie Addison's bag.

"Lie down on the floor and let me help you now, or sure as hell you're gonna die, because I should leave you here."

Ann's attention went to the motel door. It was unlocked. She was handcuffed to the heavy wooden chair. Neither of them was watching her. If she stood she could work her way to the door. . .

Engler had taken CPR and emergency medical courses inside Folsom. He wasn't sure what to do, but reasoned he should do something right now, right here to tend to Tribe's wound. If it was wrong, or it hurt him, too bad. He brought this on himself.

"Here." Engler gave Tribe the whiskey after he was on the floor. "Take a big drink," he said, tearing the bedsheet into strips. "Hurry up! Drink. Now bite down on the screwdriver. Hard."

Engler got on his knees, poured some of the whiskey on the point where the scissors pierced Tribe's face, the pain arched his back. "They're small scissors. It's not that bad. Hold still and don't you dare scream."

The activity made the door open a crack. Ann stood and shifted the chair two feet.

Engler clamped the pliers on the handles, his muscles

glistening as slowly he extracted the scissors in a small eruption of blood, skin, and tissue. Tribe's teeth nearly bent the screwdriver, his body writhed, his throat warbled in a guttural hum. Engler splashed whiskey into the wound. It was a small hole, not a tear. No stitches. Not too bad.

"Hold still, damn it." Engler put a square bandage on it, gave Tribe a cotton ball to tuck between his cheek and gum, then tied a bedsheet strip around Tribe's head to keep pressure on it. He looked like a soldier wounded in a Civil War battle.

By now Ann had moved closer to the door. If she could smash the chair against something it might break. She could run.

Engler finished working on Tribe's face, passing him the rest of the bottle. Ann stood just as Engler pointed his handgun at her and pulled back the hammer.

"We've killed three people already. Four won't matter now."

Tribe climbed into the rear end of the truck and moaned. Engler handcuffed Ann in the SUV's seat directly behind the front passenger seat, just as before. Her right wrist to the handgrip under the window. Her right ankle to the bottom frame of the front passenger seat.

They sped away into the night.

In the rearview mirror, Engler saw one police car, its lights flashing as it turned down the dirt road that led to the encampment behind the motel. If they were lucky there'd be few cars on shift at this hour. It would take time to rouse more deputies. If they were lucky. Engler eyed the rearview mirror and drove the speed limit before he began pounding his fist on the dash.

"You stupid stupid stupid goddamn idiot!"

"Fuck you!" Tribe groaned from the rear, his pain driving his rage. "If you'd just let me have my way with her none of this would've happened."

Ann gazed into the darkness.

"Shut up!" Engler screamed. "Shut the fuck up!"

"No witnesses. Remember? No goddamn witnesses! What's that I see sitting behind you? A witness? Or your little fantasy wife?"

"Keep talking." Engler's eyes blazed in the rearview mirror.

"You got some sick freaky shit happening in your head, John. Sick."

Ann worked the duct tape off her mouth to breathe just as a second police car went by them in the opposite direction. She was beyond praying, beyond hoping. She was trapped in a nightmare. If Engler and Tribe didn't kill each other first, one of them would kill her.

She had to escape. Or die trying.

61

Kimberly Sue Garner's wedding diamond sparkled as she twined and untwined her fingers under the dome light of the Carter County Sheriff's Department's car.

"I think he would've killed me." Deputy Josh Throll nodded and passed her a fresh tissue. "I never stabbed anyone in my life, he just grabbed me and told me to keep quiet if I wanted to live."

Throll reviewed the notes he took during his twenty-minute interview with Garner. She was a twenty-eight-year-old Sunday school teacher from Lone Grove. According to her, a white male had grabbed her from behind, forced her into the tent where he attempted to sexually assault her before she plunged her small blue-handled sewing scissors into his face. The pair her aunt Bell with the bad arthritis had given her. That was all Garner could tell Throll. Thirty-one witnesses, most of them young girls, saw the suspect flee into the night. No one was certain which direction, or had a usable description.

But Throll was undaunted.

He had put in eleven years with the St. Louis Police

Department, the last four as a homicide detective, before honoring his ailing mother's wish and returning to Ardmore, Oklahoma, and the farm where he was raised. He touched Garner's hands to assure her. "Kimberly Sue, I want you to think. Are there any more details you can remember, anything, no matter how trivial? It might help."

"He stunk. Like beer and BO."

Throll noted it.

"Did you call my husband at the tire plant?"

"He's on his way," Throll said, thanking Garner for her help. "I think we're done for now. Please wait here. Joleen, the counselor from the county services, is on her way to talk to you, tell you what we need."

Garner nodded, twisted her ring, and stared into the night. Throll's flashing police lights lit up the encampment, along with those of the other cars that had responded.

An Oklahoma Highway Patrol trooper had been first on the scene, followed by a night-shift officer from Healdton PD who'd caught wind of the call and came to assist. Two other Carter County deputies were stretching yellow crime scene tape around the tent. The Oklahoma State Bureau of Investigation had paged on-call forensic agents.

Throll's skills as an investigator were respected by the younger lawmen. When they saw he'd finished with the victim and was searching the ground with his flashlight at the edge of the camp, they approached him.

"What's your read, Josh?"

"Stop where you are, guys." Throll's request halted them. "Did any of the girls here, or any witnesses, say they saw our guy drive off?"

"Nothing like that, Josh."

"I think he came on foot." Throll's flashlight lit on a beer can. "I don't expect that belongs to anyone at this Bible camp."

"Hey, that's a lead," one of them said.

"Chester, seal this spot. Get your car-wreck camera and

take pictures of the can. I want OSBI to see if they can print that. And call Fred Reems again to get his dog out here."

"Josh, where're you headed?" one of the officers called.

"The motel. Bobby, come with me. Hang back a bit, watch my rear in case he's out there. You other boys stay put. Protect the scene."

Moonlit Dreams was a ramshackle fleabag motel situated off a quiet stretch of State Road 76 between Healdton and Fox. Seeing as there was not much else nearby, it seemed a logical place to start looking. Throll made a direct line to it while raking his flashlight across the rolling oil-rich plain. After a short distance, he'd realized something and reached for his radio.

"Chester, can you drive round to the motel, and grab every plate there, ask the night clerk for all registration information?"

"Ten-four, Josh."

Throll stopped, so did Bobby, who was fifteen yards behind him also sweeping the field with his flashlight. Throll watched the camp as he talked on his radio. "Chester, be quiet about it. No lights or sirens. Try not to let anyone leave the motel."

"Ten-four."

Satisfied upon seeing a sheriff's car leave the camp for the road to the motel, Throll, with Bobby behind him, resumed his trek. He searched for several more minutes, until his light picked up something that looked like trash.

What's this? Looks fresh. Take-out food box, fry tray, slaw tub, lid, foil wrapping. A grease-stained brown bag from Red-Jack BBQ, that chicken place down the road. He pulled out his pen, prodded the bag until he saw gold. A computerized receipt from Red-Jack with the date and purchase time.

"Doreen?" Throll said into his radio to his dispatcher.

"Go ahead, Josh."

"Get the night manager at Red-Jack BBQ to call me now on my cell."

"Sure, Josh."

"Hey, everything all right?" Bobby called.

"Just marking this trash for OSBI."

Throll looked around until he found a couple of sticks. He shoved them in the ground, a yard from the bag and box, a crude evidence marker. Then he continued to the motel when his cell trilled and the keyboard lit up.

"Throll."

"Hi, Deputy. Steve Suther at Red-Jack. We're just locking up. Is there a problem?"

"I need your help."

"Certainly."

"Your security camera's working okay, still recording?"

"Yes."

"Would you and your staff volunteer to stay late so I can view your tape from tonight with you, maybe talk to them about customers?"

"Sure. Can you say what this is about?"

"I'll tell you later. Be there in about thirty minutes, Steve. Now don't touch your security camera. It's very important. Please."

"I understand, Deputy."

Throll stopped walking. He found a second beer can.

"He stunk. Like beer and BO."

Several minutes later, Throll and Bobby arrived at Moonlit Dreams. They were greeted by Chester and the night clerk, a pimply-faced metal head wearing a black T-shirt, black jeans, and a black vest.

"Josh, Jason here says he only rented two rooms tonight."

Throll's eyes spotted the keys clipped to Jason's Indian beaded belt. "You got the key to the rooms?"

Jason jingled the set.

Throll took the keys, waving Jason a safe distance aside. He sent a deputy to the rear while he and Bobby drew their guns. They started with number 6 and knocked.

No response. No sounds.

They unlocked the door and entered the empty unit.

"Don't move," Throll said to Chester after switching on the light and spotting Kimberly Sue Garner's blue sewing scissors in the pool of blood on the floor.

"Chester, Bobby, we've got to seal this room."

"Right."

"And get Doreen to call in the FBI. Chester, I got to borrow your car."

"Sure, where you going, Josh?"

"To Red-Jack's."

62

After the case status meeting at the Hall of Justice, the homicide detail's secretary rapped on the lieutenant's open door. "Urgent call from Detective Gutteres in San Bernardino, Leo."

Gonzales caught Turgeon and Sydowski armed with files and departing. "Linda, Walt. Wait. It's Gutteres. Can one of you take it?"

"Send it to me," Turgeon said.

"What is it?" Sydowski said.

"Said it was urgent," the secretary said. "Also got Tom Reed out front for you, Walt."

"Reed? We were on our way to see him." Sydowski set his files down.

On the phone, Turgeon said, "Say that again"; then staying on the line she waved Sydowski to see her notes. "Hang on, Marv. I got Walt here. San Bernardino's got a shell casing with a new print. You won't believe this."

"Could you tell Reed I'll be a minute?" Sydowski asked the secretary.

Turgeon went back on the phone. "The BATF and the

FBI are helping out on the new stuff right now. Marv says a kid taking pump readings at a truck stop near Barstow saw a shell casing fall from an SUV a few days ago.''

''A few days ago?''

Turgeon ping-ponged between Sydowski and Gutteres on the phone.

''Marv says the kid got sick, then forgot about it until all the news got out. Turns out the kid had picked up the casing, put it in his pocket; and *get this*, he noted the plate on his clipboard.'' Turgeon nodded big nods. ''The kid said two big white men. No female.''

''Maybe she was concealed,'' Sydowski said. Or dumped.

''What's that, Marv? They paid cash. That's all he can remember. The time from the kid's pump records would be consistent with a vehicle en route to Baker and Death Valley. The tag matches the VIN of our burned-out desert car.''

''What about the casing?'' Sydowski said.

''Marv says BATF says the caliber matches the casings from the jewelry store. They're running the latent and going through the truck stop's security tapes for the time period. Not much there. Ball cap. Big glasses, long sleeves.''

''They're smart.'' Sydowski nodded, hoping against the odds that the new print was distinct from Tribe's. That would give them hope on both suspects.

''Reed's here, Linda, I'll talk to him. You keep working with Marv and let Leo know what's up.''

Reed's eyes were bloodshot. He hadn't shaved. It broke Sydowski's heart, knowing what he was going to tell him.

''Tom, we were coming to see you.'' Sydowski noticed Reed had a file bulging with papers and cassette tapes under his arm.

''I can identify one of them, Walt.''

Sydowski wondered how Reed could seriously identify anyone in his condition.

"Tom, we've identified one too and we're going to hold a news conference. We'll talk in the interview room."

Reed sat at the table.

"Are you okay?" Sydowski closed the door. "Getting any sleep?"

"Walt, I've been on the street chasing stuff down."

"You've got to leave that to us. We talked about this."

"No one will stop me from searching for her."

"We've got a break, but brace yourself."

"Did you find her?"

"No. We got a positive ID on one of the suspects."

"Engler. John Engler, is it him?" Reed patted his files.

"Who?"

"John Mark Engler. I did a story on him. It's all in here. Is he your guy?"

Puzzled, Sydowski glanced at Reed's file folder, then his.

"No, we've identified Delmar James Tribe, an ex-con from Folsom."

"Delmar Tribe? Never heard of him. But Engler went to Folsom." Reed slid his file to Sydowski, telling him everything as he read.

Turgeon entered.

"Linda, call Marv." Sydowski passed a few pages from Reed's file to her. "Tell them to compare their latent from the truck stop immediately against John Mark Engler, if it's not Tribe's." He tapped the page. "There's Engler's DOB, his CDC number, NCIC and LEADS numbers. Tom's got it all right here."

"Sure, with those specifics it won't take long. Be right back."

"And these cassettes, Tom?" Sydowski turned over three standard cassette recording tapes, each with sixty minutes of HF normal bias recording time.

"Tapes of my interviews with Engler. They were in storage with tons of old stuff. I'm not very organized but I never throw anything away. I've listened to them again. I think he's on the 911 tape you gave me."

Sydowski left and returned with a cassette player to run a minute or so of Reed's tape, then the 911 recording. "We'll have to pass it to an examiner," he said. "See if they can get a positive or probable voice identification."

Turgeon returned. Holding up a slip of paper. "Bingo. Direct hit. The print matches. John Mark Engler."

"Alert Leo, we're going to need a warrant for him," Sydowski said, "and we'll get the FBI to help us get both Tribe *and* Engler blasted out there together on the news ASAP. In a few hours everyone in the country will be looking for these two. Tom, this is a break. Tom?"

The smiles melted on Sydowski's and Turgeon's faces.

Reed was lost in Sydowski's file of Delmar James Tribe on a passage he'd found from a psychiatric report.

Tribe has either raped, or tried to rape, every woman he's had any substantial contact with. In many instances he hunted for victims and attempted to kill them afterward. We may never know how many times he's succeeded. . . .

Reed was wrenched back to the grave site at Death Valley. He didn't feel Turgeon's hand on his shoulder. "Tom? Tom?" He felt the hellfire heat of the desert engulfing him, burning him alive. "Walt, we should call the paramedics. Tom?" The headless, handless corpse being lifted from the shallow grave.

"Tom?"

Why did he write about Engler? Why did he write about crime and dark things? He'd been warned.

"Be careful . . . don't get too close to your subject. . . ."
Reed's darkness had manifested itself in the shape of two. Engler and Tribe.

They had taken Ann.

How could any sane person hope she was alive?

63

Tia Layne took a hit of coffee from her oversized take-out cup. She drummed her polished nails on the wheel of *Worldwide*'s rented SUV, parked near the Hall of Justice. Her concentration never left the door where she expected Tom Reed to exit.

"Something huge is popping in there, Cooter. Huge! Can't you feel it?"

Cooter was sleeping with his head pressed against the passenger window. Layne patted his knee. "You rest there, hon. You've earned it. It's been hard work but it's going to pay off. We're so close now I can smell the money."

It was Cooter's brilliant idea to hire a private investigator to report Reed's movements. The PI's late-night call had alerted them to Reed's secret trip to Oakland where they'd struck gold with Angela, girlfriend of ex-cop Donnie Ray Ball, a convicted bank robber and Folsom inmate.

This story kept getting better. Layne pulled out her cell phone. She pushed her speed-dial button for her editor in New York. Waiting for a connection, she reflected on their recent work.

In Oakland, the PI, an "ex-federal agent" who kept a fat cigar clamped in the corner of his mouth, lent Cooter his parabolic microphone and night-vision video gear, "top-of-the-line, no blooming or whiteouts." It was fantastic. They saw, heard, and recorded everything. Until Reed spotted them.

They went back to the office, sent their uncut pictures off. The PI was good. In a few hours he would hand-deliver to Layne all the criminal files, photographs, news stories, and available photos that would help Layne tell the story of Reed's link to the fugitive killers and his quest to find his wife. The total cost to Layne: five thousand bucks.

But her reward . . .

Sure, it might be measured in six figures, but how to measure the triumph of a woman who, after a lifetime of being made to feel inferior to others, proves her worth to the entire damned world?

And soon her money would be in the bank.

Come on Seth, answer. They had exclusive grainy dramatic night pictures from Oakland, Reed entering the *Star* at night, then rushing to the police. It was engrossing stuff.

"Seth here."

"Tia in San Francisco."

"London wants to know the latest in California."

"We've just about got this nailed."

"London's excited about the night footage. Thanks for rushing it to us. Legal is going through everything. The surreptitious recording, your controversial tie to this case over the previous incident. Indications are we should be clear on most of it, depending on how we present it."

"Yeah, yeah. Routine ass covering. What's the real status, Seth?"

"Still no charges."

"And?"

"London loves what you've got."

"But?"

"They said all that's required is an exclusive clip of Reed

talking about his one-man pursuit. That would guarantee you're the top story and bump the current piece, Hollywood addictions and infidelities. You'd be the *Worldwide* exclusive; 'the story behind the story that has gripped America.' Can you get Reed to talk about it on camera, Tia?''

''For how long? He won't do a sit-down.''

''Longer is better, but even a few dramatic emotional seconds. Ambush him. Coldcock him on a public street. Do whatever it takes. We can stretch a few words, slow-mo his image. You know. It would harmonize with the story's tone and our style.''

''How much?''

''One hundred.''

''Two.''

''We'll talk when you get something.''

''I know the numbers are hot for this story, Seth.''

''Tia, can you get what's needed?''

''Shit! There he is! Cooter! Wake up, baby!''

Reed exited the Hall of Justice.

Layne dropped her phone, spilled her coffee as she shook Cooter. He growled awake, grabbed the camera, microphone cords dragged on the sidewalk; Layne scrambled to catch Reed as they rushed to the stairs.

''Tom, please. Just a few words.''

As he recognized Layne, Reed's distress became disdain.

''Get away from me. I've got nothing to say to you.''

Reed walked fast down the street with Layne and Cooter in tow. No other press in sight.

''Tom, we know about your incident with the drug dealers, your meeting with Angela in Oakland—''

''It was *you* we saw. You're stalking me?'' Reed searched for a taxi.

''I'm a journalist on your story.''

''Give me a break. You're supposed to stay away from me. Back off.''

''This is a public street. Tom, you're a hero, doing what

you're doing, enduring the unimaginable, chasing down every lead on your own. A righteous one-man task force.''

"Get out of my face.''

"You must love Ann more than anything else in this world.''

Reed stopped, swallowed hard. Layne's words pierced his armor already weakened by exhaustion and trauma, steeped in guilt. His mouth moved to speak but as he walked, each step hammered his broken heart into smaller pieces, knowing what he now knew. Engler and Tribe. He was helpless.

"I'm no hero.'' Reed's eyes stung as he squinted into the sun. "My wife's the hero. I'll go anywhere, I'll do anything to find her. I've got to bring her home. *No matter what. Please just leave me alone now.''*

Reed spotted a taxi and trotted to it.

Layne stood there watching Cooter shoot everything.

They reviewed it on playback, confirming it was all there.

"I'm no hero. My wife's the hero. I'll go anywhere, I'll do anything to find her. I've got to bring her home. No matter what.''

Layne felt the corners of her mouth ascend into the beginnings of a victory grin.

64

In Albuquerque, New Mexico, Judy, the office manager for AJRayCo, was gossiping on the phone.

"If a girl with her mileage is woman enough to keep a thirty-one-year-old stallion like *that* interested, then I say, God bless."

Winn, the secretary at the city electrical department, which often contracted RayCo's electricians, giggled. "It's wild. Mack and I saw them at the Well last night, carrying on and all. Mack says, 'That her son?'"

"You're not serious?"

"I am."

"Lordy, Lordy." Judy was filing her nails staring at the portable TV at the corner of her desk. Her daytime soap was muted. "Boring today. Why don't they move the stories along? That star's been on her deathbed for months."

"So, the boys at your shop pull any pranks on you lately?"

"Not really." Judy reached for her tea. "Whatcha watching? Wait, let me guess."

"CNN. I'm a news junkie. They're doing something now on the woman who was abducted in that San Francisco jewelry store robbery. You know, where the police officer was murdered?''

"I thought they found her body in Arizona or California.''

"No, *that* woman used to work in the jewelry store. They found parts of her in each state, near Death Valley and near Winslow.''

"My God! That's awful! How do you know all this?''

"News addict, Judy. Oh, the news conference is coming on. Live.''

"What channel?'' Judy reached for her remote, surfing channels to see FBI, San Francisco police, and other officials at a table behind a mountain of microphones. Scores of news cameras were trained on them.

"Hey, Winn, that reminds me. Actually, the boys did try a new one on me a few days back. Something on this very case.''

"Really? Like what?''

"Made up a note that sounded like the kidnapped woman.''

"What? That's not even funny, Judy. You tell them that?''

"Nope. None of them owned up to it. I think it was Sparky, he's the sort who'd do it.''

"They really made up a note? It doesn't make sense.''

Judy wasn't paying attention to the news conference or what the police official was saying.

". . . we just want to update you on the investigation. Today we have confirmed the identities of the murder suspects who we believe are responsible for the homicides of San Francisco Police Officer Rod August, Leroy Driscoll, Carrie Dawn Addison, and the kidnapping of Ann Reed, during an armed robbery. Investigation confirms them as being . . .''

The camera pulled tight to the face of Delmar James Tribe and John Mark Engler. Now the two most wanted men in America.

"Look at the one guy, Judy, missing a chunk of his ear. He's frightening. What did the note say?''

"Oh, something like call the police, I've been kidnapped by two white men. It's still up on the board. Want me to fax it to you?"

"Would you? I'm curious. I mean that's just *not* funny."

Judy went to the corkboard, sifted through the untidy collection of tool sale flyers, safety codes, state regs, and insurance forms before she found the handwritten note. She fired it through the fax to Winn. It went fast.

"Did you get it, Winn?"

"Coming through now. They just said they think the men were both convicts who did time in Folsom. They're headed east. Here comes the fax. They said Winslow, Arizona, is the last place they have on them."

"Winslow? That's not too far from us." Judy studied her TV. A printed case summary filled the screen.

Suspects:

Delmar James Tribe and John Mark Engler.

Delmar and John.

In a distant region of Judy's stomach, a flicker of knowing began; it was a weak, desperate cry, welling into an anguished scream until she snatched the note from the fax tray. *Dear God.*

Winn at the other end of the line had read it. "My God, Judy, I don't think this is a joke."

Judy didn't hear her friend. She was staring at the TV, then reread the note, each word imploring her like the hand of someone drowning, someone flailing for their life, begging her to . . .

Please call the FBI now—

The TV showed another photo. A woman. Her pretty face smiling at Judy. Her name emblazoned under it. The words she had scrawled leaping at Judy from the note she held in her trembling hands . . .

Please call the FBI now. My name is Ann Reed, I was kidnapped by two men from the San Francisco Deluxe Jewelry Store armed robbery. I saw them shoot a police officer.

*We're going east. Men are named John and Del. Two white
males about six feet driving a . . .*

Judy reread the passages.

*We're going east . . . John Mark Engler and Delmar James
Tribe.*

John and Del.

"Judy? Are you there?"

Gooseflesh rose on her arms as she thought back to that
day, the electricians bringing her their work orders, job
sheets, invoices, time sheets, the note falling from the pile.
No one admitting it was a joke. Oh God. Could one of the
boys have picked it up on a job somewhere?

"Judy? Are you there?"

"Sweet Jesus, Winn, what have I done? What should I
do?"

"Call the FBI! Right now!"

"Yes."

"Right away!"

Judy's hands shook, she knocked her tea over, lifting
Ann's note in the nick of time from harm's way. Flustered,
she didn't know where to begin looking for the FBI's number
in the Albuquerque directory.

"Lord, help me."

Judy dialed 911.

65

In San Francisco, Reed watched the live broadcast of the latest news conference with Zach and Doris.

Every muscle in his body throbbed, his stomach was heaving uncontrollably, his ears pulsed; he slipped into a surreal state as he studied John Mark Engler. The task force had obtained recent photos. Over time his face had hardened, his eyes were colder.

Like looking into hell.

For Reed had devoted himself to pursuing monsters. Exposing them. Chronicling their sins, all the while believing they could never touch him. How could they? Truth was his shield and his sword. But he'd looked too long into the abyss without realizing it had also been looking into him.

"You will know my pain, Reed."

Engler. Destroyer of worlds.

The karmic wheel had turned full circle on Reed. His hopes for Ann were slipping, descending. Like a casket lowered into the grave. The press conference ended. Doris muted the TV.

"We just have to keep praying," she told Zach, then

touched Reed's shoulder. "Tom, you've barely slept in the last few days. Please rest."

Reed met her eyes. Ann's eyes.

"I'm sorry. So sorry." He heaved himself to his feet.

In their bedroom, Reed collapsed on the bed. He was sinking in a losing battle with something unseen; his soul roiling, screaming for his old friend Jack Daniel's to wash it all away, pulling Ann's pink robe to him, gripping it as he fell into an icy darkness, calling for Ann, searching for her, seeing her smiling face. *Oh, Ann.* Her voice. *Tom. I'm here.* Touching her skin. Breathing in her scent. Pulling her to him. *Tom.* Feeling her hand on his, touching him. It was so real. *Tom. Yes. I can wake up now. It was a nightmare. Tom. Ann, it was so damned real. I thought I'd lost you, I—Tom.*

"Tom. It's Turgeon. Wake up."

He blinked. How long had he been asleep?

Turgeon was holding out his glasses to him, allowing him to orient himself. Sydowski was with her. Reed sat up. The coldness coiled around Reed's heart, constricted. He braced himself. Prepared for the worst.

"We may have a break," Sydowski said. "We need your help."

"A break? Is she alive?"

Turgeon had a sheet of paper in her hand. "The FBI got this fax at the end of the news conference."

Reed heard more voices in his living room. More people were here.

"What is it?"

"Read it, Tom. We think it's from Ann."

Please call the FBI now. My name is Ann Reed, I was kidnapped by two men from the San Francisco Deluxe Jewelry Store armed robbery. I saw them shoot a police officer. We're going east. Men are named John and Del. Two white

males about six feet driving a red late-model SUV with Calif.
plate starting . . .

His spine tingled. It was Ann's handwriting. "I, where did you—"

"Is it Ann's, Tom?"

"Yes! Yes! Is she alive? Where did you get this?" He studied the back. Nothing. The front. It was a fax, 505 area code.

"New Mexico. Albuquerque," Sydowski said.

"Is she there? Give me a number. I want to talk to her now."

"Hold on," Sydowski said.

Reed searched round for his small bag, unpacked since returning from the desert. "I'm going there right now. Who do I see? Albuquerque FBI?"

"Tom, listen. No one has her."

Sydowski explained the tip and how they needed Reed to provide a sample of Ann's handwriting to compare with the note. "It came after the press conference," Sydowski said. "The FBI and Albuquerque PD traced it to a motel near the Rio Grande. Their people are all over it with help from every other agency that can assist."

"What do they know?"

Sydowski and Turgeon sat Reed down.

"As of a few days ago, it appears they were at a motel, the Sundowner Lodge in Albuquerque."

"Did they find anything to indicate—"

Turgeon was shaking her head. "All unfolding as we speak, Tom. Albuquerque's got forensics, dogs, they'll run phone tolls, check security cameras, gas stations, restaurants."

Reed ran his hands through his hair.

"It's a good break, Tom," Sydowski said before his cell phone rang. He answered, taking a few steps out of the room as Reed heard him say, "Oklahoma?"

Reed and Turgeon looked at each other.

"Walt, tell me what's going on?" Reed said.

"Hold on." Sydowski rushed to the living room, which had swelled with FBI agents and SFPD officers. McDaniel was on his cell phone writing notes, talking in whispers just as the home phone rang.

Reed looked at the detective monitoring his incoming calls. He nodded and Reed answered after the second ring.

"Yes?"

"Tom Reed?"

"Yes."

"Mr. Reed, this is Mike Sorros, I'm with *USA Today* in Dallas."

"Dallas." Something was happening, Reed searched for hints in the police faces near him.

"Mr. Reed, a source of mine in Oklahoma has confirmed that the suspects wanted in your wife's case were in a motel last night in Carter County, west of Ardmore in a rural area near Healdton."

"I don't know where that is."

"Roughly 120 miles north of Dallas, Texas."

"They *were* in Oklahoma last night?"

Reed glimpsed McDaniel, Sydowski, and the other detectives exchanging concern. They knew Reed's call was from a reporter with breaking information.

"Correct. My understanding is the Oklahoma State Bureau of Investigation and county investigators have confirmed it was Delmar Tribe and John Engler through fingerprints and possibly some security video."

"Is my wife with them? Do you know?"

"A man staying at the same motel stepped from his room to buy a soda late last night and said he saw two men leave in their vehicle, a red SUV with a California plate."

Reed squeezed the phone.

"The man, Jimmy Leverd of Fort Worth, said a woman was with them and my understanding from my source is that your wife's fingerprints were on a soda can in the motel room."

Reed closed his eyes. "You're certain about this?"

"I trust my source, Mr. Reed. I was calling for your reaction to this break in the case."

"You want to quote me for *USA Today* about the break in Oklahoma?" Reed looked at Sydowski and McDaniel, reading unease in the FBI agent's face that the press was learning information as fast as they were.

"It gives us more hope that we'll bring her home safely. We're less than twenty-four hours behind them now and we're gaining on them."

Reed did not hear Sorros ask his other questions. He stared at Zach and Doris, trying not to lose his composure.

Please, Ann. Hang on. Just hang on.

66

Angel Zelaya touched the thick cotton napkin to his lips after finishing his enchilada lunch at his favorite Mexican restaurant in southwest Houston.

Impeccably dressed in his copper suit, navy polo shirt, and glasses, Zelaya looked every inch the successful wholesale gem buyer. He was a soft spoken careful family man who attended Mass on Sundays. A father who enjoyed playing with his four children in the pool of his home in Lakewood Forest, a desirable Houston neighborhood.

What Zelaya never enjoyed, and had a personal rule against, was dealing with anyone from his past, that being the three hard years he did in Leavenworth for stealing and selling M16s to various Central American revolutionaries.

It was a lifetime ago.

So when Delmar Tribe first contacted him a few months back with the San Francisco offer, Zelaya rejected him outright. Later, after he took a call from Tribe's partner, John Engler, whom Zelaya thought more intelligent than Tribe, Zelaya was tempted. Engler said they had solid inside information on a jewelry store. The scale and quality of inventory was impressive. Zelaya considered it until he flew to San Francisco to personally assess the situation. He weighed the risks and his profit margin. He kept weighing them until he broke his rule: he agreed to do business with Tribe and Engler.

Zelaya would pay five hundred thousand cash for one million in retail. Extremely generous.

Zelaya had nearly doubled his network in South America. By having his tradesman recut, melt down, and recast, and with some substitution, Zelaya could turn his end into three, possibly three point five million. All for five hundred. The prospect prompted him to indicate to some of his trusted clients that he might soon be offering some very good numbers on new product. Very good numbers. It was risky but the bottom line was enticing, Zelaya thought, after paying for his meal and walking to the door, where he stopped cold.

Tribe's face was glowing from the big-screen TV behind the bar.

What the hell was this? Zelaya closed his eyes sadly, then took a stool at the far end of the near empty bar and ordered mineral water.

There they were. Tribe, Engler, the face of their hostage, pictures of their victims, a little map like connect-the-dots, from San Francisco, to Death Valley, to Winslow, Arizona, to Albuquerque, New Mexico, to Healdton, Oklahoma. Might as well light up Texas. Zelaya drank some of his water; then his dealer's cell phone vibrated.

"Yes?" His voice was barely above a whisper.

"We're local now. We're not far from the point. We're set."

These morons had beautiful timing. Zelaya said, "No."

"No? What do you mean, no?"

"I'm staring at your face. Is your middle name Mark?"

"What?"

"Did you call to tell me to tune in?"

"What?"

Zelaya ensured no one could overhear him. "You're live on CNN."

"Goddammit. It was Tribe. He messed up."

"I don't care. The deal's off."

"No. We've come this far. Wait. We'll move it up. We're very near."

"I'm sorry."

"We'll call you. *Angel, don't you hang up! Angel!*"

Zelaya ended the call, then consulted his Rolex. He had to see the owner of a store at a downtown shop. All legit. And boring. Then there was the church board meeting.

Walking to his gold Mercedes 450 SL in the lot, Zelaya rebuked himself for not adhering to his rule. This deal was dangerous. He should back away period. Still, the numbers were damned tempting. And he had everything in place with his network. If Engler or Tribe *did* call later, he could exercise leverage. Given the circumstances, he'd only close the project if he had a deep discount, say one hundred thousand. Greed is a sin, Zelaya reminded himself. Perhaps he'd give the church a sizable donation. He sighed as his gleaming car glided from the lot. He resumed listening to his Freddy Fender CD and pondered an evening swim with his children.

67

Ann Reed's sweating fingers tightened on the handgrip under the rear passenger window. Her right wrist was still handcuffed to the grip and her right ankle chained to the rear frame of the seat in front of her.

Engler had stopped along an empty stretch of a two-lane back road to make a call from a roadside pay phone. Tribe was lying in the far back bed of the SUV, sleeping off his wound and hangover.

They were in Texas.

After fleeing the motel, Engler had driven on dirt roads before pulling into a dense pine grove where they'd slept. At dawn they'd entered Texas. For much of the morning they'd meandered as if going in circles while keeping to rural roads. Ann had glimpsed signs indicating the distance to Dallas, Longview, or Tyler. They were somewhere in the eastern part of the state.

If felt like early afternoon. The heat was intense. Before going to the pay phone, Engler had switched off the engine and the air conditioner. Ann surveyed the area. Nothing but forests. She let her head drop to the headrest. Too exhausted and too hot to cry or think, she shut her eyes to pray but couldn't find the words. She tried to think of Tom, of Zach, her mother, but their faces were eclipsed by Engler.

Blaming Tom for his tragedy. Engler was insane. But what if Tom *was* to blame? Could she accept that? No. *Don't even think about that.* Engler and Tribe were cold-blooded killers. Hadn't she witnessed their work? Hadn't she felt Tribe's hands around her neck, all over her, violating her? She swallowed her sobs. She'd never dwelled on the concept of her own death until now. With all she'd suffered and with death so near, she grew calm, almost welcomed it.

No.

Stop thinking this way. Don't give up. Don't let them do this to you. You're still alive. You still have a chance. Come on. Think.

Ann turned to watch Engler on the pay phone, and the sun hit on something metal deep between the cushions of the seat beside her. A screwdriver. Tossed hastily into the truck last night. It glinted like hope. Ann used her free hand to slide it behind her. Out of sight.

Engler pounded the pay phone's handset three times against the cradle, then strode to the SUV and got in. The engine roared and he left rubber pulling away.

"Hey!" Tribe moaned awake.

"You're an asshole, Del! A sorry stupid twisted asshole! I should've known better. I should've damn well known better."

Tribe worked himself to a sitting position, holding his cheek.

"Because of you we're all over the news. Our pictures. Our names. Everything. Angel wants out of the deal." Engler put his thumb and forefinger together and held them up. "We were this close! This close!" He tightened his grip on the wheel. "I told him we've come too far. I swear to you we're going through with this. No way in hell are we turning back. We'll speed things up. We'll head to the meeting place tonight and give him a final chance to keep up his end. I've waited too long. I've paid too much to let this all die because of you.''

"Me!" Tribe winced, extracting a wet bloodied cotton ball from his mouth. "This whole thing went to hell the minute you flipped out in the jewelry store. Our problem is sitting right between us, brother, and it's not too late to get rid of it.''

Bang!

Ann jumped, the truck swerved, her seat belt tightened. Tribe steadied himself, cursing, looking around to see who'd shot at them. Engler wrestled with the steering wheel as the truck bucked and vibrated to a stop.

"Blew a goddamned tire," Engler said. "Get your ass out here and help me change it, Del. Move."

They'd gone over a piece of rotted board with four six-inch spikes that shredded the steel-belted radial. Tribe and Engler began unloading the rear to get at the jack and full-sized spare, leaving Ann alone.

"Please. It's so hot, can I have some air, please?" she said.

Engler looked at her. Checked her wrist cuff. Knowing the child safety lock kept her door secure, he dropped her power window before he returned to the rear. He and Tribe cursed each other as they worked.

It was a desolate stretch of back road cutting through a shady dense cottonwood forest. Ann let her head rest, drinking in the breezes that filled the truck and rekindled her hope. The networks had their pictures. Their names. It meant the police had to be close. She shut her eyes and bit her bottom lip. *God. Please.* She prayed for a patrol car, a stranger, anyone to happen by so she could scream for help.

Tools clanged and echoed with the chirping birds. The truck and Ann jerked as the jack ratcheted it up. Her feet slipped. For the first time since Engler had checked her ankle cuff that morning Ann noticed something that took her breath away. *The handcuff around her ankle was open.*

In his groggy state in the early dawn, after taking Ann to a roadside toilet, Engler had not closed it fully. The flat tire must've loosened it open. Hidden under the seat, her foot looked secure.

But it was free.

Ann's mind raced. *The screwdriver.* It was behind her back. Reaching for it with her free left hand, Ann glanced at the handgrip. She knew from an auto upholstery job she'd had years ago that most grips and armrests were screwed to the door. The screw head was capped with a plastic plug.

Her body shook as the SUV jolted up. Naturally her free hand went to the grip. She pried off the screw cap in seconds. The screwdriver was a flat-head, the screw head was a star-point. Damn. She'd have to angle it in.

Engler and Tribe were working fast, finger-twisting the lug nuts off the raised damaged wheel, not watching Ann. Her hand was sweating. She was right-handed. It was difficult gripping the hard yellow plastic handle of the tool. She had it locked on the screw head but couldn't get enough torque. It would not budge. She drew on strength she didn't have. It wouldn't budge. She kept trying. Her hand ached. *Come on.* Sweat dripped from her arm. Her hand was slipping. She rubbed her palm on her shirt. *Keep trying.* The truck shook. They'd slammed the spare on. *Come on.* Ann gritted her teeth, angled the screwdriver in again. It locked. She clenched her jaw, thought of Zach, Tom, her mother. Pictured them helping her twist. *Come on.* Her hand, then her entire arm began shaking. *Turn. Damn it. Turn.* Ann felt it give.

Oh God!

Engler and Tribe were finger-tightening the lug nuts on the raised wheel. Ann ran her sweating hand on her shirt and twisted the loosened screw, turning, the driver missing, she kept twisting, her wrist was on fire with pain, her hand was slipping, the screw coming out, seeming like the longest screw in the world, the truck shifting, the screw bobbling; then it was out. The jack whirred as the truck dropped so they could use the wrench. Ann pulled on the loosened end of the handgrip, pushed the metal cuff against the interior upholstery, wedging it, pushing it, working it, working it. *Please, dear God, help me!* The cuff slid away. She grabbed it so it wouldn't make a sound, then bent over and freed her ankle. She slipped out the open window, vanishing down the steep hill that dropped off the highway into the forest.

"Jesus Christ!" Engler came after her, tossing his keys to Tribe. "Del, take the truck to that side road. She can't get far!"

Please, God, help me. Someone help me.

Ann's heart thundered in her rib cage, tree branches snagged and scraped at her, her ears pounded as she slid and tumbled down the slope until she hit flat ground running, widening the distance, running faster. *Don't look back. Run. Run. God. Please.* She couldn't feel her tears, the splinters, the cuts tearing at her arms, her face. She was between life and death and she was running. Something whip-snapped through the leaves near her head.

The first pop of gunfire.

Ahead, Ann saw the river and the jagged banks with a drop that was nearly straight down. She jumped, sliding, rolling down the slope, then crashed into the water. The rocky bottom was mossy, slippery. It was up to her chest, about fifty yards wide. Using her arms it took a combination of running and breaststrokes to get to the other side where a rock chip hit her leg from the second gunshot.

Downstream Ann saw a small wooden bridge and Tribe driving the SUV across it. He was close. She ran in the opposite direction. Searching for a highway, a farmhouse, a farmer. Anything. *Please.*

She cried out.

Through a stand of trees fifty yards away, she saw a mobile home park and ran toward it as if it were salvation. She saw the eviscerated junked pickup trucks, saw the white sheets, T-shirts, pants, flapping on the clotheslines, the satellite dishes, children's bicycles. A dog barked. A falling-down picket fence bordered the park. Ann ran to the nearest home screaming.

"Help, call the police! I'm Ann Reed! I've been kidnapped!"

No sign of life. Ann ran to the side porch and banged on the door.

"Help me! Call the police! Somebody! They're coming after me!"

Ann ran across the lane to the next unit. A white double-wide with U.S. flags. She flew to the side door, banging on it, screaming. "Help me! Please. My name is Ann Reed. I've been kidnapped. Please!" She pulled at the door. It opened. She ran inside. A TV was on. A pot was boiling on the stove. "Help me! Help me!" Her eyes went round the place for the phone but stopped on the white woman in her late twenties standing in the hallway. She looked six months pregnant. Her brown hair tied in a ponytail, she was gripping a baseball bat with both hands. She was wearing a Dallas Cowboys T-shirt and shorts. Fear filled her face.

"Get the hell out of my house!"

"Help me, please." Ann dropped to her knees. "Call the police now, my name is Ann Reed, I was kidnapped in San Francisco. Please call the police."

"That's enough, Ann." Engler was at the doorway, holding out his wallet as if it were official ID. His handgun in the other hand. He gasped. "Ma'am, I'm Dean Weller. I work for the county, bail bondsman. This lady here's a bail jumper. Escaped my custody." He pointed his gun to the handcuffs dangling from Ann's wrist. The pregnant woman nodded slightly, thinking.

"No!" Ann said. "He's a murderer! He and Del kidnapped me. I swear, it's the truth! They've killed a police officer and two other people. They're on the news." A game show was on the TV set.

"Ma'am," Engler said, "don't listen to her. She escaped custody."

"No," Ann screamed. "I've got a son. Call the police. Please!"

Confusion masked the pregnant woman's face. She noticed the puddle of water growing under Ann's drenched clothes.

"Ma'am," Engler said, "this lady's off her medication and missed her psychiatric appointments. I swear to you, she's a county prisoner and my responsibility. There's a reward for citizens who cooperate."

"A reward?" the woman repeated.

"But I have to bring her in. Police involvement cancels the reward."

"What?" the woman said.

A girl, about three years old, stepped into the room from the sliding patio deck doors. She froze. Her big eyes went to Ann on her knees, the big man at the door with the gun. Her mother with a baseball bat. The little girl's chin crumpled.

"Misty, come to Mommy, sweetie."

Ann bolted through the opened patio door, jumping from the deck, screaming down the roadway between the mobile homes. Her handcuffs reflecting the sun.

"My name is Ann Reed! Call the police! Please. Ann Reed! San Francisco!"

An old man in a stained shirt came to his door at one unit. At another, a large woman holding a small dog looked from her window. Ann rounded a parked Mack truck, running smack into Delmar Tribe.

"Darlin'."

His big arms locked on to her so tight, her ribs cracked. Engler came up behind her. The men wrestled her into the SUV, making certain this time that the handcuffs were painfully tight. Ann screamed hysterically, her cries muffled by the closed windows. The people who trickled out of their homes barely had a chance to see the terror on her face as the SUV disappeared in a dust cloud.

68

Communications Officer Sareena Sawyer took the first incoming 911 call for police at the Communications Center in Lufkin, Texas. It came from the Big Timber Mobile Home Park, outside of Lufkin just off the Texas Loop.

Two white men had forced a hysterical white woman, blond hair, late thirties, into a sports utility vehicle. A handgun was seen. The woman appeared to have handcuffs locked on one wrist. She identified herself as Ann Reed of San Francisco.

Sawyer's fingers were a blur on the keyboard of the CAD system. Using the police radio, she dispatched units from the Angelina County Sheriff's office to Big Timber. Then she called Highway Patrol, alerted DPS, the Texas Department of Public Safety. Within thirty seconds of the first call, she got a second, then a third from the park, lighting up the 911 console.

"... one of the guys had a deformed ear and tattoos like the fella wanted by the FBI in that big murder case in California that was on the news."

Lufkin updated DPS that it had unconfirmed reports that

the incident at the park was connected to the FBI's California fugitive case and the BOLOs out of Oklahoma. DPS alerted the FBI in Houston and Dallas, who in turn alerted the FBI's San Francisco division.

Word of the break in the case got out fast. The Associated Press wire service moved a national bulletin from Lufkin, Texas. More reporters began calling Reed at his home. Tia Layne was one of them.

"Tom, please don't hang up."

"I've got nothing to say to you."

"*Worldwide* will fly you to Texas now, pay for the flight *and* all expenses, if we can accompany you."

"I don't want *your* help. I'm going on my own." Reed slammed down his phone and resumed trying to get airline flight times while packing between press calls. Reporters from Texas gave Reed the latest news. TV networks called offering to fly him to Texas. He declined.

Reed's lack of sleep and his emotional state made Sydowski and McDaniel apprehensive. Watching him, as they finalized their own arrangements to join investigators in Texas, McDaniel pulled Sydowski aside.

"If this goes down, Tom could be a problem, Walt."

"We should take him with us so we can watch him."

"No, we should insist he stay here. Put people on him. He's reckless, he'll get in the way."

"We can't arrest him, Steve. And there's no way he'll stay. He *will* go off on his own. Reporters are feeding him information. I say take him."

It went against McDaniel's better judgment but he knew Sydowski was right. They could control Reed if he was with them.

"I don't like this. It's not the way we do things, Walt."

"I know."

"I'll make calls. You've got your bag. Tell him we're leaving now."

Two hours after the first emergency call from the Big Timber Mobile Home Park, Reed was in the back of

Sydowski's unmarked SFPD Caprice as it raced south on the Bayshore Freeway to San Francisco International Airport. His stomach was clenched with tension. He'd clamped his hands together to stop shaking. Turgeon was driving. Sydowski and McDaniel were each being updated on their cell phones by detectives in Texas interviewing eyewitnesses at the park near Lufkin.

"She was wet. She must've gone through a river to escape," Sydowski said.

Alive. Reed could barely breathe. Ann was alive less than three hours ago. She escaped. She was fighting. Reed gazed at the city rolling by, deaf to the siren, blind to the pulsating red light, until he leaned forward to ask Turgeon to drive faster. That's when he saw the speedometer vibrating between ninety and ninety-five miles an hour as she knifed through traffic.

The private investigator hired by Cooter and Tia Layne tipped them to the break and the police flight to Texas.

Layne and Cooter paid a taxi to speed from their Tenderloin office directly to departures at the airport. They arrived minutes ahead of Reed but weren't first. In fact, they were behind. Cooter had been right. The San Francisco press had good sources too. News cameras dotted the cluster of press people who'd beaten them to the airport where the unmarked Caprice screeched to a halt at departures. Half a dozen officers from the SFPD Airport Bureau met Sydowski, McDaniel, and Reed, escorting them through the terminal and a barrage of press questions.

"Did you speak to your wife, Tom?"

"Tom! Please, can you make a statement?"

"What can you tell us, Tom?"

Reed's face was taut. It was all he could do to keep his composure as the cadre of officers jostled him through the news pack.

"We'll put out a statement when we know more," McDaniel said.

"What about now? Tom, share your thoughts now!"

Forgetting he knew most of the faces in the crowd, that many were friends who'd offered prayers and support, Reed waved them off. "I'm sorry, I just can't. I'm sorry."

"Excuse us!" Sydowski said, pulling Reed toward a security checkpoint.

Much had been precleared. The FBI had found a travel charter jet filled with a tour group of seniors flying directly from San Francisco to Houston. The bureau arranged seats for McDaniel and Sydowski. It took intense last-minute grumbling before they'd secured a seat for Reed. After undergoing security checks and presenting FBI and SFPD credentials, they were rushed by airport security and police to the Jetway where they hurried aboard the waiting 737.

Inside the terminal, several San Francisco reporters scrambled to ticket counters for the next commercial flight to Houston or Dallas. Tia Layne was near the front of the line, tapping her credit card against her palm, when Cooter joined her, setting his camera down.

"You get Reed?" Layne said.

"Got what everyone else got. We going to get a flight?"

"Yes. Next one leaves for Dallas very soon. We'll drive a rental to Lufkin from there. Hope your card's not maxed out."

"I'm good."

"She's alive. Do you believe it, Cooter?"

"Wild, huh?"

"The story's exploding. I called New York. They'll buy anything we can get."

A world away, in row 19 of the crowded plane, Reed let his head drop to the headrest feeling each bump in his heart as the jet crept into position before stopping on the runway to await clearance.

Acknowledging the flight attendant's request, McDaniel and Sydowski continued with final calls on their phones while Reed thought back to the time he'd first met Ann. The first time he saw her smile and touched her hand.

The turbines whined and the 737 began rolling down the runway, wings springing as it gathered speed, the ground rushing under them as they lifted off, Reed welcoming the thrust that forced him into his seat. *Faster. Goddammit. Can't this thing go any faster?* As they climbed, Reed gazed down at the earth dropping below him and was overwhelmed.

Ann was alive. But Engler was a psychotic killer with a vendetta against him. Tribe was a murdering rapist. How could Ann ever be the same? *Don't think about that.* No matter what happened, he'd be bringing her home—in the seat beside him, or in the cargo hold below.

He swore to God, he'd be bringing her home.

69

In Houston, a group of investigators met Reed, Sydowski, and McDaniel. On the phone, the Texas lawmen had let Sydowski know they didn't like the idea of bringing Reed with them. But on the ground at George Bush Intercontinental Airport, they were hospitable.

"We wish the circumstances were different, but welcome to Texas, Tom. Ira Doyle. FBI, Houston."

"Tom, I'm Jay Sander, Texas Rangers." Sander took Reed's small bag. "Y'all come this way. We've got a DPS plane waiting."

A quick round of handshakes. The group strode through the airport, exited to the tarmac. The temperature was in the mid-nineties, huge gulf clouds sailed northwest like frigates in an azure sky.

The officers and agents climbed into a van. It whisked across the busy airport to a small hangar where they stepped back into the humid air. It roared from passing jets and the twin props of the DPS plane. Reed saw a cluster of news-people on the other side of a chain-link fence. Pictures of him boarding the small plane with police were being broadcast live across the nation.

"I'm afraid we have little that's new to report," Doyle said through the headset intercom as the aircraft taxied.

"In all, we've got at least one hundred people moving on this already," Sander said. "We're flying directly to Lufkin."

Reed nodded as they lifted off, glimpsing Houston's skyscrapers rising through the hazy distance as they banked over webs of expressways and headed northeast.

When they landed at Lufkin's airport, more police vehicles and press were waiting. Bud Tarpell, with the Angelina County Sheriff's office, took Reed and most of the others with him in the lead van that rushed off to the Big Timber Mobile Home Park.

"We've got every available officer from every nearby jurisdiction that can spare them on this." Tarpell recited them: "FBI, Texas Rangers, DPS troopers, sheriffs' deputies from half a dozen counties, county constables, game wardens, TDC people, national parks people, off-duty police officers, and volunteers. We got dogs, we got aircraft. Ain't no place these fellas can hide. We've got a dragnet set up reaching into every county within several hundred miles of Lufkin. From Dallas to the gulf and to Louisiana."

Reed nodded because that was all he could do. He was a crime reporter, a veteran of many big stories. Fugitives were difficult to catch. The dumb ones, the dope addicts, the desperate ones, made it easy. But smart ones and lucky ones were another story. Engler was smart. Despite Tarpell's assurances, Reed took nothing for granted.

They came upon the park where scores of satellite trucks and news vans lined the road to the entrance. Their call signs were from Dallas, Houston, Tulsa, Tyler, Longview, Lufkin, Huntsville, Nacogdoches, Shreveport. Nearly one hundred other vehicles jammed the area. Police and news helicopters rumbled overhead.

"We'll take you right to where you want to go, Tom."

Tarpell dropped his window to show his face to the deputy at the checkpoint, who waved them in. They parked near yellow crime scene tape, which was lifted for Reed and the others as Tarpell took them to the white double-wide unit with the American flags. A pregnant woman in a Dallas Cowboys T-shirt was sitting on a chair on the rear deck talking to two women, an FBI agent and a Texas Ranger. Everyone had been alerted in advance of Reed's arrival. After quick introductions the FBI agent said, "Tom, this is Gloria Pickett, the woman who spoke to your wife."

"The woman who spoke to your wife."

Reed was at a loss. He watched as Gloria, who'd now told her story several times, twisted the little gold heart necklace that hung around her neck, and recounted it for him. When she finished, Reed removed his glasses.

"Did she look like she'd—" Reed cleared his throat. "Was she hurt? How'd she look?"

"She looked okay." Gloria nodded, trying to be precise because she wanted to help Reed. "She was panicked, looked like she'd been through a lot, considering everything. The detectives showed me her picture. Her hair was dyed. A few scrapes. Her clothes were wet like she'd come through the creek. Scared, frightened, but she looked okay."

A helicopter thumped above, then faded.

"May I go inside to see?" Tom asked Gloria, who deflected his request to the investigators.

"Forensic people are done. They're just going over a few things but it should be fine," one of the officers said.

Gloria struggled from her chair and led Reed inside. The others followed as she walked Reed through everything, narrating.

Ann was here. I was here. The man, Engler, was there. His gun. His attempt to confuse things. How Ann had dropped to her knees, pleading. Misty came in here. Ann ran out there.

Reed's eyes went to the glass of the sliding patio door and the gray-black fingerprint powder smeared on it. He stepped closer and leaned his face into the smudges. A fingerprint tech was packing up her equipment.

"Is this where my wife's hand touched the glass?" Reed said.

"Yes," the tech said. "Confirmed her prints with the California DMV. It's okay, I'm done there."

Unable to take his eyes from the black smudges, Reed let his hand hover over the spot.

Ann's hand, the hand he had held on their first date, the hand he had squeezed on their wedding day, the hand that had crushed his in the delivery room when Zach was born, the hand that had waved the last time he'd seen her, then handcuffed to the wheelchair. Oh Jesus. She was here, less than six hours ago. She was here.

70

They disappeared into the swamps, creekbeds, and deep pinewoods of East Texas.

Engler drove while Tribe used torn sections of county maps to navigate through a serpentine course of paved, gravel, and dirt back roads where they traveled undetected while scanning radio news reports.

"... the incident has focused the nationwide manhunt on Texas ..."

Over Tribe's shoulder Ann saw handwritten notes and arrows covering the maps but couldn't find their destination. At times they'd stop to consult notes as if searching for something before continuing.

Ann thought she'd heard the distant thump of a helicopter and prayed for it to be police. But she saw nothing and her heart sank. She'd lost count of the hours and grew confused as they took yet another back road through another dense forest. Gravel popcorned against the undercarriage.

"Stop! I saw it!" Tribe said.

Engler braked. The SUV was swallowed by its own dust cloud. When it settled, Engler reversed until coming upon a hand-scrawled NO TRESPASSING sign on the right side. It marked the beginning of an unmarked road, an overgrown grassy pathway invisible in the thicket.

"See?" Tribe said. "The NO is underlined and the sign's framed in bright orange, just like Driscoll's notes. He set it up good."

Engler inched their way delicately along the path, awakening branches that slapped and scraped against the wheels, the doors, the windows.

"It'd better be here like we planned it," Engler said.

The late afternoon sky dimmed under the natural canopy of the forest as they bumped along for nearly half an hour, coming to a tranquil lake, the shore lined with shortleaf pine and loblollies. They stopped near a huge thicket of underbrush covered by a sweeping natural forest roof of towering pine, willow, and cyprus trees. Undetectable from the sky. Driscoll had good friends here, graduates of the Texas Department of Corrections who knew how to help when it counted.

"I think it's here. Damn," Tribe said.

They got out and began pulling away at the boughs, branches, and under, revealing a huge sheet like military camouflage and a white late-model van. Ann saw a Texas license plate. Tribe reached under one of the wheels for keys. Soon the engine purred. Ann read the small commercial sign on the van's door. EFFCT HOSPITAL WASTE. CAUTION: HAZARDOUS PRODUCTS.

Engler looked through the van. It was filled with boxes of food, clothing, radios, blankets, medical smocks, supplies, camping gear, a tent. A full tank of gas. Everything he'd told Driscoll to do. Man, he'd done a good job. For about two seconds, Engler felt sad that he'd killed Driscoll, an outstanding wheelman. But then again, it was never part of their plan to let Driscoll live long enough to receive his cut of the heist. Engler glanced at Tribe. He studied him, thinking; then he looked at Ann, handcuffed in the SUV, and reevaluated the situation.

"I told you, Del, we've come too far to drop this."

"It's getting dark, John. Let's eat."

"Sure, then we'll load up the van and head to the meeting place at dawn. It's not far and this will get us by any road-blocks along the way."

"Not far at all." Tribe rummaged through potato chips, beer, beans, pork rinds, soda, water, snack cakes, delighted to find beef jerky.

Using the chains and handcuffs, Engler secured Ann to a pine tree, letting her sit on the fragrant pine needles covering the soft forest floor, where they set out the food.

Ann ate but not much. Fear kept her numb. The rage between the two men was gone, as if a switch had been thrown. It terrified her. It was as if they'd achieved the next level of whatever it was they were planning, making them even more determined to finish things.

She prayed police were near.

Few words were spoken as they ate. Crickets, birdsong, and the occasional splash from the swamps competed with Tribe's lip-smacking, beer guzzling, and belching. In the twilight, Ann saw a water moccasin thread across the glass surface of the lake.

Tribe saw what Ann saw.

"Snakes are beautiful, misunderstood creations. Water round here is filled with them. Gators out there too. Big ones." Tribe belched, then turned to Engler. "We get our money, I'm going to Belize. Got friends down there. I can live good on my share. Start a reptile farm."

Staring at Tribe, Engler probed his teeth with a toothpick and nodded.

"I ain't never going back to prison, John. What about you?"

Engler sucked air through his teeth, then looked at Ann.

"Del, I think you were right."

"About what?"

"No witnesses."

Tribe stared at Engler, then at Ann.

"About her, you mean?"

"Yes. Things got tense in the mobile home park. Damn near ruined it all for us. But, Del, you came through, showing up with the truck like you did. You could've left me. I mean everything was in the truck. Cash, the jewels. Everything was on the line. How come you didn't leave me, Del?"

" 'Cause we go back to C Yard, John."

"Guess I got messed up, thinking about my wife, about Ann Reed, what her husband took from me. I got a little selfish."

"John, we didn't know she'd be in the jewelry store when we came in. I understand how it messed with your head, brother."

"I forgot all about your needs, that's what got us trouble in Oklahoma."

"That was me, John."

"But I should've let you take care of your needs with her; otherwise you wouldn't have gone off like you did and get hurt, and draw attention to us."

"I won't argue with you there. So what're you saying?"

"I'm saying you're right. We should've stuck to our plan. No witnesses."

Tribe looked at Ann. "It's not too late."

Ann's heart began to race.

Engler looked at her. "I think she's grown to like you, Del."

"Think so?"

"I do. And I think you should do something about it. Especially after what she did to us. She's earned it."

Darkness was descending fast. Large things were splashing in the water. Engler grunted, fishing into his pocket. "Here's the handcuff key. I'm going to load up the van."

Engler left for the trucks. Tribe leaned back on his elbow, looking at Ann as if he'd won something. He touched the bandage on his face, tugged at it slowly, pulling it off, in an attempt to make himself presentable.

Drinking beer, he dabbed his facial wound with a tissue

and stared at Ann, rubbing the back of his hand across his mouth. Again, something huge splashed in the swamp nearby; a bird screamed.

Tribe stood and sighed as he approached Ann, working the chains around the tree upward so he could bring her to her feet. Then he gazed upon her.

"Darlin'. Darlin'. Darlin'." Tribe grinned, his big, powerful hands gripped her shoulders. "Now, now, there's no sense in crying like this."

She could smell his body odor, felt his hot foul breath panting against her skin. His widening eyes, his malformed ear, the running wound on his face, the animal cries and splashes coming from something dying in the swamp. She felt his hands slithering all over her, then his lips and tongue on her neck.

Ann raised her head to heaven and prayed as the tear tracks glistened down her face. She couldn't fight anymore. She thought of Tom, of Zach, of her mother and every good thing she'd had in her life.

Then she wished for death.

71

A sheriff's deputy came to the door of Gloria Pickett's home, said something into FBI Agent Ira Doyle's ear that made him nod.

As they stepped from the double-wide, Doyle told Reed the press wanted a statement from him.

"It's entirely up to you, Tom," Doyle said.

Buoyed by the recent breaks, Reed decided to say something. The deputy hurried ahead to alert the networks and dozens of press people.

"Seein' how you're a reporter," Doyle said, "I figure you know how best to handle this, Tom."

Reed nodded and they started walking toward the yellow tape at the end of the lane. Sydowski got close enough to Reed to say privately, "Engler and Tribe will be listening. Don't antagonize them, Tom. They've backed themselves into a corner. This is the most dangerous time now."

"What do you want me to say?"

"Assume you're talking directly to them and be careful."

Doyle went to the microphones first. "This will be short."

He paused to let a helicopter pass. "Tom Reed will make a brief statement."

The late-afternoon sun and lights hit Reed's face. He squinted into the cameras.

"I just want to say to the men who've taken my wife, Ann Reed, please let her go. She's never hurt you. Please let her go. She has a family, a little boy who needs her now, so we're begging you, I'm begging you, please let her go."

Next to Reed, some news networks juxtaposed smaller inset live footage of the dragnet on Texas highways, the helicopters, dog teams checking pickups and wooded areas as the live press questions came for Reed.

"Tom, there are reports that you know the men, or have written about them, is that true?" a *Dallas Morning News* reporter said.

"I reported on the case of one of them, yes, but we suspect Ann was taken randomly."

"Which suspect, Tom? Tribe or Engler?" a *Houston Chronicle* reporter said.

"Engler."

The networks juxtaposed inset mug shots of Engler, Tribe, then Ann Reed's photograph. Summary descriptions of the suspects, then a summary of the San Francisco case, murdered SFPD Officer Rod August, suspect Leroy Driscoll, murdered Carrie Dawn Addison, remains found near Death Valley, California, and Winslow, Arizona. Tribe sought for assault in Oklahoma. Several questions were shouted at once, but Reed heard a familiar voice.

"Tom, Tom," Tia Layne yelled, "isn't it true that John Mark Engler holds a grudge against you for your reporting of his Florida death row case?"

"That was a long time ago."

"And," Layne pushed on, "what does this mean for Ann, given the circumstances?"

Pulling Reed from the microphones, Sydowski stepped in. "I think that's all we're going to say for now, thank you."

"Wait! Tom," Molly Wilson from the *San Francisco Star* said. "Tom, some people have been portraying you as a hero for investigating Ann's kidnapping on your own. Do you agree with that?"

Reed stepped back to the microphones.

"No, I don't. Ann's been fighting for her life. What happened here a few hours ago is evidence of that fact. *She's* the hero. Not me. I'm not giving up. No one's giving up. No matter what."

FBI Agent Ira Doyle held up both hands. "That's it, folks. Thanks."

"Wait, sir, how many officers are on this case and—"

"Those questions were addressed at an earlier briefing, but we'll have releases for you shortly, thank you."

Bud Tarpell led Reed, Sydowski, and McDaniel back to his van and drove them to Lufkin's Communications Center. Reed tried to think but couldn't. He was drained by the time they rolled into the center's parking lot. Stepping from the van, he realized he'd lost track of time. It would be dark soon.

Tarpell led them into a room where nearly twenty people from various agencies, FBI, DPS, county, and more, were working, talking on phones, radios, or typing on computer keyboards.

Large maps covered one wall, several large TVs tuned to all-news networks, national and local stations. There was a table heaped with food. Near it were sofas, cots, sleeping bags. Empty desks to work.

"Washrooms and showers are just down the hall, fellas," Tarpell said. "You won't miss a thing. If there's a break it comes here first."

Reed sat on a sofa. He couldn't bring himself to eat. A young woman approached him.

"Tom, I'm Sareena Sawyer, the 911 dispatcher who took the call."

"Hello."

"I just want to say we're all praying for y'all. Everybody here's given one hundred and ten, Tom." She patted his shoulder.

"Thank you."

Alone, Reed watched TV news reports on what had remained a national story. Sydowski and McDaniel joined other investigators at a table, downing endless cups of coffee, flipping through notes and files.

Sydowski explained how San Francisco's chief of police wanted him to accompany Reed to Texas to offer San Francisco's help to the growing task force on this case. Three San Francisco people had been murdered, two in the city, one was an SFPD officer. A San Francisco woman was being held hostage, Sydowski could offer help. Still, some of the seasoned local detectives questioned Reed's presence. Sydowski said it was easier for them to keep an eye on Reed, who'd already taken a few risks to pursue matters on his own.

DPS and the Texas FBI were scouring Engler's background history for any connection to Texas. The FBI was pressing its sources who were convinced the stolen jewelry was going to be sold in Texas.

Police radio chatter and TV news reports filled the room long into the night. The hours melted into each other.

Reed's eyes grew heavy and he found himself dreaming of Ann's hand holding his in sunlight, leaving a silhouette in glass, reaching up from a desert grave. *God, please no.*

"Tom." Sydowski stood over him. "Wake up."

Reed rubbed his eyes and sat up. It was dawn. The radios were loud and heavy with a volume of excited cross talk.

"What's going on, Walt?"

"They found something. In the water."

72

At first it looked like a postage stamp in a swimming pool.

But to the spotter in the Department of Public Safety search plane making its first morning pass over a remote sliver of East Texas it was a find. "Take us closer," the spotter said over her headset.

The pilot looped and descended, then cut the speed so the spotter could focus her high-powered binoculars, steadying her line of sight until she had it.

"Looks like a body."

She radioed the location to Lufkin, concentrating the massive search operation to the region and tightening the dragnet.

A DPS helicopter marked the site, directing scores of agencies to it, deputies, DPS troopers, Rangers, the FBI, game wardens, the county coroner, local fire officials. Rescue boats were trailered and launched, their motors rumbling across the surface some seventy-five yards from shore.

On land and over the water, investigators sealed the scene. They videotaped, photographed, sketched, and made notes of the time, location, weather, water temp, conditions, as news helicopters recorded events live from above and hurried to locate the scene on the ground.

In the two lead boats police cut the engines and used oars for positioning. The corpse was facedown, arms outstretched, clothed in a light-colored shirt and blue jeans with what appeared to be a scarf around its neck.

"Okay, Earl," an older forensic investigator in one of the boats said, "you boys bring it in, let's see what we got here."

A grappling pole was extended to the waist, and after two attempts, hooked a belt loop. As the body was pulled to the aluminum boat's gunwale, the corpse flipped.

"Goddammit!"

It had been eviscerated. Instead of a stomach there was a gaping cavity of twisted ribs, with waving ribbons of fabric and visceral matter that had attracted small fish.

Several investigators winced.

A water moccasin was coiled around the neck, its head had wormed into the yawning mouth of Delmar James Tribe and had worked its way to his heart, or the few bits the gator had left.

On the tree-lined shore, police uncovered the SUV with the California plate belonging to a Los Angeles family still vacationing, oblivious of the role their family vehicle had played in a drama that had gripped the nation.

The dogs had found women's bras, tops, shoes, and slacks scattered in the forest. Crime scene experts were casting tire impressions from the vehicle that had left the area, identifying them as those commonly found on vans.

The FBI and Texas Rangers found a chain at the trunk of a pine tree, and a large knife. A detective, expert on blood-splatter patterns, found dried blood on the tree, the chain, and the ground. None of this information was relayed to Tom Reed, who was kept at a distance where he sat with local police, his face buried in his hands.

In the sky above, Tia Layne adjusted her binoculars.

"Cooter, can you pull in on Reed?" she said over her

headset of the rented helicopter. They had split the hourly cost with a small East Texas daily newspaper so they could keep up with the bigger news outlets to get the best pictures of the latest development. The networks broadcasting live pictures pulled back on the floating corpse, so as not to offend viewers by showing too much detail.

About an hour after the body was found, one of the news shows went back to Texas for more on the robbery, homicide, kidnapping case.

"Sources have just told us that the body is that of one of the two fugitives, Delmar James Tribe," a news anchor said over jittery aerial shots of the police activity on the shoreline. "Of course, the question remains, where is San Francisco businesswoman Ann Reed, the wife of San Francisco reporter Tom Reed, whom you see to the extreme right of your screen? We're going to break now, stay with us, we'll have more on this stunning case when we come back. . . ."

73

Angel Zelaya was on the FBI's list of suspected Texas buyers.

Sources told them he was active. The FBI had obtained warrants to tap every phone owned by Zelaya, his wife, their children, his jewelry wholesale business, or any of his staff. Even the cell phone he'd donated to his church.

The FBI didn't know about one particular cell phone Zelaya used that was tied to a numbered company registered in the Caribbean with a subsidiary listed to a New Orleans post office box, until a sharp-eyed agent experienced in white-collar crime investigations uncovered it.

Based on information from FBI informants, a federal judge granted a warrant allowing agents to search Zelaya's house for the cell phone.

The FBI had reason to believe it was the phone Zelaya used to conduct illicit jewel transactions and was the number being called by John Mark Engler and Delmar James Tribe. The men were dangerous fugitives wanted under a federal warrant charging them with multiple homicides in California.

Fearing Zelaya's home was under surveillance by Engler, Tribe, or their associates, two burly FBI agents wearing jeans, T-shirts, and tool belts arrived at dawn in a carpenter's van. They pressed the doorbell of Zelaya's 2,900-square-foot custom ranch house with the wagoneer's porch that swept along the front. Zelaya was groggy when he came to the door rubbing his eyes as he studied the warrant.

"I don't own that phone anymore," he said. "It was stolen."

An FBI agent reached into his tool belt, pulled out a cell phone, and dialed the number of Zelaya's "stolen" cell phone. Seconds later a girl, who looked to be about seven years old, trotted to the door.

"Daddy!" She had a ringing cell phone in her hand. "Your phone!"

Zelaya kissed his daughter, took the phone from her, then said to the agents. "Permit me to call my lawyer."

"Sure, but we'll hold this." The agent took Zelaya's phone.

Her name was Conchita Flores. She pulled into the driveway in her BMW. She was a Harvard grad, tall and dressed in a tailored business suit. Upon arriving, she had a twenty-minute conversation with Zelaya behind the closed door of his large book-lined study, emerging with a yellow pad full of notes. "Gentlemen, please come in and close the door," she said.

The agents entered. Zelaya, still in his robe, was seated behind his desk. Flores sat next to him, studying her pad. "There's coffee," she said to the pad, then looked at the agents. "Has my client been charged?"

"Not yet, but he faces accessory charges for starters."

"He'll cooperate fully in exchange for dismissing them."

"No deals. You take yours black, Tim?" one agent said to his partner.

"Then he'll choose never to answer his cell phone again."

"We've got records of calls placed to the line from every location where the suspects have been. Milk, no sugar."

"Circumstance."

"He did time in Leavenworth. Shared a federal prison cell with one of the suspects sought in three homicides and one million in stolen jewelry. He flew to San Francisco before the heist. Your client is the buyer. See where this is going?"

The lawyer stuck out her chin. "I don't."

Her client did. "I'll do whatever you want," Zelaya said.

"Where are they?" The agent sipped his coffee. It was strong. Colombian.

"Somewhere out of Lufkin."

"The entire country knows that. Where are they headed?"

"I don't know, I blew them off in the last call, they'd drawn heat out of Oklahoma and I didn't want to hear from them again."

"Are they coming here?"

"No, they were going to call me with a meeting point, but I swear I blew them off. Look, I had no part in this, they called me—"

"Angel." His lawyer cautioned him in Spanish to be quiet.

One of the agents requested Zelaya in Spanish to cooperate.

Zelaya agreed to help.

His wife made breakfast and the agents waited with Zelaya and his lawyer.

They passed time watching news reports and staring at the phone. The agents called in updates to their supervisor; the lawyer and Zelaya's wife discussed children, fashion, and upcoming social functions, indifferent to the fact that Zelaya was the thread holding Ann Reed's life.

It was early afternoon when the cell phone rang.

Everyone exchanged glances. The agents knew the tap should pick up the conversation, but the senior agent acted fast and reached into his tool belt for a microcassette recorder and an ear-jack microphone.

"Angel," he said, going over what they'd advised him, "remember, agree to meet them, get details of their location." The phone rang a second time. "Here, like I showed you, this goes in your ear, like an earplug, it will record the call." The agent plugged the jack end of the device into the recorder and switched it on.

"Hello," Zelaya said.

"It's me," Engler said. "Let's deal tonight."

Zelaya nodded.

"I don't know, you've drawn too much attention. Your numbers are too high. I told you it was off."

"The price went down. Emergency clearance rate. Two hundred."

"That's still high and the risks are now too great."

"We can do it tonight."

"Where are you?"

Engler took time to consider his answer.

"Are you alone, Angel?"

"Yes."

"How safe is this phone?"

"Safe. Tied to a numbered company. Not even registered to me."

"Have you noticed any new vehicles parked near your house or business? Like repair vans, utility vans, or trucks?"

"Nothing, man. I'm at home and it's all quiet. This phone's untraceable."

"Let's do it then. Two hundred?"

"Too much."

"Come on. You were set to go five."

"That's before you became a celebrity."

"Two hundred, Angel. That's a big cut."

"I can go one-fifty."

"All right. One-fifty, cash. But you got to come with a small RV."

"What?"

"A small RV. This is good fishing country, you'll blend in and the RV's good for travel. One-fifty and a small RV."

"Where can I get one?"

"Rent it, buy it, I don't give a damn, just get one or kiss one million in product good-bye."

The senior agents nodded for Zelaya to make a deal.

"Okay, okay. One-fifty cash and a small RV."

"Come alone, tonight. Here are the directions . . ."

74

It was an island on the Pacific side of Costa Rica with white sand beaches, nodding palms, and forests fragrant with orchids. Engler had read about it in prison. He imagined how he could lose himself in one of its villages, start a new life where the past couldn't touch him, where he could live free.

He carried that dream every moment of every day. It got him through the long haul. Got him past the pain Tom Reed had caused. Engler's hatred for Reed had never died. He had fed it to fate. Whatever happened, happened. He'd decided to work on getting to his island.

Engler needed one clean score. It all came together in C Yard where he'd met Tribe. Partnering with a sexual predator was a risk, but Tribe's connection to the job was Engler's ticket to the island.

They were patient old cons, taking their time to develop their plan when they got out, working on Caesar, on Carrie, on Angel. It all came off until fate went to work at the jewelry store and gave Engler a divine gift. Tom Reed's wife, Ann. It blew his mind. Wife for wife. Life for life.

Tribe could never grasp the cosmic importance of such an event because he was a subhuman twisted being who was a slave to bestial forces.

It wasn't personal, Del, but you were a liability.

The universe had entrusted Engler with the duty to right a wrong. Tribe understood few things. His animal needs, and that they'd agreed to leave no one alive who could identify them.

No one, Del. No witnesses. That was the deal, partner. That's what Engler had told Tribe before he slit his throat, disemboweled him, then dragged his body to the swamp.

"That's just the way it is," Engler said aloud, peering through the cobwebs covering the filthy cracked glass of the window.

Still no sign of Zelaya.

It was a small farmhouse built just before the Second World War, hidden deep amid thirty acres of pinewood forest in the corner of an East Texas County northeast of Huntsville.

"Belonged to my grandpappy who kept his still there. Been overlooked by county surveyors," Driscoll had boasted one night in the garage he'd rented in San Francisco where they'd planned the heist. Engler insisted he draw him a detailed map to it.

Floor planks creaked as Engler left the window for the dust-covered table to inspect the gym bag filled with jewelry. It glittered in the twilight.

He checked on the propane camping lanterns Driscoll had supplied in the van. Engler hid the truck in a far corner, deep in the forest. Lanterns looked fine. He checked on his arsenal: three assault rifles, a Mac-11, an AK-47, and an M16, four handguns, semiautomatics, two Glocks, a .45 Smith & Wesson, and a Beretta, grenades, a bag of ammo, trip wires. He tore into a pack of beef jerky and paced.

"Come on, Angel."

Engler could make it to the gulf tonight. He had a connection there where he could buy his way onto a Panama-bound cargo ship, then make his way to Costa Rica. Then to the West Coast. He was so close. He just needed Zelaya's cash and the RV to get him out of here.

Engler shrugged. If Zelaya didn't come to him, he'd go to Zelaya in Houston. Zelaya had children. One way or another, Engler would see to it that Angel held up his end.

It was coming up on the hour. Engler turned up the radio and gnawed on his jerky, waiting to catch the latest news updates. He scanned the stations.

"Unconfirmed reports have identified the victim as Delmar James Tribe, one of the two fugitives. The national manhunt has led to a dragnet in East Texas involving the FBI and scores of law officials from across the state. Tom Reed, husband of the abducted woman, arrived at the Lufkin mobile home park where his wife was seen pleading for help. He spoke to reporters there. WTTX's Melody Honeycutt was there. 'Tom Reed, a crime reporter from San Francisco, made an emotional appeal for his wife. "I just want to say to the men who've taken my wife, Ann Reed, please let her go. She's never hurt you—" ' "

Engler rubbed the muzzle of the Smith & Wesson across his lips, then heard the sounds of grass brushing against moving metal, then the low squeak of brakes, prompting him to switch off the radio and go to the window.

An RV had stopped in bushes at the far end of the property. No one moved from the driver's door. The light reflecting on the windshield made it impossible to see if Zelaya was inside the cab.

Little chickenshit. Afraid to get out. To hell with him. Engler had no time for games. He shoved his handgun in his waistband, grabbed his assault rifle, then stepped from the farmhouse.

75

Captain Vern Stinton, commander of the Department of Public Safety SWAT team, was a bumpy-faced big man, whose eyes lit with anger upon seeing Reed.

"I own this damn scene. I don't like him or you being here. It's not the way I do things." Stinton nodded to Reed. "Just keep the hell out of my way and we'll get along."

McDaniel and Sydowski nodded.

Stinton went back to studying sketches and rough maps of the property. His crew had set up in an abandoned barn, shielded naturally by a hill a hundred yards from the farmhouse where Engler was.

Once the FBI had obtained directions to the site from Zelaya, no time was wasted. DPS Aircraft Section dispatched a single-engined 206 Cessna from Region One out of Garland near Dallas. It conducted covert surveillance, flying so high it could not be heard or seen, but was able to pinpoint the site with high-powered telescopic equipment and guide Stinton's SWAT team.

Some sixteen members, most of them Highway Patrol troopers called in from Madisonville, Crockett, Lufkin,

Groveton, Huntsville, and Tyler, rolled to the command post
where they were briefed.

They suited up in camouflage gear, crept up to the building, which had dense forest cover. In silence they'd set up
an inner perimeter on the farmhouse. Stinton assessed the
updates first from the scouts on the best points; then the
other team members took positions, reporting by radio to
Stinton and his commanders who directed the operation from
the command post.

"We're sending the RV to the extreme edge, where he
can see it, to draw him out for a takedown," Stinton said.

Reed, Sydowski, McDaniel, Ira Doyle, and a small number of federal, state, and county emergency officials ob-
served.

The Highway Patrol had sealed an outer perimeter, setting
up roadblocks to keep back the press and the rubberneckers
who were gathering at the far boundaries, straining to see
something.

Inside the barn, where temperatures were nearing ninety
degrees, the SWAT radio crackled with a report from one
of Stinton's scouts.

"We see him inside."

"What about hostages? See anything?"

"Nothing."

Stinton shook his head.

Reed shut his eyes. What did Engler do with her? They'd
found Tribe, the chain around the tree, the blood, the clothing
strewn about. Jesus. Reed stepped out of the barn and ran
a hand over his sweating face. Sydowski followed him.

"Tom, we don't know anything until we can get in there."

The soft radio talk of Stinton's team leader spilled from
the barn. Sydowski and Reed listened as one of the scouts
said, "Okay, the RV's just edged up to the far end."

Stinton waited. His team relayed more whispered updates.

"There's movement. He sees it. Hasn't drawn him out
yet. Wait, there's movement. Yup, here we go. He's stepping

out to meet the RV. He's armed. Looks like an AK. Repeat, suspect is armed.''

"Head's up, everybody.'' Stinton told his snipers to line up a clear shot.

76

Engler couldn't take his eyes from the RV. A white twenty-five-footer cab-over bed, roof AC. Looked like a rental. Tinted glass.

The tall grass and overgrowth reached his waist. He grew weary as he walked, resting the AK-47's barrel on his shoulder, thinking how Angel was such an asshole sitting out there.

"This is Sergeant Paul Harris—"

The bullhorn shattered the quiet. Engler dropped to the ground.

"—of the Texas Department of Public Safety—"

Police. Goddammit. Angel set him up. The farmhouse was some thirty yards away. Engler began crawling back on his stomach as fast as he could, cursing Zelaya.

"Halt! Release your weapons and raise your hands—"

Engler's sweating fingers tightened on his AK-47. He rolled and fired several rounds toward the sound of the cop's voice. Engler was twenty yards from the farmhouse when police returned fire, rounds whip-snipping through the grass, thudding into the earth, soil erupting near his head.

"Halt!"

Fifteen yards now. Engler heard the RV's engine start. More gunfire. The truck pursued him. Engler rolled to his back again and let go three staccato bursts, the RV's windshield blossomed, chrome peeled, the engine growled as rounds plunked into metal, popping headlights, shattering windows.

Engler crawled five yards more as the RV's engine roared and it retreated, vanishing backward into the forest.

"You mothers!" he screamed into the dusk. "You son-of-a-bitching mothers!" Engler squirmed in the tall grass, unloading a spray of automatic fire in all directions, before returning unscathed into the farmhouse.

Stinton ordered his team to cease firing and called for status reports.

They came back fast. No hits. No casualties. Stinton puffed his cheeks and exhaled, embracing a degree of relief that was short-lived.

"Sir," a scout said over the radio. "From here, it looks like he's got the place trip-wired with grenades. We can't get tight on the house."

Damn. Stinton rubbed a hand over his spiky brush cut. Damn.

His squad leader's voice came over the radio: "Gas him?"

"Not yet. Everyone get comfortable, make sure you got cover. Get the negotiator on the bullhorn. Let's try talking to him."

Reed paced just outside the small barn, his jaw dropping at the RV limping back to the command post, bumping along flattened rear tires, remnants of punctured glass tinkling from metal dangling like war wounds. The vehicle stopped and half a dozen heavily armed SWAT members in camouflage and body armor stepped from it.

Near the farmhouse a bullhorn crackled from the forest.

"John Engler, this is Sergeant Ralph Langer. Are you hurt, John? Can we get you anything?"

Inside, Engler was panting, shaking his head as if hearing a joke. His hands trembled as he loaded his weapons, strapping them to his body, stuffing his handguns in his waistband. *Let's see, I'm good for homicides in California and Texas. Death penalty states. Just fired on police. What could they possibly offer me? A cheeseburger and an execution date.*

"John?" Langer called. "Why don't you come out, son?"

Son? The guy sounded twenty and he was calling him son. Christ. Engler had spent more time in a cell than this guy had spent on the planet.

"Are you hungry? We can send in some food. Why don't you release anybody you got there with you? How about a trade, John?"

Engler stomped toward the window.

"I've got Ann Reed with me! The next shot fired at me means the second one goes into her head! Understand?"

"Take it easy, John. I understand."

Engler scanned the woods but it was futile. He saw no police but felt them all around, sensed their breathing, their hearts pounding, their fingers on the triggers, itching, craving to take him out, to be the hero.

"I'm never going back to prison!"

"John, how about you let me hear Ann as a sign of good faith, that she's with you and she's okay? Can you let me see her or hear her?"

Engler rubbed his lips. Studying the jewels, now useless to him. His breathing quickened. He took stock of his arsenal, his options, his sorry life.

"John? How 'bout it, partner, you going to let me talk to Ann?"

Engler turned.

"Get Reed. Her husband, Tom Reed. I know he's around. I heard him on the news. You get him, I want to talk to him."

77

Stinton hated the situation.

"What do you think?" He turned to his two sergeants advising him at the command post. "If I let him talk to Reed, it could turn to crap in a heartbeat."

"Could antagonize him further," Bolander said.

"He's already fired on us, I'd say he's beyond that," Rikker said.

Stinton gritted his teeth, hating the notion of having a civilian this close and now possibly involved. It could all go to hell. He had to study every option. He stepped outside the barn and approached Reed.

"If I allow it, would you want to talk to Engler, over the bullhorn under our supervision?"

"I'll do whatever it takes."

Stinton chewed on the possibility before returning to the barn and conferring quietly with his sergeants. "This is not consistent with policy and procedure," Stinton said. "But it's my scene and I'm exercising discretion. What if she's in there wounded? We can't waste time."

"You're thinking on letting the husband talk to him?" Rikker said.

"It might be all we need to distract the suspect," Stinton said. "To draw him out or provide a kill shot. We make no deals. We can't fire on the house in case she's inside. We want a clear shot. This may be our only way."

The sergeants agreed. Under the circumstances it was the best option.

At the command post SWAT team members put body armor and a helmet on Reed as Stinton briefed him.

"Just keep him talking. Make no promises. Urge him to surrender."

Reed, exchanged a glance with Sydowski, nodded to Stinton, then went with the team members. They led him on foot down the roadway to the farmhouse. Reed double-timed it with his escort. They moved in silence. Reed's pulse quickened as they neared the perimeter edge where Sergeant Langer was crouched behind an unmarked patrol car. Not far away, Reed saw two snipers covered with branches. Their rifle scopes were trained on the farmhouse.

It was weatherworn, its wooden frame was gray and leaning from age. It rose like an ancient ghost house amid a sea of overgrown grass and bush.

"Mr. Reed, Ralph Langer. Negotiator." He extended his hand.

The bullhorn rested on the hood of the car; connected to it was a remote handheld microphone that allowed Reed to crouch down behind the fender, out of the line of fire. Langer demonstrated. He passed the remote microphone to Reed.

"Real simple to use, press here, keep your mouth about two inches back, and talk in a normal tone."

Reed nodded.

"Talk to him. Keep him calm. You can't make any promises. That's up to us. Okay?"

"Yes."

"You're good to go, Tom."

Reed raised it to his mouth, depressed the switch.

"John, it's Tom Reed." His voice carried over the silence. Night was falling. The house darkened.

"Hey, asshole," Engler called back, "bet you thought you'd never hear from me again."

"Where's Ann?"

"Not even a hello, how are you?"

"John, I can't change your past."

"You twisted it."

"John, where's my wife?"

"*Your* wife? Where's *my* wife?"

Reed looked at the ground as if he'd find an answer there. "Take me, John." In the command post Stinton winced, then got on his radio to Langer, who waved a hand to Reed indicating that was the wrong thing to say. Reed ignored him. "Let Ann go. She's never harmed you. It was me. I was wrong. Your fight's with me. Take me."

Nothing came from the darkness for a long moment.

"I don't want you, Reed. I'm happy with your wife. We make a good couple. She's a looker. You know why I had to kill Tribe? You know what he is and what he did to her?"

Reed's knuckles whitened on the microphone.

At the command post, Stinton was whispering radio calls to team members tight on the house. While Engler was distracted with Reed at the front, they'd been working on one of the trip wires at the rear.

"We might be able to go tear gas, flash-bangs, and a full-bore assault, Captain."

"One step at a time. He may have a hostage."

At the rear, the bomb tech was disarming the trip wires while out front Reed was nearing his breaking point.

"John," Reed's voice echoed, "what do you want?"

"I want you to atone for what you did to me."

"I'm sorry for what you went through."

"No, Reed, that's not enough—that's not—"

Tear gas smashed through the windows followed by a flash-bang as two SWAT team members stormed the rear and released gunfire in short bursts. Engler pivoted, spraying the doorway with AK-47 fire. The officers retreated as Engler advanced, tossing the tear gas back, throwing his own grenades and unleashing a volley of gunfire.

"Mothers, son-of-a-bitch!"

In the chaos, the lantern smashed against a wall and within seconds, flames licked up aged crisp wallpaper. In moments, half the living room was engulfed. Engler worked in vain to smother the fire with curtains but it ripped through the tinder-dry frame building. Engler coughed, touched something wet on his chest. He tore his shirt to see the two bleeding bullet wounds above his heart.

Outside, Reed's eyes widened.

Firefighters and paramedics at the command post were alerted.

"Hold your fire," Stinton ordered. "Drop back, hold your fire!"

Nearly one-quarter of the building was ablaze.

"Ann!" Reed called on the bullhorn standing. "Ann!"

"Tom, get down! Get down!" Langer said.

Reed fought off the arms pulling him and ran to the burning house.

Langer alerted Stinton, who alerted the SWAT team.

"Hold your fire. We have a civilian breach from the south." Stinton turned. "Son of a goddamned bitch!"

Reed ran faster than he'd ever run in his life, not feeling, hearing, or fearing anything, thinking only of entering the house to find Ann. He came up fast, surprising SWAT members aiding a downed partner whose body armor had taken one of Engler's shots. Yelling, one of them tried stopping Reed but he broke free and entered the blazing house.

The heat began baking Reed's skin, the lack of oxygen was suffocating, he dropped to his hands and knees, squinting in the smoke and debris. He scanned the small house, searching tiny smoke-filled rooms, finding no one, seeing nothing.

"Ann! Ann!"

Reed came to Engler, lying on the floor, blood flowing from his wounds. Reed grabbed him. "Where is she!"

Engler stared into Reed's face and started to grin.

"I'm not going back to prison. I was out and you put me back. I'm not going to die an old man in a cage."

"Where's Ann!"

"You'll know my pain, Reed. You'll never find her."

"Tell me!"

Engler's eyes fluttered.

"John! Tell me! God, help me!"

Hands gripped Reed's shoulders, dragging him just as the roof gave way in an explosion of fire that collapsed on Engler.

"You'll never find her!"

SWAT members and firefighters pulled Reed clear of the inferno. No one could save Engler. Reed's rescuers carried him over fifty yards from the house. Gasping, he looked into the sweaty faces of police, firefighters, and paramedics gathered around him.

"Did you find her?"

No one answered as he searched their eyes for a flicker of hope.

"Anyone? Did you find her? Did you find anything?"

Each of them shook their head as the blaze crackled and helicopters circled.

Reed choked on his anguish as flames lit the night sky.

78

Sparks and ash whirled to the stars as the old farmhouse burned.

Firefighters were kept back because it was not known how many live rounds or unexploded grenades were among the ruins. Cartridges popped amid the red-hot debris.

Reed stood there all night watching the black-gray smoke rise from the coals, carrying the stench of soot, cordite, and charred flesh over the pine woods. Radios clattered with cross talk as emergency lights strobed.

Stinton, the SWAT commander, approached Reed. Two county fire officials joined him, faces sweaty and sooty under their ball caps.

"I'm sorry, Tom," Stinton said. "We got to let it burn out. It's too dangerous to get close. If there was any other damn way . . ."

Reed's eyes never left the ruins.

He felt nothing. Not the heat. Not the night. Not the earth under his feet. Sounds faded, his mind swam, taking him far into a dark, calm surreal sea. Was he dreaming? Was this shock? Again and again in the blackness, he met Engler's eyes, his words stabbing his heart.

"You'll know my pain, Reed. You'll never find her."

His memory took him back to that night in the newsroom, the warning from his friend the religion editor, *"Don't get too close . . ."*

All through the night, Reed kept vigil over the smoldering ruins like a mourner at a funeral pyre. They offered him coffee. He refused. They offered him water. He refused. They offered him a sandwich. Reed shook his head.

He wanted Ann.

Over the years she'd grown fearful of his obsession with crime stories, his addiction to get closer and closer. She'd agonized over the toll it was exacting, his drinking, fracturing their lives. How she'd begged him to quit. How, after the last close call with Zach, he'd finally agreed, and how he'd intended to retire the day she was taken. *Intended.* Hell is full of good intentions. *Oh, Jesus. Ann, I'm so sorry.*

A breeze sent smoke into his eyes. All he could see were images of Ann, on the campus, their first date, in her wedding dress, opening her first store, holding Zach in her arms minutes after he was born. He thought of Ann's mother, Doris. God was a goddamned deal breaker.

And Zach.

"She can't be dead because she's my mom."

Reed's body shook as dawn broke. The fire was out. He heard people murmuring and turned to see several dozen news reporters with notepads, microphones, and cameras crowded against yellow plastic scene tape, some forty yards away. Police had bowed to their protests to get closer.

Sydowski, McDaniel, and Doyle took him aside.

"We can put you in a vehicle out of sight if you want, Tom."

He shook his head, watching firefighters douse the ruins to cool them.

"As soon as it's safe, they'll send the ca—" Sydowski stopped himself and said, "They'll send the dog in."

Reed knew he'd meant to say cadaver dog, the dog that can detect the scent emitted by human remains.

"The arson guys and SWAT guys saw women's clothing in the ruins, Tom. I know this is goddamned awful, but you've got to—" Sydowski swallowed, put his hand on Reed's shoulder. "You've got to brace yourself."

Reed looked up at the sky.

"How do I tell my son, Walt? How do I explain this?"

Sydowski was a veteran of four hundred homicides and a widower. "There are no answers, Tom. You have to love him and tell him the truth, hang on to those around you and live each day as best you can."

Reed's knees gave out and he slipped to the ground.

The news cameras clicked and whirred recording the moment pulling close on his anguish. The twenty-four-hour networks carried it live.

Sydowski bent down to comfort Reed, putting his arm around his shoulder, staying with him as they watched the cadaver dog poke its snout amid the aftermath. Networks split the screen, juxtaposing the dog with Reed's reaction.

A DPS helicopter thundered as it circled, while higher up, news choppers took shots from the sky. The dog located Engler's remains, a blackened boot stuck up from a tangle of a rippled window frame. The cameras pulled in. Then police radios crackled. A sheriff's deputy jogged to Reed and Sydowski, keys jangling on his utility belt.

"They found a van, about a quarter mile deep into the forest!"

The deputy led them to the location, far from the farmhouse. Reed heard a dog yelping and took stock of searchers scouring the surrounding terrain. The van was driven directly into a large bramble and was invisible.

"Everyone hold back," a K-9 officer shouted. "We got to protect this scene." White-gloved DPS investigators had opened the doors. The interior had tools, shovels, a pickax, and appeared to be drenched in something that had dried brown. Reed saw it.

Blood.

The dog was barking, straining to leave.

"Okay, she's got a scent trail."

The officer unleashed the dog and let it go. Radio traffic increased. Helicopters hammered in the sky. The small group followed. Reed chased the dog as if it were hope until he realized where it was leading.

Tears filled his eyes.

The dog was making a direct line to the smoldering farm-house.

Reed's running slowed to a walk. He felt the weight of all his fear crushing him, forcing him to the earth. Oh God. If he could hold her one last time. To tell her how much he loved her. One last time.

"Tom!" Sydowski yelled over the choppers. "Over here!"

The dog was sniffing at the ground beyond the farmhouse. The K-9 officer was saying something to his radio, the others were pulling away tree branches, boards, a cinder block, revealing a hole.

"A well!" The sheriff's deputy dropped to his knees and unholstered his flashlight, so did the K-9 officer and a second deputy. Their beams shot into the darkness. Reed dropped to his chest, shielded his eyes.

Twenty feet down, he saw Ann's terrified face squinting at the light.

She was wedged like a peg, nearly entombed in the shaft.

Radios crackled. The site swarmed with firefighters, para-medics, police, and rescue crews set to work on extracting her.

News spread that Ann Reed had been found. *Alive.* More networks broke into regular programming to broadcast the story. The growing number of press at the police tape was allowed access to the story. A quick attempt at a media pool failed. All news crews demanded access to the well site. They'd arrived in time to witness Ann Reed hoisted from it. Her dyed blond hair was matted, her face masked by dirt, arms covered in scrapes and cuts. Reed pulled her to him.

372   *Rick Mofina*

"Ann! Oh God! Ann!"

She locked her arms around him and he held her.

As paramedics began a quick examination, cell phones trilled incessantly. Reporters relayed events to their desks, some were running live on-scene commentary with their pictures.

Across the country, in Tom and Ann's San Francisco home, Zach and Doris screamed with joy at the live pictures. The police officers and FBI agents assigned to the house high-fived each other.

Throughout the Bay Area, the staff at Ann's stores squealed and began jumping. In the *San Francisco Star*'s newsroom, reporters and deskers gathered around the large TVs to cheer, some hugged, others blinked back tears. Reed's editor, Bob Shepherd, shook his head grinning. In all his years in the news business, he'd never seen a story like this. Damn.

In Texas, deputies and firefighters led Ann and Tom through the throng of newspeople to the ambulance and patrol cars cutting a swath through the grass. Molly Wilson elbowed her way to Reed and Ann, hugging them both, sharing their joy. Reed gave Wilson a few words, invited her to meet them at the hospital, before climbing into the ambulance, with Ann. The highway patrol cars gave them a police escort.

After the ambulance left, Texas authorities advised reporters of a short, upcoming on-scene news briefing. The air was electric. Everyone at the farmhouse was uplifted by the way things had turned out. Every face bore a smile. Except two.

Tia Layne was screaming at Cooter.

"I don't believe this. We missed it all because you forgot to charge the batteries? *You fool! We got nothing! Nothing!*"

Cooter kept tapping the battery against his knee. "Could be a loose contact."

"What do I tell Seth?" Layne's cell phone trilled. "Tia Layne. *Worldwide*."

"Ms. Layne, Molly Wilson, *San Francisco Star*."

"What is it?"

"I've just learned that yesterday the San Bernardino County Sheriff's office swore out a warrant for your arrest on charges against you in that little matter of the report you stole out of the Baker office."

"What? No one's told me. Who told you?"

"Sources close to the investigation. What's your reaction and could you look over your left shoulder, please?"

"What. Why?" Layne turned, opening her mouth as Henry Cain, a news photographer with the *Star*, fired off a few unflattering frames. Wilson crinkled her eyes and waved before walking toward her.

"Here you go." Wilson's bracelets jingled as she placed a faxed copy of the warrant and charges in Layne's hands.

"This can't be happening to me."

"Nice quote. You'll make a nice little sidebar. Thanks, we have to run."

In the ambulance, the paramedic asked Ann to lie down to be comfortable while she checked her signs.

"Are you aware of any serious physical injuries, Ann?" She shook her head. The woman had a kind face.

A Texas Ranger rode with them in the back. An FBI agent was up front.

Reed held Ann's hand and stroked her cheek. The paramedic prepared her stethoscope and blood pressure equipment.

"Ann, they're both dead," Reed said. "We know all about them. The police will talk to you at the hospital."

Ann nodded. Then, on the brink of hysteria, she began sobbing.

"Tom, oh, Tom. Del wanted to—I was chained to the tree—he was getting ready to ra—" Ann covered her mouth.

"Then John came up behind and cut his throat. I saw the knife just slice him, then—"

Reed caressed her head, pulling back so the paramedic could take her pressure, then shine a penlight in her eyes.

"Looking good so far, Ann."

Ann blinked.

When the paramedic removed Ann's shoes to check her feet, a small object slipped from the toe of the right one. The paramedic caught it.

"Goodness, this looks important."

The paramedic passed it to her. Ann's face brightened at the sight of the piece of jewelry that had been her lifeline, her talisman since she'd picked it up from the jewelry store that terrible day. Ann smiled, pressing it into Reed's hand.

"This is for you. For our anniversary."

It was a small gold pocket watch with a fine chain.

Reed ran his fingers over its design.

"Open it," she said.

He popped it and read the inscription.

For all time, Love, Ann.

Tears rolled down his face.

Ann pulled Tom to her and they held each other as sirens wailed and the morning sun climbed in the eastern sky.

ACKNOWLEDGMENTS

My thanks to Inspector Ed Erdelatz, San Francisco Homicide Detail (Ret.), Peggy Hill, Wendy Dudley, Mildred Marmur, Jeff Aghassi, Peter Bloch, Ann LaFarge, Laurie Parkin, Steve Zacharius, Doug Mendini, Joan Schulhafer, and everyone at Kensington. And to Barbara, Laura, and Michael. A very special thanks to Donna Riddell, John and Jeannine Rosenberg. My thanks to booksellers everywhere, who make it all happen. And to you, the reader, I hope you enjoyed the trip.

For a sneak preview of
Rick Mofina's next novel—
coming from Pinnacle Books
in 2004—
just turn the page. . . .

1

Waiting alone at Jake's Bar & Grill in North Beach, Molly Wilson finished her second diet cola, then pressed redial on her cell phone. Four rings. She got his machine again. Damn.

"It's me. I'm at Jake's. Where *are* you? Call me."

Nearly an hour late and not a word. This was not like Cliff. Maybe he'd left her a message at work. She tried her line there.

"You've reached Molly Wilson of the *San Francisco Star*. I'm either on the phone or . . ."

She keyed in her password. Three new messages since she'd left the newsroom. An editor with a question she'd already answered. Some reader with a weird story idea. A hang up. She'd been getting of lot of those lately. But nothing from Cliff. She ordered another soda and brooded.

In the six months they'd been together, he was never late. Except tonight. Maybe he'd figured out what was coming, sensed that she'd reached a decision on their relationship. Cliff was a great guy. She'd never set out to hurt him. She'd set out to have fun, and they did have fun. But she didn't want to move in with him. In fact, she thought they should cool things. See other people. It just wasn't working out for them. She was going to tell him tonight. Give him back his key. End it.

Then what? She hated this. She tried Cliff's cell phone, wanting this night to be over, to retreat to her apartment, soak in her tub, listen to Cat Stevens. Eat a gallon of butterscotch ripple. Cliff wasn't answering his cell.

She drummed her glossed nails on the table. Then stopped. She felt someone was watching her. Wilson pushed back her auburn hair and inventoried the place. Filled with after work office types. Nothing unusual until she noticed two men nearby warming stools at the bar, ties loosened, stealing glimpses of her, then the big screen TV overhead.

Of course. She was on *Eyewitness 24-Hour Action News.* It was her weekly eight-minute spot with Vince Vincent, host of *Crime Scene,* where they talked about crime in San Francisco.

The show always taped at noon. Wilson was still wearing the same sweater and matching blazer, which complemented her eyes. There she was with Vincent at a studio desk against San Francisco's skyline at night.

He was saying, "Molly, according to the new justice department figures, which crime are you most likely to become a victim of in the Bay Area?"

"You're most likely to have your car vandalized, especially if you live downtown. If you live in the suburbs, you're more likely to have your home burglarized."

"What about violent crime?"

"The odds of your being murdered, or a victim of a violent crime, are very remote."

Watching the set over the bar, Wilson shook her head. Vincent was worried. No sensational crimes in weeks. His ratings were slipping.

"But, Molly, *violent crimes do happen here.* We've got gangs, drug wars, murders of every sort. Look, the city is still reeling from the recent jewelry heist homicides. And who could have predicted the chilling case of the globe-trotting cyber killer who took direction from St. John's Book of Revelation? All of those cases arose in San Francisco."

"Sure, Vince, but the fact is your likelihood of being victimized by such a crime is virtually nil . . ."

The two guys at the bar were now grinning and offering her little waves. Wilson shrugged them off.

She'd been on the show for a year and had become a minor local celebrity. Still, it was a gig she could easily give up. The extra two hundred bucks she got every week was sweet but the show attracted crazies and jerks. Like the pair at the bar.

Wilson could handle them. She was a seasoned reporter who'd been up close to every kind of tragedy you could imagine. There was little she couldn't handle. But not tonight. She wasn't up for these two. Not now. Oh no. One was headed her way. That was her cue.

Wilson grabbed her bag, tossed a few bills on the table, gave a message to her waiter in case Cliff called, then left.

Outside, an evening breeze rolled up from the bay and Wilson was struck by an odd sensation. It was as if somebody were just waiting for her to leave Jake's.

And now they were watching her.

This was stupid. She took stock of the street. Nothing but a few window-shoppers. She was just being silly, put off by those drunks at the bar. And Cliff. Where was he? She waved it off, flagged a cab and got in.

"Upper Market," she said. "I'll give you the address when we get closer."

Against her better judgment, Wilson was going to Cliff's place. Breakups should always be done on neutral territory for a quick escape in case it goes badly. Like the time one creep grabbed her hair, called her a stupid bitch and stomped off cursing her. Or the guy who went mute and just stared. Well, she'd been dumped too. And it had hurt. That was life.

The lights of San Francisco rolled by and Wilson wondered if ending things with Cliff was a big mistake. Seriously. What was wrong with him? He was considerate, intelligent, had a sense of humor, wanted a family. A strong, handsome guy. Nothing was wrong with Cliff. So why dump him?

It was her. She'd searched her heart but felt nothing for him. She didn't love him. Didn't see a future with him. They lacked passion. And that was with every man she'd met. She couldn't connect beyond the physical. Since college in Texas, her life had been a string of superficial relationships.

Wilson felt a pang of desperation and touched her fingertips to the corners of her eyes. She was in her thirties now. Her clock was ticking. But she'd been pregnant once. *God, please. I don't want to think about that.* It was a lifetime ago. She was young. Scared. It haunted her. Rising from deep inside every time she ended a relationship. She would never forget the young father's anger all those years ago, telling her that she'd be punished for not having his baby. It was a long time ago. *Stop thinking about it.* But, here she was, the woman who has dated five hundred men. And not one could reach her heart. Was this her punishment?

Just stop it.

Wilson thought of Tom Reed, the reporter who sat next to her at the *Star.* Look at what he had with Ann, his wife. The real thing. They had a beautiful son. They were far from perfect but they had a fire that could melt steel. They had endured more than their share of heartbreaks and had emerged stronger. What they had was epic. Wilson was in awe. Would she ever find something like that?

"Miss?" the driver said. "The address, please."

Wilson recited it as the cab climbed the serpentine hills of Upper Market. She used to like the way the fog rolled up the steep streets of Cliff's little oasis. Smiled how he joked about being sheriff when she pointed at the community signs that demanded suspicious persons be immediately reported.

The creak of brakes echoed in the stillness as the cab stopped at the small Queen Anne–style house. Cliff's apartment was upstairs at the back. His sapphire Intrepid was parked out front. He must be home.

"If you shut off your meter and wait, I'll go back with you," she told the driver.

"How long, Miss? I gotta make a living."

"Fifteen minutes. Please."

He slid the gearshift to park and killed the motor. It ticked in the tranquillity.

Get this over with and make a clean getaway, she told herself as she approached the front. The exterior lights were on, but the place seemed oddly dark. She saw no interior lights. The wrought iron gate moaned as Wilson took the tiled walkway to the rear stairwell. The yard was lush, private, bordered with rosebushes, shrubs, eucalyptus trees. A couple of sturdy-looking palms.

Her footsteps echoed as she ascended the wooden staircase to his door. Inhaling the fragrance of the flowers cascading from the boxes on his balcony, she pressed the buzzer, heard it sound through his apartment. Then nothing. She buzzed again. Waiting, she put her ear to the door. Not even a hint of movement. She banged on the door. Waited. Again, nothing.

This is strange. His car's out front. He never goes anywhere without his car. Wilson reached into her bag for her key to his apartment. She slid it into the slot, but it went in too fast. *What the—*

The door was unlocked. Wilson turned the handle. It creaked open, inviting her to enter.

"Cliff?"

No one responded from the darkness. She reached inside, flipped on a light.

"Cliff?"

The first room was the kitchen. She saw his jacket draped over a chair. His car keys were on the counter, along with his cell phone, wallet, loose change, unopened mail.

"Cliff, it's Molly."

She moved to the living room. In the darkness the red message light of his answering machine was blinking like something terrified.

Wilson switched on a lamp.

This was not right. It was too quiet. Something began to bubble deep in her gut telling her this was all wrong. The next room across the darkened hall was his bedroom. Instinct warned her to leave now but her hand hovered over the doorknob. Her skin nearly exploded. The cabbie out front had blasted his horn.

"Jesus. Asshole."

Wilson took a breath and opened his bedroom door. The room swam with a surreal dim blue glow from the enlarged display of the digital clock on his nightstand. Her stomach tightened.

Oh God.

Cliff was on the bed. Facedown.

She inched toward him.

He was dressed in jeans and a T-shirt. A huge damp, dark blue halo encircled his head. Something resembling raw meat had erupted from the side, glistening in the eerie blue light.

Resting on Cliff's lower back was his service weapon, a 40-caliber Beretta. Next to it, open for display, his official San Francisco police identification. It read:

Cliff Hooper
Inspector Homicide Detail.